The Family at Red-Roofs

Those Dreadful Children

Enid Blyton

ARMADA

This Armada *Enid Blyton Two-in-One* was
first published in the U.K. in Armada in 1988
by William Collins Sons & Co. Ltd
Published pursuant to agreement with
Darrell Waters Ltd and Lutterworth Press

Armada is an imprint of the Children's Division,
part of the Collins Publishing Group,
8 Grafton Street, London W1X 3LA

Printed and bound in Great Britain by
William Collins Sons & Co. Ltd, Glasgow

CHAPTER ONE

The House on the Hill

THE little white-washed house on the green hillside seemed to smile in the warm sunshine of the bright May day. It sat there snugly in its big patch of gay garden, a white cherry tree out in the front garden, and a golden laburnum hanging over the gate. The gate was painted green and white, and there was a name on it—*Red-Roofs*.

It was easy to see how it got its name, for the pretty gabled roofs were a deep, warm red. Four tall chimneys stood there, but no smoke came from them today. The casement windows were closed to the warm sunshine, and no curtains hung behind them. The brass door-knocker was dull and tarnished.

Red-Roofs was empty. It looked sweet and smiling enough from a distance, but if anyone stood at the front gate it had the lost, forlorn look that all empty houses have.

Up the winding hillside lane came a little family party, talking excitedly.

"That must be the house! Look, Mother, it is, isn't it? It's got red roofs, so it must be the house."

"Daddy, it's pretty big, isn't it? It will take us all nicely, I should think!"

"What a darling house! Oh, I do hope we can have it! Here we are at the front gate—and, oh, look at this laburnum cascading down like golden rain!"

Six people stood at the front gate. One of them, the smallest, hung over the green and white gate, her eyes wandering all over the little white house. She was Shirley, the nine-year-old, youngest of the family of Jacksons. We can see them all plainly as they stand there.

Mr. Jackson is tall and broad-shouldered, ruddy-faced, with a twinkle in his eye. Mrs. Jackson, is small, hardly up to his shoulder, with rather an anxious little face and kind blue eyes. Then there is a big girl, taller than her small mother, her dark curly hair blowing in the wind. She is Molly, sixteen years old, and the eldest.

The two boys are as pleased as the others about the house. There is fourteen-year-old Peter, tall and well made like his father, but with serious eyes. Michael is much smaller, only eleven, serious-faced and a little sulky-looking. There they all stand at the gate, their eyes fixed on the smiling white house.

"It's *much* nicer than the house we live in now," said Shirley, climbing up the gate. "Oh, do let's have this one and live in it, Daddy, please do!"

"Have you got the keys, Dick?" said Mrs. Jackson to her husband. "Let's go in and see it. I must say it looks just the kind of thing we want. After living for so long in a poky little house in a noisy street, with only a back yard for a garden, this would be marvellous!"

There was a jingling of keys as Mr. Jackson took them from his pocket. He looked for the right front-door key. He had two or three, for the family had come out that Saturday afternoon to look over other houses besides *Red-Roofs*. He disentangled it from the rest and pushed open the front gate.

The path to the front door was made of crazy paving, in the cracks of which small flowering plants pushed up. Shirley was careful not to tread on them. The front door was painted green like the gate, and the brass knocker was in the shape of a smiling head.

There was a porch over the door to keep off the rain from waiting visitors. Mr. Jackson put the key into the lock and turned it. The door opened into a small square hall, quite empty except for a few bits of straw and a scrap of torn paper. The children's feet clattered cheerfully over the red tiles.

8

Then there came a torrent of shouted exclamations and remarks. "I say, what a darling sitting-room—with doors opening on to the back garden! Come and look, Mother! You'd love this!"

"What a nice big dining-room! We could all have our meals here without being crowded. It's got built-in bookshelves, too—how lovely!"

"Bags I those for all my books!" said Peter at once.

"And bags I the cupboard underneath for my toys!" said Shirley.

"I like the brick fireplaces," said Mr. Jackson, running his hand over the red bricks that made the fireplace. "They look so cheerful and cosy, and they send out such warmth, too, because all the bricks round get hot as well."

But nobody was interested in the fireplaces at that moment. Mrs. Jackson was in the small, bright, cheerful kitchen looking anxiously to see if the larder was nice and big and cold, and if the stove looked easy to manage. She liked the kitchen. It was tiled in black and white, and the last tenant had left the black and white linoleum on the floor. It would be nice if they could buy that.

There came a clattering of shoes on the wooden floors upstairs and more shrieks of delight.

"Mother! There's a *lovely* bedroom for you and Daddy —ever so big—with a basin for running water!"

"And *could* Shirley and I have this bedroom at the back?" called Molly. "Mother, it's got apple trees in full bloom touching the window—and they do smell delicious. And there is a climbing rose round the window, too—it will soon be out! Oh, Shirley, wouldn't it be lovely to have a bedroom like this, instead of ours looking out on the dirty street where the trams rush up and down!"

"We could look out each morning up the green hillside," said Shirley, "and hear the birds sing instead of the bells of the trams ringing!"

The boys had found a nice big bedroom which they at once marked for themselves. It looked out over the front garden, straight on to the dazzling white blossoms of the cherry tree. It must have been used as a kind of study,

9

because there were built-in cupboards and shelves there, as there were down in the dining-room. The boys immediately thought how marvellously they could arrange all their crowded belongings.

"There's another bedroom, too," said Molly, going round a corner of the passage. "*Two* more bedrooms—both tiny, but perfectly sweet. Shan't we feel grand to have five bedrooms after having only three! Mother, look—what shall we do with these bedrooms? Shall Shirley and I have separate rooms, do you think?"

"We shall see," said her mother. "Anyway, I hope we shall be able to afford help in the house now, so we shall want a room for a maid—and it would be nice to have a tiny spare room to put up a friend now and again. I have lots of old friends I would like to see again."

The children explored the cream-painted bathroom, the linen cupboard with its wooden shelves, and the little loft up in the roof, where trunks and boxes could go. Then out they went into the garden.

It was a funny, sloping garden, with little green lawns set round the flowery beds, a tiny copse of fruit trees at one side, crazy-paving paths here and there, and a rather neglected kitchen garden which Mr. Jackson at once made up his mind to tackle—if only they could have the house!

"It's a very nice little place, isn't it, dear?" said Mrs. Jackson, smiling up at him. "Just what we want. And it's not too far from the shops and the children's schools. Perhaps it's a bit far for Shirley to walk to the High School. We might have to buy her a bicycle."

"Oooh!" said Shirley in joy. "I should be like Prudence then! She's got a lovely bicycle, hasn't she, Molly?"

Molly nodded. Prudence Williams was the girl she sat next to at school. Her people had plenty of money, so Prudence had a good many things that the Jacksons hadn't. But then Prudence and her brother Bernard were the only two children and, as Mrs. Jackson often said, the bigger the family the less each child could have. Still, the Jacksons didn't want their family to be any smaller. They couldn't spare a single member of it!

Mr. Jackson looked up the green hillside. There would be fine walks here. He could keep a dog at last. He wanted *Red-Roofs* as much as the children did. He took from his pocket the paper that gave particulars of the house and its rent and rates.

"It's expensive," he said, looking down at his wife. "Two pounds ten shillings a week—and you've got to remember that Molly won't be leaving school and earning money for a while yet, if she wants to take her Kindergarten exams and train as a teacher at the High School. She will be three years more doing that—she can't start till she's over seventeen, anyhow. And there's Peter wanting to be a doctor. He *may* get that scholarship if he works hard—but it's likely we shall have to save up a good bit to help him along for many years."

"Yes, I know," said Mrs. Jackson, the worried look coming over her face again. "We've got to do the best we can for our children—but all the same I do think they deserve a nicer home than we've got at present. It was all right when we first went there, you and I—a quiet little road and nice people there—but now that it's all been built up round about and the neighbourhood has gone down and down, it's not so good. Well—if we can't afford *Red-Roofs*, let's go and see one or two more houses, not so expensive."

"Oh, *Mother*!" cried four bitterly disappointed voices. "Daddy! Do say we can have this house, oh, do!"

Mr. Jackson wanted *Red-Roofs* as much as anyone else. He looked up at the little white-washed house with its glowing red roofs.

"Well," he said, and jingled the money in his pockets, "well—we'll risk it. Nothing venture nothing have! I'm hoping to have a big rise in the firm soon, and be head of my department—then *Red-Roofs* would be a nice house to ask my friends to. I must say I like it very much myself."

Shirley flung herself on him. "Oh, Daddy! Can we have it, then? When will it be ours? Can we go and say we want it? When can we move in?"

"We'll go right back to the house agents now," said Mr.

11

Jackson firmly. "We'll decide it this very day. Come along. I'll lock up the front door again and we'll go."

So off they all went, swinging the little green and white gate open, turning round to look at the pretty house as they went. It seemed to smile and say, "I shall soon be yours! How nice to own a family like you! I shall like you all."

They went down the hill to the town that lay at the bottom, stretching along the valley. The Jacksons lived at the other end of the town, the dirty, busy end. This was the quiet, pleasant end. They found the house agents' office and trooped in.

It was not very long before everything was settled. There were documents to sign, references to be given and so on— but the Jacksons went away with the keys of *Red-Roofs* in their possession, and that was all they cared about!

"We shall move in next month!" said Molly, pleased. "What an excitement it will be! I'll help you to pack everything, Mother. How long have you taken the house for, Daddy?"

"Three years," said Mr. Jackson, "and maybe at the end of that time I shall be able to buy it, instead of renting it."

"We're going to have fun at *Red-Roofs*," said Molly. "We really are!"

CHAPTER TWO

Moving In

MOLLY JACKSON was in the sixth and highest form at her school. She was a popular, hard-working and responsible girl, and she was glad that she was soon going to start her training as a teacher. Her school had a fine kindergarten for the little ones, and an excellent training department attached to it.

"I shall start being a student in September," Molly told herself in glee. "I shall be seventeen by then, half grown-up! The K.G. children will call me Miss Jackson. I shall feel quite important."

Some of the other girls in her form were leaving that term to take up various kinds of work. One or two were going to train as hospital nurses. Some were going into offices. Others were going on to college.

"What are *you* going to do, Prudence?" asked Molly. "Have you made up your mind yet? Surely you're not going to stay at home and do nothing?"

"Well, there isn't any need for me to take a job," said Prudence. "I don't see why I should. I should enjoy being at home, and going to parties and plays, and lazing about and reading. I can understand *you* don't want to do that—living in that poky house of yours in that dirty street! I'd want to get out of it and have a job as quickly as possible if I lived there. I can't think why your people don't move."

Molly went red. Prudence had a fine big house with a tennis court and a pretty pond. She had a lovely bedroom all to herself, with blue wallpaper, blue cushions on her chairs and a blue eiderdown. She always had pretty dresses

13

and smart coats, and she was nice to look at—why did she always spoil things so by talking in that snobbish manner?

"Well, if you want to know, we *are* moving!" said Molly, rather snappily. "After all, we are a bigger family than you and cost more to bring up, so money isn't so plentiful. But we *are* moving at last—into *Red-Roofs*, that dear little house up on the hillside, the other end of the town."

Prudence looked at Molly in surprise. "That's quite near us," she said. "I've always thought it was such a pretty house. Dear me, you *are* going up in the world!"

Joan Rennie heard the last part of the conversation and came up. She lived in the same part of the town as the Jacksons, and was a plain and homely girl, kind and dependable, with a delicate mother to fuss round. She was leaving that term to go into an office.

"Oh, I wish you weren't moving so far away!" she said, dolefully. "I was hoping we'd still be near enough to see something of one another after I've left, Molly. It will be horrid to leave school, I think—all the familiar routine we know, the fun and games and friendships. I'm not looking forward to it at all."

"You're such an old stick-in-the-mud," said Prudence. "Fancy wanting to stay on at school—a school like this, anyway. I never did like this school—I always wanted my people to send me away to a decent boarding school, but Daddy doesn't believe in them, so I had to come here. And I can tell you I'm jolly glad to be leaving!"

"There's one thing you didn't learn at school which most of us *have* learnt," said Joan, in her straightforward way, "and that's loyalty! You're always talking against your people or your school, or your friends or something."

"I am *not*!" cried Prudence, and she glared at Joan. "How dare you talk like that—you plain, common thing!"

Joan laughed and walked away. She had no time for Prudence, with her airs and graces, her little sneers and gibes. She thought it a great pity that the girl was not going to a job; maybe she would have learnt what it was to work then, and get down to things. She had never bothered to use what brains she had at school.

Prudence talked to Molly with tears in her eyes. She could always squeeze a tear or two out when she wanted a little sympathy. "Isn't she a beast?" she said. "Well, anyway, Molly, whatever she says, I shan't drop *you* when I leave. Now that we are going to live near one another we'll see quite a lot of each other."

Molly was too simple and trusting to see that these sudden sentiments sprang from resentment at Joan's remarks, and not from affection for herself! She took Prudence's arm and squeezed it hard. "That's nice of you," she said. "Joan shouldn't have said that. All the same, I like her. She's always been one of my best friends. But it *would* be nice, when we move away from our old friends, to have one or two like you near us, Prudence. So do let's see a lot of one another. I shall pass your house whenever I go to the K.G. each morning for the next three years or so."

"I think you're silly to want to be a teacher," said Prudence. "Always keeping a lot of silly kids in order and teaching them that h is for hat and m is for mat. I shan't waste my time like that, you can be sure! I shall have a jolly good time and then get married to somebody rich."

"Well, you're pretty, and you've got lovely manners, and money enough to dress well," said Molly, without the least trace of envy in her voice. "That's all right for you. But I *have* to earn my own living—and as I love children and like being with them, I don't see that I could do anything better than teach them and enjoy their funny little ways."

"When are you going to move?" asked Prudence. "Soon?"

"At the beginning of June," said Molly, feeling suddenly excited at the thought of living in the dear little house on the hill. "Golly, it will be fun!"

Peter, Michael and Shirley were finding it fun, too. Already things were being cleared up and packed into big crates sent by the furniture removers.

"I'm longing for the day we move," said Shirley happily. "It will be exciting."

"Not for you, Shirley," said her mother. "You are to spend the whole day at school and have your lunch and

15

your dinner there. So are Michael and Peter. You would only be in the way."

"*Oh!*" said the two boys, indignantly. "We shouldn't be in the way. We could help, you know we could."

"I want to help too," wailed Shirley. "What's Molly going to do? Isn't she going to stay at school too?"

"No, Molly must stay at home that day and give me a hand with the move," said Mrs. Jackson, firmly. "Now don't make a silly fuss, Shirley. Think how lovely it will be for you to go to school from this dark little house one morning—and go home in the evening to lovely *Red-Roofs*, up on the green hillside!"

"Yes—it will be exciting," said Shirley, and the boys agreed with her. It was a shame not to share in the move itself—but still, there would be plenty to do when they got to their new home in the evening—enough to last them for a week or two. There would be toys and books to arrange in the new cupboards and shelves, and there would be all Michael's bits and pieces, tools and instruments to pack away carefully somewhere. Michael passionately adored taking things to pieces and putting them together again. He could mend a clock or a watch, and even tinker about with a wireless set till he got it right. Mrs. Jackson was always complaining of the way he left his things about, but now he would have the joy of a cupboard all to himself. He would soon show his mother how tidy he could be once he had somewhere to put things!

May slipped away, and June came in, bright and warm, full of flowers and sweetness. It was a fine time to move. The little old house looked queer with its carpets up and its belongings packed away into crates. The back yard was full of straw and papers and rubbish.

The great day came at last. Shirley, Peter and Michael went off to school with excited faces. That night they would sleep at *Red-Roofs*! They said good-bye to the dark little house they had lived in all their lives, but they could not feel very sad about it. It had been so cramped and dark and noisy, far too small for such a big family.

Molly stayed behind to help her mother. Her father had

THE SECOND VAN WAS STILL AT THE DOOR

a day off too. The sixteen-year-old girl felt very responsible and grown-up, for she had been given many things to do. Her mother was to go with the first van of furniture to *Red-Roofs*, and she and her father were to be in charge of the furniture that was to be put in the second one.

"Go into every room and see that nothing is left behind," her mother said. "Daddy will go with the men in the second van, but you, Molly, must stay behind and see that everything is all right. The gas-man will come and see to the gas. The electric light man will come and turn off the electricity. You can borrow a broom from Mrs. Johnson next door and sweep out the straw from the rooms while you are waiting. Then lock up the house and take the keys to the house agent. After that catch the tram to the other end of the town, and walk up to *Red-Roofs*."

"You can trust me to do everything all right, Mother," said Molly, happily. It was nice to be treated almost as a grown-up, and left in charge like this.

She did everything just as she had been told, and about half-past twelve was walking up to her new home. There it was, shining white on the hillside, its red roofs glowing. There were creepers of various kinds climbing up the walls, and roses were out on an early rambler. No curtains were up yet, so the house looked rather empty, but a great bustle was going on! The second van was still at the door, and men were carrying furniture into the house. A woman who had been engaged to help in the move was busy unpacking a big crate. Mrs. Jackson was directing where the furniture was to go.

"Oh, Molly—that's good, you're here!" called her mother. "The men have put your bedroom furniture upstairs in your room. Go up and see if the bed is where you want it. If it is, start making your bed, and then make all the others up too. The linen and blankets are in that big crate over there."

Soon Molly was working hard and happily. It was fun to see order come out of chaos and confusion, fun to see a neat and cheerful little bedroom coming out of a mess and muddle! She rejoiced when she looked round her new room. True, she was to share it with Shirley, and Shirley was not a very tidy little person—but all the same it was lovely to have a room like this, even if it had to be shared. The casement windows opened out on to the garden, and the fresh hillside breeze blew straight in. The sun slanted in too, and made everything very cheerful.

There was not much furniture in the room—a single bed for Molly against one wall, and a smaller bed for Shirley nearby. A big cupboard would hold their things, so there was no wardrobe. There was a triangular-shaped wooden washstand that fitted neatly into a corner, small and compact. There was a big and roomy chest-of-drawers which the two girls had to share, and two chairs. The carpet was on the floor—a new one, patterned in blue like the walls.

"Once I get my few pictures on the walls, and a vase or two of flowers, and some of my books and ornaments, it will all look simply lovely," thought Molly. "But I mustn't stop for that now—I must get along and make the other beds. Goodness, how hungry I am!"

So was everyone else. Moving was a hungry job! Mrs. Jackson called up to Molly.

"Come down and have some sandwiches before we do anything else. We've all worked so hard we could do with a rest."

So Molly went down the stairs, and, sitting in the sunny little garden, the Jackson family munched their sandwiches contentedly—the first meal at the dear little house.

CHAPTER THREE

Settling Down

WHEN Shirley and the boys came racing up the hill at seven o'clock that evening in the golden June sun, *Red-Roofs* was ready for them. The carpets and linoleum were down, the curtains were up, the furniture stood in its place. The beds were made, clothes were hung in the cupboards or laid away tidily in drawers, and crockery was set out on the kitchen dresser. The woman had gone, after having scrubbed and polished and tidied.

A lovely smell of cooking came from the kitchen—Molly was frying bacon and eggs for the family supper! She was a good little cook. Mrs. Jackson was lying down for a few minutes, tired out. Nothing much remained to be done except one or two more crates to be unpacked—crates of pictures and books and toys—and Michael's collection of tools and "bits and pieces."

Shouting and yelling, the three younger children tore up the front path and into the open front door.

"Mother! We're home!"

"I say—doesn't everything look super?"

"Golly—they've got everything straight already!"

"Oh, doesn't the dining-room look lovely and big—our table looks quite small in it. And what's this little door in the wall—oh, it opens into the kitchen! Hallo, Mollykins!"

Peter had discovered the hatch in the wall connecting the kitchen and dining-room, through which food and plates could be passed. He opened it and stuck his head through, making Molly jump.

20

"Molly! Isn't everything lovely! I say, you must have worked jolly hard."

"We did," said Molly. "It was fun, though. But there's still plenty to be done. It's a good thing to-morrow is Saturday, because you and Michael and Shirley can unpack your toys and books and arrange them yourselves. Mother has given us each a cupboard of our own for our things, and a book-shelf each."

"This is the loveliest house that ever was!" said Shirley, dancing into every room, her eyes shining. "It's a happy house too—it's a house where everything comes right! It's our own dear house, and we'll live here for ever and ever!"

"Idiot!" said Peter, giving his little sister a friendly slap. "Have you seen your bedroom? It's lovely. So's mine."

Each room had to be minutely examined and exclaimed over. Mrs. Jackson, lying exhausted on her bed, could not help smiling at the excited calls and exclamations.

"Look—we've got a new carpet in our bedroom—it's blue like the walls."

"Mike, look here—our room's got a big window-seat, a proper one we can sit on and look out."

"I say, Molly, doesn't Daddy's old grandfather clock look fine in the hall here—and its tick sounds ever so much louder!"

"Hurrah! We're in *Red-Roofs* at last! Molly, is supper nearly ready? I'm frightfully hungry."

"Nearly," called Molly. "Lay the table, Shirley. You'll find everything in the sideboard cupboard and drawers as usual, and I've got the plates warming out here."

Soon they were all six sitting down to supper—and how they enjoyed it! It was such fun sitting in a strange room, a room where there was plenty of space for all of them, and where the windows looked out on to beds of gay flowers. Shirley thought that the bacon and eggs tasted nicer than any she had ever had before. She was very happy. So was everyone. It was a great thing to leave behind the cramped, stuffy life in the old small house, set chock-a-block with dozens of others, exactly alike, in a noisy street.

21

"Things will be much easier here," said Mrs. Jackson. "Especially if I can get a nice woman in to help."

"This is a place where I can ask Prudence and my other friends without feeling ashamed of it," thought Molly. "It's lovely to have a nice home."

"I can work in this garden every week-end, and in the sunny evenings too," said Mr. Jackson, thinking out loud. "I could get a man in once a week perhaps—there's quite a lot to be done."

The boys had their own plans too. Peter was very fond of the country, and loved birds and animals, trees and flowers—and now, here they all were at his doorstep. What a good time he would have! And Michael thought secretly of a shed he had discovered at the end of the garden— suppose Daddy would let him have half of it for his own work-shop? Then he would never need to scatter his things in the house, and be told to tidy them up just when he had got them how he wanted them. He could make as much mess as he liked down in that little shed.

"Have we got a bottle of lemon squash, dear?" said Mr. Jackson, suddenly, to his wife. "I feel we ought to drink to the happiness and success of our new life in this nice little house. After all, from this house the children will go out into the world, train for their work in life, and grow into men and women. We should drink to their success. To-night is a stepping-stone—we leave behind us our struggles and our handicaps, and face the future with hope and contentment."

Everyone was very much impressed. Molly got up and found a bottle of lemon squash standing on a shelf in the larder. They all filled their glasses.

Mr. Jackson held up his. "To the happiness and success of you all!" he said. "To *Red-Roofs* and all it means to us!"

Everyone drank solemnly. Molly suddenly felt tears in her eyes and was rather ashamed. She blinked them away. Her father smiled at her, and lifted his glass again.

"To our Molly and her success as a teacher," he said. "We shall be proud of you, Molly. To our Peter, and his success in years to come as a doctor! To our Michael, and his success too, whatever he chooses to be. And to our little Shirley, bless her!"

"To our dear little family!" said Mrs. Jackson, in rather a shaky voice.

"And here's to the best father and mother in the world!" cried Molly, and emptied her glass in a gulp.

It was the happiest evening the little family had ever spent. Shirley didn't want to go to bed at all, though her eyes were almost closed. She went up at last, when Molly promised to come in a few minutes. The boys soon went too, looking forward to the next day, when they could unpack their possessions. Then Molly went, yawning, feeling tired but happy. She switched the light on in her bedroom, and saw that Shirley was fast asleep in her little bed, her dark hair tumbling over her face. The room looked friendly and cosy, and Molly's heart sang as she undressed.

She drew back the curtains ready for the morning, and leaned out of the open window. The scent of the roses came in and she sniffed it eagerly. Nobody had ever sniffed the night air at the other house—it would have smelt of back yards and dustbins, rather than of roses!

She got into bed and drew the blankets up to her chin. She thought gratefully of her father. He always worked so hard, and now his hard work had enabled them all to have this lovely home. She thought of her mother too, frail and easily-tired. She had worked hard for the children, cooking good meals for them, looking after their clothes, keeping them happy, and often going without things herself in order to give them treats.

"We must pay them back somehow," thought Molly, half asleep. "We must all turn out well, whatever happens! We can't let Mother or Daddy down after all they have done for us! I'll pass all my exams with honours, and one day I'll have a fine school of my own, and give Mother lovely presents. And Peter ought to do well, with his brains—he might be a very famous surgeon, perhaps. That would be lovely. Michael is clever too—I should think he'll be an engineer of some kind—or perhaps a scientist who makes a

23

great discovery, or an inventor who invents something marvellous."

Her thoughts turned to Shirley, pretty little harum-scarum Shirley, alternately teased and petted by the boys and Molly. Shirley was rather spoilt, but she was the youngest and she'd grow out of it. She was selfish and thoughtless sometimes, wanting her own way—but she seemed such a baby compared to the rest of them. She would be a credit to the family too, whatever happened, Molly was sure.

Molly fell asleep, her dark curls spread over the pillow. She had happy dreams. So had everyone in the house that night. Peter awoke once and lay in surprise, wondering where he was, for he could dimly see the unfamiliar outline of the bedroom. Then he realized with a happy shock that he was in his new home, he was at *Red-Roofs*. He lay contentedly for a minute or two, thinking over all he meant to do, before he fell sound asleep again.

The next day was Saturday. Everyone awoke about half-past seven, and nobody wanted to stay in bed for that extra minute or two that is usually so delicious. Mrs. Jackson was down first, preparing the breakfast. Mr. Jackson strolled out into the garden, whistling like a schoolboy. Yes, he would certainly get a man to come in once a week—the rest he could manage himself. And he would get a dog. How the children would love that!

Molly rushed down to set the table and chatter in her usual cheerful way to her mother. The boys tore out into the garden to have a look round in the morning sun. Shirley took her best doll to show her the whole house. Mrs. Jackson said she was getting too big for dolls, but Shirley couldn't bear to part with even the oldest one.

"We ought to be able to finish practically everything today," said Mrs. Jackson, pouring out the tea at the breakfast-table. "I'll unpack the pictures with Daddy and put them up. You children unpack your own belongings. We'll put the crates into the garden and you can unpack them there. You won't make a mess in the house then."

So that morning the four children worked busily. Molly

unpacked her pile of books and arranged them on the book-shelf allotted to her. She stowed away her work-box and knitting into her own cupboard. She set out her vases and few little ornaments here and there in her bedroom. Shirley watched approvingly and went to pick a few flowers for the vases.

"You'll have to try and be tidy now, Shirley," said Molly, looking round the spick and span bedroom. "We can't have such a nice room as this spoilt by clothes thrown about everywhere."

"Oh, of course I'll be tidy," promised Shirley. "Everything will be easy in this house. There's room for everybody and their things. I'll make my own bed each morning, and I'll sweep and dust our room too, if you like."

Molly smiled. She knew Shirley's eager suggestions and promises—but they were not always followed out or kept! "We'll see how you get on," she said. "Let's see what the boys are doing now."

The boys were having a lovely time. They had arranged all their own books and belongings, and Peter had put his most treasured possession, a small second-hand microscope, carefully at the back of his own cupboard. He had saved up for two years for this, and already used it a great deal. He never let any one else use it, but only allowed them to look down the eye-piece occasionally if he were there. He had once fought Michael and given him a black eye when he had found his brother trying to use it by himself.

"Nobody else in the whole school has got a microscope of his own!" he told Michael fiercely. "Nobody else at all. I went without sweets for ages to buy that—and you don't suppose I'm going to let you mess about with it and break it, do you? You know I'm going to be a doctor—and I *must* have a microscope for that! It's the most precious thing I have, and I'll knock your head off if you touch it again!"

Michael had been far too scared to touch it after that. At the other house it had had to stand on the top shelf of the dresser, and Peter couldn't even bear his mother to move it when she dusted the shelf there. But now his precious, beloved microscope was safe—safe at the back of his own cupboard, which had a key and could be locked. Peter was glad.

All the remaining things were unpacked and arranged that day. The empty boxes were piled into a corner of the garden to await the carrier to take them back to the removal firm. Molly and Mrs. Jackson went down to the town to do a little week-end shopping. How good it was to walk back up the hill to *Red-Roofs*, instead of taking the tram to the old dark house at the other end of the town.

"We'll have a real, restful day tomorrow," said Mrs. Jackson, who looked tired out after all her efforts. "I'm so glad to-morrow is Sunday, the day of peace and rest. We shall enjoy walking over the fields to church. Everything is done now. All we need to do is to sit back and enjoy things."

"Oh, there are still a few things to settle," said Mr. Jackson, with a smile.

"What?" asked Molly, in surprise.

"Well—we must find a maid for your mother—a man for the garden—and a dog for us all!" said Mr. Jackson, lighting his pipe. "Don't you think those are good ideas?"

Mr. Jackson liked the idea of the man for the garden and Mrs. Jackson liked the idea of a woman to help her But the children only heard one word—DOG! A dog for the Jackson family, something they had always longed for—a real, live DOG!

CHAPTER FOUR

Jenny Wren

THE Jackson family soon settled down at *Red-Roofs*, and after a week or two it seemed that they had never lived anywhere else.

"I can't even remember what the kitchen was like at the other house," said Shirley. "Where did the dresser stand? And did the bathroom window look out to the front or the back? That house seems like a dream now."

"I've got quite used to going another way to school," said Michael. "At first it seemed awfully funny to take different roads to school—and once when I wasn't thinking I took the old way after school, and found myself standing opposite our old house instead of *Red-Roofs*! "

Everyone laughed. Michael had these queer absent-minded fits at times.

"Thinking of some wonderful new discovery or invention, I suppose?" said Peter sarcastically.

"Well, as a matter of fact I was," said Michael, quick to defend himself. "You know that wireless set of Paul's I'm trying to put right for him? Well, I thought of a way to solve the difficulty—you see, if I put a bit of wire on the . . ."

But nobody wanted to hear. Once Michael started off on his endless explanations of something extremely complicated and technical, people faded away from his company. It sometimes made the boy very sulky and angry.

"You get so serious over your 'bits and pieces'," complained Peter. "You only just mess about, really, and it's a bit of luck when you put things right."

27

"It is *not*," Michael flared. "I have to think out and follow all sorts of theories. It isn't fair of you all to laugh at me as you do. I may be only mending things now, and taking them to pieces and putting them together again — but you just wait till I think out something entirely new and make it myself. You'll sit up then!"

But his family did not take him very seriously, and often laughed at his queer ways and fits of dreaminess. Mr. Jackson sometimes got cross over remarks in his end of term reports.

"Has excellent brains, but dreams too much!" he quoted from one report. "No good having fine brains, my boy, if you don't use them."

Then Michael would retire into his shell, look as black as thunder, and scowl fiercely at anyone who approached him. He would go and brood over his precious "bits and pieces" as everyone called his tools, instruments and material, until a bright idea would send the scowl from his face and he would begin to work happily.

It was Michael who found Miss Wren for them. He came home one day and announced that Miss Wren was coming to see his mother at six o'clock that evening.

"Miss Wren, Michael dear?" said his mother, astonished. "Who is she? And why is she coming to see me?"

"She wants a home," said Michael. "She's being turned out of her cottage, and she's got nowhere to go. She's got her own bed and chest of drawers and things, and our maid's bedroom is unfurnished, isn't it? I thought as you wanted someone to help in the house you might like Miss Wren. She's always working hard whenever I see her."

"But, Michael—we don't know anything at all about her!" said Molly. "Don't be so silly. You can't go round promising bedrooms to people. Mother, isn't he stupid?"

"I'm not stupid," said Michael, obstinately. "I'm sensible. Here's a woman who wants a home, and here are we who want a woman to help in the house. Well, then—the two things fit, don't they?"

Mrs. Jackson began to laugh helplessly. "Oh, Michael—

you do have such queer ideas," she said. "How did you get to know Miss Wren?"

"I mended her clock for her," said Michael.

"But how did you get to *know* her, and where does she live?" said Mrs. Jackson. "You must tell us something about her."

"She lives down near the mills at the other end of the town," said Michael. "In one of those old tumble-down cottages. I went down there one day to see the mills at work, and I fell down just outside Miss Wren's cottage. She was out in the yard, and she took me in and bathed my leg and bound it up. She sounded awfully cross, but she was very kind, and it's only put on, that crossness."

"She sounds rather queer," said Molly.

"Perhaps she is, a bit," said Michael, considering. "She's got a terrific sense of fairness, though. If anyone does her a bit of kindness she can't rest till she pays it back. I like that. Well, anyway, I was jolly grateful to her, because my leg was pretty bad, and I knocked my head, too. She gave me a drink of milk and a bun. Then I noticed a clock on her mantelpiece, a fine old clock with a pendulum. But it wasn't going."

"So you brought it home and made it go!" said Peter with a grin.

"Yes, I did," said Michael. "Fair's fair, isn't it? as Miss Wren keeps saying. Anyway, she said that I'd done more for her old clock than she'd done for me, and she said I could have a look through a lot of the things that once belonged to her brother. He was a clock-maker. So I did, and she let me have a lot of jolly useful tools."

"So that's where you got those fine little tools from!" said Peter. "Why didn't you tell us all this, you funny boy?"

"Oh, I thought you'd laugh at me for having a friend like Miss Wren," said Michael. "You're always laughing at me. She's funny to look at—screws her hair up into a kind of bun thing at the back, and wears skirts down to the ground! And she's awfully independent, and speaks sort of sharply, so that you feel a bit afraid at first, but you get used to it and don't notice it after a bit."

29

"She doesn't sound awfully pleasant," said Mrs. Jackson, not liking the sound of Miss Wren very much. "Whatever made you tell her to come to me?"

"I've told you," said Michael impatiently. "She wants a home and you want a woman. Can't you give her a home and let 'her work here? She's always working in her own home, so I expect she would work here."

"Well, I'll see her when she comes, but I don't expect she would do for us at all," said Mrs. Jackson. "And, Michael dear—please don't go round telling people to come and see me without discussing things with me first. I don't want all the queer old women of the town coming here."

Michael put on one of his scowls. As if he would go round doing that! He only knew one old woman, anyway. Well, if his mother didn't like Miss Wren, he couldn't help it. He had done what he thought was a good thing—but so often his "good things" turned out to be wrong after all.

Miss Wren came up the garden path and went round to the back door at exactly six o'clock. The whole family were looking out for her, and Shirley began to giggle. Certainly Miss Wren was queer-looking. She was very small, and had a wizened face like a brown monkey's. Her hair, which was thin and wiry, was screwed into the tightest little bun at the back, out of which two or three very coarse hairpins stuck. She wore a hat which was garlanded with pink roses, a plain white blouse, and a black skirt that reached her ankles. She wore black cotton gloves and carried a stout umbrella.

"We can't possibly have *her*, Mother!" said Molly in a low voice.

Shirley giggled again and her mother spoke to her sharply. "Go into the garden, Shirley."

Michael opened the back door and grinned at Miss Wren. He was almost as tall as she was, although he was only eleven. "Hallo," he said. "Mother, this is Miss Wren."

"Evening, mam," said Miss Wren in a sharp voice.

Mrs. Jackson looked at the brown monkey-face and unexpectedly she liked what she saw there. The voice was sharp, the whole figure was queer and dowdy, but those brown eyes were gentle and very kind.

"Good evening," said Mrs. Jackson. "Come in. My boy Michael said you were coming."

"He's a nice boy, that one of yours," said Miss Wren, coming in and standing stiffly by the kitchen table. "Knows what fair's fair means, he does. Won't take no advantage of nobody, but gives back any kindness he gets with more of it thrown in."

Michael went red and disappeared into the garden. He couldn't bear to hear himself talked about, whether it was good or bad. Mrs. Jackson looked at Miss Wren and laughed.

"Yes, he's a good boy, but dreamy sometimes," she said. "I don't quite know what to say to you about his idea of your coming here, Miss Wren. I expect he has told you all sorts of tales about our having an empty room, and you probably thought we might let you have it or something. But actually we want a maid, someone who will help me to run the house and take some of the cooking off my hands."

"I see, mam," said Miss Wren. "Well, I couldn't give up my independence like that, no, I couldn't, and that's flat. It's true that I go out working by the day to oblige a lady sometimes—but I've been used to my own little bit of a home; I'm not dependent on nobody and never could be. I couldn't be nobody's slave."

"Of course not," said Mrs. Jackson, amused. "We don't want a slave, as you call it. I'm sure you wouldn't like being here, having to work to somebody else's time-table instead of to your own, living in someone else's house instead of in your own cottage."

"Well, I shouldn't," said Miss Wren, still standing very stiffly, her face more like a monkey's than ever. She looked round the spick-and-span kitchen. She saw the refrigerator, the larder with its stone shelves, the neat boiler on the hearth, the half-tiled black and white walls. "Nice place you've got here," she said. "It must be a pleasure to work in a kitchen like this. You should see mine! I haven't even a tap in it—have to go a quarter of a mile to a pump. We're badly off in those old cottages by the mills. Don't wonder

31

they're condemned and will soon be pulled down. But it's hard on people like me who's got nowhere else to go. You wouldn't believe how high the rents are in decent cottages nowadays! "

Mrs. Jackson bent down and opened the oven of her gas stove. She pulled out a tray of new-baked buns. Miss Wren looked at them with approval.

"Try one," said Mrs. Jackson, and scraped one free of its tin. "Peter, take some to the others—they love them when they are new."

When Peter came back he was surprised at what he saw. Miss Wren and his mother were washing up the cooking and baking dishes together. Miss Wren had draped an overall round her and was washing, while his mother dried the things.

"Just giving a bit of a hand," said Miss Wren, seeing Peter's surprised face. "Must do something in return for that nice bun. Fair's fair, you know."

Michael came in a little afterwards and spoke to Miss Wren. "Come and see my bedroom. Mother, can I show Miss Wren my bedroom? I've told her a lot about it."

Miss Wren not only saw his bedroom, but the whole house, too. Michael took her into the little empty room at the end of the landing which was to be the maid's room.

"This was the room I said we had empty," he told her. "It's such a dear little room, and I could just see you in it, somehow."

"I couldn't accept no charity from anyone," said Miss Wren sharply. "I couldn't afford to pay the rent of a room like this, and to get it for nothing I'd have to lose my independence, and that's a thing I won't do, not for anyone. Anyways, your mother could never make do with a little old thing like me—she wants a smart girl, that looks nice when she answers the door and all. Oh, you naughty boy— just see the marks you've made on the clean wall with your dirty hands! Now you go straight downstairs and get a wet cloth and bring it up here to me."

Michael grinned. Miss Wren's bark was so much worse than her bite. He went downstairs to get a wet cloth.

"Mother, you do like her, don't you?" he said. "I know she's funny, but she's awfully nice really, and she's always doing kind things for people. I believe she'd come, only she thinks she's too old and dowdy for you. She just loves that little room."

"Well, dear, I do like her," said his mother, "but she'd never come—she's too independent—and besides, we don't know anything about her at all. If her references were all right I'd certainly try her, poor little old thing—she looks lonely and lost somehow."

Michael said no more, but climbed the stairs and presented Miss Wren with the wet cloth. She was soon rubbing away at the wall.

"Mother likes you," said Michael. "I knew she would. My mother always knows when people are nice. She would like you to come here, I know, and live with us, and have this room, and pay you wages, and . . ."

"So that I lose my independence, like I said!" said Miss Wren fiercely. "No, thank you! Now don't you say any more about it!"

"All right," said Michael, and put on his sulky look.

Miss Wren noticed it at once. "Now don't you look like that!" she said sharply. "Spoiling your nice face! Ashamed of yourself you should be."

She went downstairs, washed out the cloth, patted herself down, settled her hat straight and said good-bye. "It's been a pleasure to meet your family, mam," she said, her dark brown eyes fixed on Mrs. Jackson's. "And to see your nice little house. And it's a place I'd like to come to if I didn't have to lose my independence, so it is!"

She went out of the back door, and was soon walking down the hillside. She had a tram to catch home—but she didn't catch it. Instead she sat down on a wooden bench and shut her eyes. She saw that little room again, with its windows opening on to the garden. She saw her furniture there—her small bed, her old chest of drawers, her comfortable chair, her best carpet. She saw herself in that beautiful kitchen, putting things into that wonderful refrigerator, standing things on those cool larder shelves,

33

wiping over those black and white tiles. She saw herself standing out in that lovely flowery garden, pegging up clothes that would dry dazzling white in the sun. No soot from the mills, no dust, no dirt.

Then she spoke to herself. "Well, fair's fair. Suppose I take that little room for myself and give back work in exchange; that's fair enough, isn't it? I don't want wages, and I'm old now and get a bit tired—but I'm worth a room to myself. And that boy Michael's there. He's a nice boy, for all his funny ways. I've a good mind to go back and tell them what I think is fair. I won't be their maid, I won't give up my independence, not for nobody, but I'll work in return for my room, because fair's fair."

So, to Mrs. Jackson's astonishment, Miss Wren knocked at the back door and walked in again, twenty minutes after she had left. She expounded her idea of what was fair to Mrs. Jackson, who listened seriously.

"I see, Miss Wren," she said. "You would like to come and have that room, with your own furniture in it, and in return you will work in the house for me. But I should give you money as well, please understand that."

"No, thank you," said Miss Wren firmly. "I have a few shillings a week of my own, and that's all I want. I'm not taking no charity. I want the room and you want a bit of help in the house. You give me one and I'll give you the other. That's fair, and a bargain. I don't want nothing else. I'll keep my independence that way. I don't come on any other terms."

And so, when references had been taken up, and Miss Wren had sold the bits of furniture she didn't want, she arrived at *Red-Roofs* to add to the happy little household there. Mrs. Jackson had been worried about the question of wages, but Mr. Jackson had laughed at her.

"You can always give her nice presents," he said. "Make it up that way. Anyway, she mayn't be worth much. We shall have to see."

Miss Wren arranged her bits of furniture in the little room. She garbed herself in enormous white aprons over her black skirt. She scared the tradespeople with her sharp

34

tongue. She fed all the birds in the garden with scraps and crumbs. She scolded Shirley for her untidiness. She ordered Mrs. Jackson to lie down every afternoon. She made Peter sweep up the dried mud that dropped from his boots on to the carpet. She was an absolute dragon.

And yet they all liked the new little dragon immensely! She kept the house spotless, and as for the little kitchen, it twinkled everywhere you looked. She could bake the most delicious pies. She would scold Michael for something he had forgotten, and the next moment she would hand him out a hot jumble from the oven.

"She's like a funny little bustling bird," said Peter. "A little busy bird with a loud voice!"

"A wren!" said Molly at once. "Of course—she's like a Jenny Wren—loud-voiced and busy and small. She's a Jenny Wren."

So Jenny Wren she became, and she, like the others, settled down at *Red-Roofs* happily, busy in her little kitchen all day long and retiring to her nest at night.

"Good night, Jenny Wren," Shirley would say at half-past seven when she went to bed. "Good night, Jenny Wren."

"What sauce to call me Jenny Wren at my age!" Miss Wren would say, but her gentle brown eyes would twinkle, and everyone would smile. Jenny Wren liked her new name, and her new family, and her new home, just as much as her new family liked her!

CHAPTER FIVE

Bundle

THE next excitement was the dog. The children had badgered their father continually since he had suggested a dog for them.

"I want a terrier," said Peter. "They're sharp and neat and trim."

"Oh, *no*," said Michael. "Let's have a big dog—a fierce one, like an Alsatian. Or what about a Great Dane?"

"No," said Mrs. Jackson decidedly. "Certainly not. Good gracious, a Great Dane in this little house would be ridiculous! Every time he sat down he'd rattle all the ornaments, and when he wagged his tail he'd send everything off the table!"

Shirley at once longed for a Great Dane. A dog that did things like that would be marvellous. Molly wanted a Sealyham. Prudence had a Sealyham, and it would be nice to have a dog like hers.

"Pooh! Always copy-catting that silly Prudence!" said Peter. "For goodness' sake! Who wants a short-legged dog like that wandering about? Gracious, if its legs were much shorter they wouldn't reach the ground!"

Shirley had not heard his joke before, and she squealed with laughter. Mrs. Jackson looked round humorously. "Everyone wants a different kind of dog! We shall have to get a mongrel, a mixture of all the different breeds!"

"No, thank you," said Mr. Jackson decidedly. "I haven't waited all these years to have a mongrel dog, nice as they can be. We'll have a pedigree dog worthy of *Red-Roofs*."

"What kind?" said Peter. But again nobody could agree. And then the dog itself decided for them!

It was Sunday afternoon and the six Jacksons had left Jenny Wren in charge of the house and had walked over the hill and down the other side, where one or two farmhouses were dotted about. Red and white cows were in the fields and sheep grazed on the hilltop.

36

They sat down beside the hedge and took out their tea. They had a lovely view in front of them. They munched their jam sandwiches and looked contentedly over the valley below and the hills rising beyond.

Shirley suddenly gave a squeal. "Oh! You bad, wicked dog! Oh, Mother, this dog has eaten my sandwiches. Oh, you bad dog, I'll smack you!"

Everyone turned to look at the little thief who had crept through the hedge and had gobbled up poor Shirley's sandwiches. It was nothing but a puppy, about ten weeks' old—a black, silky cocker spaniel, with long drooping ears that almost touched the ground. He gazed mournfully at six accusing pairs of eyes. Then he unexpectedly rolled over on his back and lay there, quite still, his four paws in the air.

"Do you think that's his way of saying he's sorry?" said Shirley, in surprise. "It must be. Roll over, little dog. I've forgiven you. Oh, Mother, isn't he sweet?"

He really was. He looked at them all with big, sad brown eyes, and his look melted everyone's heart. Molly stroked his soft ears. Peter patted him. Michael tickled him. Shirley hugged him and he licked her cheek.

The spaniel would not leave them. He begged titbits from each of them in turn, he pawed their arms, he butted them with his black nose, he looked at them so meltingly that one and all thought him the most marvellous puppy they had ever seen.

"I think the person he belongs to is very, very lucky," said Shirley, as they got up to go home. "You must go back to your home, now, puppy. We are going home too."

But the puppy had no intention of going home. He liked this family. He liked their voices and their smell and the touch of their hands. He meant to go with them.

"Go home!" said everyone, but still the puppy followed them, his tail down and his eyes looking beseechingly at them. Mr. Jackson stopped in exasperation.

"This silly animal will go right home with us if we don't send him off. I wonder whom he belongs to."

"Let's ask this shepherd," said Molly, and she called to

an old man in the field nearby. "Do you know whose puppy this is?"

"Aye, missie. He belongs to old Lassie's last litter. Farmer Thomas owns him," said the shepherd, and pointed with his stick to the farmhouse not far off.

"We'd better take him there," said Mr. Jackson, so they all trooped across the field-path that led to the farm. Molly knocked at the old farmhouse door. A loud voice roared to them to come in. Mr. Jackson opened the door. Sitting at tea was a big burly farmer, his wife at his elbow serving him with some kind of hot dish.

"Excuse our coming along like this," said Mr. Jackson, "but this puppy of yours attached himself to us and wouldn't leave us. So we brought him back."

"Ah, he's a wanderer, he is," said the farmer. "Won't stay to home, that he won't. Be glad when I get rid of him, so I will. Folks is always bringing him back."

"Get rid of him? What do you mean, get rid of him?" said Shirley, in alarm.

"Sell him, missie," said the farmer. "He's the last one of the litter. You don't want a dog by any chance, do you?"

Away flew all thoughts of Alsatians, Great Danes, Sealyhams, and terriers from the minds of the six Jacksons! Want a dog? Well, they wanted the little spaniel, there was no doubt about that at all!

"Daddy!" said four urgent voices, and Molly slipped her hand through her father's arm. "Daddy! Can we have him?"

"Well—how much is he?" said Mr. Jackson, doubtfully. "Is he a pedigree dog?"

"Can't you see he is?" said the big farmer, wiping his mouth and getting up to go to the door. "He's a fine dog, that little fellow. You can have him for three guineas, and that's dirt cheap."

It was cheap for a pedigree spaniel, but to the children it sounded a small fortune. Three guineas for a puppy! Goodness gracious!

"I'll give him to you for your birthday, Dick dear," said

Mrs. Jackson. She could see how much her husband liked the little creature.

"No, Mother. Let's *all* buy him! " said Michael suddenly. "All of us, so that he belongs to us all and not to any special person. I've got some money in my money box and so has Shirley, and the others have some money in the post-office savings. Let's *all* buy him! "

Everyone thought that was a fine idea. Then the dog would belong to the whole family. He would be a Jackson dog.

"Right," said Mr. Jackson, and he felt in his pocket for his wallet. He took out three pound notes, and three shillings from his trousers' pocket. He handed them to the farmer. "Here you are. Send me the pedigree along when you've time. We live at *Red-Roofs* over the hill."

"Ah," said the farmer, pocketing the money. "Nice little house that. Lucky house too, so people say. Everyone's had good luck there so far. Hope you will have too."

"Oh we shall! " said Shirley. "We've had good luck so far, because we've got Jenny Wren and now we've got this darling puppy. What's his name?"

"Oh, he answers to anything," said the farmer, with a grin. "Call him what you like."

So the puppy went home with the Jackson family after all, just as he had made up his mind to do. He ran along beside them, wagging his plume-like tail, his pink tongue out, his eyes sparkling. He didn't mind leaving the farm. These were the people he wanted. They belonged to him.

The children were delighted with him. They took him to see Jenny Wren as soon as they got in, and it was she who really named him. She stared at the little dog, and spoke sharply as usual. "Dear dear—dogs just dirty the place up, and make twice as much work for anyone. But I warn him, if he starts chewing up any of my things, he'll get a wallop with a broom-handle! What's his name?"

"He hasn't got one, Jenny Wren," said Molly. "We'll have to think of one. What about Tinker?"

"No," said Michael. "There was a Tinker in our old street and he was a horrid dog. Let's call him Scamp."

Nobody liked that. It didn't fit the puppy at all.

"Silky?" said Shirley, stroking his black silky coat. "Or Paddy-Paws?"

"Shadow," said Peter, whose favourite book once had been about a dog called Shadow.

The puppy stood and stared up at them, trying to understand what they were saying. He wagged his tail at every new name. He didn't seem to mind what he was called. Then he got tired of listening and darted to a nearby rug. He pulled it up and began to shake it to and fro as if it were a rat, making funny growling noises all the time. Jenny Wren gave a squeal of horror and snatched it away from him.

"Bad dog! A bundle of mischief you are, and a bundle of trouble you'll be!"

"Oh!" said Molly. "That's his name—Bundle! A bundle of mischief, a darling soft silly bundle of dog! Bundle!"

"Wuff," said the puppy, and wagged his tail hard. Everyone agreed in delight that his name should be Bundle. "It's just right for him," said Molly. "And it's good to call, too. When you give a dog a name, it must be one that is easy to call. Come here, Bundle!"

"That *was* a good idea of Jenny Wren's," said Michael. "Jenny, you've named the new Jackson. Let me introduce the two of you—Mr. Bundle Jackson, Miss Jenny Wren!"

"You've more nonsense in you than the dog!" said Jenny Wren, in her usual sharp voice, but her eyes had a pleased twinkle. Bundle would find a friend in her, and she would find a friend in him. He would never go short of food and fresh water while Jenny was about.

And so it was that Bundle came to join the little family at *Red-Roofs*, and quickly became one of them, accompanying them everywhere they went, burying bones in the garden, scratching at doors to be let in or out, and chewing up slippers and rugs and cushions in spite of Jenny's constant threats of "walloping with a broom-handle." He was soon "that nice little spaniel of the Jacksons at *Red-Roofs*," and took his rightful place as one of the important members of the family.

CHAPTER SIX

Prudence Comes to Tea

MOLLY related to her school fellows all the happenings at *Red-Roofs*. She was a friendly, unreserved girl and she poured out everything. Her friends knew of the blue carpet in her bedroom, the spotless refrigerator in the kitchen, the crazy paving paths in the garden, Jenny Wren's coming, and, of course, they heard every day about Bundle the spaniel.

Joan Rennie was pleased to hear it all. It was nice to see her friend so happy. Prudence listened with a rather supercilious air. How stupid to revel in all these simple things, she thought. She had had a beautiful bedroom, a dog of her own, a bicycle, and goodness knows what ever since she could remember.

Molly brought Joan home to tea, and showed her everything. Joan admired it all, and adored the spaniel puppy. He pranced round the girls' feet, his long ears flopping about. He could bark in a high puppy bark that made everyone laugh. His tricks were endless, some of them laughable, others more serious that brought down Jenny Wren's wrath.

Prudence came to tea too, dressed in a fine silk frock, patterned with red and blue that suited her to perfection. She was very much the great lady that day, rather languid and haughty, looking down her nose at everything, much to Molly's disappointment. She had so badly wanted Prudence to admire everything as Joan had done.

"I'm afraid this new carpet of yours won't wear very well," said Prudence, rubbing her foot along it. She had a small and dainty foot, and Molly was always conscious of

41

her own much larger feet when she was with Prudence. "It's not a very good one, you know."

Shirley was in the room. She was always rather in awe of Prudence, and although she thought she was marvellous in many ways, she hated her with all the strength of her loyal little heart whenever she thought Prudence was upsetting Molly.

"This carpet is a very good one," said Shirley, in a loud voice. "It cost fifty pounds. I'm sure yours didn't cost as much, Prudence!"

Molly cast a look of surprise and horror at Shirley, who stood there, very red and hot. She knew Shirley was telling untruths—the carpet had only cost a few pounds. Shirley made a rude face, marched out of the room and banged the door.

"What a dreadful child!" said Prudence, languidly. "Badly brought up, I suppose, because she's the youngest. I wonder you don't deal with her, Molly."

"Shirley's all right," said Molly, shortly. She wasn't going to have Prudence criticizing her little sister! She could turn up her nose at carpets and chairs and beds, if she wanted to—but not at any member of Molly's family!

Mrs. Jackson disliked Prudence's airs and graces. The boys sniggered every now and again and Prudence looked at them coldly. Both boys thought her very pretty and dainty, but her affected little voice grated on them, and when Michael suddenly imitated it when he asked for the jam, it sent Shirley, and Peter too, into fits of laughter.

Molly glared at Michael. It was too bad of him to be so rude when Prudence came. He had been very nice when Joan came to tea, and had even taken her down to the shed to show her his "work-shop" as he now called it. Molly did badly want to make a good impression on Prudence, and things hadn't gone at all well so far.

"Michael, don't be silly," said Mrs. Jackson. Michael put on a scowl. He never liked being scolded in public. He didn't say another word all through tea, not even when he was spoken to. Prudence thought he was a very disagreeable boy.

"Funny manners your brothers have," she said, after tea, when they went into the garden, with Bundle careering round them. "I'm glad my brother has better manners, I must say. You've met him, haven't you, Molly?"

Molly had. Bernard was as good-looking as Prudence, but the girl had found his good manners quite overpower·ing. He had opened the door for her every time she left the room with Prudence, he had offered to carry even the flower she had picked when she had walked round the garden, and had made conversation the whole time in a very grown-up way. Molly privately thought that she much preferred her own downright brothers, even if they hadn't nearly as good manners as Bernard.

Prudence frankly sneered at little Jenny Wren, and hardly waited for her to be out of the room before she laughed.

"What an odd creature!" she said. "So that's Jenny Wren you're always talking about! Really, Molly, I wonder your mother doesn't give her a proper uniform, and train her well. I should think all your visitors laugh when she answers the door."

"Well, they don't laugh twice," said Molly. "Jenny Wren has got a very sharp tongue—so you be careful she doesn't overhear what you say, Prudence."

Jenny Wren disapproved highly of Prudence. Whenever she came near the girl she gave her such a cold look that Prudence felt quite shrivelled. How could the Jacksons like such a person, she thought. Just like them.

She didn't even like Bundle very much—and Bundle captured everyone's heart from the very first moment, as a rule. "He's too boisterous!" complained Prudence. "Always rubbing round your legs, and barking for something. He isn't properly trained. Now my Sealyham really knows how to behave."

Molly thought of Prudence's heavy, fat, over-fed dog. Certainly he never barked, and he would find it almost impossible to run. Bundle was a thousand times nicer!

"Bundle is a dear," said Molly. "He's only a puppy yet.

Give him a chance, and he'll grow into a fine dog—and not as fat as yours, I hope!"

Prudence had enjoyed her afternoon. She loved turning up her nose at things, loved making people feel small. Secure in her own position, with rich parents and a beautiful house, fortunate in her looks and figure, she was a spoilt and selfish girl. People couldn't help admiring her prettiness and daintiness, and when she wanted to be charming there was no one who could be sweeter than Prudence. But Molly's two brothers were not deceived, and neither was small Shirley!

When Prudence had gone, after a gracious good-bye and many thanks for *such* a pleasant time, the boys had a wonderful half-hour imitating her.

"Thank you *so* much, Mrs. Jackson!" began Michael. "What a wonderful house you have! To be sure, Molly's carpet won't last very long because it isn't a good one—and Shirley's eiderdown is only silk one side—and Jenny Wren doesn't wear a cap—and the refrigerator *is* rather small for such a big family, isn't it—and although your boys are *sweet*, it's a pity they haven't better manners—still, I *did* enjoy the afternoon, dear Mrs. Jackson. Thank you *so* much!"

Shirley squealed with laughter. Then she too mimicked Prudence, getting up and walking across the room in the rather affected, but very graceful manner of the older girl. "What a beautiful garden you have, Molly! But if I were you I'd get a man in to do it properly. It's a shame to see so many weeds. And couldn't you get a few new rose-trees next year—these look very old and overgrown. But still, it's a *lovely* garden!"

Peter did his bit too. He sat down at the table and pretended to be Prudence at tea. "Oh, thank you, Mrs. Jackson, yes, I'd love to try the cake. Is it really home-made? Of course, I *love* home-made cakes, but I wonder if you've tried the cakes at Lymington's in the High Street? *Such* lovely ones, and they look as nice as they taste. Is that marrow jam? How perfect! But I wonder why it goes so runny, don't you? Now, when our cook makes it . . ."

Molly came into the room and frowned. She felt exhausted after having coped with Prudence for three hours. She was bitterly disappointed too, and sad. Somehow Prudence had taken all the glow and sweetness from everything. She had unerringly put her finger on any little failing or fault in the house, in the garden, and in the family too. Still, she wanted Prudence for a friend. She wanted to dress like Prudence, she wanted to have as nice things as Prudence had, she still wanted to model herself and her family on Prudence's.

So she was very angry with Peter. "Shut up!" she said. unexpectedly bitter. "No wonder Prudence thinks you're all a bad-mannered crowd! Taking her off like this—and you did it in front of her too! *I* heard you talking in a high voice, pretending you were Prudence, at tea-time, Michael. I think you're all mean! And Shirley, how dare you tell such an awful untruth to Prudence? I'm ashamed of you, I really am!"

"She's awful!" said Michael. "People think she's pretty and has lovely manners—but you just look at her bad-tempered mouth with its thin lips, and the way she screws up her eyes when she says something nasty. I hate her!"

Michael banged out of the room. Molly pursed up her mouth and went up to her bedroom. She sat by the window and cried to herself.

Wasn't *Red-Roofs* as nice as she had thought? Wasn't her family as admirable as she had always felt it was? Was she, Molly, wrong in being proud of the pretty new house and garden, and of all her household, not forgetting darling Bundle? For the first time a doubt of herself and her own judgment crept into her heart.

Bundle flung himself against the door, burst it open and threw himself on Molly. He licked her hand, tried to get on on to her knee, looked up at her with his brown, soulful eyes, and butted his cold little nose against her leg.

"Oh, Bundle!" said Molly, laughing through her tears. "I don't care what anyone in the world says about you! I love you and I think you're the dearest, darlingest puppy in the world. You've made me feel better already."

45

Molly confided to her mother that night that Prudence hadn't liked anything very much. Mrs. Jackson smiled. Molly was sitting close beside her, on a stool, knitting. Her mother put her arm lightly round the girl's shoulders.

"I'm sorry for poor little Prudence!" she said. "And you should be too, Molly."

Molly was intensely surprised. "Sorry for *Prudence*!" she said, hardly believing her ears. "Mother, whatever do you mean? Why, Prudence has everything a girl could want. She's unbelievably lucky, I think. I only wish I was as pretty as she is, and had her charming manners."

"What is the good of a pretty face if there is a spiteful heart beneath it?" said Mrs. Jackson. "Has Prudence any real friends, dear? She knows the meaning of riches and good food, a car, servants and things of that kind, but does she know the meaning of kindness, loyalty, humility and charity? I don't think so. Those are the real things, the things to be desired. Prudence is not a happy girl and never will be. I am very sorry for her. My little Molly is worth ten of her!"

"Oh, Mother, I'm not!" said Molly, but she felt happy in knowing how much her mother thought of her.

"You should try and help Prudence a little," said Mrs. Jackson. "It would do her good to come here and see a loyal and united family, where kindness and give-and-take and loyalty are shown every day. There is not much of that in Prudence's home, you know. Her father and mother quarrel, Bernard is wild and unruly, and Prudence herself is wilful and selfish. She is very much to be pitied."

This was all very surprising to Molly, who, in common with most of the girls in her class, thought Prudence was the luckiest, prettiest, most-to-be-envied girl there. Even Joan admired her looks and dresses.

"Well, I'll ask Prudence again," she said at last. "But I don't expect she'll want to come after Shirley's silly behaviour and the boys' bad manners."

"Oh, those will be quite good for her," said Mrs. Jackson. "I don't mean that I shall encourage them to behave badly, of course, but to them Prudence rings false, and they treat her accordingly. You can't complain of the way they behaved to Joan, can you?"

"Oh, *no*," said Molly, remembering the way Shirley had shown Joan all her dolls, and how the boys had taken her round the garden and down to the "work-shop." "No, Mother—they were really sweet to Joan, and she thought they were marvellous. And so they are."

"So we all are when we are with people we like and who bring out the best in us," said Mrs. Jackson. "So would Prudence be, too, if she could forget her pride and her habit of sneering at everything, and could really like and admire somebody else. Then she would try to please them instead of hurting them, and we should see quite a different side of her. But I don't think poor Prudence likes anyone but herself at the moment."

"Mother, I do think you are terribly wise," said Molly, rubbing her curly head against Mrs. Jackson's arm. "I really will try to help Prudence. I see her in a different way now—your way. I won't envy her any more."

"She probably envies *you* and your happiness and united family," said Mrs. Jackson. "Poor Prudence!"

CHAPTER SEVEN

End of Term

MOLLY'S last term rapidly came to an end. The school was to break up on the twenty-fifth of July. There was to be a garden party for the parents at the end, and all the girls were to wear white dresses and to manage the tea themselves.

Molly couldn't help feeling a little sad when she thought that no longer would she go to her familiar place in the sixth form each day. Miss Jenks, the history mistress, would not scold her again for forgetting her dates. Miss Kenton would not mark her compositions, "Could do better, I am sure," and Mam'zelle would not lift her hand to the ceiling and cry, "Ah, this Molly! She should be in the kindergarten!"

Nearly all the sixth form girls were leaving, but most of them were glad. They discussed their future lives eagerly. Few of them were starting work till September, but one or two began the following week. Joan Rennie was one of these.

"I shan't see very much of you, I'm afraid, Molly," she said. "My hours are long—nine till six—and I shall want to do some work in the evenings till I am as good as the other girls in the office."

"Poor Joan!" said Prudence, in a tone of great commiseration. "It *is* hard luck having to start work so soon. *We* are going abroad, you know. Don't you wish you were coming with us?"

"No," said Joan, politely but firmly. "I don't. I should be bored living the life you want to lead, Prudence. I've got brains, and I want to use them. As a matter of fact, I think every girl ought to have some kind of work to do,

48

whether she needs to earn her living or not. Even if my people were rich, which they are not, I should still take a job. I like working. I like using my brains."

"I suppose you think because I've never bothered to go in for swotting up for exams that I've got no brains!" said Prudence, flaring up. "Well, you're wrong. I've got plenty of brains, and if I had to earn my own living I'd do it a lot better than you!"

"I'm sure you've got brains," said Joan. "But they haven't shown up very strongly yet, have they, so you can't blame us for not knowing about them, Prudence. You're nearly always bottom, and you don't even play games well. Still—I dare say you *have* got wonderful brains, and *if* the day ever comes when you feel like earning your own living, I'm sure you'll get a most wonderful job and earn at least a thousand a year!"

Prudence flushed and turned away. She had never liked the plain-speaking Joan. Plain-spoken and plain-faced! How anyone could like Joan Rennie, Prudence simply did not know. Molly, remembering that she had said she would help Prudence, tried to pour oil on the troubled waters.

"What are you going to wear for the garden party, Prudence?" she asked. And, just as she had expected, Prudence forgot Joan's direct words, and began to talk eagerly of the pretty dress her mother had brought from London for her.

The party was a great success. All the girls served the tea well, and waited on their guests prettily and efficiently. The mothers of the girls were there, and Prudence's mother was, of course, by far the best-dressed there. But Molly, glancing from Mrs. Williams' rather discontented face and perfect figure to her own mother's sweet, faintly anxious face and dark simple frock, felt that she would not exchange her mother for any other there, and certainly not for Mrs. Williams.

The Headmistress made an excellent speech. She spoke of the girls who were leaving and the jobs they were going to. She wished them luck, and reminded them that loyalty, honesty and conscientiousness in their work mattered as much as quickness or brilliance. She picked out specially one or two girls she was very sorry to lose, because of their good influence on the others, big and small.

"Joan Rennie we are very sorry to part with," she said. "She has a sterling character, and whatever work she takes up will be well done. I think she will go far. Then I hope also that Fanny Wilson, with her great gift for music, will bring honour to her school. Fanny not only has a gift for music, but has a talent for really hard work. When these two things go together, there is no saying what heights they will lead to."

Everyone applauded. Fanny was popular and very gifted. She sat blushing, a golden-haired girl with very blue eyes, her long, nervous fingers locked in her lap.

"I would like to speak of all my girls who are leaving," said the Headmistress, glancing round at the rows of young, eager faces. "But there is not time. Still, I think I must speak of one more."

Prudence sat erect, feeling certain that the Headmistress must be going to mention her. She had always been careful to be polite and charming to the Head, had never got into any serious trouble, and had always brought her flowers on her birthday and sent her a beautiful present of some kind at Christmas. Then, too, her father and mother had always presented the best prizes—prizes for sports, gym, and various subjects. But it was not Prudence that the Head spoke about. It was Molly.

"There is one girl we are not going to lose," said the Head, and she smiled at Molly. "Molly is certainly leaving the sixth form, but she is going to the kindergarten to learn the serious business of teaching others. Molly is going to take the Froebel exams, and she will be with us for the next two or three years, learning her profession, taking her exams, and working with the little ones of four to eight. We are all delighted about this, because Molly is the kind of girl we certainly do not want to lose sight of. She has a fine character which will be a splendid influence in the lower forms."

The Head had to pause because clapping broke out.

Molly was fiery red and more surprised than she had ever been in her life. Goodness gracious—she hadn't for a moment guessed that the Headmistress, awesome and dignified, had known all this about her! She glanced at her mother. Mrs. Jackson was sitting proudly upright, and a small tear ran down her cheek. She was very much touched by this public praise of her elder daughter.

"Well, I won't say much more," said the Head. "I shall know how Molly goes on, because she will be under my eye, so to speak—but I hope each one of you will keep in touch with me, come to me for advice and help if you need it, and let me know how you get on."

All the girls who were leaving made up their minds at once that they would do as the Head said and keep in touch with her. They all determined to do well, to work hard, and to be a success. All but Prudence, who, annoyed at not being mentioned, and with no job to go to, sat rather sullenly through the rest of the speech. She wouldn't keep in touch with the Head, but she would show her that she, Prudence, was the most marvellous girl she had ever had in her silly school! She would be a great social success, she would go everywhere and do everything and in the end she would make a most wonderful marriage, have the finest wedding ever held, and send an invitation to the Head. Poor, silly little Prudence!

The boys and Shirley broke up on the same day. All four children had their reports, as usual. It was always a ceremony opening them and reading them. Bad work, laziness, lateness—all these might be glossed over during term-time, but any glaring fault always appeared in the end of term reports!

On the whole all the reports were good. "Too dreamy," appeared once more in Michael's report, but on the other hand he was top in maths, science and history. Shirley's was very good, although the word "untidy" occurred twice. Mrs. Jackson nodded her head and looked at Shirley over her glasses.

"Well, if I were giving you a report on your *home* behaviour last term, I should certainly have put 'untidy' more

51

than twice!" she said. "I'm getting tired of seeing 'dreamy' in Mike's report, and 'untidy' in yours, Shirley. These things are pointed out so that you can get hold of them and conquer them, you know. Now don't let me see them in *next* term's report!"

Molly had a fine report and Peter's was very satisfactory, too. Once upon a time he had had the word "lazy" appearing far too often, and then, after a serious talk with his father, Peter had made up his mind never to let it appear again. And, to his father's delight, the boy had enough strength of character to keep his resolution.

"You see, Peter, if you really do want to be a doctor, you'll have to work hard for years and years, and to take no end of exams," his father had told him. "It's just no use at all thinking of being a doctor if you're lazy. You might just as well give up the idea."

Peter had wanted to be a doctor as long as he could remember. When he was six or seven he had run a hospital of Molly's dolls, bandaging them and visiting them in a most professional manner. Now that he was fifteen, growing up, he was a serious, kindly fellow, given to sudden jokes, always ready to help anyone in trouble, but having little patience with shams or frauds.

"Peter will never suck up to old women or selfish people who think they're ill when they're not!" said Michael. "You won't make a fortune that way, Peter."

"I should hope not!" said Peter indignantly. "And, anyway, who cares about making fortunes? I'm going in for doctoring because I want to cure people, to give them back their health and happiness, not to squeeze money out of them all the time."

"You will be a fine doctor, old son," said Mr. Jackson, making up his mind for the hundredth time that whatever it cost him to get Peter through his medical exams, he would manage it somehow. The boy was meant to be a doctor, there was no doubt about it—and people who had a real vocation for anything ought to be helped to follow it.

The reports were dealt with, discussed thoroughly, and

then filed away with the dozens already collected. Now for the holidays! The four children felt thrilled.

"Are we going away?" asked Michael, not very hopefully. The matter had not been discussed at all by his parents as it usually was. The children felt certain that because of the expense of the new house and the move there would be no money available that year for a seaside holiday. Well, never mind—two months at *Red-Roofs* would be marvellous!

"Well, Michael, I don't quite know yet," said Mr. Jackson. "There is something in the wind at the office, but I haven't heard what it is yet. It affects me, I know, and means a change of some kind, even though, as you know, I have just become head of my department. It can only mean a change for the better again, but I can't quite see how yet."

"Oh—so you are waiting to know, Daddy, before you make holiday plans?" said Molly.

"Yes," said her father. "Perhaps I am to get a bonus— an unexpected fifty pounds or even a hundred—and if I do we will all go off for a few weeks together. We'll see."

"Oooh!" said Shirley. "What a lot of money that would be. When will you know, Daddy?"

"To-morrow," said her father. "I'll tell you the news, whatever it is, to-morrow evening. Now I'm going to go out and see if Daw has come."

Daw was the man who came to help in the garden each week. He was a young fellow about seventeen, shy and clumsy. He had an enormous shock of hair that fell over his forehead, startlingly blue eyes, very white teeth, a big nose and enormous ears that stuck out at the side of his head.

He did odd jobs in people's gardens, and was a hard worker, but found it difficult to speak more than a few words at a time. Whenever anyone said anything to him he would shake back his black hair, look down at his feet, and say, "Ar," very wisely.

"He says 'Ar' to simply everything," complained Shirley, who was a great chatterbox and liked to talk to everyone.

"When I told him my doll Josephine had got measles, he said 'Ar,' just like that, and when I told him I'd broken up, he said 'Ar,' too, and even when I asked him what his Christian name was, he only said 'Ar.' It *can't* be 'Ar.' I've never heard of anybody called 'Ar.' "

"Might be short for Arthur," suggested Michael, grinning at Shirley.

"Or Archibald," said Peter. "Only somehow Archibald doesn't fit him."

Nobody knew what his Christian name was till he had to sign a receipt for something one day. Then he signed himself J. Daw in large childish, straggling letters.

"*J.* Daw," said Peter, looking at it. "What's J. stand for?"

For once the boy did not answer "Ar." "Jack," he said. "J. for Jack."

"Jack Daw! " said Peter at once, and yelled to the others. "I say, listen to this—his Christian name is Jack and his surname is Daw—so he's Jack Daw. We've got two nice birds in our household now—Jenny Wren and Jackdaw! "

A grin appeared on Jackdaw's face. It seemed that he saw the joke and liked it. He looked shyly at the four children round him, showing his white teeth and blue eyes.

"You're not really a bit like a jackdaw, you know," said Shirley, looking up at him. "Jackdaws are always chattering away to one another, but you hardly ever say anything. Still, your hair is as black as a jackdaw's feathers, so it's quite a good name for you."

"Ar," said Jackdaw, and went on with his grass-cutting, a smile still on his brown face. He liked being called Jackdaw. Although he never said a word about it, he liked working for the Jacksons, too. They were friendly to him. Mr. Jackson paid him regularly, and told him he was a good worker. Mrs. Jackson sometimes gave him a bun hot from the oven. Little Shirley often came to work with him, trying to do the things he did. And Master Michael was that clever with all the things he did in his workshop down in the shed.

Jackdaw liked smiling Molly and serious Peter, too, though he never knew what to say to them when they spoke

54

to him. He spoke more often to Jenny Wren than to anyone. She was sharp with him if he said "Ar" too often.

"Ar!" she would say. "Ar! Is that all the language you know? Think of some other word, boy, for goodness' sake! Why, 'Ar' isn't even a word. I don't know the meaning of it. Now, each morning when you come, you say 'Good morning, miss,' to me, proper and loud, like that—and don't you dare to say 'Ar' instead of 'thank you'!"

So, to Jenny Wren, at any rate, Jackdaw found a few other words besides "Ar." He mumbled "Good morning" and he stammered "Good night." He tried to remember "Thank you," but when he forgot Jenny Wren pulled him up as sharply as she would have pulled little Shirley.

Jackdaw had no mother and no father. He lived with a silent grandfather, and had done for years, which was perhaps why he had no conversation at all. He had a great love of gardening and of animals, and Bundle adored him, tearing into the garden as soon as he heard the click of the back gate when Jackdaw came. He adored Bundle, too, and always brought him a bone or a titbit of some kind.

"He's a nice fellow, if he is a bit dumb," said Mr. Jackson. "We're lucky to have him. He's absolutely honest, a very hard worker, and he's got the green thumb."

"What's that?" said Shirley, interested at once. "Which thumb is green? Fancy, I haven't noticed! But then Jackdaw's hands are always so black that maybe the green is hidden."

The others explained to her, with laughter, that the "green thumb" was only a saying. "It's said of people who can make things grow well in the garden," said Molly. "Now don't you go asking Jackdaw to show you his green thumb."

"It wouldn't be any good," said Shirley. "He would only stare at me and say 'Ar.' All the same, I like him. I like both our birds, the old one and the young one—Jenny Wren and Jackdaw. I think we're lucky to have them—but then, as the farmer once said to us, this is a lucky house!"

CHAPTER EIGHT

Unexpected News

MR. JACKSON went to the office next day wondering what news it was he was going to hear. He knew it would not be bad news, but he could not quite make out what it was. Surely he was not going to be transferred to another town, just when he had got his family settled in so well at *Red-Roofs*? That would be very bad luck, and a great expense.

He had told Mrs. Jackson this, and she had agreed with him that it would indeed be bad luck. "Don't say anything to the children till we know," she had said. "It would only upset them and make them miserable—and we don't know yet for certain if that is the change that the directors are thinking of. It may be something else. Anyway, dear, it is promotion of some kind again, already, so don't worry about it!"

The children were waiting for their father when he came home that night. They knew he would have news for them. They looked forward to a family discussion. That was one of the nice things about their parents—they always explained things to their children. They took them into their confidence, they told them when money was scarce, or when it was plentiful; they allowed them to share not only in the thrills, but in the worries that come to every family.

It made Molly and Peter very dependable, responsible children. Even Michael and Shirley were learning these things too, and would be glad of them when they grew up. None of them ever betrayed their parents' confidence or talked about their family matters outside the household. They all knew loyalty to one another.

Mr. Jackson came up the hill, and walked up the front path. The children ran to him, Shirley as usual hanging on his arm. Molly scanned her father's face. It was not worried, but it was serious. She longed to know what his news was.

"Hallo, children!" said their father. "Where's Mother?"

That was always his first question, and had been for years. "There she is," said Shirley, "at the window. Daddy, what's the news?"

"Wait till I get indoors!" said Mr. Jackson, with a smile. Shirley was always so impatient and eager. She couldn't wait a moment for anything.

When he was sitting stirring a late cup of tea, brought to him by Jenny Wren, Mr. Jackson told his news.

"It's good, but it's a bit upsetting," he said. "I've been offered very good promotion again—but I have been told that it entails going to America for six months, to represent my firm."

There was an astonished silence. Mr. Jackson had never been away from his family for even one night. He had spent every single holiday with them. How could they possibly do without him for six whole months?

"Daddy! You mustn't go!" cried Shirley, at once. "I should miss you too much. I couldn't bear it. You're not to go!"

Mr. Jackson patted Shirley's shoulder, but his eyes turned to his wife. She sat opposite him, looking anxiously at him. What was the best thing for him to do? Six months was a long time—but it would come to an end—and would her husband's position in the firm be very much higher because of a successful journey? Mrs. Jackson thought a great deal of her responsible, clever husband, and she was glad that after so many years of hard work his firm should recognize his good qualities and fine brain.

"Must you go, Daddy?" said Molly.

"Well—I can make my own choice," said her father. "I haven't been *ordered* to go—but it would, of course, be a great thing for me if I made a successful trip, and brought back orders for my firm. In fact, it might almost double my salary next year, and make a directorship not very far off!"

"Gracious!" said Molly. She looked at her father. "Do you want to go, Daddy?"

"I don't want to leave my little family," said her father, "especially as we have just settled down in a new house and there are so many new responsibilities. And your mother hasn't seemed very well lately, so it would worry me to leave her."

All four children gazed at their mother. "Mother! Haven't you felt well? You never said a word about it," said Molly, reproachfully. "You might have told me."

"Mother never makes a fuss about herself," said Peter. "All the same, Mother, I've thought you looked a bit queer sometimes. Wait till I'm a doctor! I'll cure you of anything you ever get wrong with you!"

Mrs. Jackson smiled. "There's nothing wrong with me," she said. "I'm only just a bit tired sometimes, that's all. As for Daddy saying he wouldn't like to leave me because of that, well, that's ridiculous. I'm perfectly well; and although we shall all miss him dreadfully, I think he ought to go, of course. It will be a grand trip for him; he's always wanted to travel a bit."

"I can manage everything, if Daddy tells me what he wants done," said Peter, suddenly looking very serious and grown-up. "I'm turned fifteen now."

Mr. Jackson looked at his elder son and felt proud of him. "All right, Peter," he said. "You shall take some of the responsibilities on your own shoulders. You shall help your mother with the bills that come in, you shall check all the amounts, work out the electricity and the gas, do all the things that *I* do for your mother."

"I could do that," said Michael, half jealously. "I'm better than Peter is at maths, much better."

"That isn't the point," said his father. "Peter's go to do it all some day, when he's grown-up, and whether he is good at it or not makes no difference. He must learn to do it somehow. Mother, bless her, isn't much good at figures and bills and things. She can sign the cheques after you've worked out all the figures to see if they are right,

58

MR. JACKSON TOOK SHIRLEY ON HIS KNEE

Peter. I shall be very pleased with you if you can do it properly."

"Daddy, I could really do that too," said Molly, feeling a little left out, as she was the eldest.

"Well, it should be the man's job," said Mr. Jackson. "A man should always shoulder that kind of responsibility —you can help in the household, Molly dear—share the responsibility of that with your mother. You can help her with the ordering and planning."

"What can *I* do?" said Shirley. Then her face crumpled up and she wailed loudly. "I don't want you to go. I shall miss you so. You're not to go!"

They all felt the same as Shirley did, but they knew that their father must go—it would be very silly not to take the chance offered to him, and after all, six months was not such a very long time—he would be back in the spring.

Mr. Jackson took Shirley on his knee and wiped her eyes with his handkerchief. "I shall miss you all too," he said, "but you must write and tell me everything—how Molly is getting on in the kindergarten—how Peter is getting on with his scholarship exam—and Michael with his maths—and you, Shirley, with all your lessons in a higher form. And you must all have your photographs taken together so that I can take one with me."

Shirley cheered up at once. She loved having her photograph taken. She sat still on her father's knee, while the discussion went on.

"When must you go?" asked Mrs. Jackson. "Soon?"

"Yes," said Mr. Jackson. "Almost at once, I'm afraid. Next week."

"Oh!" said everyone in dismay. "What about the summer holiday?" said Michael. "Can't you go with us?"

"No, I'm afraid not," said his father. "But you can all have one, if you like. I can give you fifty pounds to spend on a really good holiday by the sea. Go in September—it is always such a fine month—then, when you come back, you will soon start school, winter will come quickly, and then we can look forward to the spring, when I shall be home again!"

It wasn't nice to think of their father going so far away in such a short time. Why, there would hardly be time to settle anything! Mrs. Jackson felt sad and worried. It was true that she hadn't felt well lately, and she had put it down to the worrying business of moving. But she still felt very tired, and it was horrid to think that the one on whom she leaned, and went to for comfort and help, was going away just when she needed him.

But she knew she could not possibly stand in his way, so she swallowed her own feelings, and smiled round the little company.

"Well," she said, "this certainly looks like being a lucky house! Daddy has got this fine chance offered him, and when he comes back he will probably be richly rewarded. Six months will soon go."

Jenny Wren listened to the news in silence when she was told. She glanced sharply at Mrs. Jackson. She, like Peter, had noticed that her mistress had looked "right down queer" sometimes.

"You'll miss him, mam," she said at last. "But never you mind—we'll get along together all right. You see if we don't!"

Jenny found Mr. Jackson alone one night when she took in a letter that had just come. "I'm real sorry you've got to go, sir," she said. "I guess you're a bit worried about Mrs. Jackson, aren't you? But don't you worry— I'll look after her all right."

"Will you, Jenny Wren?" said Mr. Jackson, taking his pipe out of his mouth, and looking at the queer little monkey-faced figure before him. "Will you make her take things easy if she gets over-tired? She's had a hard life really, bringing up four boisterous children with not a soul to help her, and not ever being very strong herself."

"I'm right down fond of Mrs. Jackson," said Jenny Wren, earnestly. "Just you set your mind at rest. I promise, cross my heart, that I'll look after her for you."

Mr. Jackson felt relieved. Jenny was so dependable

and so staunch, and carried out her idea of "fair's fair" every day of her life.

"Well, Jenny, as you often say, 'Fair's fair,'" said Mr. Jackson, "and although you will only take presents from us and not wages, I'm going to put thirty pounds in your name in the post-office savings bank—a little present in advance for the kindness I know you will show to my wife."

"I'll not touch the money!" cried Jenny Wren, indignantly. "What, buy my kindness? Never! I don't want your money. What I do I'll do because I want to, and not because I'm being paid for it. Do you want me to lose my independence?"

"Now, now, Jenny," said Mr. Jackson, laughing. "You must see my point of view too. Fair's fair, you know. I should feel much happier if I know I have tried to recompense you in some way for your hard work and kindness. So I shall do what I said."

"And I'll not touch the money, so it will all be wasted," said Jenny Wren, still more sharply. She went out of the room, scowling. But in a second or two she was back again.

"But if I don't touch it, it's not to say I don't think well of you for offering it, and I thank you very much," said Jenny, disappearing like a jack-in-the-box as soon as she had spoken.

Mr. Jackson had a few days off before he left. He spoke to Jackdaw about the garden and the boy promised to come three times a week and keep it in order, instead of one. "Ar," he said, looking at his master as if he wanted to say a good deal more. "Er . . . ar."

Peter and his father had long talks together about everything. Peter was surprised to find what a lot there was in the upkeep of a house, and the many many things that had to be attended to regularly—rent—and rates—and water —and electricity—and gas—and insurances. It was amazing.

The boy followed all his father's explanations intelligently and seriously. He meant to carry out his suggestions to the letter. He felt proud to think that his father considered him grown-up enough to leave in charge like this.

"My salary will be paid into the bank regularly," said his father, "and your mother can draw out any amount and sign any cheque. As well as my salary, there is a sum of about a hundred pounds there—that, I am afraid, is all I have as capital at the moment, because of the expenses we have had this year. Fifty of that can go for a summer holiday for all of you. You need not worry about spending it, because I shall get a big bonus when I come back, and probably double my salary."

Peter felt a real man of the world as he listened to his father talking. It would be nice to think he was the man of the family, when his father was in America. Molly had always been the oldest, the head one—but now he suddenly felt that even she was under his protection. She was only a girl—two years older than he was, but still, only a girl!

The days fled away. There was a lot of packing to be done, and Mrs. Jackson discovered that practically everything of her husband's needed either to be washed, cleaned or mended. So she and Jenny Wren were busy from morning to night.

The day for good-byes came at last. Shirley woke up with a horrid heavy feeling, and wondered what it was. Was she going to the dentist? No. Was there an exam that day? No, of course not—it was holiday time. Then she remembered. Daddy was going away! Shirley hated good-byes. She wished the day were over. She wished her father weren't going. She wished she were going with him if he had to go. No, because then she'd leave her mother behind. Well, she wished they could all go too—Jenny Wren as well, and Jackdaw—and Bundle too of course.

It was not a nice day at all. Everyone tried to be cheerful and bright, and everyone talked as if six months were nothing at all—but in their hearts they all thought the same thing—six months is terribly, terribly long!

The taxi came to the door at ten o'clock. They were to say good-bye to their father at the door, not at the station. He said he couldn't bear that. One by one the children hugged him and wished him good luck. Last of all he took his wife into his arms, and she clung to him.

Jenny Wren shook hands solemnly. Jackdaw, who was there for the day, came up and tried to say something. Jenny Wren had tried to teach him to say "Good-bye, sir. and good luck," but all that came out was his usual earnest "Ar."

Bundle couldn't understand anything. Why all the fuss? He whined round the group of legs, and tried to get into the taxi with his master. He was most indignant when he was hauled out by Peter.

"You can't go to America, Bundle!" said Peter, in rather a shaky voice. "You're not enough of a tough guy to mix with the dogs out there!"

But nobody laughed at the feeble little joke. The taxi door slammed. The driver started up his engine, and the taxi plunged forward. Mr. Jackson leaned out and waved. Everyone waved frantically, and Bundle barked himself hoarse and wagged his tail hard.

But when the taxi turned the corner and was out of sight, Bundle put his tail down—and poor Shirley broke out into a wail. "Tell him to come back! I don't want him to go. Fetch my Daddy back. He's not to go away and leave us."

"Now you come along and help me make some cakes," said Jenny Wren's brisk, sharp voice, and she put an arm round the little girl's shoulders. "Come along, you can mix everything together, stir it well, and then scrape out the bits to eat them."

This was a great treat, and Shirley, though still wailing, allowed herself to be pushed into the kitchen. Michael, upset by Shirley's wails, retired hurriedly to his "workshop" and busied himself in pulling an old clock to pieces to try to make it strike again.

Mrs. Jackson looked very white. "You go and lie down for a bit, Mother," said Peter, gently. "You've had a hard week. You go and lie down."

"I think I will," said Mrs. Jackson, and she went upstairs, keeping a brave face as long as Molly and Peter were there to see her.

"Well, good-byes are beastly, I must say," said Peter, in a would-be-cheerful voice. "Let's go out for a walk with Bundle, Molly. Come on!"

Molly thought that was a good idea. She always liked doing something strenuous when she felt upset. So the two set off over the hill, with Bundle at their heels, capering about in his usual mad manner, his long silky ears flapping as he ran. Somehow the sight of the mad little dog comforted the two children, and they soon began to talk together of the summer holiday.

Mr. Jackson had said they could decide everything as soon as he had gone. He knew that it would take their minds off his departure, and make them look forward happily to something in the future. So the two discussed it, wondering where to go, and how long for.

"Swanage!" said Molly, remembering lovely holidays there. "Let's go to Swanage."

"No. Carbis Bay—then we can take that little railway to St. Ives and watch the fish-market in the morning," said Peter, remembering a holiday he had had with another boy. "You'd love that, Molly, really you would."

"Well, we'll talk it over with the others to-night," said Molly. "Mother looks as if she wants a good holiday. I vote we go to a hotel or a good boarding-house, not to rooms—then Mother won't have to bother about shopping or anything. It will be a real change for her."

"Home, Bundle, home!" called Peter. And, feeling much more cheerful from their walk, Molly and Peter went back home. That night they would decide all the details of their summer holiday!

CHAPTER NINE

A Horrid Day

THE next few days seemed very queer without their father. It was odd to come down to breakfast and not see the familiar figure at the table, drinking hot tea, and poring over the newspaper, relating the news in fragments to the family.

"We shall have a cable as soon as he arrives," said Peter. "The liner will dock in a few days' time. We'd better start writing letters now, hadn't we, Mother—then Daddy will get them not very long after he's arrived."

So quite a lot of letter-writing was done. Molly wrote a long, newsy letter, putting in everything and everybody—the whole family, Jenny Wren, Jackdaw and Bundle too. She related the silliest little happenings, knowing that her father would love to hear them all, and feel that he was still sharing in their daily life. She told how Bundle had pulled a string of sausages off the table, and had rushed off in fright when they all fell on top of him. She told how Shirley had picked the first beans in the garden that day, and how Peter had chased out a wandering cow.

There were other letters to write beside those to their father. They had to write to find room at a seaside place for their holiday—and this was not going to be easy, because they had left it rather late to book rooms.

Peter and Molly wrote to various places chosen by the family, and everyone waited eagerly for the answers to come. One sounded just right.

"They have two double bedrooms and one nice single room looking out on the sea!" said Peter, looking up from the letter, in excitement. "That would do for you, Mother, wouldn't it? *Our* bedrooms would be on almost the top floor, but that doesn't matter a bit. This hotel has its own swimming pool, filled with sea water—that sounds fine. Shirley can practise her diving nicely there."

"What about dogs? Will they take dogs?" asked Michael. "We simply must take Bundle. We can't leave him behind."

"Dogs are welcomed, but must be kept on a lead in the public rooms," read out Peter. "So it's all right, Bundle —you can come too! "

Bundle thumped on the floor with his tail. He listened to every discussion with the utmost attention, his head on one side, his melting eyes turned on first one speaker, then on another, his long ears flopping down at each side of his "beautiful face" as Shirley insisted on calling it.

"I'll write and book the rooms at once," said Mrs. Jackson. But Molly said she could do that easily. She meant to save her mother any little task she could. So the letter was written, and put on the mantelpiece to be posted when next anyone went out.

But before it was posted something happened that put the letter quite out of everyone's mind. They were all sitting at dinner, when Mrs. Jackson suddenly gave a long sigh, and said, in a faint voice, "Molly—I don't feel very well."

Molly leapt to her feet at once, and ran to her mother's side. Mrs. Jackson was very white, and looked as if she were going to faint. Molly and Peter between them half carried her to the sofa, where she lay moaning.

"Are you in pain, darling?" asked Peter in a gentle voice.

His mother nodded. "It's silly of me," she gasped. "I ought to have said something before, but I thought it would pass. I've had pain for a long time now. I just thought it was indigestion."

"Jenny! Jenny! " called Shirley, hurrying to the kitchen. "Come quickly. Mother's ill."

Jenny Wren came. She told Peter to telephone to the doctor at once. She had no idea what was the matter, but she knew it was serious. She gave Mrs. Jackson a hot-water bottle, and spoke to her gently and cheerfully.

"Now don't you fret. We'll soon have you put right."

"Do you think—do you think just a day or two in bed

will put Mother right?" said Shirley, with rather a white face. She could see her mother was in great pain—much worse than the earache Shirley had had, or even when she fell down and hurt the back of her head so badly.

The doctor was in and came at once. He sent all the children out of the room, but kept Jenny Wren there. Molly was indignant at being sent out. The four of them sat in the kitchen, looking aimlessly round at the shining tiles, neat boiler and dazzling taps—but they didn't see anything except a mental picture of Mother in pain in the other room.

The doctor made his examination and stood up with a grave face. "Where's Mr. Jackson?" he said.

"Gone to America," said Jenny Wren. "On the way now. Why—is it serious?"

"Serious enough," said the doctor in a low tone. "Have to be an operation, and that very soon. Is there anyone I can go to—a brother or sister or anyone?"

"No," said Jenny. "One is abroad and another is ill. There are only the children and me. You can tell me anything. What can I do?"

The doctor looked at Jenny Wren's sharp little monkey-face and liked her.

"We shall have to get an ambulance and take Mrs. Jackson to hospital," he said.

He had spoken a little more loudly, and Mrs. Jackson heard the word "hospital." She roused herself out of her pain and spoke feebly.

"I won't go to hospital. What's to be done can be done here. I can't leave the children."

"You leave things to us now," said the doctor gently. "Don't you worry. We'll manage everything beautifully, and things will go marvellously. Now I must just go and telephone. Where is the 'phone?"

Jenny told him. He went into the hall, and the children heard his footsteps and thought he was going. Molly came out, followed by the others, just in time to hear the doctor telephone for an ambulance. They looked at one another with scared faces. An ambulance! That meant that Mother was going away—she must be very, very ill.

The doctor put down the receiver and saw the silent, frightened children. Molly went to him and spoke in a low tone so that her mother could not hear.

"Doctor Ransome! What's the matter with Mother? Where is she going? Will she be away long?"

"She will have to be taken to the hospital, and there she will have an operation to set her free from the terrible pain she must have been having for a long time," said the doctor. "There is something wrong with her stomach—you would hardly understand if I told you—and, indeed, I must have my own opinion confirmed before I feel quite certain about it. But she is very ill, and must have the greatest care and attention for some time."

"But what shall we do without Mother?" said Michael in a bewildered voice. Home without either father or mother—why, that was impossible. Such a thing had never happened before, and couldn't happen now. But it *was* happening—and nothing could stop it.

"Doctor Ransome, she will get better, she will, won't she?" said Shirley, a great fear in her voice.

The doctor nodded at once. "Oh, yes—it's not so desperate as that! But all worry must be kept from her, because worry will be the very worst thing possible. She must know and feel that everything is all right at home, or she will make a very poor recovery."

All four children immediately resolved that not one moment of worry should harass Mother. Whatever went wrong, whatever worried *them*, not a single hint of it should reach their mother till she was better.

"Can I go and see Mother now?" said Molly.

The doctor nodded. "Yes. Go and see what she has to say to you, but just assure her again and again that you can manage all right. I'm sure that little woman I spoke to in there will help you a lot. Your maid, isn't she? She seems a very sensible sort."

Molly crept quietly into the dining-room, where her mother still lay on the sofa, very pale. The meal still stood

69

on the table, plates half full, the food quite cold. Her mother looked at Molly and spoke urgently to her.

"Molly, darling, promise me something before I go to the hospital. Promise me that you will send a cable to Daddy to ask him to come back at once. I can't be very ill and away from home and leave all you children like this. He must come back."

"Of course, Mother," said Molly, patting Mrs. Jackson's hand gently. "Of course. Don't you worry. Daddy will be back in no time. Now don't worry at all. You'll probably see him in about two weeks' time, and by then you will be feeling well again, and everything will be all right."

"I shouldn't call him back, I know," said Mrs. Jackson faintly "But I want him with me. And I want him to look after you, too, while I'm not here. Perhaps he could go over to America when I'm better."

"Of course," said Molly. Then she turned and looked out of the window. She heard a heavy van coming up the hill—it was the ambulance. At the same moment Jenny Wren appeared at the door, a suitcase in her hand.

"I've packed all your night things and everything you'll want for a day or two," she said in a brisk but kindly voice. "And don't you fret. Aren't I here to look after the family? Can't I manage them as well as you can? Haven't you been a good friend to me—well, fair's fair, and I can return a little of your kindness now. I'll come and see you soon, and ask you what else you want and bring it. Everything will be all right, you'll see if it won't, mam! "

Everything happened after that with the curious unreality of a nightmare. The doctor and an ambulance man carried Mrs. Jackson gently on a stretcher. The door was shut. The doctor had got in with Mrs. Jackson. Jenny wanted to go, too, but he shook his head.

"She wants you to stay with the children," he said. "I'll ring you up in the morning."

The ambulance drove down the hill. Jenny shut the door quietly and turned with a fairly cheerful face to the children. "What about finishing your dinner?" she said. "I'll hot it up again. Nothing like getting something inside you to make you feel better."

"I couldn't eat anything," said Molly, sitting down suddenly in a chair.

"Nor could I," said Shirley at once. "I think I'm going to be sick."

"Oh, no, you're not," said Jenny Wren immediately. "Now you bring the dish of meat into the kitchen for me, Shirley. Careful now. And you, Michael, bring that vegetable dish. We'll soon have them hot again."

Once in the kitchen, Jenny Wren faced the two younger ones with the air of a conspirator. "I'm right down sorry for poor Molly and Peter," she said. "They've took this badly, haven't they? I wish they'd eat something—make them feel better, it would. Couldn't you two manage to eat a good dinner just to put heart into the others?"

"Well—if it would help Molly and Peter, I would," said Shirley, forgetting about feeling sick, in the importance of being a help to the older ones. Michael nodded, too. He still felt hungry, but if the others didn't feel like eating because they were so upset he somehow felt that it would be shocking to tuck in to his food. Still, to help them, he certainly would.

"Just scrape the vegetables off these plates into the dishes for me while I go and get the other dishes," said Jenny Wren. She left them busy, and went back into the dining-room.

Molly looked at her. "Yes, take everything away," she said. "I couldn't possibly touch anything. I feel so miserable."

"Now, look here, Molly," said Jenny Wren, bustling about round the table, "it's selfish to talk like that, with poor little Shirley and Michael feeling all upset and unhappy. What they want is a good meal to make them feel better—and even if you don't feel like eating, you and Peter ought to make yourselves eat for the sake of the little ones."

"All right," said Molly. "Warm up the things and I'll eat something just to encourage the others. Peter will,

71

too, if it really will be any help. I only hope Shirley won't be sick—she said she felt sick."

"She'll be all right once she sees you eat," said Jenny Wren, and went off to the kitchen with a very small twinkle in her eye. Soon all four children were once more sitting round the table, with the reheated food in front of them. Molly and Peter ate to encourage Michael and Shirley, and Michael and Shirley ate valiantly to help the older ones, all of them pleased to see the apparent effect of their efforts. And by the end of the meal they all felt very much better, and much more inclined to take a cheerful view of things.

"Anyway, it does mean that Daddy will soon be back again," said Michael. Everyone felt relieved at the thought of their father being home once more. Molly felt sorry for him when she thought of him receiving the cable.

"What shall we say in the cable?" she said. "How do we send a cable? Do we just go to the post office?"

"I know how to," said Peter quietly. "Daddy gave me his various addresses with the dates he would be there, and told me exactly how to cable. It's easy. The thing is —what shall we put in the cable—so as not to scare Daddy too much, I mean?"

"Better wait till to-morrow, then we shall get definite news from the doctor," said Jenny Wren, serving Michael with another helping of pudding. "We'll make up a cable together then—one that will bring him back at once, and yet won't worry him too much."

The rest of that day was queer. The children mooned about, missing their mother and not knowing quite what to do with themselves. Jenny Wren set them various tasks, and they did them, but they had no heart for anything.

"Poor Mother," Molly kept thinking. "Poor darling Mother—she must have felt ill and in pain so often and gone about her work and never said anything—and yet she always smiled at us and never grumbled or snapped. I do hope she will soon be all right. What shall we put in the cable to-morrow? We *must* send it off soon, because I promised Mother."

CHAPTER TEN

"Here is the News . . . "

THE doctor telephoned the next morning. Jenny Wren was at the telephone before anyone else could get there, firmly resolved that if there were any bad news she would hear it first, and not any of the poor children.

But the news was not bad. It was fairly good. "Mrs. Jackson had to be operated on almost immediately," the doctor's voice came over the 'phone. "She stood the operation very well, but she is very weak, and must have no visitors for some time. The children can write, but see that they put nothing at all in their letters to worry her. Tell them to put all the cheerful little details in that they can to assure her that everything is going well at home."

"Yes, sir, I will," said Jenny, overjoyed to know that her mistress was over the worst. "I'll see to that. They are good children, sir, and wouldn't dream of worrying her. They are going to send a cable to their father to tell him to come back—it won't be long before he's here."

"Well," said the doctor, "his return will probably hasten Mrs. Jackson's recovery; but there is no urgent need for him to come back, you know. Mrs. Jackson will make quite a good recovery, I am sure. The only thing is—she simply must *not* have any kind of worry at all."

"I'll tell Molly and Peter that," said Jenny Wren, whose opinion it was that it would be a pity to bring Mr. Jackson back if there were no need for it. Couldn't she manage perfectly well in running *Red-Roofs*? Of course she could!

She put down the receiver and told the waiting children the news. They looked more cheerful at once, especially when they heard that the operation was over successfully.

"And the doctor says there's no real need to bring your father back," said Jenny Wren. "So perhaps it would be a pity to send him that cable."

"I promised Mother," said Molly. "I shall have to send it. I promised her, you see."

So the next thing to do was to make up the cable and

send it off. It must be short, because of the expense. Eventually it was done. "Please come back, Mother ill, but getting better," the cablegram said. That would tell Daddy of the seriousness of the illness, but would comfort him, too, because he was told Mother was recovering.

Peter went down to the post office to send it off. When he came back it was almost dinner-time, the house was tidied up, and Michael was in the garden helping Jackdaw.

"Put the news on, Molly," yelled Peter, putting his head in at the window. "I want to hear about the cricket."

Molly switched on the wireless. The familiar pips sounded, and then the smooth voice of the announcer.

Molly was helping Jenny Wren to lay the table for the midday meal. She went in and out of the room, only half hearing what the news was. Peter sat outside in the garden, whittling at a piece of wood, waiting for the cricket scores to be announced. Shirley was down in Michael's "workshop" with Michael, watching him take a portable wireless to pieces.

The news went on and on—and then something was said which made everyone listen in amazement and horror. Molly stood transfixed, a dish in her hands. Jenny Wren stood with the oven door handle in her hand, forgetting to shut the door. Peter leapt to his feet and Michael, listening with half an ear, away down in the workshop, could hardly believe what he heard.

"We have to report a grave accident in the Atlantic. The great liner *Albion* was nosing her way along in a thick fog when she collided with another ship. She swung round and endeavoured to get clear, when by some mishandling the two ships once more struck one another. We regret to announce that both ships sank within three hours. Many lives have been lost, but the great majority of passengers and crew are safe, picked up by ships called there by wireless."

"The *Albion*!" cried Peter, rushing indoors. "Why, that's Daddy's ship! He was on it!"

"Oh, Peter!" said Molly, rooted to the spot with fear. "How dreadful! Oh, do you think Daddy is all right?"

"He can swim, can't he?" said Jenny Wren at once. "Well, he'll be all right, then. A strong man like your father could swim for hours. The sea wouldn't be rough. He'd be all right. Anyway, he'd be bound to be in a lifeboat, I should think.

"Many lives were lost," said Molly, repeating what she had heard. "Oh, Peter! This is dreadful news. Thank goodness Mother isn't here to hear it! "

Michael came tearing up the garden, followed by Shirley, who hadn't yet grasped this new disaster. "Did you hear?" cried Michael. "Daddy's ship is sunk! "

"Sunk! " said Shirley in amazement. "What do you mean?" The little girl stared around at the scared faces of the others, and burst into tears. Jenny Wren put her arm round her and comforted her.

"Now don't you take on so! Ships often have accidents and often get sunk. Your daddy will be safe all right, you'll see! We'll get the names of all those who were saved, and your daddy's will be in the list."

"No good sending that cable after all," said Molly, with a little break in her voice. "Oh, Peter—haven't we had bad luck lately?"

"Yes," said Peter, who suddenly looked rather old and grown up. "Yes—we have. First, Mother having to go to hospital like that, and now this news about Daddy's boat. Doesn't look as if *Red-Roofs* is quite as lucky a house as that farmer made out! "

The wireless was still going on. It was playing gramophone records now. Peter turned it off. "What do we do now?" he said in a voice that suddenly sounded strangely like his father's.

"We'll all have dinner," said Jenny Wren firmly. "No good making wildgoose plans yet. We'll get news as soon as possible, you see if we don't. We'll get a cable very soon—maybe to-morrow, or the day after. But whatever we do we must keep this from your mother."

"Oh, yes! " said Molly. "It would never do to worry her with news of this kind. It's a good thing we're not to be allowed to go and see her yet—I don't know how

75

we'd manage not to tell her about the sinking of the *Albion*."

This time the four children really could not manage a big meal. It had been a real comfort to them to feel that they could cable to their father to come back—now probably he would not get the cable at all. They must wait for him to cable his whereabouts to them before they could communicate with him again.

Everyone was miserable that day. Jenny Wren hovered round the little flock like a watchful hen, and encouraged Bundle to do his naughtiest tricks. Anything to make a smile flicker across Shirley's face, or to lighten the sadness on Molly's!

When the doctor 'phoned again that night with news of Mrs. Jackson, Jenny Wren told him of the day's happening. He listened in silence.

"It's bad," he said. "Very bad. We can't possibly tell Mrs. Jackson any of this. I'll give instructions for the nurses to remove any wireless sets near enough for my patient to hear. It would put her back very considerably, dangerously, indeed, if by any chance she heard this bit of news. Dear me, what a dreadful thing for these four children; their mother away seriously ill and their father's ship sunk. Well, well, things aren't always as bad as they seem. Maybe they'll get a cable to-morrow to say he's all right."

Mrs. Jackson's report was good. She had had a quiet day, though she was very weak. The children were glad to hear this. Shirley went to bed feeling more cheerful. Mother would soon be better, surely, and they would hear from Daddy, and things would soon be ordinary again. Shirley didn't like her little world being set upside down so quickly. Molly went to tuck her up and found her asleep. She hoped she would be able to go to sleep as quickly as little Shirley, but she didn't think she would. She had lain awake for hours the night before, and she knew Peter had, too, because she had heard the creaking of his bed as he tossed and turned.

No cable came the next day. The children read the paper

from end to end for news, and turned the wireless on at every news-time. Names of the survivors of the two shipwrecks began to trickle through. It was agony to listen to them, expecting to hear the name of "Jackson" every moment—and never to hear it after all. Molly felt quite sick each time.

When three days went by and the list of survivors was completed, the children almost gave up hope. Jenny Wren was very anxious, too. She went to a friend of hers, a man who worked on a newspaper, and begged him to find out all he could for her. He presented her with two lists; one a list of the missing passengers, and another the list of the saved. Mr. Jackson's name did not appear on either.

Jenny was puzzled. "He must either be saved or *not* saved," she pointed out to the young man.

"Can't have been on the *Albion*, perhaps," said the young man, getting impatient.

"But he was," said Jenny. "Why, I saw his steamer ticket lying on his dressing-table, so I know."

"Well, there were a lot of little and big ships that went rushing up to help," said the young man. "Maybe he's on one of them and she hasn't sent in her list of survivors yet. Sorry I can't help you any more, Miss Wren."

Taking the hint to go, Jenny Wren walked out of the office, feeling almost in despair. She felt nearly certain now that Mr. Jackson had been lost—else surely he would have managed to send a cable. All ships carried wireless now. He could have wirelessed his safety, even if the ship which had rescued him had not gone into port, but had proceeded on her own voyage. It was strange.

After a week the children made up their minds that their father had been lost, but they could not bring themselves to admit it to one another. They all felt that as long as he was not in the list of missing men he might turn up. So they still talked of "when Daddy comes back"; but their hearts were heavy, and they felt lost and forlorn. It was not at all the same gay, merry little family of a week or two before.

Then came a letter stamped with the name of their

father's firm. It was addressed to their mother. Molly had been opening and answering all her mother's letters, and she now opened this one. She read it, gave a little sob, and handed it to Peter. It was a letter of condolence to their mother, and because the man who wrote it put down in black and white how sorry he was to hear of the loss of their very valued employee, Richard Jackson, it seemed to come home to the children for the first time that they might never see their father again. To read a letter like that made it all seem suddenly real and shocking. Molly put her head down on her arms and cried bitterly.

The two younger ones were not there. Peter came round to his sister and put his arm round her. "Don't Molly, darling," he said. "I shall howl, too, if you don't stop."

Molly didn't stop, and soon poor Peter felt the tears running down his cheeks, too. He kept thinking of his father swimming in the water, waiting to be picked up. Poor old Daddy, thinking of his little family at home and longing to be with them.

Jenny Wren, suddenly coming into the room, was astonished to see Peter and Molly so upset. She saw the letter on the table and picked it up. She read it slowly, and realized that its coming had somehow taken away all hope of their father's return. Jenny blinked away her own tears, and then spoke in her usual voice.

"Come now! We've got to make plans, not give way like this! You two are old enough to shoulder your burdens bravely. Anyway, this letter says six months of your father's salary will be paid to your mother—that's something. You won't be completely penniless as I've been, many and many a time."

Peter rubbed his eyes, and a cold feeling crept round his heart. Money! He hadn't thought of that at all. His father earned the money that kept the Jackson family going. Who was going to earn the money now? Something would come from the insurance, but not much, and whatever it was must go to Mother. Then there was the hundred pounds in the bank, and the six months' salary. But beyond that there was nothing, and they had just moved into *Red-Roofs*, which, nice as it was, needed help in the house and in the garden, too.

Peter sat thinking all this out, and Molly, drying her eyes, glanced at her fifteen-year-old brother. How like Daddy he looked, sitting like that, his mouth set, and his forehead wrinkled up as he thought hard.

"Peter, what are you thinking?" she asked.

"Molly," said Peter, looking anxious and worried, "we've got to be careful of money now, you know. I've suddenly realized it. We've got to be most awfully careful. No more will come in now, as it did when Daddy earned it."

Molly stared at him, and in that one moment the girl grew up. Year after year she had accepted the fact that bills were paid, presents were given, clothes were bought, and her Saturday pocket money given to her with the others. Now she saw money not as something to be received, but as something vitally necessary to be earned and worked for. Daddy had earned his own living and the living of all his little family. Now he wouldn't do that any more; but they had to go on living, so they must earn money themselves.

Jenny Wren went out of the room to answer the back door. Peter and Molly looked soberly at one another. They had to decide everything for themselves. Mother was ill and could not be worried at all. She must not know for a long time about Daddy being lost, though how they were to keep the news from her they could not imagine.

Somehow the two of them had to find a way out of their difficulties. "We'll have to talk things out, Molly," said Peter. "I'm the man of the family now, more's the pity, and you are the woman of the family till Mother comes back. We've got to make our own decisions, and they won't be easy. Everything will be different from what we had planned."

"Hush! here come the others," said Molly as she saw Michael and Shirley pass the window on their way indoors. "Don't say anything in front of them, Peter. We'll talk tonight when they've gone to bed."

CHAPTER ELEVEN

New Plans

JENNY was out that night, so, after Shirley and Michael had gone to bed, Peter and Molly sat in chairs opposite one another in the sitting-room, with Bundle between them, and talked everything out.

"It's no good my thinking of being a doctor now," said Peter straightaway. "Not the very slightest bit of good. Even if I won all kinds of scholarships, I'd still have rather a hard job to keep myself—and I must begin to think now of keeping other people. The bit of money Mother will have out of the insurance and what Daddy left as capital is so little that it's not worth thinking of. It would keep her for a few years, and that's all."

"Peter! You can't give up thinking of being a doctor!" said Molly in horror. "Why, you know you've always said you could never, never be anything else! It's what you've dreamed of all your life! Somehow we'll manage—but you *must* be a doctor."

"It's no good arguing that," said Peter patiently but firmly. "I've made my mind up. I'm leaving school—I mean I'm not going back. I'll go and see the Head before he goes away. I must take a job of some sort that brings us in a little money. I could earn a pound a week somehow, I should think."

Molly stared at this suddenly-grown-up young brother of hers, and her throat felt rather tight. She swallowed hard once or twice before she could speak. He was talking as if it didn't matter at all that he had to give up his lifelong ambition, his secret dreams, his magnificent hopes—and yet it must be the hardest thing he had ever had to do.

"I can't train as a teacher either," said Molly in a low voice. "I realize that. I can't afford to spend nearly three years as a student now, being kept all the time instead of earning my bit, too. Shirley and Michael must still be educated. But whatever can I do?"

"We'll see," said Peter. "I don't want you to go out earning money, and, anyway, you'll have to be at home looking after things till Mother comes back because we can't possibly afford to keep Jenny Wren now. We can't give her the presents Daddy gave her instead of wages. You would have to keep house till Mother comes back, then perhaps you could take a job as governess or something. You're so good with little children, aren't you?"

"Yes, I could do that," said Molly. "I could teach on my own, though not nearly so well as I could if I had taken the proper teaching exams and gone through my training. I might be able to get some sort of a job. Do you think I could earn a pound a week, too?"

"I should think so," said Peter, considering. "We could keep things going for a bit, and perhaps when Uncle Ned comes back from abroad he could help us for a time till we both earned more money, and till Shirley and Michael leave school."

"Yes—perhaps he would help us a little," said Molly, brightening up. "He isn't well-off—but we'd only ask him to *lend* us money, not give it—because I'm sure you will be earning a lot of money, Peter, with your brains when you are a little older."

Peter was not so sure. He knew that an untrained and inexperienced youth was not worth half so much as anyone with even a little good training. That was what his father had always said. The best and most worthwhile jobs always went to those who had taken the trouble to train for them. That was why Peter had worked so hard this last year or two—he wanted to win scholarships that would help him in his further training, but now it was all no good. He could not afford either the time or the money. He must go to work at once.

"What about *Red-Roofs*? Shall we have to leave it?" said Molly fearfully. She did so love the little new house. She knew they would have to leave it—of course they would—but if only they needn't!

"The rent is paid till the end of the year," said Peter. "I know that. So we can stay here till then, and in the

81

meantime we must look out for something a lot smaller and cheaper—something more like our old house; I'm afraid, Molly."

The girl's heart sank into her shoes. Go back to a small, dark, stuffy, smelly little house again, after having tasted the delights of *Red-Roofs* and its lovely garden? How miserable she would be! She sat so still that Bundle, sitting by her, wondered what was the matter. He gave her hand a gentle lick. She jumped.

"Oh, Bundle! I didn't know you were there!" Then a dreadful thought struck her. "Peter, we shan't have to part with Bundle, shall we?"

"Well—he costs a little in biscuits and bones," said Peter reluctantly. "We have to rule out any unnecessary expense, you know."

"Peter, is Bundle an unnecessary expense?" said Molly in a trembling voice. "I feel as if he's most awfully necessary—and Daddy did love him so."

Bundle listened to this conversation with every appearance of anxiety, looking from one to another with such earnest, beseeching eyes that Peter could not bear it.

"Don't let's talk about old Bundle now," he said. "He understands every word. Let's talk about him when he's not here."

"All right," said Molly. "What about Jackdaw? I suppose he's an unnecessary expense now, too? But we shall be very glad not to have to buy vegetables or fruit, Peter. Do you think we could manage the garden ourselves?"

"We'll have to," said Peter. "We can't possibly afford Jackdaw—or Jenny Wren—or a window-cleaner, or a telephone, or lots of other things! We'll have to turn to and do most things ourselves now. You must take a few lessons from Jenny before she goes, Molly. It's a good thing you're such a fine little cook already."

Molly sighed. Life suddenly seemed terribly hard and difficult. She felt very grown-up—and she didn't like it at all. She had always wanted to be grown-up, and had thought what a fine thing it would be to make her own decisions and carry them out, but now that she had to it wasn't nearly so fine as she had thought. Things were going to be such a struggle, just as they had seemed to be easy and happy.

"Peter, we must back each other up in every way," said Molly earnestly. "We shall often be tired and miserable but for the sake of the others we'll have to smile and pretend we don't mind—especially for Mother's sake. It will break her heart when she hears about Daddy."

"I know," said Peter sadly. "Things will never be the same again. Last week we were planning a lovely summer holiday together—good gracious, there's the letter we wrote to that hotel still on the mantelpiece! What a good thing it wasn't posted. And this week here we are, tearing our plans to pieces and going together into a completely new life, not at all what we had hoped."

Jenny Wren poked her head in at the door. "How long are you two going to jabber away like this? Do you know the time? It's quarter to eleven! You may think you're heads of the house and grown-up, but let me tell you that a quarter to eleven is no hour for girls and boys to sit up to!"

"All right, Jenny," said Peter. His face, thin and troubled in the last week or so, caught at Jenny's heart.

"Well, you stay up a minute or two more and I'll bring you in some cocoa," she said. "Got it hotting on the stove now."

"Bring three cups, Jenny Wren," said Molly, suddenly making up her mind to break the news to Jenny that night. Jenny would have to find another room and another job, and she had better be told at once.

In a few minutes Jenny brought in a tray on which stood a large jug of cocoa and three cups and saucers. She set it down on the table and began to pour out the cocoa.

"What have you two been talking about, so solemn and grave?" she asked, her sharp eyes going from one to the other.

"Jenny Wren, we've been going into money matters," said Molly, taking the plunge. "And, oh, Jenny, we can't possibly afford to keep you, and you'll have to go, but I don't know how in the world we're going to do without you now! Peter isn't going to be a doctor now; he's going to take a job—you see, there's so little money. And I'm not going to be a K.G. student because I must earn my living, too. So I shall look for a job as nursery governess."

All this came out in a torrent, and Jenny listened in amazement. She set her cup down on the table and looked serious. "I don't know which is worse," she said, "too much money or too little! Well, well, we mustn't tell your mother any of this for a while. But you can set your minds at rest about one thing—I'm not leaving you! What, leave you when you're in a fix? That's not my way. Fair's fair, and you've done a lot for me. If I can't do a bit for you, then I'd be a poor stick."

The children stared at Jenny, hardly knowing what to say. "But, Jenny," said Molly, "we can't afford to pay you a penny, or give you a present, or even to keep you in food."

"Who's asking you to?" said Jenny, very fierce all of a sudden. "Now you tell me that! Who's asking you to, I say? Didn't I just want a room to live in with my few bits of things, and didn't I get it here? You gave me my food and my room, yes, and you gave me presents, too, and all I gave you was my poor bit of work, for I'm a little old woman now, and not much good. Well, you listen to me. I'll still have my room, and I'll give you work in return for it. But I'm paying for my food from now on, as I ought to have done before, for fear of losing my independence!"

"Jenny, don't be silly," said Peter. "How could you pay us for your food, even if you wanted to? Anyway, you don't eat more than a few shillings' worth every week!"

"And I can earn those few shillings easy!" cried Jenny, getting all worked up. "Yes, I can. I can go out two days a week and work for the ladies I used to work for—and the work I do here will pay for my room. I'll keep my independence then, like I ought to before—and I'll still be with you."

"Dear Jenny, it won't do," said Peter, smiling at the

generous little woman in front of them. "We can't exploit you like that."

"I don't know what you mean by 'exploit'," said Jenny Wren, two tears unexpectedly running down her cheeks. "If you don't want me, say so right out, can't you? Then I'll go and gladly. But I'm happy here—you're like my own folks to me. But I'll go if you don't want me! "

She picked up her cup and began to march out with loud sniffs, almost as if she meant to walk out of the house then and there. Molly and Peter rose in alarm. Molly caught her by the arm and made her spill the cocoa.

"Jenny Wren! Don't go! Stay here as long as you like. We can't do without you! Oh, if only you'll stay it will make things so much happier! But don't pay us for your bit of food."

Jenny set down her cup and looked at the mess on the floor. "Such carelessness! " she said, sniffing. "Messing the carpet like that! All right, I'll stay—and if you want to know, I promised your father I'd look after your mother for him—and a promise is a promise with me. So I should have stayed anyhow, however you tried to get rid of me. When folks are kind to me, you can't expect me to run away when they're in trouble. Fair's fair, isn't it? I'll go and get a cloth to wipe up the mess."

Still sniffing loudly, Jenny Wren went into the kitchen. Molly looked at Peter, half laughing and half crying. "Isn't she a dear?" she said. "She's a kind of anchor, I feel. I should feel lost if she went."

"So should I," said Peter. "It will be nice for Mother to have someone to look after her a bit when she comes home. I shall feel relieved to know Jenny Wren is here when you and I and the others are either at school or at work."

So that was settled, and nobody said any more about Jenny going. Nobody said anything about Bundle going either, especially after Jenny said that there was one thing about Bundle, he cost almost nothing to feed! The children hardly believed this, but they wanted to so badly that they did—and Bundle was safe.

Jackdaw proved very difficult. He came the next day and Peter tackled him. He told him about the loss of his father in the sinking of the *Albion*, and said that now he would have to go out to work himself, and so would Molly. "So, Jackdaw," he said, "you'll have to stop coming here, I'm afraid, because we've got no money to pay you after to-day."

"Ar," said Jackdaw, profoundly. He shook back his mass of untidy hair and looked at Peter out of very blue eyes. He opened his mouth as if about to say something and then shut it again. He opened it and made a great effort. "Ar," he said. "I'm right sorry. Ar, I am that. But don't you worry, I'll do the garden."

This was the longest speech that Jackdaw had ever made and it left him quite exhausted. He shut his mouth, opened it again to heave a huge sigh and then began to wheel away his barrow.

"What does he mean?" said Molly to Peter. "He can't do the garden any more. We can't pay him."

"He won't come after to-day," said Peter. "You'll see. He's got to earn his living as we have. He can't afford to work for nothing. He doesn't mean anything by what he says."

But Jackdaw did. True, he did not come in the daytime, he got himself other odd jobs then, but three times a week he turned up regularly in the evenings and worked away with a will in the garden, pleased to see Shirley working with her little spade or fork beside him, or to peep into the "work-shop" at Michael's invitation, and see his latest "mending" or invention.

Nothing Peter could say made any impression on Jackdaw. The boy tried to explain to him time and again that he must not come, that he would not be paid, and that he, Peter, forbade him to come any more.

"Ar," Jackdaw would say, in a very deep manner, nodding his black head, and that was all Peter could get out of him.

"You leave him be," said Jenny Wren, when Peter asked her to try and get it into Jackdaw's head that he wasn't to come any more. "You leave him be. There isn't all that amount of kindness in the world that you can afford to turn it down when it comes along. It'll do Jackdaw good to give a little something for nothing. Does us all good, that does. Won't hurt Jackdaw. He likes coming here—same as I like living here. You lend Jackdaw a few books now and again, and he'll be that pleased! He likes reading though I don't believe he understands a word he spells through! "

So Jackdaw, to his immense pride and delight, had books lent to him by Peter. He apparently didn't care in the least what they were—they could be a history of Greece, a tale of some animal, or even a dictionary—he took them all home with the greatest joy, and showed them to his grim and silent grandfather.

"It's a poor return for the good work he does," said Peter to Michael, "One day maybe I'll be able to reward him a bit better. He's teaching me a lot about the garden. I'm getting as good as Daddy was! "

A week or two went by, and the children's mother made such good progress that the doctor said they might visit her. "But mind, not a word about your father yet," he said. "I've told her he can't come home yet, and she's quite happy about that now she feels better. But any sudden shock or worry will cause a terrible relapse, and set up a lot of trouble again, so don't say anything. She will never be very strong again. I'm afraid you must tell a few untruths just at present. Say you have heard from your father, but have left the letters at home—and just make up a few things to keep her happy. She is still weak, and doesn't want to hear any details, I'm sure—just you hold her hand and say that everything is all right."

So the next day they all went off to the hospital, Jenny Wren too, laden with flowers out of the garden. Molly could hardly keep the tears back, she was so glad to know she would soon be seeing her mother again.

CHAPTER TWELVE

Peter Gets a Job

MOLLY was taken in to see her mother first. The ward was full of sick people, but Molly had no eyes for any one except her mother. She had a shock when she saw her, so white and thin—and so *old*-looking. "Why, she looks like a little old woman!" the girl thought, and her heart sank. What would Mother do when she heard about Daddy?

Her mother smiled at her, and tears ran down her white cheeks. It was so sweet to see someone she loved after all that long lonely time. A nurse hovered near to see that she did not exhaust herself. "One minute alone, and then the others can come in for four minutes," said the nurse. "No longer this time, I'm afraid."

The minute fled by. There seemed no time to say anything. "We are all getting on all right," said Molly. She took her mother's hand. "Everything is fine, except that we miss you and want you back."

"Is Daddy all right?" said Mrs. Jackson. "I am not allowed any letters, you know."

"Quite all right," said Molly, bravely, with a lump in her throat.

"Doctor says he's not coming back, and I'm glad now that I didn't bring him back," said Mrs. Jackson. "I hope he's having a lovely trip."

Molly nodded and changed the subject. "Bundle sent you a bark," she said. "Oh—here are the others."

They came in, tiptoeing, Peter looking round him with intense interest, for he had never been inside a big hospital before. How he had hoped to work in one—and now that would never be. He looked round for his mother, and, like Molly, he had a shock when he saw her lying so white and thin.

THEY CAME TIPTOEING INTO THE WARD

Shirley did all the chattering and the boys were content to let her. Jenny Wren sat and smiled, adding a word of comfort at the end. "Everything's fine, Mam. All you've got to do is to get better quickly."

Mrs. Jackson smiled back at her, feeling that that was the one thing she couldn't do—get better quickly! She knew it would take her a long time to get back her strength.

"I don't much like being in a hospital," she said. "I would much rather be in a nursing home, with my own room. I feel I would like to be alone, and think about you all."

"Do you think you'd get better more quickly then?" said Peter, gently.

"Perhaps," said Mrs. Jackson. Then the nurse came up, and good-byes were said. "You can come again next week," said the nurse. They filed out, looking now at the patients in the other beds. They thought that none of them looked so white as their own mother.

"I wish we could get Mother into that nice nursing home not far from us where she could have her own room and nurse, and the very best treatment too," said Peter, as they rode back home on the tram. "But nursing homes are so terribly expensive. Hie—where are you going, Jenny Wren? This isn't where we get out."

"Going to the post office," said Jenny. "You go on and get out, I'll come along as soon as I can. You put the kettle on for tea, Molly."

"Well—she's wasted half her ticket!" said Michael, in surprise. "I suppose she must suddenly have thought of something she'd forgotten."

Jenny Wren had. She had suddenly remembered the thirty pounds that Mr. Jackson had put into the post office savings bank for her, in her own name. She had the book in her bag. She would get the money—but not for herself! No! She would get it out, and she would arrange for Mrs. Jackson to go to that nice nursing home! Wasn't that exactly what Mr. Jackson would have done himself? Jenny Wren felt intensely pleased with her brilliant idea. She had sworn that she would never touch the money—but this was a wonderful way of spending it.

In a few days she had arranged everything. Through the doctor she had managed it all very nicely. He approved of the removal to the nursing home, especially as the hospital was very full and needed its beds. Mrs. Jackson still needed expert treatment and the utmost quiet—she could not possibly come home. The nursing home was a very good idea, he thought.

"But what about the money?" he said, doubtfully. "I thought you told me it was very short."

"I'm managing this, sir," said Jenny. "The children don't know anything about it."

When Jenny told them of the new arrangement they were astonished. Molly stared at Jenny Wren, puzzled. "But what about the money?" she said, at last. "Where's it coming from?"

"Don't you worry about that," said Jenny. "Your father gave me some money before he went—and I suddenly thought he would like it spent this way. That's all."

"You never told us of this money before," said Peter. "It must be money he meant for you to spend on yourself, Jenny. You're not to use your own money like this."

"I didn't tell you about the money because I'd forgotten all about it," said Jenny, truthfully. "And don't you go telling me what I can or can't do with my own money—I can spend it how I like."

And before any more could be said she had gone out of the room and closed the door firmly behind her.

"We shall simply never be able to repay her," said Peter, in despair. "But isn't she a brick? What luck that you fell down outside her cottage that day, Michael! "

Peter was now trying to find himself a job. He and Molly had said nothing to the two younger ones about the money difficulties, or the fact that they would have to leave *Red-Roofs* at the end of the year. It would only puzzle and worry them. They would both get themselves jobs, and then tell the others that they had changed their minds about the future, and had decided to go to work straightaway.

Peter went to the Headmaster and explained everything to him. Mr. Grey was a kind and shrewd man, and he listened to the boy in silence. He knew Peter's great ambition to be a doctor, and he had secretly thought that the boy was exactly the right type for that high profession. He was intelligent, responsible, of a strong character and very kind.

"Must you give up your ideas?" he said to Peter. "Is there no relative you can turn to for help, temporarily? You cannot hope to earn much if you start out suddenly, without any training, at fifteen. It is really a great waste of your good brains too."

"We've no relative who can help us at present," said Peter. "When my uncle comes back from abroad I will go and see him and perhaps he will allow us something till I can get on in the world and can repay him. But till then I must do the best I can."

"You would have won that scholarship," said the Head. "There's no doubt about that. Couldn't you still work for it, Jackson, even if you take a job? You will not be any the worse for going on with your education, even if you take a job. I can help you with books and papers and advice."

Peter flushed. This was more than he had dared to hope. He loved his school work, and badly wanted to pass the exam he was working for—and perhaps he could win that scholarship after all, even if he hadn't the chance to use it! It would have to go to the next boy.

"Thank you, sir," he said. "I think I'd like to go on with my education—if you really wouldn't mind helping me. I can't thank you enough. I don't know what to say."

"That's settled then," said the Head. "I'll work out a syllabus of work for you, and supply you with the books you'll need. Once a week you can bring in your work to me, and I'll see if I can keep it up to scholarship standard! But it means working at night you know, when you're tired out after your job. It won't be so easy as going at it fresh each morning in school!"

"I know that," said Peter. "But plenty of boys have had to do that before—and it won't hurt me to tackle it too."

"I'll try and find you a job as well," said the Head. "But that's more difficult. You want a job where you can use your brains—no errand boy work for you! I'll see what I can do."

But Peter found his own job. He answered an advertisement that stated "Junior Clerk wanted. No experience necessary, except knowledge of typing."

"Well—I can type," said Peter to himself, thankful that he had tackled his father's typewriter when he had the chance. "Junior clerk—what sort of work does he do, I wonder? Well, if they told me, I bet I could do it. I wonder what the salary is."

It wasn't much—twenty-five shillings a week! But to Peter, still not more than a schoolboy in his ideas of money, it seemed a lot. He called at the office that needed the junior clerk, and sat first of all in a room with about a dozen other youths, all of them older than he was. Each had come after the job, and they talked and fidgeted, falling silent as one boy after another went in to be interviewed and came out again.

Peter had with him a letter from his Headmaster, giving his report on the boy's character and abilities. When he went into the big office to be interviewed, the man there looked at him sharply, and almost turned him down at once. He was only a schoolboy! Peter said "Good morning" and handed him the letter.

"This will tell you a little about me," he said, and the man read the report. He looked at the serious-faced boy in front of him. He thought he would probably get more work out of a boy of this sort, responsible and serious, than he would out of the others, although they had had more experience.

He asked Peter a few questions, and then returned the letter to him. "Let you know by to-morrow if you've got the job," he said. "Send in the next boy."

By the first post the next day Peter had a letter saying that he was engaged as junior clerk in the firm of "Jameson and Morris, Publishers." He was to arrive there at half-past eight each morning, and to leave at six o'clock each night. His duties would be explained to him, and his salary would be twenty-five shillings a week.

The little family were thrilled. Peter had a job! Twenty-five shillings seemed a lot of money and even Jenny Wren agreed that it was. She could make it go a long way. Now if Molly got a job too, things wouldn't be so bad—they could make do for a little while.

Peter was to start his job the following week. It had been a surprise to Michael and Shirley to hear that he was not going to return to school again, but Peter had not made much of it. He had merely said that he was still going to do school-work in the evenings and try for the scholarship, and that as he had the chance of this job, he thought he had better take it.

Shirley had accepted it without thinking, but Michael was puzzled. He had known how much Peter had set his heart on being a doctor—and one could not train as a clerk and yet be a doctor too, surely! He questioned Jenny Wren so closely that he soon knew the truth—money was terribly short, and poor Peter had to make the best of it! Michael listened gravely, and felt hurt that Peter had not taken him into his confidence.

He went to Peter. "Is Molly getting a job too? Is that why she keeps looking at the advertisements in the paper? Why don't you tell me and Shirley anything? It's mean of you. Even if Shirley isn't old enough to know things, I am. You just tell me everything, Peter, or I'll get it out of Jenny!"

"Keep your hair on!" said Peter. "You and Shirley aren't old enough to share in this earning business, so what's the good of worrying you about things? If you could help in earning money, we'd tell you, but you can't —you've got to go to school."

"I'm almost twelve!" said Michael, indignantly. "Boys of twelve often earn their own living."

"Not nowadays," said Peter. "You can't leave school till you're at least fourteen, you know that."

"I could deliver newspapers or do something like that," said Michael, fiercely. "Why don't you and Molly let me share? You think I'm a silly kid, like Shirley—well, I'm not. I've got as good brains as you have—better in some ways, because I can handle figures and you can't."

"Shut up, idiot," said Peter. "We're not leaving you out of the plans, really, it's only because you must go on going to school, and at any rate for two years you can't do much. Molly and I can keep things going."

Michael went out of the room and shut the door loudly. He scowled. Always treating him like a baby! Why couldn't they tell him things? Why must he always be lumped with Shirley and her dolls? He was just as near Peter in age as he was to Shirley—well, almost!

He went to his work-shop and shut himself in. He took up the clock he was mending, and went on with his work, but his fingers trembled too much with rage and grief, and he had to stop. He leaned back and began to think—and when Michael really began to think, things happened!

CHAPTER THIRTEEN

Molly Finds a Job Too

MOLLY could not get a job. Nobody seemed to want a nursery governess just then. True, it was the summer holidays, and most people were away—but still, it did seem peculiar that nobody wanted someone to look after their children. She could have got a resident job, but she wanted to be at home. She was not going to leave her family just now—not till her mother came back at any rate.

Molly had avoided her old friends recently. She did not feel she could discuss her problems with them, except perhaps Joan Rennie. She suddenly wondered if her Headmistress would help her—give her advice at any rate. After all, she had told the girls to go to her if they wanted advice —and Peter's Head had helped him considerably.

So Molly went to her old school and went in at the familiar door. She made her way to the Headmistress's drawing-room. But nobody called out in answer to her knock. A surprised maid saw her and asked her what she wanted.

"Isn't the Headmistress in?" said Molly, disappointed. The girl shook her head.

"No. She's away abroad. She won't be back for three weeks."

Molly went away with a sinking heart. Three weeks! She couldn't wait all that time. On the way home she passed Prudence Williams' house. She stood there outside the gate, hesitating. Should she just go in and see Prudence for a few minutes? It would be nice to feel herself a schoolgirl again and chatter about old times—and after all Prudence had been her friend.

As she stood there a voice hailed her. "Molly! Come in! I thought you must be away, because I haven't seen you for ages."

It was Prudence, waving a tennis racquet and looking very cool and sweet in a short white silk frock with a scarlet belt. Molly went in. She gazed in admiration at Prudence, who really looked most attractive.

"You do look lovely," said Molly, and the spontaneous admiration warmed Prudence's heart. She slipped her arm through Molly's.

"Come into the garden where the swing-seat. is, and we'll have a good old talk," she said. "Can you stay to tea? Good! Everyone's out, so we'll have a nice old talk. I'm just about fed up to-day."

"*You*, fed up!" said Molly, astonished, looking at the pretty girl disbelievingly. "Whatever can you be fed up about?"

"Well, Daddy's always in such a foul temper nowadays," said Prudence, banging on the ground with her racquet. "He's always going for me and Mother because, he says, we are extravagant! Extravagant! I ask you, what's the sense of not being extravagant if you've got plenty of money? Daddy's a mean old stick—can't think what's come over him lately! And Mother gets cross with me, too, though goodness knows why. She treats me as if I were a schoolgirl still, and I'm not. I just won't put up with it. There's always some row or other on here. Either Daddy and Mother are going at it hammer and tongs, or Daddy's finding fault with Bernard—and my word, you should have seen Bernard's last report, it was awful—or Mother's going for me, or I'm howling at Bernard, or one of the maids is being sacked. Honestly, it's like a lunatic asylum sometimes."

Prudence paused for breath. Molly stared at her in surprise. What a dreadful home life! She didn't know what to say. Only about ten minutes ago she had envied Prudence because she had her mother and father at home, and plenty of money to keep everything going happily and easily, but now Molly no longer envied her friend.

Prudence noticed her silence. She also noticed that Molly looked rather thinner, and she wondered why.

"How are things with you?" she said. "How are those awful brothers of yours, and is Shirley any less spoilt? What's your news? Are you going away? We were going abroad, you know, but now Daddy has put his foot down on it, and says he won't throw money away on a holiday like that, so we've had to cancel the rooms and everything. My word, it's no wonder I'm fed up!"

"Haven't you heard any news of our family?" said Molly after a pause.

Prudence shook her well-shaped head, secretly amused. As if she was ever likely to hear news of nobodies like the Jacksons!

Molly told her all that had happened—her mother's illness, the sinking of the boat her father had been on, the lack of all news of him, the shortage of money, the need to find jobs at once. She told how Peter had already got a job and was soon to start.

"But *I* can't get one!" she said desperately. "I never knew it was so hard as that to get a job—at least, I suppose if I didn't mind what sort of a job it was, I could get one easily enough. But I do want to be with children."

Prudence had listened to Molly's recital in horror. How could so much happen to anyone in so short a time? It sounded unbelievable. Thank goodness her own father had plenty of money, and she, Prudence, would not have to earn her own living.

"Poor Molly," she said, patting her friend's hand. "What an awful shame! I wish I could help you. I wonder if Mother knows of anyone who needs a governess. I'll ask her when she comes home to-night and let you know."

Molly knew Prudence's ready promises of old, and she did not place much confidence in this one. But she thanked her, and then changed the subject. She knew Prudence would soon be bored if she spoke any more of her troubles. Soon she was listening to a tale of all the wonderful tennis parties and dances that Prudence had been to, the brilliant way she had played and danced, the partners she had had, and the compliments she had received. Molly did not need to say much. Prudence loved to hear herself talk, and she liked condescending to people like Molly, who was just a nobody, and could listen in open-eyed admiration to the happenings in a life like Prudence's.

But Molly did not listen with such admiration as Prudence thought. Molly was no longer a schoolgirl. Hard things had come to her, and she was seeing many things in a new light. She was feeling real responsibility for the first time, and she could now weigh up Prudence's life and character in a way that would have surprised that pretty young lady very much if she could have seen into Molly's thoughts.

Still, Molly enjoyed going out to tea and having a change and talking to somebody else. She got up to go about half-past five, and said good-bye.

"I'll tell Mother about all your troubles the very minute I see her!" said Prudence earnestly when she said good-bye. "I'll do the best I can for you."

Molly went up the hill to *Red-Roofs*. She felt she would rather have her own little family, with all its troubles, than Prudence's quarrelsome, cat-and-dog life, in spite of its money and ease. She remembered what Jenny Wren had said once—that she didn't know which was worse, too much money or too little!

The others were interested to hear what Molly had to tell them about Prudence, and Michael made them laugh by suddenly imitating her again. "Perhaps Prudence's mother will find you a lovely job," said Shirley, slipping her hand into her big sister's.

"I don't think so," said Molly. "No good hoping for anything from Prudence—she was always ready to promise, but she always forgot to keep her word."

But, to everyone's great surprise and excitement, a telephone call came from Mrs. Williams the very next morning. Jenny Wren answered the call, and went to fetch Molly.

"Someone for you," she said. "Very la-de-da—a Mrs. Williams, I think she said."

"Oh," said Molly, and rushed to the 'phone at once. "Hallo!" she said breathlessly. "Good morning, Mrs. Williams."

"Is that you, Molly?" came Mrs. Williams' rather affected voice. "I'm *so* sorry, dear, to hear of all your troubles, but I think I can help you."

"Oh, thank you," said Molly. The others hung round her, trying to make out what was being said. Could it be a job for Molly?

"My sister needs someone for her three small children," said Mrs. Williams. "Such little dears! Perhaps you would like to go there? The children are three, five and seven, two boys and a girl, just the ages for you, dear."

"They sound lovely," said Molly, "but—but—I couldn't go away from home, Mrs. Williams. I mean, I couldn't sleep at your sister's. I could only go there for the day. You see, I must be at home to keep a hand on things till Mother comes back."

"Well, you could take the tram each day," said Mrs. Williams. "It's only half an hour by tram. You would have to be there at nine, and you could leave when the children were in bed. Then you would always have the evenings at home, though, of course, my sister would rather have someone sleeping in. Still, I dare say if I spoke well of you and pressed her, she would consent to have someone daily."

"Oh, thank you," said Molly again. She wondered what Mrs. Williams' sister was like. Would she live in a big house, too, with a big staff, and have beautifully dressed children, and expect a really marvellous governess? Molly felt she would never do if she did.

"Well, would you like to take the job?" asked Mrs. Williams. "I'm afraid I must know at once, or my sister will probably engage someone else. She will pay you a pound a week, but you will have to pay your own tram fares."

"Oh, dear!" said Molly. "They would take up nearly all my wages! I would bicycle there, but I haven't a bike."

"Prudence has an old bicycle. You can have that," said

Mrs. Williams. "You could bicycle there more quickly than the tram would take you. Well, will you let me know in half an hour's time? Then I will telephone my sister. Oh, by the way, if you were daily you would have all Sunday off, but no half-day. Well, let me know in half an hour."

Molly put down the receiver and went into the sitting-room, followed by all the others. She told them briefly what Mrs. Williams had said. She had already made up her mind to take the job.

Peter was doubtful. He thought the hours were long, and somehow he didn't like the sound of the job. But Molly's mind was made up. "You know you can't pick and choose when you've *got* to find a job," she said. Peter knew that only too well.

"All right," he said. "Take it, then. After all, you can always chuck it if it's awful."

"I shan't give it up easily," said Molly. "I know how important it is to hold your first job down, and I shall try my best. Three little children—they ought to be sweet at that age. I must think out how to teach them and keep them amused, and give them handwork to do. It will be fun! "

Molly rang up Mrs. Williams in half an hour's time and told her she would take the post. Mrs. Williams sounded relieved. She told Molly the address and her sister's name, and promised to ring up her sister and tell her she had engaged a nursery governess for her.

"Thank you very much for your interest and help," said Molly. "It's awfully good of you. Please give my love to Prudence and thank her, too."

Molly and Peter were to begin their new work on the same day—new, grown-up lives. How strange they would feel!

CHAPTER FOURTEEN

Off to Work

THE Jacksons felt more cheerful again that weekend. None of them could feel really happy, because the loss of their father was always at the back of their minds, but at any rate their mother was on the mend, almost ready to be moved to the nursing home, and the two elder ones had got jobs. That was something.

Jenny Wren worried a little as to how Mrs. Jackson would take the news of her husband's loss, and how they were to keep it from her till the doctor said she might know. Fortunately she was not allowed any letters, or, indeed, to read anything, so she did not ask to see her husband's letters, but was contented to know, through Jenny or the others, that he was getting on in America. It was becoming increasingly difficult to keep up the deception, for the Jacksons did not find it easy to be deceitful. Sometimes, indeed, Jenny wondered if Mrs. Jackson suspected something, but if she did she said nothing about it.

Neither Peter nor Molly could tell their mother of their jobs, because then she would realize that something strange was afoot. They impressed upon both Shirley and Michael that they were not to say a word either. Shirley found this very difficult, but she did not let out the secret. Mrs. Jackson was still very weak, and found it hard to concentrate on any news for long, so the children simply talked cheerfully of *Red-Roofs*, the garden and Bundle in the few minutes they were allowed to see her.

Monday morning came. Molly had fetched Prudence's bicycle, and Jackdaw had obligingly oiled it and cleaned it and mended a puncture for her. He was quite one of the family now. The garden was looking trim and neat, for not only Jackdaw worked hard in it, but Jenny Wren, too, and all the children. There was something very satisfying about gardening, Molly thought; it seemed to heal your mind when you felt depressed and miserable.

Molly set off on her bicycle and Peter ran to catch a tram. The others stood at the front gate and waved to them. Michael half envied the two of them, setting out to earn their own livings. He was an independent boy, and felt that he would like to be on his own, too. Well, he had a plan. Now that the other two were going to be away all day he could start to carry out his plan!

Michael meant to take in work as a watch and wireless mender! He didn't really mind what it was he mended so long as it was something mechanical, something with screws and levers, valves, wire, nails and things of that sort. He had a genius for these, and they seemed to do exactly what he wanted them to do. Suppose he got broken clocks and things from people to mend and charged them for the mending? He would be earning *his* living then, and could put his share towards the expenses of the house. Then Molly and Peter would see that he was one of the older ones, too, someone to be trusted, confided in, not a baby like Shirley, who still played with dolls and toys.

So while Molly and Peter rushed off to their new jobs small Michael, serious and scowling, made preparations for his new job, too. First he tied a board beside the front gate. He had made it and painted it, with Jackdaw's willing help.

"Michael Jackson," it said. "Mender of watches, wireless sets, etc."

Jackdaw admired Michael's idea very much, and had promised to get him things to mend from among his own friends, though how he would ever find enough words to tell his friends puzzled Michael. Jenny Wren was in the secret, too. She thought the world of Michael, and secretly loved him the best. His curious mixture of maturity and childishness appealed to her, for she was much the same type herself.

Michael's "workshop" looked very professional now. Jenny Wren had helped him to set up a proper bench, and had given him a chair of her own and some shelves.

The boy was very proud of his little den. He kept his many tools and instruments carefully and tidily, and always knew where everything was. He had borrowed many books on the subject he was interested in, and already had a vast store of information far beyond his years.

Shirley stared in amazement and delight at the board by the front gate. As soon as she realized what Michael meant to do, she badgered him to tell her how she could earn money as well. "You're too little, and besides, you're a girl," Michael said. "Go and play with your dolls."

"I shall never play with dolls any more," said Shirley at once. "I'm growing up fast. I'll give all my dolls away. To-day, if you like."

"No, don't do that," said Michael hurriedly, knowing that Shirley would cry her eyes out after she had done such a thing. "That would be silly. Now are you going to be quiet? I've got something to do."

"Well, tell me what I can do to earn money, and I'll be quiet," said Shirley. "But if you don't tell me I'll sing at the top of my voice all morning."

Michael groaned. Shirley had a dear little voice, but she didn't sing in tune. "Well," he said after a moment's thought, "you *can* be a help if you like and earn a bit of money. In fact a very great help."

"How?" said Shirley in excitement.

"Well, the things I mend have got to be fetched here and taken back when they are mended," said Michael, "and they are difficult to carry. But you have a fine doll's pram, so would you like to be my errand boy and fetch the broken clocks and things in your pram for me and take them back? They would be quite easy to wheel."

"Oh, *yes*!" said Shirley in delight. "Fancy wheeling things like that in my pram! Much better than dolls. Yes, I will, Mike. Is there anything to fetch this morning?"

"There's this clock to take over the hill to *Four Chimneys*," said Michael, pointing to a wooden clock which was ticking away merrily. "There will be half a crown to pay. You can collect the money for me, and ask if there is anything else to be mended."

Shirley put the clock carefully into her big doll's pram and set off happily. "Now we are all earning money," she said. "How much will you give me for each errand?"

"Twopence," said Michael. "You will soon earn a lot! Won't Peter and Molly be surprised at you?"

Molly bicycled to her new job. It took her almost twenty minutes, but she was there at last. She found the road and looked for the house. She was surprised to find that it was quite a small one, no larger than *Red-Roofs*, and not nearly so pretty. She got off her bicycle and went to the front door. It badly wanted a coat of paint.

She heard the sound of a child crying indoors, and a voice raised in exasperation. She rang the bell, and there was silence. Then someone came to the door and opened it.

It was a woman of about thirty-two or three, who had once been pretty, but was now faded and tired. Her mouth had the same discontented twist as Mrs. Williams' and Prudence's, and there were frown-creases on her forehead. At first sight Molly did not very much like the look of her.

"Oh—are you Miss Jackson?" she said. "I am Mrs. Lacy, Mrs. Williams' sister. Come in. I'm all behind this morning somehow. You see, my maid left last week, and I haven't got anyone else yet, and it's such a business getting my husband off in the mornings and seeing to the children and everything. I shall be glad of your help."

Molly went in. She took off her hat and then went to see the children. The seven and three-year-olds were boys, grubby little things with untidy hair and dirty overalls. The five-year-old was a small girl, who stared at Molly unblinkingly, her thumb in her mouth. They all had dark, straight hair and sloe-black eyes.

Molly did not know whether to kiss them or shake hands as Shirley had been taught very early to do. The children's mother spoke impatiently to them.

"Say 'hullo!' to Miss Jackson. She's come to look after you. You must be very, very good with her."

The three-year-old boy immediately burst into floods

of tears. Molly bent over him, trying to comfort him, but he beat her away with his little fists.

"He doesn't like strangers," said Mrs. Lacy. "Stop that row, Alfred, or I'll smack you."

Alfred stopped. He evidently knew that his mother could be relied on to slap him if she said she would. He staggered away to a corner and sat down with his back to them.

"Well, I'll leave you to make friends with them," said Mrs. Lacy. "I've got the breakfast things to wash up and the dinner to cook. When the children are a bit used to you, you can dress them properly and take them to the shops with you. I want some shopping done."

"But don't you want me to teach them any lessons?" said Molly in surprise.

"Well—not just at first," said Mrs. Lacy, wrapping an overall round her. "Now children, Mummy's going to wash up. Be nice to Miss Jackson and show her all your toys. Then she will wash you and dress you nicely and take you for a walk."

Left alone with the grubby little children, Molly felt strange. She didn't quite know what she had expected, but certainly it wasn't this. She had vaguely hoped for a little schoolroom of her own, with three well-behaved children sitting at small desks, learning simple things in delight, just as the children did in the kindergarten at school. She had planned to have a rug on which the smaller ones could sit to play with bricks. She had thought of stories she could tell them. She hadn't somehow thought of a messy little sitting room with three grubby, half-dressed children staring at her out of dark, gipsy eyes.

Mrs. Lacy liked somebody to talk to. She kept drifting back into the sitting-room, pots and pans in her hands, telling Molly this, that and the other. She told her of all the maids she had ever had, who, according to her, had all been cheeky, dishonest or careless. Then she spoke of Mrs. Williams and "that stuck-up niece of mine, Prudence," whom she evidently cordially hated.

"Of course, my sister's had all the luck," she said, polishing a dish vigorously. "She married well, and I expect you've seen her lovely place. But she never asks me or the children there. Ashamed of us, I suppose. Well, if you only have a bit of money to make do on, you can't live in *her* style, can you, and I must say she's a selfish snob. She might make things easier for me than she does. But she won't. Just turns up her nose at me and the kids."

Molly disliked hearing all this. She thought it was very mean and disloyal of Mrs. Lacy to speak against her sister as she did. After all, she, Molly, was a complete stranger. In just the same way Prudence, too, spoke against her people. Mrs. Jackson was right—there was something badly wrong with Prudence's family. Molly said nothing but busied herself in tidying up the children's toys, which were all over the floor.

"She's taking my things away!" wailed Terence, the seven-year-old, and Crystal, the little girl, set up a howl too.

"They really get on my nerves," said their mother. "Take them up to the bathroom and wash them and put on their clean clothes, Molly. I can't call you Miss Jackson, after all—you look so young!"

Molly trailed the three children up the stairs to the dirty, untidy bathroom. She had to clear it up before she could even wash the children. She did not like the dirty little house, nor its stale smell. She thought of clean, sweet-smelling *Red-Roofs* and longed to be there. She didn't think she was going to like this job at all.

It took her until twelve o'clock to get all the children ready. She was horrified to see the time, but it was impossible to make the children hurry. They were spoilt, irritable and had no idea of what it meant to be obedient.

"Oh dear! I shall have to make them understand they've got to obey me before I can do anything with them at all!" thought Molly, almost in despair. "Alfred, come away from the water. Crystal, don't pull your pretty dress about like that. Look how you've messed it up already—and you did look such a pretty little girl."

Alfred burst into one of his loud wails. He did this at

107

regular intervals, apparently for no reason at all. Molly could not find one, at any rate.

But at last the children were ready and Mrs. Lacy gave Molly a list of the shopping she wanted done. "You'll have to hurry to be back by one," she said. "Take the push-chair with you for Alfred. The others can hold on to the handle."

Molly set off, but it was not possible to hurry to the shops with two small children hanging on to the handle of the push-chair. She felt harassed and worn by the time she got there, and she was really ashamed of the dirty push-chair and filthy cover. She would wash that, and clean the push-chair as soon as she could!

She did the shopping and then turned to go back. It was one o'clock already. She hadn't the heart to make Crystal and Terence hurry, so she did not get back till twenty-past one, half afraid that Mrs. Lacy would scold her and make her feel she wasn't a bit of good. But there was no sign of dinner when she got back. The hungry children began to wail.

Mrs. Lacy was talking to her next door neighbour out in the garden. She hurried in when she heard the children. "Good gracious, are you back already?" she said. "Lay the table for me, there's a dear, Molly. Terence you show her where everything is kept. Crystal, leave Alfred alone. If you make him cry, I'll smack you."

Somewhere about two o'clock the badly-cooked meal was ready. Molly, who had been too excited to eat much breakfast, was as hungry as the small children.

"I don't know what's the matter with the stew," said Mrs. Lacy ladelling out helpings. "It doesn't look very nice, and yet I took a lot of trouble over it. Can you cook, Molly?"

"Oh, yes," said Molly. "Mother often had a stew like this for us, and I know exactly how she did it."

"Aren't you a clever girl?" said Mrs. Lacy, opening her baby-blue, rarther faded eyes, very wide. "Next time we have a stew you shall do it for me and let me see how it tastes."

After dinner Alfred and Crystal were put out into the garden on rugs to sleep. Privately Molly thought that Terence could do with a sleep too, for he looked white and cross. She suggested this, but Mrs. Lacy said no. Terence never would have a rest in the afternoon, and he was so strong-willed it wasn't a bit of good forcing him. So Terence dragged round after the two of them, getting in their way, and finally bursting into tears when his mother slapped him.

"I'll have a bit of a lie-down now," said Mrs. Lacy, when the dinner-things had been washed up. "I'm going out to tea, Molly, but you can manage the children all right, can't you? You'll find the tea-things in the kitchen, and you can cut the bread-and-butter, can't you? The children's milk is in the larder."

Molly dealt with the children firmly. When their mother, after an hour's rest, departed at half-past four, Molly felt she had a freer hand. She was genuinely fond of children, knew how to interest them, and could be kind and firm at the same time. She told them little stories and got them really interested, and soon the spoilt, half-neglected, badly-managed little things began to feel that Miss Jackson was somebody to be liked.

"Are you the new maid?" asked Terence. "We always called our maids by their names. Why can't we call you Molly?"

"I'm your governess, you see," said Molly. Then she laughed. "But you can call me Molly, if you like. I feel more like Molly than Miss Jackson."

"We've never had a governess before," said Terence, solemnly. "What is a governess? I go to school in term-time and Crystal is coming next term too. But Alfred is too little."

Alfred set up one of his usual howls. Molly comforted him, and looked at Terence in surprise. "You go to school?" she said. "But—I thought I was to teach you all!"

Terence said nothing more, but stared back at her. Young women came and went in his home, but he hoped this one would stay. He liked her.

CHAPTER FIFTEEN

Clock-mender and Errand-girl

MRS. LACY did not come back till half-past six. Molly was upset. She had no idea what time the children should be put to bed, but she felt that the two little ones ought to go before six o'clock. So she began to run the bath water and to get things ready for the night. She had hoped to be able to leave at half-past six, but there seemed no chance of that!

She bathed Alfred and Crystal and had just put them into their cots when Mrs. Lacy came back.

"Good gracious! Have you got Alf and Crystal into bed already?" said Mrs. Lacy, approvingly. "That's good. Terence doesn't go till seven."

"Well—he's tired—and he didn't have a rest in the afternoon," said Molly, looking at the white-faced little boy, who certainly looked as if he might fall asleep at any moment. "Shall I pop him in now? The bathwater's nice and hot."

"I suppose you're wanting to go off now," said Mrs. Lacy, in a suddenly irritable voice. "I knew that was what it would be when Catherine told me you wanted a daily job. Get here late and go early. *I* know!"

"It isn't that at all, Mrs. Lacy," said Molly, hurt and upset. "It's just that Terence is so tired."

"I'll put him to bed myself and you can go home," said Mrs. Lacy, sulkily. "Come to-morrow at the same time."

Molly did not know yet Mrs. Lacy's odd sulks and tempers, and she was sad as she put on her hat. She had hoped to have a word or two of praise for her handling of the children. She said good night, took her bicycle and

110

rode off, hearing Terence beginning to howl as he saw her leave.

The girl was tired. She rode home quickly and was so glad to see *Red-Roofs* on the hillside that she almost burst herself riding all the way up to it. She put her bicycle into the shed and ran indoors.

"Well, we'd almost given you up!" said Jenny Wren, and Shirley ran to hug her. "Why, child, you look tired! Sit down and I'll get supper."

Oh, it was good to be home and sit down quietly. It was good to see little Shirley again and hear her chatter. It was nice to see old Peter coming in, serious-faced as usual, asking her how she had got on.

They were soon exchanging all their news. Now that Molly was rested a little, her day did not seem to her to have been so hard and she made the others laugh as she related various incidents. Then it was Peter's turn.

"Well, I'm not a junior clerk, that's plain!" he began. "I'm just odd-job man and office-boy, and errand boy, and goodness knows what! I'm at everyone's beck and call. The things I've done to-day! I've cleaned two typewriters (though Mike would have done it much better than I did) and I've brewed tea twice for the whole office, and carried dozens of cups about. And I've washed up too, and I've even cleaned the windows of one of the offices! I've posted hundreds of letters, bought pounds' worths of stamps, run a score of errands, and sharpened about a thousand pencils. And I haven't used my brains once. A pity—but there it is!"

Molly sensed disappointment under Peter's gay tone. "Is it a good job, do you think?" she said. "Is it one that will lead to something, Peter?"

"Oh, when you begin, you always have to do a bit of everything," said Peter. "All the same, I do hope I get a chance of using my brains somehow. Why, Shirley could have done what I did to-day!"

"You'll never guess what *I* did to-day!" began Shirley in an important voice. "I earned my living too. I've got sixpence already. You can have it at the end of the week."

Molly and Peter laughed. "Whatever do you mean, Shirley?" asked Molly.

Then Shirley poured out what she and Michael were doing. Michael was still at work in the shed, and had not yet appeared, so Shirley had a fine time telling all the details.

"A watch and clock-mender—and a mender of wireless-sets—and a board at the front gate!" said Molly, amazed. "You're making this up, Shirley. I didn't see any board."

"You came in at the side-gate with your bike," said Shirley. "And Peter ran in without noticing it. But the board is there."

The two older ones went out to look. There was the board, true enough! Molly stared at it in horror.

"We can't let Michael do that! We can't. What ever will people say? It's really ridiculous. Mike, where are you? Come here!"

Michael came out of his workshop, looking rather dirty, for he had been hard at work all day. He had had a barograph to mend, a kind he had not seen before, and it had rather worried him. He had been reading a book about them, but so far he did not quite see how to put this one right. He was not in the mood to be scolded.

"Hallo," he said, not seeing Molly's frown at first. "How did you and Peter get on?"

"Michael, you must take that board down!" said Molly. "It's ridiculous! And there's no need for you to earn your little bit of money. We're not so poor as all that. People will think we're ready to go into the workhouse if we let you act like this."

"What's the matter?" said Michael, with one of his familiar scowls. "Why shouldn't I have a board up at the gate to tell people what I can do for them?"

"It's silly," said Molly.

"It isn't," said Michael, suddenly fierce. "Wouldn't Peter have a board or a brass plate up on his front gate if he was a doctor? And don't dentists? Well, why shouldn't *I*? It's true I don't mend people, only clocks

112

and things, but I don't see that it matters. The board is only to tell people I am a mender."

"And you've made silly little Shirley into a sort of errand-girl," said Molly, whose tiredness was making her really irritable. "I won't have it!"

Shirley burst into tears and wailed. Jenny Wren came running out in surprise. "She won't let me help, she says I'm silly," wept Shirley.

"And she says I'm ridiculous!" said Michael, still scowling. "All because I wanted to help, and this is the only way I *could*. I think it's mean. Takes the heart out of a fellow."

Peter felt sorry for the crestfallen little boy. "Don't worry, old thing," he said. "Molly's just tired, aren't you, Mollikins? When we've all had some supper, we'll think things are grand. Of course you wanted to help—and he can have his board up, can't he, Molly?"

Molly felt terribly, painfully sorry for her unexpected outburst. How could she have hurt her little brother and sister like that? She must be more tired than she had thought.

"Yes," she said, soberly. "Of course he can. Sorry, Mike. Don't cry, Shirley. You shall be an errand-girl if you want to, and we shall love to have the money you earn too. My word, if all the Jackson family work together like this, we shall soon be rich!"

Michael lost his scowl. He saw that Molly's under-lip was trembling a little. Jenny Wren saw it too. "Now do come in to your supper," she said, "arguing like this in the garden—enough to frighten all the birds away. I've got such a nice supper too. Can't you smell it?"

And at that moment a most delicious smell did come out of the kitchen. "Stew! Onions!" cried Shirley, cheering up at once. "Am I going to have any? Can I have a proper supper to-night instead of bread and butter or biscuits?"

Shirley did not usually share in the supper often provided for the bigger ones, but this time she did. "Yes, you shall," said Molly, willing to offer Shirley almost anything she wanted, to make up for her burst of ill-temper.

"Let's come in. Michael, you haven't heard about my funny day yet. I'll tell you all about it."

Their mother would have been proud of her little family that night, if she could have seen them sitting round the table, eagerly discussing their various "jobs". Here were four children—for Molly was only seventeen, and looked younger—children who a few weeks back had no responsibilities at all; and now each child had set to and discovered some sort of work that would bring in a little money to a home bereft of father and mother. Jenny Wren thought they were all wonderful—even little Shirley and her eager acceptance of the character of errand-girl.

Shirley had put away her dolls that day. Yes, she had stuffed Josephine, Angela, Rosebud, Daisy, Betsy-May, Belinda and Amelia Jane into empty drawers, face downwards. She could not belong to the older group of children if she still played with dolls, she felt certain of that. Jenny Wren had discovered all the dolls that afternoon, because the drawer had stuck on one little stuffed arm, that hung out helplessly.

She showed Molly the dolls that evening and tears came into the big girl's eyes as she saw poor Shirley's efforts at being "big".

"She's not to do that," she said. "I shall take them all out and give them back to her."

"No, don't do that," said Jenny Wren. "She's done a very big thing—given up something she still loved very much in order to throw in her lot with you. Let her do it, and be proud of her, Molly. She would rather have your admiration for what she had done, than the comfort of her dolls."

So Molly gave unstinted admiration to her little sister and praised her highly, which gave Shirley enormous pleasure. She adored Molly, and thought there was no one in the world like her big sister.

"But don't you think you could just have *one* doll to look after?" said Molly, as she finished tucking Shirley up for the night.

"No, thank you," said Shirley, firmly, putting away the

picture of chubby, smiling Angela that came floating into her mind. "Good night, Molly. I wish you hadn't got to go away to-morrow again."

Molly wished it too. It was no good pretending—she was disappointed in her job. It wasn't what she had hoped for at all. Still, maybe when Mrs. Lacy got another maid in the house to see to things, and she, Molly had got the children in hand, things would be better. But all the same, if Terence went to school in September—and Crystal too—surely Mrs. Lacy wouldn't want a governess for little three-year-old Alfred. It was puzzling. Never mind, maybe things would sort themselves out and come all right.

Both Molly and Peter talked very cheerfully to one another that evening about their jobs, though each was nursing disappointment in their hearts. Peter had hated his first day. He had been "chivvied about" as he called it, almost every minute. Everyone had used him as an errand-boy. He could see that one was necessary in a firm like Jameson and Morris, but why call him "Junior Clerk"?

Peter did not realize that many boys like to go into the offices of a publisher right at the bottom and work their way up, learning each section as they go—and maybe even reaching the head of the firm. He had never wanted to be a publisher. All his heart had been set on doctoring. He considered it a waste of time and a waste of his good brains to spend his days making tea for the other clerks and secretaries, doing up parcels and licking stamps. He turned with thankfulness to his school-work. He meant to work hard at his books each night, and go on with his education as if he were at school.

But although he had done little brainwork that day in the office, he was tired. He could not concentrate. His thoughts slid away from the page in front of him, and he found himself yawning.

"Go to bed, Peter," said Molly, yawning too. "You're tired."

"I've got some work to do," said Peter, looking worried. "You know I've made up my mind to try for that scholarship, Molly, even though I can't take it up if I win it.

115

But after all I've done half the work already, and it would mean a lot to me if I had the honour of winning it. So I really must work each night."

"Yes, but go easy for the first few nights, Peter," said Molly. "Give yourself a chance. Hallo, Jenny Wren! You always come in at the right moment with your cups of cocoa. Give one to Peter—he's yawning his head off, but he won't go to bed. A cup of hot, milky cocoa will finish him off and send him to sleep. Then he'll *have* to go to bed!"

"You'd better go, too," said Jenny Wren, her sharp monkey eyes looking at Molly's tired face. "You've got to be off in good time to-morrow, both of you, and you want a good sleep."

So, after two cups of cocoa each and a final chat, the two said good night. Molly went upstairs, leaving Peter to clear away his books. The boy stood for a moment in front of a photograph of his father. How hard he must have worked to keep a whole family going, thought Peter. It was difficult enough to earn a pound or so a week; he felt he would never be able to earn enough to marry and keep a growing family himself. It wasn't so easy to be grown-up as it looked!

CHAPTER SIXTEEN
Busy Day

MOLLY went off the next morning again and so did Peter. Michael retired to his "workshop" to tackle the barograph once more, and Shirley went to help Jenny Wren do the washing up. Michael was looking cheerful. He said he had dreamt how to fix the barograph. Nobody really believed this, but it was quite true. Michael often found solutions of his mechanical difficulties in his dreams at night, and put them into practice the next day. As Jenny Wren often said, he was "a bit of a genius"!

Mrs. Lacy appeared to have forgotten her unkind words of the evening before. She greeted Molly with a smile, and told her to get the children ready to go out.

"Better do the shopping a bit sooner this morning," she said. "Then you might be back early enough to help me with the cooking. Can you do fritters?"

"Yes," said Molly, and went to get the children ready. Terence was pleased to see her. Alfred once more broke into wails and Crystal stared solemnly at her. Molly smiled at them all. She thought they would be dear little children once they were really clean, nicely dressed and had better manners.

The day passed very much as the one before had, except that Molly did most of the cooking for the midday meal and all the washing up. Mrs. Lacy announced that she had a bad headache and must go and lie down. So Molly put the children down to have a rest—the two younger children, that is—for once again Terence wandered about in the kitchen, irritable and tired, instead of resting with the others. Molly talked to him quietly, telling him about Shirley and all that her little sister did. Terence became intensely interested in her, and in Bundle, too. Soon, Molly thought, he would want to do all the things that Shirley did, and it would be quite easy to handle him. He was

117

a serious, old-looking child, white through lack of sleep and too little fresh air.

Mrs. Lacy stayed in to tea that day, but declined to have it with the children. "You have tea with the children in the garden," she said to Molly. "I've still got a headache. The children get on my nerves then. Bring me a pot of tea and some bread and butter and a slice of cake before you have tea yourself."

So Molly prepared a dainty tray of tea for Mrs. Lacy and took it into the cool drawing-room to her. Mrs. Lacy was curled up on the grubby sofa, reading a novel. She did not say thank you or even look up at Molly, but went on reading. Molly secretly thought that it was no wonder the children's manners were so bad!

"I shall even have to teach them to say please and thank you!" she thought to herself as she tried to prevent Crystal from snatching at the bread and butter, and made her ask politely for it. "Now say thank you, Crystal," she said.

Alfred resisted all efforts Molly made at teaching him to say please. He simply opened his mouth and yelled when Molly held the cake away from him till he said please. Mrs. Lacy called peevishly from the window.

"For goodness' sake, Molly! What's the matter with the children to-day? Can't you keep them quiet? What's Alfred yelling about?"

Alfred yelled more loudly. When he had quietened, Molly explained to Mrs. Lacy. "Alfred doesn't want to say please, that's all. But he'll soon learn. Terence has learnt, and he says it nicely—don't you, Terence?"

Alfred howled again, one eye on his mother. "Oh, give him the cake, Molly!" said Mrs. Lacy, exasperated. "I can't stand this. He's too little to learn things like that yet. Really, I should have thought you would have had more sense—working him up like that. You can have your cake, Alf but be quiet, or I'll come and smack you."

Alfred felt victorious. He had soon learnt that howling got him most things, so he howled even when there didn't seem much to be got by it. Unexpected howls often produced sweets, biscuits and chocolate—"anything to keep him quiet," his mother said. Molly was quite taken aback by his flouting of her ideas. She felt almost inclined to howl as loudly as Alfred! How *could* Mrs. Lacy find fault with her like that in front of the children?

The girl gave Alfred his cake, and he snatched it off the plate. Molly did not ask him to say thank you, fearing another howl. But Terence spoke up.

"Say thank you, Alf," he remarked. "Didn't you hear *me* say thank you?"

"Tankoo," said Alfred in an angelic manner.

"There!" said Mrs. Lacy, who was still watching. "A little of Terence's example, and Alfred is quite ready to learn, Molly. It's just no use going on at him."

Molly said nothing. She felt that it was no use at all arguing with Mrs. Lacy. Their ideas about things were quite different. What was the good of telling her that Terence had only just learned to say "thank you" himself that day, and was showing off his recently-acquired manners?

All the same, Terence should have a word of approval from her. So Molly smiled at Terence and said, "Well done, Terence. How clever of you to teach Alfred his manners! "

Terence immediately made up his mind to teach Alfred more manners. He liked this Molly, and he hoped she wasn't going to have a row with his mother and go off in a huff, as nearly everyone did. He sat a little closer to her and tried to imitate her in all that she did.

Mrs. Lacy went out at half-past five, saying she was just going to slip along to the shops for an evening paper.

"Shall I begin to put the little ones to bed soon?" said Molly, suspecting that Mrs. Lacy might quite well be more than a few minutes.

"Yes, if I'm not back by six," said Mrs. Lacy. "But don't worry. I shan't be long! Be good children! "

Alfred opened his mouth and howled. Molly let him. She knew by now that Alfred's howls meant nothing at all. The more notice that was taken of them, the more

119

he would howl. Therefore it was best to take no notice at all, and maybe he would get tired of it. Poor Alfred! He was not a very attractive child just then, but it was not his fault. Constant mishandling had turned him into a bad-tempered little bundle of nerves. Cuddled one minute and slapped the next, he never knew a moment's security.

Molly, with her instinctive understanding of young children, knew this. Now, when Alfred howled, she immediately began to show Crystal or Terence something interesting, and at once Alfred would stop howling and stagger over to see what she was showing. Then she would show it to him, too, and that finished that little outburst. A mother more intelligent than Mrs. Lacy would have seen and understood Molly's sure handling of the little boy, but Mrs. Lacy, peevish and spoilt herself, saw only that Molly apparently took no notice of "poor little Alf" when he howled.

Six o'clock came and no Mrs. Lacy. Molly sighed and began to run the bath water for the two little ones. She had them both in bed at half-past six, and Alfred was already asleep.

"Would you like to go to bed, too, Terence?" she said, seeing how listless the little boy was.

"No. You tell me a story," said Terence. So she took him on her knee and began to tell him all Bundle's funny tricks. He listened, entranced.

The clock struck seven. No Mrs. Lacy. "It's too bad," thought Molly. "She knows I can't leave the children by themselves. I *must* stay till she comes back."

She put Terence to bed and he fell asleep as soon as his head touched the pillow. Molly cleared up, then took a book and sat down. She was tired. She wanted to be at home with her own family. She was hungry, too, for she had not had very much lunch that day.

Mrs. Lacy came home at a quarter to eight with her husband, a dark-eyed, black-haired man whom Molly disliked at sight.

"Oh, Molly!" said Mrs. Lacy, "you still here? I met my husband by chance coming from the station and went to see some friends. I'm afraid we stopped rather late. Are the children all right?"

"They're in bed and asleep," said Molly. "I must go now. My family will wonder what has become of me."

Mrs. Lacy had one of her quick changes of mood. She looked black and said sullenly, "You might have laid the table for our meal while you were waiting. Mightn't she, Claude?"

Claude always agreed with his wife, and he nodded. Molly flushed. "I'm sorry," she said, "but I'm afraid I never thought of it. I was expecting you every minute, you see."

She rode home, troubled and sad. It was beginning to dawn on her that Mrs. Lacy hadn't wanted a governess at all—she had wanted a little maid-of-all-work, someone to push all the various jobs on to—cooking, housework, children. She wanted someone whose every minute would be taken up with her house, her children and herself. She resented Molly going home to her family. The girl felt unhappy as she cycled quickly back. Mrs. Williams must have known that Mrs. Lacy didn't want a governess. She must have known that Terence went to school and that Crystal was going with him the next term. It wasn't kind of her to deceive Molly like that.

The girl did not know in the least what to do about it. She did not feel able to stand up to either Mrs. Williams or Mrs. Lacy about it. Also she knew that it was bad to give up one's first job too easily or too soon. Weak characters always did that, and Molly was not weak. So she supposed she would have to go on with the job and hope it would turn out better than it seemed.

The others had given her up and had had supper. Jenny was anxious about her and hit her anxiety under an assumed sharpness.

"Well well, here you are at last! We've had our supper. Couldn't keep it waiting any longer. Whatever made you so late? You really must try to get home sooner, Molly. I thought you must have had an accident."

"No," said Molly, sitting down meekly to the warm

plate of food that Jenny set in front of her. "No, Jenny Wren. Mrs. Lacy went out and didn't come back till a quarter to eight, and I couldn't possibly leave the children all alone in the house, could I?"

Jenny Wren made no answer. She had formed her own opinion of Mrs. Lacy the day before, from various things that Molly had let drop, and Jenny Wren was beginning to feel certain that the job Molly had was not at all what she had meant to get. Still, there was no use saying anything just yet. So Jenny cut some bread for hungry Molly and brought her in a good helping of chocolate blancmange. Bundle sat by her legs and occasionally put a friendly paw on her knee. Molly ate in peace, glad to be quite alone for a little while.

Peter was working hard at his books in the other room. Michael was clearing up in the workshop. He had mended the barograph, and it was going well. He was debating how much to charge for his work. Would three shillings and sixpence be too much? he wondered.

Shirley was in bed, waiting for Molly to come up and say good night to her. She went up as soon as she had finished her supper. Shirley flung her arms round her.

"Molly! Are you tired? Why were you so late? I did miss you to-day. Do you know, I took a wireless set back to Mr. Harris, and fetched a clock from Miss Wilson, and I've earned another fourpence. That's tenpence. Isn't it good?"

Molly sat listening on the bed. She felt like a mother now, listening to Shirley's little chatter. She was sorry to have to be away so long each day from her. It was lucky that Jenny Wren was there to have the little girl around and listen to her endless talking. She felt certain that Shirley had missed her mother almost more than anyone. She went downstairs.

"Got good news for you to-night," said Jenny Wren, scouring out a dish. "Doctor Ransome says we can get your mother moved to the nursing home this week. Won't it be nice for you all to have her so near? One or other of you will be able to pop over every day."

CHAPTER SEVENTEEN

August goes by

THE days went by, beautiful, warm summer days, with bees buzzing in the hollyhocks in the garden, and raspberries ripening each day for tea or supper. August was magnificent that year.

Mrs. Jackson was installed in the nursing home and looked with weak delight from the windows that opened on to the green countryside, instead of on dismal walls or roofs, as her hospital window had done. She was near her children now—they could see her often. She had a room of her own where she could lie in peace, instead of being continually bothered by the busy happenings of the big ward. She could lie and think.

Bundle, once he had discovered where Mrs. Jackson suddenly and unaccountably lived, made his way solemnly to the nursing home every single day. Sometimes he went with one of the children and sometimes by himself. He would trot down the hillside, take the path that led to another slope, gambol down the drive to the front door and into the cool hall. He would wait cautiously to see if anyone were going to turn him out, and then when the coast was clear he would scamper along the hall, go up a flight of stairs and come to the door of the room where Mrs. Jackson lay.

If it were slightly open he would slide his black nose round and look in. Mrs. Jackson would see the door move and look round. Then Bundle would caper in, his paws rattling on the polished linoleum, his tongue out in ecstasy. His tail would wag so hard that it moved the back of his body from side to side with it.

He never attempted to jump on the bed. He merely went over and put his head up near Mrs. Jackson's fingers. She looked down into his speaking eyes and smiled. Her hand stroked the soft silky head and Bundle was quite content. He would stand there as long as she stroked him, his tail wagging.

Mrs. Jackson loved to see him. The first time the nurse had come into the room and found Bundle there she was angry and horrified, and was about to shoo the dog out when Mrs. Jackson stopped her.

"Don't, Nurse! " she said. "He's our dog, and he's come to see me all by himself. He's such good company. Couldn't I keep him for a little?"

The nurse looked at Mrs. Jackson and saw that she had a little colour in her cheekss for the first time, so she relaxed her stern look and nodded.

"Very well—as he's your own dog. But any messing about or getting on the bed and out he goes for good and all! "

Bundle looked at her, his head on one side, listening. He could tell by the tone of her voice that if he were good he could stay. Well, he meant to be good. He was never the bad, mad Bundle of mischief and trouble that he could be sometimes at home. No, in the nursing home he was a model dog, a paragon, the ideal canine friend. Mrs. Jackson often smiled to herself when she compared this calm, self-possessed, well-behaved dog with the mad little puppy of *Red-Roofs*. He was like the children—suddenly serious and grown-up. But wait till she got back and took the reins again. They would all of them revert to their young childish ways and be as young as they really were! And when Dick came back, what a time they would have!

The children were glad to have their mother so near. They were still only allowed to see her for a few minutes at a time, and this little time they filled with easy chatter of home happenings. Mrs. Jackson herself talked very little, for it was still an effort to answer questions, or to follow any story for long. She hardly heard what they said. She

124

was content to watch their well-loved faces and hear their voices.

She always asked if they had heard from their father, and trying not to look straight at her, the children said the same thing, "Daddy's all right. Having a good time. He sends you his love."

"She'll have to be told some time." Peter said gravely to Molly. "But who is going to tell her? I simply can't, Molly. Can you?"

Molly thought about it. "No," she said, "I couldn't possibly. The doctor will have to."

But Jenny Wren settled the problem by saying that *she* would tell her when the time came. "This is a woman's job," she said, "not a man's job, nor a child's job. It's my job, so don't you worry your heads about that. I'll do it. But she shan't be allowed to hear a word till she's strong enough to bear it—and you needn't worry too much how she'll take it, poor thing. We're never given anything that's too much for us to bear. Your mother's got more strength and courage than you think. Look how all you children have faced everything—well, don't you suppose that your mother can be as strong as her children?"

This sounded very sensible to Peter and Molly, and they were relieved that Jenny Wren would take on herself the dreadful task of breaking the news to their mother. They both had more than enough to cope with now without worrying about anything else.

Molly's fears had come true. Mrs. Lacy was now quite frankly using her as a little maid-of-all-work, making her do the housework, most of the cooking and giving her the care of the three children as well. Molly did not mind what she did, but she resented being deceived about the job, and she hankered after the work she really would have liked—the actual teaching and training of little children.

"You see, Peter," she said one evening when they were sitting together talking for a few minutes before going to bed, "you see, I do feel that teaching is what I could do and do very well. Just as you used to feel that doctoring was the only thing possible for you. Well, it's a dreadful waste washing up dishes and cleaning taps all my life, when my real gift is teaching. If I hadn't a gift for that I wouldn't care. But I feel somehow it's wrong to waste a real gift. Or doesn't it matter, Peter?"

Peter stared at a big vase of flowers. He, too, had often asked himself that question. When you had a gift, a real vocation for something, *was* it wrong not to use it and follow it? But if he, Peter, had followed his, it would have meant that the Jackson family would fall on very bad days, and that, too, would have been wrong. Life was a puzzle. Sometimes Peter felt very grown-up and sometimes he felt terribly, horribly young. These were the times when he most missed his father. Daddy had solved many of the problems that were worrying Peter, and he could have helped him so much. It would have been fine to talk to Daddy. That was what parents were for, as much as to provide food and shelter. They could hand on to their young ones the things they knew and had learnt about life and its puzzles. It was hard to have to find things out all by yourself.

Peter was finding his job very distasteful too. He was quite the youngest in the office, and the others, amused at his seriousness, teased him, used bad language, offered him cigarettes, laughed when he refused, and made him work at endless little jobs all day long. The boy served every one of the seven offices. He was packer for them all, errand-boy for them all, typed out dozens of letters when someone was too lazy to do it, and made hundreds of pots of tea. As he often said "Shirley could do it all quite well— except for the typing! "

It was always a pleasure for him to turn to his work in the evenings. He could use his brains then. He could concentrate on something worth while and think about it. If he wanted to work out an essay in his mind he could go into the garden and do some weeding, and think quietly while he did it.

He had conquered his tiredness in the evenings now. He could work till half-past ten quite easily. He was making very good headway with the tasks that his Headmaster set him. Mr. Grey was pleased.

"You're doing very well," he told the boy. "That last essay of yours would win top marks in any exam. You could get that scholarship easily if you keep going like this. But don't overdo things, Jackson. You get Sunday free, don't you? Well, make it a complete rest and do what you like."

So Peter did, and Sunday was a red-letter day to all the family; a welcome break from the hurry and bustle of the week, when the material things about them could take second place. It was not altogether without a little sadness, because the children seemed to notice the absence of their father and mother more than ever as they set off in the morning to the little grey church over the hill, but they always came back refreshed in spirit and comforted by the knowledge that they were not alone in the task they were trying to do. In the afternoon they saw their mother; they took Bundle for a walk; they lazed and they read. Jenny Wren even went so far as to say that if anyone wanted breakfast in bed they could have it. But nobody did. They were all young and eager and restless, and breakfast in bed was no treat. They wanted to enjoy Sunday all together and not to miss a minute of it.

Molly and Peter both stuck their jobs well. They grumbled to each other but to nobody else. They grieved because they had gone into the wrong kind of work for them, however much it might have suited others with different gifts. But both were determined not to give up.

Sometimes Molly came home very late, and Jenny was angry—not with Molly, but with the inconsiderate Mrs. Lacy. Mrs. Lacy would suddenly think that she would like to go to the cinema with her husband and would ask Molly to stay until she came back. "Can't leave the children alone, can we?" she would say, smiling at Molly. "And I must have a bit of pleasure sometimes. So would you mind staying, Molly dear?"

Molly never said no. She had an idea that if she did and went home, Mrs. Lacy would leave the children alone in the house, rather than forgo her own pleasure. And Molly had got fond of the three little things, and could not bear to think of Alfred howling with no one to comfort him, or of Terence wanting a drink and no one to get it for him. Also she was haunted by the fear that the house might get on fire and the children be burnt. Mrs. Lacy never could remember to see that the kitchen fire was safe when she left it.

Molly did most of the cooking now. She liked cooking and she knew that at least they would all get well-cooked meals if she cooked them, but she resented Mrs. Lacy's laziness. It would be so easy for her to learn how to make a good cake instead of a heavy one that gave the children indigestion and made them sick. It would be so easy, too, to learn to fry bacon properly instead of frizzling it all up. But Mrs. Lacy did not mean to learn anything if she could help it. She never thought it was her own fault if anything went wrong with the cooking, but blamed the stove or the saucepan or the way the wind blew.

She talked incessantly to Molly about her friends and relations. They all seemed to have treated her disgracefully at some time or other, and she was especially bitter with Mrs. Williams and Prudence. "Stuck-up, that's what they are," she would say to Molly. "And after all, Catherine was brought up the same way as I was, wasn't she? Anyone would think the way she behaves that she was born with a gold spoon in her mouth—well, she wasn't. She was born and brought up in a tiny little house, along with seven others. Our mother kept a sweet-shop—and yet to look at Catherine having a bridge-party, you'd swear she was cousin to a duchess, wouldn't you? As for Prudence, well—I'd just like her to see her maternal grandmother thirty years ago! She'd have a fit. But don't you tell I told you all this, or Catherine would half-kill me."

"Mrs. Lacy, please don't tell me all these things," Molly said desperately one day, "I don't really think you ought to. And I don't like hearing them. After all, Mrs. Williams got me my first job, and Prudence has always been a friend of mine."

Mrs. Lacy gave a loud snort. "Catherine got you your first job—that's quite true! But she didn't do it to give *you* help! Did you imagine that she did? I told her I'd come and plant myself on her, kids and all, if I couldn't find someone to give me a hand with the house and everything pretty soon—and she was so scared that I meant what I said, that she somehow got hold of you and sent you along! *That's* how you got this job!"

Molly's heart sank. She couldn't help believing Mrs. Lacy. She remembered Mrs. Williams' affected, hypocritical voice over the telephone. She wondered if Prudence knew all this that Mrs. Lacy had told her. Surely Prudence might have warned her if she did. Molly felt very hurt and bitter. She left Mrs. Lacy and went to the children. They all loved her now, and it was somehow comforting to see their dark eyes smiling at her and to feel their hands reaching for her.

"All the same, I shan't stay here now," Molly thought. "I'll find a job at teaching somehow, and this time I'll be a bit more careful."

CHAPTER EIGHTEEN

Breaking the News

SEPTEMBER came in, a warm and mellow month. Apples began to ripen on the fruit-trees at *Red-Roofs*. Jackdaw and Michael, Jenny Wren and Shirley picked them in the evenings and stored them very carefully away on straw up in the loft.

"Jackdaw, we must handle them very gently, mustn't we?" said Michael. "Or they won't keep."

"Ar," said Jackdaw, and added unexpectedly. "Treat 'em like eggs."

So, as if they were as fragile as eggs, the pickers handled them delicately, placing them one by one in the baskets, carrying them up to the loft, and putting them carefully down in the straw there.

"We shall be glad not to have to buy apples in the winter," said Jenny Wren, thinking that stored fruit would save the housekeeping quite a lot. "And I've bottled goodness knows how many pounds of plums and greengages, and we've got enough home-made jam to last us a whole year!"

"Jenny Wren, aren't you clever?" said Shirley, earnestly.

"Clever! Clever to bottle fruit and make jam!" snorted Jenny. "Why, them's things every girl and woman ought to learn. And if I'm spared to be here when you're a growing girl, you'll be learning them too, I promise you that. Yes, you'll know how to keep a house clean and sweet, how to cook and how to bottle and preserve and pickle, how to sew and knit and mend and everything else, if it rests with me!"

"Oh," said Shirley, rather alarmed at this catalogue of future achievements. "Well—I rather thought I'd be an artist, Jenny. I shouldn't need to learn all those things then, should I?"

"You'll be a woman and a good housewife before you're an artist," said Jenny, firmly. "And if so be you *are* an artist, it's not going to make you a worse one for knowing how to cook, and run a house, is it? Now just look at that —dropping two perfectly good apples on the ground! No, don't put them into the basket for storing—they'll be bruised now, and won't keep!"

"Well, they'll do for eating," said Shirley. "We want some for eating now, don't we?"

"That's no reason for dropping them, butter-fingers," said Michael. "Is it Jackdaw?"

Jackdaw showed all his white teeth in a wide grin. "Ar," he said, and then again, more wisely—"Ar."

Jackdaw seldom entered into any conversation at all, but he enjoyed hearing the constant chatter of the Jackson family. He listened eagerly to every word, and occasionally contributed his "Ar." Shirley, always imitative, developed the same manner of answering questions.

"Have you put on your overall?" Jenny Wren would call. And back would come the answer in Shirley's clear high voice.

"Ar!"

"Have you fetched my clock for me?" Michael would yell. And back would come an answering shout.

"Ar!"

"Now just stop that," Jenny Wren would say. "You're getting as bad as Jackdaw, Shirley."

"Ar!" Shirley would say, and rush away from Jenny's exasperated snort.

The September days went by quickly. Michael began to think of school again, and he didn't like the idea. He had enjoyed working on his own like this. Shirley, too, had stuck faithfully to her job as errand-girl, and both the older children had to admit that Michael and Shirley together were doing extremely well.

"The two little ones nearly always have a pound or so to contribute at the end of each week," said Peter, one

131

Saturday when he had done the weekly accounts. "It's simply amazing, Molly. Look, this week Mike has brought in eighteen-and-sixpence—and little Shirley has presented us with a shilling and eight-pence—just over a pound between the two of them. And last week Michael actually gave us twenty-six shillings—more than either you or I earned. That boy's a good little fellow, I must say."

"Yes. I feel ashamed now when I think how I scolded him for his board up by the front gate," said Molly. "You know, Mike's clever, Peter. You and I went out and got ourselves the wrong sort of job, though we didn't know it at the time, but young Michael just sat down and made his own job and brings in as much and more money than we do. I should never have thought he had it in him."

"Well, this trouble has shown us what old Mike really can do," said Peter. "It's changed him too. He isn't dreamy or sulky any more—he's alert and cheerful."

"He's doing the work he loves," said Molly. "That makes a lot of difference to anyone. I wish *you* were doing the work you loved, too, Peter—I mean, studying with the idea of being a doctor, as you used to. You've got rather gloomy and serious lately."

"Have I?" said Peter in surprise. "Gosh—I mustn't do that. But this is such a different life I'm leading now— there's no proper fun and talk and games and loyalty like there is in school-life. I don't understand half the silly jokes the fellows at the office make, and they laugh at me for being a mutt. They think I'm older than I am, of course. Well—I shall grow into it all, I suppose, but somehow I don't feel as if I want to."

He looked closely at his listening sister. She was pretty, and he loved her unruly curly hair and her big, wide-set eyes. But nowadays she always seemed to have little lines between her eye-brows—worried, frowny-lines. Peter didn't like them.

"We're all changing," he thought with a sigh. "Even little Shirley, who has just put away her dolls. I suppose it can't be helped, but it's a pity it all came so suddenly.

132

To grow up too quickly isn't very good, perhaps. It's a thing that should be done slowly."

Mrs. Jackson suddenly began to make headway at the nursing home. Her colour came back, and her cheeks filled out. She began to look young again, instead of old. Her eyes had a glow in them. The children were delighted.

"We'll have her back again soon, surely!" they said to one another. "Won't that be lovely! We'll have to put up the flags we save for grand occasions!"

"Yes, she'll be back soon," said Jenny Wren. She was glad to see Mrs. Jackson was responding to the expert treatment she was getting, especially as the thirty pounds would soon all be used up. The doctor had been very good about his fees, but Jenny Wren had been quite horrified at the costs in a good nursing home. Why, thirty pounds went nowhere!

Each of the children was thinking the same thing at intervals—"Mother will soon have to be told about Daddy. Next week she is to be allowed to read—and she will want to read his letters."

Jenny Wren knew this too. She meant to tell Mrs. Jackson very soon, but she was not looking forward to the task. One day the doctor told her that Mrs. Jackson was well enough to know everything—but it must be broken very gradually and gently, so that the shock did not come all at once.

Jenny did not tell the children that she was going to break the news to their mother so soon. She went off alone to the nursing home one day, leaving Michael in charge of Shirley. Bundle was shut in the house so that he would not follow her. He whined dismally and scratched frantically at the front door. But Jenny Wren did not want anyone with her, not even Bundle, that day.

She had gone after tea, and when she got home both Peter and Molly were back from their jobs, Molly unexpectedly early because Mrs. Lacy had taken the children for the night to a friend of hers, so there was no one to put to bed.

Shirley had told her that Jenny Wren had gone to see

their mother, so Molly went into the kitchen to see if she could prepare supper. Michael followed her. He was hungry. Peter called to them.

"Jenny Wren's coming. Ask her if we can have lemonade with our supper for a treat. I know she's made some to-day."

Jenny marched into the kitchen and rushed up to her bedroom without saying a word. Molly stared at Michael. "What's the matter with Jenny?" she said. "Her eyes looked awfully red."

Michael's heart went cold. Surely his mother was all right? They called Peter, and Shirley came running in. "Jenny Wren's been crying," said Molly. "Do you think anything's happened?"

"Sh. Here she comes," said Peter. Jenny came into the kitchen and went to the oven.

"What's the matter, Jenny Wren?" said Shirley, in alarm, for she had never seen Jenny with such red eyes before.

"I told your mother the news to-day," said Jenny, opening the oven door with unnecessary violence. "Upset me a bit, that's all."

The four children stared at her in silence for a moment. "Jenny—was she—was she—awfully upset?" said Molly, with a break in her voice.

Jenny stood up and looked at them. "She didn't believe it," she said. "She *won't* believe it. She just lay and listened to all I said—and then she smiled in that quiet way of hers and said, 'I don't believe it, Jenny. Dick isn't drowned. He'll come back. I should know if he was dead.'"

"Poor Mother!" said Molly. "She doesn't *want* to believe it. She daren't. She's just going to go on and on hoping, when there isn't any hope."

"That's what I think," said Jenny, a tear suddenly running down her cheek again. "She's too weak to face up to it, that's what it is. So's she going to pretend to herself, like many a one has done before. She wouldn't do that

134

if she wasn't weak and hadn't been so ill—she'd have found the strength to look it in the face and accept it."

"Did you tell her everything—how the two ships sank—and that many lives were lost—and that lists of all survivors have been published weeks ago?" said Peter.

"Everything," said Jenny Wren. "I told her how you had all turned to and got yourself work, too, and how well we were managing—and all she said to that was 'But Jenny Wren, it's all unnecessary. Mr. Jackson won't like to think the children have given up our plans for their future, when he comes back'."

"Poor darling Mother!" said Molly. "She's been out of touch with real things so many weeks—she's still in a sort of dream-world of her own. She'll gradually realize all these things are true, and had to be, Jenny. Anyway, it's a good thing the news doesn't seem to have been a shock to her."

"She's coming home next week," said Jenny Wren. "She says she won't stay a day more than she needs to, now. She wants to get back and see what we are all doing. But she cried, poor thing, when she heard how you and Peter go off to work each day, and how Michael and Shirley do their bit too. And well she might—I'd be right down proud of such children too!"

Jenny Wren gave a loud sniff and marched out of the kitchen into the dining room, where she began to lay the table for supper, making quite a lot of noise. She always made a noise when she was upset.

"Leave her alone for a bit," said Molly. "Dear old Jenny Wren—we're like her own family to her, and she takes things to heart terribly. Fancy having Mother back next week. I can hardly believe it. My goodness, that *will* be something to look forward to!"

"I'll go and look out the flags this very minute!" said Shirley, and rushed up to the loft full of joy and excitement.

CHAPTER NINETEEN

Trouble for Prudence

MOLLY went as usual to her job the next day. She found Mrs. Lacy in a great state of excitement, longing to talk to somebody.

"What do you think of your great friend Prudence now, and her stuck-up family?" she greeted Molly. The girl looked at her in amazement. She had no idea what Mrs. Lacy meant.

"Haven't you heard?" said Mrs. Lacy, with relish. "Mr. Williams has gone smash."

"Gone smash?" said Molly. "What do you mean?"

"What I say," said Mrs. Lacy impatiently. "Can't you understand plain English? His business has gone smash. Over-reached himself—been too clever—borrowed money he couldn't repay—and now he's gone smash. No wonder he's been in such a foul temper lately, always going on at Catherine for extravagance! Well, he's got the reward he deserves—and so has that stuck-up Catherine."

Molly was horrified—horrified not only at the news, but at Mrs. Lacy's pleasure in it. After all, it was her own sister and niece that were to suffer. "Oh, how can you talk like that!" she said in a trembling voice. "You ought to be sorry for them—and go and help them."

"Now don't you dare to talk to *me* like that!" said Mrs. Lacy, flying into one of her tempers. "I know my own family better than you do, and Catherine's not one I'm going to pity. Do her good to live in a small house and do her own work, and go without new clothes for a bit—and, my word, what a shock it will be for dear, darling Prudence to turn out into the world and work hard! No more parties for her. She'll have to get a job."

"Poor old Prudence!" said Molly, knowing what a blow

this would be for her old friend. "I must go and see her. She'll want to talk to somebody, I know—you do when you are in trouble."

"Their trouble is their own making," said Mrs. Lacy sourly. "It'll do both Bernard and Prudence good to come down in the world a bit. What job Prudence will get I *don't* know! Hasn't a scrap of brains, that girl."

"She could come to you and have the job I have here," said Molly. "You could at least do that for her."

"She hates me," said Mrs. Lacy, "and I wouldn't have that conceited creature here with my own children for anything. No, thank you. Ah, I'd like to have seen Catherine's face when she heard the money had all gone!"

"Mrs. Lacy, *please* don't talk like that," said Molly desperately, thinking that Mrs. Lacy's face and voice were unbearable to look at and hear that morning. "It's—it's not right."

Mrs. Lacy flew into a rage again. "Not right!" she yelled. "What do you mean by telling me what's right and what's not? Insolence! Impertinence! I'm fed up with you—nasty goody-goody little prig! I suppose you think I can't do without you now—well, you're mistaken. You can go!"

Frightened by their mother's angry voice, the three children burst into tears. Terence, recognizing that here was a row which would probably mean Molly's disappearance, ran to her and pulled at her arm.

"Don't go," he sobbed. "Don't go, Molly. I want you. Let Mummy go instead. You stay with us. We love you."

This was too much for bad-tempered Mrs. Lacy. She struck at Terence and hit him on the left side of the head. He wailed dismally. Molly gave an exclamation of horror, for the blow had been a hard one. "How can you do a thing like that?" she said, with tears in her eyes. She picked Terence up to comfort him. Mrs. Lacy went quite mad with fury. She wrenched the screaming boy out of Molly's arms and gave the girl a push.

"Coming between me and my children now, are you?" she shouted. "I never did like you—always thinking you

137

knew better than I did. I don't know how I kept you so long. Well, you can go. Terence and Crystal are going to school next week, and I shan't want you any more. Put your hat on again and go."

Crying bitterly, Molly found her hat and put it on. She did not dare to kiss the weeping children good-bye, though it tore her heart to see their woebegone little faces. Alfred's howls echoed after her as she went down the front path. What a terrible ending to her first job!

She wanted to go and see Prudence, but her eyes were so red that she did not like to. So she rode quickly home and gave Jenny Wren a shock when she appeared in the kitchen.

"Gracious goodness, child, what's the matter?" said Jenny in alarm, dropping the saucepan into the sink and wiping her hands on the towel.

"Oh, Jenny—I've lost my job—and Mrs. Lacy said such awful things," wept Molly miserably.

Jenny put her arms round her and hushed her like a small child. "There now! You cry if you want to. Do you good; but what there is to cry about over a mean, selfish, lazy woman like Mrs. Lacy beats me! Lost your job, indeed! You mean *she's* lost the best little helper she's ever had in her lazy, dirty life. There now—don't take on so! What's it matter what a person like Mrs. Lacy says? It's a good thing you've lost the job, so it is; it wasn't a job at all, just slavery, I call it. Best thing you ever did! "

All this was poured out without a stop, and Molly felt comforted to have such a staunch friend. Jenny Wren had such a fund of common sense. She saw things so clearly, and made other people see them clearly, too, which was a great gift. Molly saw the morning's happenings with new eyes as Jenny Wren went on talking.

"I didn't want you to keep that job and you didn't want to either. Don't I know? Sooner or later this was bound to come, and I expected it when school-time for Terence and the little girl got near—and you wouldn't expect Mrs. Lacy to give you notice in a decent way, would you, her being what she is? No, I guess everyone she's ever had has gone in the same way, with nasty names and high words and shouting—and no money!"

Molly remembered that Mrs. Lacy had not paid her for that week, and she had not thought to ask her for her money. Jenny Wren was right. This kind of ending was bound to come with a person as unreliable and ill-balanced as Mrs. Lacy. It was just as well it had, except for the sake of those three poor children. Molly did not like to think of their unhappiness that day—the badly cooked late dinner—the smacks and scoldings and threats. She said so to Jenny, dabbing at her eyes.

"Oh, children have short memories," said Jenny, giving her a pat. "They'll have forgotten by next week, and the two elder ones will go to school. So don't you fret yourself over that. And now tell me what blew up all of a sudden."

Molly, now almost recovered, gave Jenny Wren a full account of what had happened. Jenny washed up the breakfast things and Molly dried them as they talked.

"So old man Williams has gone smash," said Jenny thoughtfully. "That'll be a fearful shock for his wife. My, how she has fancied herself, poor thing! It comes hard on people like that. She'll just crumple up under it, and won't she give Mr. Williams a bad time? What about that friend of yours—silly young bit, I thought she was —what was her name—Prudence, was it now?"

"Yes," said Molly soberly. "Jenny, Prudence will be awfully unhappy. I can't think what in the world she will do. I really can't."

"I don't see why she can't do what all you four children have done when *you* found that your future wasn't as bright as you thought it was," said Jenny, wringing out the dishcloth and hanging it up. "Set to, use her brains and go out to a job! Seventeen or eighteen, isn't she? My word, if she can't do some kind of useful work at that age, she's a poor stick!"

"I'll go and see her after tea," said Molly. "I won't go now, because my eyes are so swollen—and won't it be nice to have an unexpected day at home! I *shall* enjoy it!"

After tea Molly got on her bicycle, which she now meant to return to Prudence, and rode off. She came to Prudence's lovely house and went to the front door. The maid opened it and took Molly up to Prudence's room. The girl was there, sitting huddled up in a chair, looking white and shaken, her eyes red and swollen. She jumped up when she saw Molly and flung herself in her arms.

"Molly! Oh, Molly! Have you heard? Oh, Molly, nobody's come near me all day, not a single one of my friends. I'm so glad to see you! I supposed that you wouldn't want to know me after all this—this terrible disgrace!"

She began to weep bitterly, hiding her face in the back of the chair. Molly was very sorry for her. Was this poor, tear-stained, ugly, dishevelled little thing the bright, smiling, superior Prudence she had always known? How she had gone to pieces! Molly took her friend's hand.

"Prudence, I'm your friend—of course. I shan't desert you for something that isn't your fault. It must be a dreadful time for you."

"It is, it is," wept Prudence. "You don't know everything either. Daddy's run away. He's gone abroad so that he can't be arrested and put into prison—and he's taken Bernard with him! We haven't got any money at all now. Mummy's almost off her head, and she screams at me whenever I go near her. Oh, Molly, what am I to do? The maids will know everything to-morrow, and they'll go. What's to become of us?"

Molly was horror-struck at all this. To have money troubles and unhappiness—these things she understood—but to have them come in such a way was terrible. Troubles that came with shame and disgrace must be doubly hard to bear. She felt painfully sorry for Prudence. She sat there in silence, not knowing how to comfort the girl.

The door opened and Joan Rennie came in, her plain face worried and anxious. She was surprised to see Molly there. "Why, Molly!" she said. "You've heard, too, then? I came to tell Prudence I'd do anything I could to help her. Prudence, I'm so sorry—I came along as soon as ever I heard."

"Oh, I didn't know I had two such good friends," said Prudence, tears running down her cheeks again. "Oh, it does make things better when you've got friends. You will help me, won't you? I'll have to get a job, but I don't know how to, or what to do either. We're giving up this house. We'll get a little money from the furniture, but not much, because most of it will have to go to pay debts. What Mother will do I don't know. She always did dislike me, and now she seems to hate me. She says she's going to live with my aunt, Mrs. Lacy, for a bit, but there's no room for me there. I shall be without a home and parents —nobody cares for me at all! "

After this long wail Prudence went off into floods of tears again. "Let her cry," said Joan. "She's had an awful time, you can see. I think I could get her a job in my office if she's willing to learn shorthand and typewriting; but I can't possibly have her to stay—we've no room at all."

Molly remembered their own little spare room. "I could have her for a while," she said. "We've got a little room. But, oh dear—Prudence doesn't like my family at all—do you, Prudence?"

"I do, I do! " wept Prudence. "I always thought you were lucky to have a family like that. I always envied you, because you loved one another and stuck up for each other. I only pretended to look down my nose at you all because I was jealous. Oh, do let me come, Molly! "

For the first time in her spoilt and selfish life Prudence was getting down to the real things and admitting them to herself. Molly was surprised to hear what she said. She put her arm round Prudence. "Now, you pull yourself together a bit," she said. "You can come home with me to-night if you like, if your mother says so. It would be better for you not to be here when the maids go and the things are sold. You'd hate that. Get your things, see your mother, and come along straightaway. Things are never so bad as they seem, you know! "

CHAPTER TWENTY

Jackdaw Springs a Surprise

AFTER a stormy, ill-tempered interview with her mother, Prudence packed her things and went off with Molly.

"Only take what you want for a little while," said Molly, "and take sensible things, Prudence, because you'll have to help in the house a bit. Don't pack an evening frock, or even a tennis frock."

"No, I won't," said Prudence, and she didn't. She was very quiet as she said good-bye to Joan and went up the hill with Molly. She was glad to be away from her home, glad to shake off the disgrace and trouble she felt there. She looked at Molly thankfully. What a good friend she had been.

"But I say, Molly," said Prudence, suddenly struck by a thought, "what about your job with my aunt? It will be pretty beastly for you, with my mother there soon."

"I've left my job," said Molly, and told Prudence very shortly why. "I don't envy your mother going there," she said. "I'm afraid she won't be very welcome."

"Mother's thick-skinned," said Prudence, and the subject dropped. Prudence wondered what Molly would do. She, too, would have to get a job, that was plain. There would be two of them wanting work. Perhaps Joan could help Molly as well.

Jenny Wren was not too pleased to see Prudence coming back with Molly, and the boys were frankly disgusted. Prudence felt their diasspproval, and her eyes filled with easy tears. "I won't be a nuisance," she said in a pathetic manner.

"You won't have a chance to be," said Jenny Wren, in

her sharp way. "If we put you up here, you've got to give a hand and help. Fair's fair, you know."

And Prudence certainly had to help, for Jenny made her do all kinds of household jobs, tasks that Prudence had never done before, and which she was certainly not very good at now. But Jenny Wren, knowing that Mrs. Lacy had made Molly do a hundred times more, showed little sympathy if Prudence flopped down into a chair and declared she was tired out and must have a rest.

"Well, five minutes you can have, but a young girl like you ought to be ashamed, getting out of breath and puffed just because you've swept the stairs down!" said Jenny Wren. "Shirley's better than you are at doing a job —you haven't even taken the dust out of the pan!"

There was a great deal to do in the next day or two, because Jenny Wren had declared that the whole house must be cleaned from top to bottom to welcome Mrs. Jackson home. So every room was turned out, every carpet swept, every floor cleaned, every picture taken down. Prudence had never in her life been so busy, but somehow she found enjoyment in it. There was no spite or ill-temper at the Jacksons, and if anyone got cross it was soon over, and "sorry" was being shouted down the garden or up the stairs. Prudence grew to love the harmony and friendliness at *Red-Roofs*, and wished she could live there always.

The flags were up outside the front door when the doctor brought Mrs. Jackson back in his car. Bundle was waiting with the others at the gate, all of them impatient to welcome the homecomer. They saw the car rounding the corner and a shout went up.

"She's coming! She's coming! That's the car!"

The car stopped outside the gate and the doctor smiled at the eager group there. They rushed forward to open the door and help their mother out. She could walk now, with the help of someone's arm, but she was still feeble.

She was crying with joy at being home again, and seeing the crowd of happy faces welcoming her. "Mother! You're back at last! Are you all right? Welcome home, darling! We're so glad you're back!"

143

Mrs. Jackson, smiling through her tears, quite unable to say a word, was taken straight upstairs to her bedroom. It was full of flowers and loving messages. Flags not only hung outside the front door, but were festooned up the stairs as well.

"I might be a queen," said Mrs. Jackson, finding her voice at last.

"So you are!" said loyal little Shirley. "The queen of *Red-Roofs*. Hurrah!"

There was a cake at tea-time with "Welcome home, Mother!" written on it in Jenny Wren's best icing hand-writing. There were little buns made by Molly herself, and there was a dish of the reddest, ripest apples from the garden. Mrs. Jackson lay in bed exhausted, but full of great happiness. How lovely it was to be loved like this— it made her feel better at once. Only one thing was lacking, as she said to Jenny Wren—her husband was not there to welcome her, too. "But I shall be here to welcome him instead," she said.

Jenny Wren said nothing. It seemed to her very pathetic that Mrs. Jackson still would not realize that Mr. Jackson would never come back. Well, it was no good discussing that. She and the children must just let her think what she liked. In the meantime money still had to be earned, so Peter must go on with his job and Molly must get an-other—whatever Mrs. Jackson said.

Prudence was not there when Mrs. Jackson came back. She had gone to see someone at Joan's office—someone whom kind and dependable Joan had interested in her, and who had promised her a job if she could get herself trained.

"I have a little money of my own in the post office," said Prudence. "I could use that—and perhaps if the people I am staying with now would let me live with them till I am trained, I could pay them for my board and lodg-ing, too."

So it was arranged that Prudence should use her own bit of money, pay the Jacksons weekly for her room and board, which would help them, too, and go down to a commercial school in the town each day to learn typing and shorthand. Her big, lovely home had been shut and sold to someone else. The furniture was gone. No one had heard a word of her father or brother. Her mother was living with Mrs. Lacy, quarrelling bitterly, and threatening to go off every day, but not doing so because she hadn't enough money to live anywhere except at her sister's. Jenny Wren privately thought that it was a good punishment for both sisters to be forced to put up with one another, but Molly grieved for the three children, and wondered what they thought of all the quarrelling and ill-temper.

Peter was still in his job. He worked hard in the evenings, and his Headmaster thought there was no doubt but that the boy would win the scholarship. What a pity he would have no chance of using it! He could so easily have taken up medical work and done well at it with a start like that. Peter was looking white and thin. Work all day and work each night was too much for a growing boy. Molly was worried about him.

"It wouldn't be so bad if he liked his job," she thought, "but he hates it more and more. Poor old Pete. I must see that when school begins next week, and Michael goes back, _he_ doesn't do what Peter is doing—work all day and then do another job at night! He will have to give up this mending in term-time, even though it does bring in a very welcome sum of money. Still, there is Prudence's bit of money each week now—and I shall soon get another job. The Headmistress will get me one, I'm sure."

Molly had been to see her old Head, and this time she had been back from her holiday. She had listened with the utmost sympathy to Molly's recital, and she was deeply disappointed to know that the girl would not be able to come to the K.G. department and train there, as she had hoped. She did her best to persuade Molly to try, to come, but the girl was firm. She had to earn money. She could not afford to train and pay fees and have herself kept for almost three years now. She had to get some work.

Mrs. Jackson, in her strong conviction that her husband

would come back, tried to make Peter give up his job, and Molly to stop hoping for work. But the two children, although very gentle with their mother, were firm. She was amazed to find how grown-up they were, amazed to hear all they had done. But she was sad, too. It was not right that they should grow up as quickly as this. She was afraid it would harm them.

"Harm them!" snorted Jenny Wren when she told her this. "Can't you see how strong and full of courage those children of yours are? Don't you think the world of their determination and independence? Well, all I can say is if they were *my* children I'd go down on my knees and thank God for them every night of my life!"

"So I do," said Mrs. Jackson. "When I see that poor little Prudence, with no backbone, no loyalty, no courage, I feel proud of my own four—yes, even of little Shirley, who has put away her dolls."

A wet tongue licked her hand and she smiled. "Yes even of you, Bundle," she said, looking down into a pair of melting brown eyes. Bundle was her inseparable companion these days. He lived in her room or lay beside her when Peter helped her down into the garden. He made himself her devoted slave, her fierce guardian, her faithful friend.

Jackdaw was delighted to see her back again. He presented her with a magnificent bunch of roses from his own garden at home—the first beautiful autumn roses.

"Oh, how lovely, Jackdaw!" said Mrs. Jackson, smelling them and feeling very much touched. "Are they from your own garden?"

"Ar," said Jackdaw, showing his white teeth and flashing a pair of startlingly blue eyes at her.

"Thank you, Jackdaw, for coming here at night to help us," said Mrs. Jackson. "When Mr. Jackson comes back he will be glad to repay you."

"Ar," said Jackdaw, looking alarmed. He had not known that Mrs. Jackson would not believe that Mr. Jackson was lost at sea. He edged away from her.

146

"Will you ask Jenny to put these in water for me?" said Mrs. Jackson and held out the roses.

"Ar," said Jackdaw and fled thankfully to the kitchen. Mrs. Jackson watched him go, thinking how lucky it was that her little family had had people like Jenny Wren and Jackdaw to help them in their time of trouble. You never knew who your friends were till trouble came, she thought. It was the same with poor little Prudence. All her grand friends had deserted her now; not one ever came near her. But the Jacksons and the Rennies had stood by her valiantly, and, if only Prudence would realize it, this trouble of hers might be the making of her. She was losing her old, silly ideas and superior manner and gaining a whole set of new and better ones.

It was good to feel how much better she, Mrs. Jackson, was getting every day. Soon she would be able to do her tasks in the household. If only she could have news of Dick! This was her constant thought, and it never left her, day or night.

Then one day, just as Molly was setting out to go to an interview that the Headmistress had arranged for her, an extraordinary thing happened. Jackdaw arrived at the back door holding a picture paper in his hand, in such a state of excitement that he could not even say "Ar." He merely stood at the back door, opening and shutting his mouth like a goldfish, waving the paper about. Jenny Wren looked at him in the greatest amazement.

"What's bitten *you* all of a sudden, Jackdaw?" she said sharply. "Stop waving that paper. Haven't you got a tongue in your head? Why aren't you at work?"

Jackdaw swallowed two or three times and rubbed his nose, trying to find words. "You look there," he said at last. "Ar—you look there!"

Jenny Wren took the paper, still eyeing Jackdaw as if she thought he had gone slightly off his head. She looked where Jackdaw's dirty forefinger pointed, his whole hand trembling with excitement. Jenny Wren stared. She stared for quite a long time. She saw a smudged, rather spoilt copy of a picture she knew very well, for it was standing

147

on her bedroom mantelpiece at that very moment—a photograph of the four Jackson children!

How did it come to be in this picture paper? In growing astonishment Jenny Wren read the few lines beside the picture. They were strange and exciting words.

"Who knows these four children? This photograph, marred by immersion in the sea, belongs to one of the survivors of the ill-fated steamer *Albion*. He gives his name as Harrison, but has lost his memory owing to shock, and does not remember his address or his profession or circumstances. The only clue to his identity is this photograph, which was found in a leather case on his person. The mystery deepens when we know that no passenger of this name was on the *Albion*, nor on the other wrecked ship, the *Swift*. It is possible that he is unknowingly giving a wrong name. He knows these are his children. If we can find them, happiness and health will come back to this bewildered man."

"Ar," said Jackdaw, and jabbed with his finger at the picture again, his blue eyes like stars.

"Bless you, Jackdaw!" said Jenny Wren in a choking voice. She took the paper and rushed into the sitting-room, where Mrs. Jackson sat peacefully shelling peas. She looked up in surprise at the excited Jenny, and was even more surprised to see Jackdaw's brown face looking in at the door, too. This was the greatest moment of the garden-boy's life. He was beside himself with excitement and joy. He had brought the most marvellous news to the family he liked so much. Wouldn't that little Shirley be pleased!

"Look there, mam," said Jenny, putting the picture in front of Mrs. Jackson. "Look *there!* Did you ever think to see that picture in a paper? And you read what's beside it, too! Oh, mam, oh, mam—it's too good to be true, that's what it is!"

"Ar," said Jackdaw, feasting his eyes on Mrs. Jackson's face, which was astonished, delighted and overjoyed as she read the lines and scanned the picture. She turned to

148

Jenny Wren, her face as radiant as a young girl's, her eyes bright with springing tears.

"I told you he wasn't lost," she said. "Didn't I tell you? He'll come back to us! My darling Dick, I knew you weren't dead! Oh, Jenny, Jenny!"

She held out her arms to the little monkey-faced old woman, and the two of them shared her happiness. Jackdaw, rather alarmed now, retreated quietly to the kitchen. He stood rubbing his nose, staring blindly at Bundle on the hearthrug. "Ar," said Jackdaw. "That's something, that is. Ar."

What the "something" was Bundle didn't know. Jackdaw went out, walking back to his work, which he had left without a word the minute he had suddenly seen the surprising photograph in the paper the cook had been reading. No boy could have been happier than Jackdaw that day. It was the finest thing in the world to bring good news to a brave and lovable family like the Jacksons.

After their first overwhelming delight, Mrs. Jackson and Jenny Wren made plans to get into touch with Mr. Jackson at once. "I'll go off to that young man who's on a newspaper," said Jenny, dabbing her eyes happily. "He'll know what to do. He'll thank me good and plenty for going to him, no doubt about that! It'll be a scoop for him—me telling him we're the family the world is looking for. Now, just you stay here and rest after your shock—for shock it is. The children will soon be in from school, and Molly will be back. You rest here and think what to say to them when they come!"

CHAPTER TWENTY-ONE

All Together Again

MOLLY came back first and went to tell her mother about her interview, but she did not get a single word out. One glance at her mother's face told her the news.

"It's Daddy," said Mrs. Jackson. "He's all right, Molly. Just lost his memory, that's all. I knew he'd come back to us, I knew he would."

Molly felt as if she was in a dream. Daddy alive—coming back—taking the head of the household again. The girl burst into tears of joy and ran to her mother. Mrs. Jackson patted her and told her about the picture, showing her the photograph. "Everything will be all right now," she said. "Everything. I can hardly wait till Dick comes home."

The two discussed it all excitedly. Then Molly ran to telephone to Peter. He must know the news at once. He mustn't wait till the evening—he must know now, this very minute!

She managed to get on to Peter after a lot of delay. "What is it, Molly?" said Peter in rather an impatient voice. "You know you are not supposed to ring me up here. Is anything wrong?"

"No, no—everything's right!" Molly's voice rang out gladly. "What do you think? Daddy's alive! He's coming back! Oh, Peter—he's only lost his memory, and that will come back soon, won't it? Peter, isn't it an absolute miracle?"

"I can't believe it," said Peter's voice after a pause of amazement. "Molly, this is the best news in the world. I'll try and get the day off and come home. We must all be together to-day! Oh, Molly, I'm so terrifically glad!"

Then there was the joy of waiting for Shirley and Michael to come home. Was there ever such marvellous news to break to anyone? Molly could hardly wait for the two children to come. Peter got the day off and came tearing back, flinging his arms round his mother, a boy suddenly made young again with joy.

"Here they are!" yelled Molly at the front gate. "Shirley, Mike, buck up!"

In surprise the two young ones came hurrying up, Shirley wheeling her bicycle. "What is it?" shouted Mike. "What's happened? Why is Peter home?"

"Mike, Shirley, Daddy's found, and he's alive!" cried Molly. "Isn't it marvellous?"

"He'll be home soon," added Peter, rejoicing in Shirley's swift look of utter amazement and joy. Michael gave an enormous whoop and whirled Molly round and round.

"Golly! What news to tell the boys! How did you hear? Is it really true? No kidding?"

"Of course not," said Molly, trying to disentangle herself. "As if I'd make a joke of a thing like that. Come on in and we'll let Mother tell you all about it."

"Dear old Daddy, he'll be back," sang Shirley in her clear little voice, and danced up the path, feeling that nothing could ever make her unhappy again.

It was a very happy half hour. Nobody thought about dinner. Jenny Wren came hurrying back to tell them her news. The young newspaper man had been "knocked all of a heap," as Jenny Wren said. He had done a lot of excited telephoning, and had sent a very, very long cable to America, and promised them news that very afternoon.

"So now we'll have a bit of dinner—if we can eat any—and wait to hear what the young man says," said Jenny Wren, bustling happily into the kitchen. Bundle followed her, hearing the word "dinner." He couldn't understand what all the terrific excitement was about. He had joined valiantly in it, of course, leaping about, barking, licking, whining, and pulling at anyone's sleeve to get a bit of notice. But everyone had been curiously unaware of Bundle that morning—he had got absent-minded pats, but the excited chatter and laughter had gone on above his silky head without a stop. Bundle was rather out of the picture, he felt.

Nobody ate much dinner. They were glad Prudence had gone to see her mother that morning. They wanted to be just themselves, Jenny and Bundle that day.

The telephone rang at half-past two. It was the young newspaper-man, very important and excited. He had got the news for them. America had cabled through to say that the man who had called himself Harrison had been told that his real name was Jackson, and bit by bit he had been told about his family and home—and now he had suddenly remembered everything, and was in a great state of happiness, mixed with anxiety. But he would be fit to travel almost at once, and was coming home on the first liner that left for England.

This news electrified everyone. Why, he might be leaving the very next day! He might be home in a week!

"My paper is trying to arrange for him to travel by air," went on the young man importantly. "We feel that he should be reunited with his family as soon as possible. We shall be very pleased to pay all expenses and to hire a car for him to travel home from the airport. So he may be back in a day or two."

"It's a dream," said Molly, happy tears overflowing down her cheeks. "It's not real. I shan't believe it till I see Daddy himself."

Everyone felt a bit like that. Things were happening so quickly—too quickly to keep up with, as Shirley said. That afternoon the telephone rang incessantly. All kinds of newspapers were ringing up about the news, for it had caught everyone's attention. People wanted to share in the happiness and thrill of the Jackson family. They wanted to rejoice with them, see pictures of them, they wanted to know how they had faced what seemed a disaster, and how they reacted to such an unexpected miracle.

"I suppose we mustn't mind all this publicity," said Mrs. Jackson with a sigh, as a press photographer, the fourth one that afternoon, appeared at the gate.

152

"The whole world wants a bit of your happiness," said Jenny Wren wisely. "It's a nuisance for you, but it won't last long. News soon gets stale, like yesterday's loaf. Well, well, there's not all that amount of happiness in the world but what we can't share a bit of ours. We've been handed out a great dollop all at once, so we'll let others have a lick of it, too. Fair's fair!"

All the same, Jenny Wren was a perfect dragon with all the press people who came—the eager newspaper reporters, the photographers, the film representatives. The Jacksons had never been in the full glare of publicity before, and they found it bewildering.

"I'll be glad when Daddy's home and this is all over," said Molly, tired of being photographed again. "Oh, Mother, I shall never sleep to-night!"

Nobody slept very much, not even little Shirley, who usually slept like a top. She dreamt of ships and aeroplanes, each of them with her father on board. Fancy having both Daddy and Mother back again! Why, things would be the same as they used to be then.

Peter went off to the office next day as usual. "I'd better not give in my notice or anything," he said to Molly. "We'll make sure Daddy's all right before I do anything. Just in case, you know. We've had so much bad luck that I hardly dare believe in any good luck yet."

The young newspaper-man became a great friend in the course of a few days. He was always telephoning them or coming to see them. He said Jenny Wren had done him the greatest good turn she could have done anyone by giving him such a scoop. Shirley could not imagine what a "scoop" was. She kept thinking of the scoop that Jenny Wren used when she did the cooking.

Jackdaw was photographed, too, and duly appeared in all the picture papers as "the boy who took the news to *Red-Roofs*." He was so proud of this that he became almost talkative. "You look there," he said to all his friends, pushing the paper into their hands. "Know who that is? It's me, see? Ar! Ar! Ar!"

Bundle was photographed, too, and the newspaperman

had the snap enlarged and framed for the children. They were delighted. Daddy would like that! Bundle adored the newspaper-man, and behaved most ridiculously with him, rolling over on his back with all four feet in the air whenever he saw him. It was a mad, glad household those days. The flags were got out again and put up. The newspaper-man produced a whole lot more, including some bunting that was used at dances in the town hall. *Red-Roofs* looked very gay.

Daddy was travelling home. He was on the Clipper, flying fast over the Atlantic. He was approaching the homeland every hour. He was landing on the airport. He was photographed as he landed. He was photographed as he got into the fast car that was there to motor him all the way home. He was astonished, for he had not realized all the excitement his adventure had caused.

The young newspaper-man kept telephoning to Molly: "He's about half-way here." "He's in the next town—message just come through." "Just coming along to snap you all greeting Mr. Jackson, if you don't mind."

Everyone was at the front gate, Mrs. Jackson, too. The miraculous news had acted like a strong tonic, and she was now her old self, looking even younger. She trembled as she leaned on Peter's strong arm.

"Here's a car!" yelled Shirley and made everyone jump. The little girl could not wait at the gate. She tore down the hill to the big car, feeling absolutely certain that it was the one bringing her father home. She danced in front of it, yelling at the top of her voice. "Stop! Stop! Daddy, get out, quick!"

Her father leapt out and swung Shirley into his arms. He looked none the worse for his adventure. His face was brown, his eyes twinkled as much as ever, and he seemed even taller than before. "My little Shirley!" he said, and Shirley clung round his neck like a monkey, shouting "Daddy! Daddy! You've come back!"

The others rushed down the hill pell-mell to meet him. The press photographers who had taken their stand near

EVERYONE WAS AT THE FRONT GATE

the front gate, ready to click their cameras at this dramatic home-coming, rushed down, too. Click! Click! Click!

But the Jackson family heard no clicks. All they heard was their father's well-known voice, ringing out happily. "Molly! Peter! Mike! My darling wife, are you better again now? Oh, it's good to be home!"

Bundle dashed round madly, trying to get in between the legs. Here was somebody he had known and loved, but had forgotten! He must lick him and welcome him, too, but how difficult when there were so many legs everywhere.

The little family went into *Red-Roofs*. Jenny Wren was peeping out of the window as they went in. She would not push herself forward just then. The family belonged together, and for just this once she must keep outside it. But they did not let her. Molly tore into the kitchen and lugged her out.

"Daddy! Here's dear old Jenny Wren! Daddy, we couldn't have done without her! You wait till you hear all she's done!"

To Jenny's overwhelming amazement and delight, Mr. Jackson gave her a hug and a smacking kiss on her withered brown cheek. "Well, I never!" said Jenny Wren, retiring to the kitchen again. "Knocked all of a heap!" as she said to herself, "Well, I never! *Well*, I never!"

It was a wonderful reunion—one of the happiest moments in all their lives. Nobody could get near enough to Daddy somehow—squeezing and hugging weren't enough! There was a terrific noise—talking and laughing and barking, and Shirley's excited voice over everyone's, with "Daddy, this" and "Daddy, that!"

That evening, when the first tremendous excitement had simmered down, and this curiously unreal happening had become something real and solid and true, all the news was exchanged and many, many questions were asked.

"What happened to you, Daddy, when the ship went down?" asked Shirley, and Mr. Jackson related the whole story briefly and dramatically.

"We had plenty of time to get into the lifeboats, and I got into one that was very full. I saw someone struggling in the water and leaned out to pull him in—but he pulled me overboard. Then something hit me hard on the head, a floating bit of timber, I imagine, and I don't remember any more at all till I woke up and found myself in hospital."

"How did you get there?" asked Michael.

"I was picked up by my lifeboat again and another ship took everyone on board, and then steamed off to the nearest port," said Mr. Jackson. "It was terrible when I woke up—or came round, as they called it—because when they asked me who I was I could only think of the name of Harrison."

"The name of your firm! " said Peter. "Poor old Daddy —you'd got it on your mind that you were working for Harrison's, and so you thought your name was Harrison when it came flashing into your mind. Didn't you remember anything?"

"Nothing at all," said his father. "It was the queerest and most horrible experience I've ever had, losing my memory. You see, your memory is like an anchor to a ship—it keeps you pinned down to yourself. When you lose it the little ship tosses away on an unknown sea, and you can never anchor anywhere for long. You're lost, quite lost. How I tried to remember if I had a family—and who they were—and then they suddenly showed me that photograph of you and I knew you were my children. But I couldn't even remember your names! "

Mrs. Jackson slipped her hand in his. "Poor Dick," she said. "What gave you back your memory?"

"Well, apparently the picture of the children was flashed over here to England, and they were recognized, their names given, and everything found out," said Mr. Jackson.

"That was old Jackdaw—he brought the paper to Jenny Wren! " said Molly, "and Jenny went down to see a newspaper-man, a friend of hers, and he did the rest."

"Oh, so that's what happened, is it?" said Mr. Jackson. "Well, suddenly the doctor came along and said to me, 'Do you remember Molly—and Peter—and Michael—and little Shirley?' He spoke of Bundle, too, and as he spoke your names something went 'click' in my mind, like a camera taking a picture—and everything came back to me! I yelled out 'I'm Dick Jackson! My home's at *Red-Roofs* in England. I want to go back'."

Tears ran down Mrs. Jackson's face. She knew so well what her husband must have felt. "I knew you would come back, Dick," she said. "I always knew it."

"Yes, you did, Mother," said Shirley. "How did you know?"

Mrs. Jackson shook her head. "I don't know how I knew. I just did. Oh, Dick, it's been hard without you. But now we're all together again, and nothing else matters. And the children have been so marvellous! "

Then it was the children's turn to talk—and how they talked! Molly told of the job she had taken and given up. Peter told of his job. Michael related the tale of his and Shirley's work, and everyone told about Jenny Wren and her loyalty.

"And Jackdaw, too—he came three times a week in the evening, and he wouldn't take a penny," said Peter. "He let us lend him books, but he wouldn't have us do anything else."

"He still says 'Ar,'" said Shirley, imitating Jackdaw perfectly. "Ar. Just like that."

Everyone laughed. They laughed easily that night because they were so happy."

"Well," said Mr. Jackson, stroking Molly's soft curly hair, "well, you're a family to be proud of, I must say. Mollikins, you'll go to the Headmistress to-morrow and ask if you can begin training as a kindergarten student straight away, just as we had planned. Peter, you'll give notice on Saturday and return to school. I should think, with your evening work, you will be well up to the standard of the other boys and will get that scholarship all right. Then on to the medical school you'll go, and in a few years' time we'll see you a fully-fledged doctor! "

"Oh, Daddy! " said Peter, overjoyed at the thought of doing what he had so much wanted to do and yet had given up so willingly.

158

"Michael and Shirley, you have both shown us that you are great little people," said Mr. Jackson. "When the time comes for you to choose what you want to be, I shall listen to you and help you as much as I can."

"Woof!" said Bundle, not wanting to be forgotten in this great moment. Mr. Jackson looked down at him.

"And you, little dog, shall have a grand new collar with your name and address on it, for you are six months old now and growing up fast. What a family I have got!"

It was a happy family that night that went up the stairs to bed at *Red-Roofs*. They were all together again. They could do the work they wanted to do. Daddy was back and Mother was almost well again. Molly and Peter could look forward to a happy future. Jenny Wren would always be looked upon as a friend and given a home in her old age. Bundle would grow up, faithful and loving—and even poor little Prudence would find a niche at *Red-Roofs*, for out of their own happiness the Jackson family could spare some of her.

"They all look so sweet and young again," said Mrs. Jackson to her husband. "Oh, Dick, they all began to look so old and worried, poor little things! Now Peter has got back his old merry laugh, and makes his sudden jokes again, and Molly is a happy young girl. Michael is a little boy, instead of a hard-worked wage-earner, frowning all day long—and my dear little Shirley has taken all her dolls out of the drawer she stuffed them in!"

So she had! When Molly went to tuck up her little sister that night she stared in surprise, for there were dolls everywhere! Two were in bed with Shirley. Amelia Jane sat on a chair. Rosebud lay on the floor. Josephine was in Molly's own bed. It was lovely to see them all again. Shirley laughed, half embarrassed, as her big sister stared round the bedroom.

"They wanted to come out and be happy, too, now that Daddy's back," she said. "They just broke their hearts in that drawer, Molly. It doesn't matter having them out again, does it—because you do know I'm big now, not little."

159

"Yes, I know it," said Molly, kissing the anxious little face on the pillow. "You're very big—you earned a lot of money. I'm very proud of you, darling."

And there we must leave the family at *Red-Roofs,* all asleep but Jenny Wren. She is getting into bed, a queer little figure in her long flannel nightdress, her hair scrimped back tightly.

"Well, well! " she says as she settles herself comfortably into bed, "I never did enjoy a day so much in my life. Those children met their troubles well, and stuck by one another. 'Tisn't always that courage and goodness get rewarded like this—but fair's fair, I say. You reap what you sow, no doubt about that! "

Yes, Jenny Wren, we reap what we sow, and may our harvest always be good!

Those Dreadful Children

by Enid Blyton

Those Dreadful Children was
first published in the U.K. in a single volume
in hardback by Lutterworth Press, London
First published in Armada in 1967
by Fontana Paperbacks

CHAPTER ONE

At the Bottom of the Garden

Two children stood on a garden-roller at the bottom of their garden. A third one tried to get up too, but there was no room for her.

"Let me up," she wailed. "I want to see too."

"Wait," said the others. "We'll let you see in a minute."

The two on the garden-roller were looking up the garden of the house that was built at the bottom of their garden. The two gardens joined at the foot. The children's garden was neat and trim, and full of flowers. The other garden was untidy and overgrown.

"They've gone, Margery," said John, her brother. "The curtains are down. The garden-seat is gone. The house is empty."

"Let me *see*!" cried Annette, scrabbling at their legs. "You're horrid! Let me see too!"

Mother came down the garden, hearing Annette's voice. "Oh, let her see," she said. "She's so much smaller than you are."

"We were going to let her have her turn," said John, frowning. "Mother, have the Healeys gone? The house looks quite empty."

"Yes, they've gone," said Mother. "The two old ladies were really too feeble to look after themselves any longer. So they have sold their house, and gone to live with a niece. I went to say good-bye to them yesterday."

"Who's coming to live in their house?" asked Margery. "I hope it's a family with children."

"Well, it is," said Mother. "A family with four children. One is just a baby. The others are about your ages."

"Oh!" said Margery, thrilled. "We shall be able to make friends with them then. When are they coming?"

"Not till next week," said Mother. "The house is being painted and cleaned first. I hope the new people will look after the garden a bit better than the old ladies did. Really, it is quite a disgrace."

"Four children!" said John. "I hope there's a boy for me."

"And somebody for me," said Annette. "I want somebody to play with too. Don't I, Mother?"

"Yes, dear," said Mother, putting her arm round small Annette. Annette was spoilt. She yelled when she couldn't get her own way. She sulked if she was scolded. She was pretty when she smiled and looked happy, but very ugly when she frowned or pouted.

"Margery and John always play together, and they leave me out," said Annette, cuddling up to her mother. "I want somebody to play with too."

"I only hope they'll be *nice* children," said Mother. "I don't want you to make friends with badly-brought-up children. I don't know anything about the family, except that they are called Taggerty. We'll have to wait and see what they are like."

She went back to the house, taking Annette with her. Margery and John went on looking over the wall, jiggling the roller a little.

"Four children! That sounds good. Mother won't let us make friends with many of the children here—except those stuck-up Fitzgeralds, and they're boring. I hope they'll be fun, Margery!"

"John," said Margery in a whisper. "Do you think

166

we could slip over the wall and see the empty garden and peep in at the windows of the house? We've never been into this garden."

John looked doubtful. "Would it be all right?" he said. "I mean—suppose somebody saw us?"

"Well—let's go this evening then, when there's nobody much about," said Margery. "And don't tell Annette. We don't want her to come too. She'd only make a noise or something."

"All right. We'll slip over the wall this evening," said John. "I've always wanted to explore the garden at the bottom of ours. I know it's awfully untidy and overgrown—but it looks exciting and mysterious somehow—plenty of places to hide in—almost like a jungle."

They heard their mother calling and slipped down from the roller. It was tea-time. Annette was already sitting in her place, washed and brushed. Margery and John went to get themselves ready, too.

"You're late for tea," said Annette, when they came back. "I was first. Mother, John hasn't washed his hands properly. I can see some black on them."

John glared at Annette and put his hands under the table.

"Let me see your hands, John," said Mother. "And don't glare at poor Annette like that. Oh, dear—you really *must* go and wash your hands properly. Are *your* hands clean, Margery?"

John left the table, still glaring. Annette took no notice at all, but helped herself to plenty of honey. Nobody said that Annette was a little tell-tale.

After tea, the children went out into the garden to play. John wouldn't play with Annette, and she sulked.

"You're unkind to me! You're a horrid, sulky boy. Mother said you *were* to play with me!" wailed Annette.

John took a hurried glance at the windows of the house. "Be quiet, Annette! Don't make such a noise. We'll play hide-and-seek if you like. You can find us when we call cuckoo."

Margery and John ran off, leaving Annette to count a hundred before she came to find them. "We'll hide at the back of the garden-shed," said John. "She never thinks of looking there. We can keep away from her then. I'm cross with her. I shall be cross with her for two days."

Margery knew he would, too. John remembered things too long. If anyone offended him or made him angry he thought about it for a long time, and wouldn't forgive them. He seldom flared up or quarrelled—he just said nothing, but went on thinking little bitter thoughts that made him most unpleasant for some time.

They squeezed behind the shed. They had to push a bush out of the way first. It hid them nicely. They settled down in the small space there, and whispered to one another.

"As soon as Annette goes to bed we'll hop over the wall. I do hope we shan't be caught."

"We might find a window open, and creep into the empty house," said John, daringly.

"The windows will all be shut," said Margery. "They always are, in an empty house."

"I'm coming," yelled Annette, suddenly. "Look out, I'm coming."

She couldn't find them, of course. She hunted everywhere, and then burst into loud wails. "Where are you? You are hiding away from me on purpose. Come out and let me find you."

John and Margery knew they would have to come out or Mother would come running to see what was the matter with Annette. They came out of their hiding-place without being seen and jumped on Annette, who screamed in fright.

"Oh, don't! Where were you? I looked simply *every*where. I don't like hide-and-seek. Let's play something else."

When Annette was called in to bed, the other two went down to the bottom of the garden. They got up on the roller and then climbed to the top of the wall. John slid over first and then helped Margery. In a few seconds they were standing in the untidy garden, looking round in excitement.

"Come on. We'll go up this path. Look how the trees meet overhead."

"And look at that funny old summer-house! It's got three windows and a wooden seat running all the way round inside it! I wish we had one like that. We'd play houses in it."

They went up the path. Certainly the garden was very overgrown and neglected—but how exciting it was! There was a big tree that dropped long thin branches to the ground all round its trunk, so that under it was a big cave of green. It was a weeping willow, graceful and beautiful. The children pushed aside the drooping twigs and went into the green cave.

"Oh, it's lovely!" said Margery. "John, I do hope we can make friends with the Taggerty children. It would be lovely to play here. And, oh, look! There's a pond!"

So there was. Goldfish swam about in it, and the water looked clear and cool. "It would be nice to paddle there," said Margery longingly.

"But Mother wouldn't ever let us," said John. "Look at the lawn, Margery. The grass is like a hayfield, and all the flowers in the bed are overgrown with weeds. What a shame!"

Both John and Margery were good little gardeners.

They had gardens of their own and kept them beautifully. Margery pointed to some fine rose-trees, unpruned but full of lovely roses.

"Look there! Did you ever see such roses! Oh, what a shame to let the garden go wild like this. I like the part at the bottom, where it's all thick and green and mysterious—and I love that big cave-tree, with its long twigs drooping right down to the ground. But this bit would look much nicer if it was trim and neat."

They went to the house. They peeped in at the kitchen window. It was empty and bare. A tiny mouse scuttled across the floor and Margery jumped.

"Oooh! A mouse! I'd hate to go inside there if mice are about."

Margery was scared of mice and bats, moths and beetles, worms and earwigs. She was afraid of strange dogs, and hardly liked to stroke a cat in case it scratched her. The children had no pets, because Mother liked her house to be clean and spotless—and she said pets made it dirty and muddy, and covered everything with hairs.

They tiptoed to another window. They spoke in whispers—not because there was anyone to hear them, but because it was exciting.

There was no window open at all; so they couldn't possibly get into the empty house, even if they wanted to—and Margery didn't want to, now that she had seen a mouse. Still, it was thrilling, just peeping in.

The old ladies had left nothing in the house at all, except a pile of newspapers in a corner of the scullery. One of the taps there dripped, and the evening sun caught the drips and made them shine. Otherwise there was nothing to see.

A distant bell rang and John frowned. "There's our bedtime bell. What a pity! We could have had a wonderful game under that cave-tree."

170

It was thrilling, just peeping in

"And we could play houses in that summer-house," said Margery. "John—the Taggertys aren't coming till next week. Do let's creep over here each evening and play, till they come. The painters and cleaners will be gone then, and there will be no one to see us."

"I don't think it's a very right thing to do," said John, who was always rather afraid of doing anything that might not be quite right and proper, "but we shan't be harming anyone. So let's!"

"Yes, let's!" said Margery thrilled. "Come on, we must get back now without anyone seeing us. We'll come again tomorrow—but mind, not a word to Annette, or she'll tell."

CHAPTER TWO

In the Other Garden

JOHN and Margery couldn't help feeling that it was rather an exciting secret they had between them. They whispered about it, and Annette was cross because they stopped whenever she came near them.

"You might tell me," she whined. "You might! You've got a secret and you won't tell me. When I find out what it is—and I shall—I shall tell Mother about it. Then you will wish you'd told me."

"We might be whispering about your birthday," said John. That made Annette look sweet again.

Margery and John waited impatiently for Annette to go to bed that night. As soon as she was called they ran down to the bottom of the garden. Margery had her best doll with her.

"I want to play houses with her in that summer-house," she said. "You can be the father, I'll be the mother, and she's our child. What shall we call our house?"

"No, let's play caves in that big drooping tree," said John. "We'll play that once we are inside that tree. We're absolutely safe. It shall be our cave."

"John, do you think we might pick one or two of those lovely red roses that are lost in the tangle of weeds?" asked Margery, when they were making their way through the overgrown bushes and trees.

"Well, they don't belong to us," said John.

"I know. But do they belong to anybody just at present?" said Margery. "They will bloom and fade and die—and nobody will enjoy them. I'd love to pick just two. I don't see that it would matter."

"If everyone thought that, there wouldn't be a flower

172

or a plant left in the gardens of empty houses," said John. "No, don't pick anything, Margery. We oughtn't to be here at all, really."

They had a lovely game in the cave-tree. The light under the drooping, green-leaved twigs was green and cool and rather mysterious. It was fun to part the long, graceful branches and peer out into the bright evening sunshine.

"Any enemies about?" Margery would whisper.

"None," John would whisper back. "We can make a dash for the summer-house!"

Then, pretending that enemies might be after them at any moment, the two would dash to the little summer-house and fling themselves inside.

Margery didn't like the summer-house as much as she thought she would. She saw a spider run along the ceiling and it made her shiver. "I'd like to clean this house up from top to bottom," she said. "I'd chase away all the earwigs and spiders, and clean it nicely. Shall we bring some cloths and clean it tomorrow, John?"

"You can, if you like," said John. "I don't want to. I'd rather play in the cave-tree. I wish those Taggertys weren't coming for weeks. I do so like this garden all to ourselves."

"Well, it might be better fun when they *do* come," said Margery, "because if we make friends with them, they will let us come and play here—and six children could have a lot of fun together in that cave-tree and this summer-house, and in that tangle of bushes and trees at the bottom, too. And what fun to have a pond to sail ships on. I wish we had one."

The two children climbed over the wall, the next night. Then came the third night. It was not so fine as it had been. When a few drops of rain fell, John pulled Margery under the cave-tree. It was quite dark

173

there that evening, because there were big clouds low down in the sky, full of rain.

"We'll shelter here," said John, in a whisper. "I only hope Mother doesn't start calling us. But I think she's out now. This is a lovely cave, Margery. Not a drop of rain is getting through."

He was right. The long, drooping branches waved a little to and fro in the wind, but no rain came through at all. The ground was perfectly dry to sit on. It was fun to sit there and hear the rain pattering outside.

Then suddenly the two children heard another noise. It was the sound of voices and hurrying feet. And the sound came from the back entrance of the house and garden!

John clutched Margery. "It's somebody coming in here! I hope it isn't the Taggertys."

Margery hardly dared to breathe. Her face went red and she sat absolutely still. The voices sounded very lively indeed, and the feet pattered to and fro.

"Bother this rain! What a pity, just when we wanted to see the house and garden in the sunshine. I say— look, there's a pond. Mummy, there's a pond!"

"John! We must go," whispered Margery, in a panic. "They'll find us here. Quick, let's go."

"No, we'll be seen," said John. He was frightened too. "Oh, Margery—I wish you hadn't picked those two roses this evening!"

Margery wished she hadn't, too. It was the first time she had picked any of the flowers, but she had seen two perfect red roses, and hadn't been able to stop herself from breaking them off the rose-stems. There they were, beside the trunk of the weeping willow. Where could she hide them?

There was nowhere. In despair, Margery sat her doll on top of them. There—now they wouldn't be seen.

"Pat! Look here! There's a washhouse!" cried a

voice. "Won't Bridget be pleased? She's always wanted a proper washhouse for all our clothes. Now she'll have one."

"Let's look at the garden. Goodness, Maureen, isn't it overgrown!" cried another voice. "Blow this rain! Come on, we'll look all over the garden. It's a big one. Bigger than the ones we've had before. We'll have fun here."

Another voice came on the air—a younger, more childish voice. "Take me, too! I want to come, too!"

"Say please, Biddy, then!" said Pat's voice. "And don't whine like that."

"Please!" said Biddy's voice, and then all the pattering feet came nearer.

"There's a summer-house!" yelled Pat. "Look! We can play houses and schools. And look at all these lovely trees to climb. I say—what's *this* tree?"

Margery and John clutched one another. They could see the toes of three children under the ends of the drooping willow branches. And then somebody parted the branches and looked inside.

It was a boy's face, a merry face with dark-blue eyes and curly dark hair. The boy was ten, just about John's age. He stared inside the cave-tree, and saw Margery and John at once.

"Look, Maureen," he said, startled, and pulled aside more branches for his sister to look inside the tree with him. "Children! Hey, you, what are you doing here? This is *our* house and garden!"

Margery looked as if she was going to cry. John stood up. "We only came in to have a look, because the garden was empty," he said. "You're not living here yet. Don't tell your mother and father."

"Why should we? We're not tell-tales!" said the boy, and came right inside the drooping ring of branches. "But you just clear out, see? I won't have anyone in *my* garden without my permission."

175

He looked very fierce. He also looked very dirty. His hands were black and he had a smear across his face. There was a hole in one of his socks and his jersey had a tear in it.

The girl came through the branches, too. She was the same age as Margery, about eight. She too looked dirty and untidy. Then came a third child, about five. She was Biddy. She had the same blue eyes and dark hair of the other two, and she was just as untidy. Her red hair ribbon was undone and trailed down her back.

"Where do you live?" demanded Pat.

"I shan't tell you," said John, afraid that Pat might tell his father and mother. "It's no business of yours. We've done no harm. We'll go."

"No you won't! You're our prisoners!" suddenly cried Pat, and with a truly deafening yell he produced a rope from round his waist and rushed at John, meaning to tie him up.

John was not used to this sort of thing. He tried to push Pat away, but the boy soon got him on the ground, and Margery stared at them in horror.

"John! John! You'll dirty your jersey! Oh, John, get up!"

But then it was poor Margery's turn, for Maureen and Biddy suddenly flung themselves on her, too, and she also was rolled on the ground. She screamed. What would Mother say to her dirty dress?

There was a real rough-and-tumble for a few minutes, and when it was over, John found that somehow or other his hands were tied behind his back. He was indeed Pat's prisoner.

"You rough beast!" he shouted to Pat. "Undo my hands. I'll kick you if you don't."

"Kicking not allowed," said Pat. "Don't be an ass. It's only a game."

Margery sat up and dusted down her dress. It was

176

in a dreadful mess. "Don't dare to touch me again!" she yelled at Maureen and Biddy. "Look what you've done to my frock! Mother will be furious."

"No harm done," said Maureen, dimples coming in her cheek as she grinned at the angry Margery. "A button off—but what does that matter?"

"What does that matter?" echoed Biddy, jumping up and down in glee at the sight of Margery's angry face. "Oh look—there's a doll!"

"Let my doll alone!" screamed Margery, who was now quite beside herself with rage and fright. "If you dare to touch her, I'll—I'll—I'll . . ."

But it was no use. Biddy had got the doll and was nursing her. Then Pat saw the two red roses under the doll and he picked them up.

"Oho! You've been picking our roses," said Pat. "Haven't you?"

John and Margery were both truthful children. They had been taught never to tell stories, and they never did. But how dreadful to have to own up to picking somebody else's flowers!

"I picked them," said Margery, at last. "I didn't think it would matter. They were fading. I'm sorry now —I wouldn't have picked them if I'd known you were coming and might want them."

"She's a thief," said Biddy, importantly.

"Shut up, Biddy," said Pat, at once. He turned to Margery. "You'd no right to pick our flowers. But you can have them. We'll take your doll in exchange."

"No, oh no!" cried Margery, in the greatest alarm. But Maureen was already running out of the willow-tree with the doll. Margery tore after her.

A voice came from somewhere. "Children! Do you want to see over the house? I've got the key now."

Maureen flung the doll to Margery. "Here you are. That's our mother. I was only teasing you."

"Keep the roses too, if you're so badly off for flowers," called Pat, in a scornful voice. He took Biddy's hand and they all ran to the house.

"What horrid, rough, unkind, dirty, *dreadful* children!" said Margery, almost in tears, as she picked up her doll and hugged her. "I hate them."

"Beasts," said John, looking down at his torn jersey. "Springing on us suddenly like that and getting us down on the ground. I never knew such rough children in my life!"

"I don't want to know them," said Margery. "Come on, John, let's go while we can. They may come back at any minute."

They peeped out between the willow branches. They saw a crowd of people in the empty house, and heard the sound of lively, excited voices.

"They had nice faces, those children," said Margery remembering. "Lovely blue eyes. But what awful manners! Mother would hate them, I'm sure. She'd never let us know them. Anyway, I shall never, never be friends with them after what they did with my doll. Poor Angela! I thought she'd be broken. Let's go home quickly, John."

They ran hurriedly down the garden, and got over the wall. They heard their bedtime bell as they climbed over. John looked down at his clothes in dismay.

"Mother will have a lot to say," he said. "And you look pretty awful too, Margery."

Mother *did* have a lot to say. She couldn't bear the children to be dirty or untidy. "Your jersey, John! Your dress, Margery! And where's that missing button? What *have* you been doing?"

They didn't tell her. They both thought the same thing. "Those dreadful children! We'll never speak to them again!"

CHAPTER THREE

The Taggertys Move In

NEITHER Margery nor John dared to climb over the wall into the other garden again in the evenings. It had been a great shock to them to be caught like that by the Taggertys, and given such a rough time. They talked about it to one another when Annette wasn't there.

"We can't possibly be friends with them. They were so rough and dirty and horrid. The way they got us down like that!"

"Yes—and the way they took poor Angela and then threw her back, and made her fall on the ground," said Margery. "Thank goodness she wasn't broken. I've never broken a doll in my life, and I simply couldn't bear it if Angela got hurt. Horrible children!"

"It's quite certain Mother will never let us know them," said John, "so that will be all right. I wonder when they will arrive."

The Taggertys moved in one day the following week. John had to take a message for his mother to someone living two doors away from the Taggertys' house, and as he passed by he saw two big removal vans backing up to the front gate.

"They're moving in!" he thought, and stood for a minute to watch. Some of the furniture was carried into the house as he watched. John thought it wasn't very nice furniture. It looked shabby and old, not like theirs at home, which was always fresh and shining and spotless.

A big, plump woman, with untidy hair and a loud

voice, came out of the house. "The next lot is to go into the room on the right," she told the men, in a cheerful voice that could be heard all down the road.

"That must be Mrs. Taggerty," thought John. "She looks quite jolly—but isn't she untidy! Just like those dreadful children."

He wondered when the children would arrive. There was no sign of them then. Only Mrs. Taggerty seemed to be there. Perhaps the children would arrive later. He went along to deliver his message and stayed for a while with his mother's friend, waiting whilst she wrote an answer for him to take.

Just as he passed the Taggertys' house a shabby old car drew up, and out of it tumbled three children. Yes, Pat, Maureen and Biddy. John saw another woman in the car, holding a big white bundle. That would be the baby. A man sat at the wheel, smiling. He had a long thin face, very deep-set blue eyes, and a mass of dark, wavy hair, grey at the edges. He looked nice.

"That must be Mr. Taggerty," thought John, slipping quickly to the opposite side of the road, so that the children wouldn't see him. He didn't mean to speak to them at all.

The children poured into the front garden, shouting in excitement, laughing in delight at coming to a new home. They didn't see John. Mrs. Taggerty came to the front door and they flung themselves on her.

"Mummy! We've come at last! But what a pity, the vans got here first."

"We had a puncture! It took ages to get the wheel off. We nearly went mad, it took so long."

"I want to see the men putting the furniture into my bedroom. Have they done it yet? I want to tell them exactly where to put everything."

Mixed up among the children's legs was a dog. It was a curious-looking dog, black and tan, with such a long tail that it waved about like a plume. The dog was as excited as the children. It plunged about, barking madly. John didn't like the look of it at all.

"What a dog! It's a terrible mongrel! It's not a terrier, or a spaniel, or a retriever—it's just a mix-up. And look at its awful tail!" he thought. "Well, I hope it never comes into *our* garden. If I catch it there, digging up our beds, I'll chase it out with a stick!"

"Get down, Dopey, get down!" yelled Pat, as the dog, trying to get the boy's attention, leapt right up at him and licked his face. "Mummy, Dopey was quite mad in the car. We had to open a window and let him put his head out all the time. Daddy said he wanted to make sure we were taking the right road."

"Woof," said Dopey, in an excited doggy voice, and pawed at Mrs. Taggerty.

"Good dog! Go indoors then!" said Mrs. Taggerty. "Patrick, try to keep him out of the men's way, or they'll be falling over him and dropping wardrobes down the stairs."

Dopey disappeared into the house with a bound and a deep "woof". The children followed. The removal men went in with a dressing-table. Mr. Taggerty got out of the car and helped the woman with the baby to the pavement.

"Come on, Bridget." he said. "We'll have to wake up Michael, I'm afraid. Well, what do you think of the house?"

John didn't wait to hear or see any more. He sped home to tell Margery and Annette all about everything. He called them excitedly. "Margery! Annette! I've got something to tell you."

They listened eagerly to his story. Margery didn't at all like the sound of the big dog.

"I hope he doesn't come here. I should be afraid of him. Oh dear, I do wish the children were nice—it

181

would be such fun to have three to play with, living just at the bottom of our garden."

"How do you know they're not nice?" said Annette. "You haven't even spoken to them."

John and Margery didn't say they had. They knew Annette would go rushing to tell Mother if she knew they had been into the Taggertys' garden, and seen the children.

Mother, too, heard that the Taggertys were moving in. "I'll just wait and see what kind of people they are before I make friends with them, and go calling on Mrs. Taggerty," she said. "Anyway, Mrs. Wilson will know—the friend you took a message to this morning, John. She lives only two doors away and will be sure to know what they are like."

"I didn't think they looked very nice when I passed by today," said John. "I saw the children going in. They were awfully noisy and excited."

Although Margery and John had quite made up their minds not to speak to the Taggerty children any more, they couldn't help going down the garden to see if any of them were in their garden too.

Annette was standing on the garden-roller, looking over the wall. From the other garden came the sound of shouts and calls, laughter, woofs and shrieks.

"They're in the garden," said Annette.

"You needn't tell us *that*!" said John. "We can hear."

"I've seen the big dog," said Annette. "He's called Dopey. And they've got a big cat, too. I've seen it."

"What's it like?" asked Margery.

"It's black, with four white feet and a white bib." said Annette. "And they call it Socks. Isn't that a silly name for a cat?"

"Yes, very," said John. "Socks! I suppose they call it that because it looks as if it's wearing white socks."

"Socks and Dopey! What queer names for animals," said Margery. "Is Socks friendly with Dopey, Annette? Did you see?"

"Oh yes. Dopey chases Socks, and Socks chases Dopey," said Annette. "And when Socks is tired of being chased, she just runs up a tree. There she is now, look!"

The children looked. They saw a large black cat, with four white feet, sitting solemnly on the branch of a tree looking at them.

"Doesn't she look haughty?" said Margery. "She looks as if she doesn't want to know us at all!"

"Well, look haughty back, then," said John. "We don't want to know *her*. Dreadful children, a silly dog and a haughty cat! Look out—here come the children. Let's hide."

Pat, Maureen and Biddy appeared through the tangle of bushes at the bottom of their garden. Biddy was as black as a sweep, and her hair-ribbon was, as usual, undone, and trailed down her neck.

Margery and John ran to hide under a nearby bush. Annette wasn't quite quick enough. Pat saw her head above the wall just before she got down from the roller. He called to her.

"Hey, you! What's your name?"

Annette didn't answer. She scrambled down and fell off the roller, grazing her knee. At once she set up a terrific yell. Pat's head appeared above the wall.

"What's up? What a row!"

Annette pointed to her knee. The graze was so slight that it could hardly be seen.

"Cry-baby!" said Pat. "My little sister wouldn't howl for a graze like that!"

Annette was angry to hear herself called a cry-baby. "Nasty boy!" she said. "I'll tell my mother you called me a cry-baby."

"Dear little tell-tale!" said Pat, and grinned. "Run away and tell her. Cry-baby! Tell-tale!"

Annette was so surprised and angry at this speech that she stood there with her mouth open, ready to howl, but quite forgetting to in her astonishment at hearing someone speaking to her so rudely and unkindly.

"If you don't close your mouth the flies will get in," said Pat. "Hey, Maureen, come on up here! There's a funny cry-baby over the wall with her mouth wide open."

But before Maureen's head appeared, Annette was off up the garden to find her mother, screaming in anger. How dared that boy talk to her like that?

Mother appeared at once and comforted her. "Poor little Annette! Don't take any notice of such a rude boy! Did you hurt your poor knee? Why didn't John and Margery look after you?"

"They hid away," sobbed Annette. "They don't look after me at all. They're horrid, too."

"Now you choose a sweet out of the sweet-tin and go and play in the nursery," said Mother. "And don't go and look over the wall any more, in case those children are there. If that's the way they behave we won't have anything to do with them."

CHAPTER FOUR

Daddy's Little Surprise

MARGERY, John and Annette did keep away from the garden wall for the next two days. They heard the shouts of the Taggerty children, and they heard the deep woofs of Dopey. Once they heard the baby crying.

"I saw Pat looking over our wall this morning," said John to Margery. "I don't think we'd better let him see us, because he doesn't know that we live here. He might go and tell Annette he saw us in his garden last week, if he sees us—and then she'd tell Mother."

"I suppose Annette really *is* a tell-tale, just as Pat said," said Margery. "Fancy his telling her that! If *we* did she'd complain to Mother and we'd get a scolding. Mother always treats Annette as if she was still a darling baby, but she isn't. John, I wish I could see that baby next door. I do like babies. They're better than dolls because they can really move and make noises."

"*I* don't want to see the baby!" said John, scornfully. "It will be like the rest of them—dirty and rude —and smelly too, I expect."

"Oh, I shouldn't like it very much if it was smelly," said Margery. "I hope it isn't. I like the smell of babies

185

usually—such a nice fresh *baby*-smell—of baby-powder
and soap. I wonder if it's a boy or a girl."

Mother went to see her friend, Mrs. Wilson, to ask
her about the Taggertys. "Are they nice?" she asked.
"What about the children? One of them wasn't very
polite to little Annette the other day."

"My dear, they're *awful*!" said Mrs. Wilson, wrink-
ling up her nose. "Not at *all* the sort of people for our
road. A great pity they came, I think."

"Oh, dear," said Mother. "What a shame! As they
live at the bottom of our garden I rather hoped they
would be nice. The children would like to play with
others living so near."

"They've no manners at all," said Mrs. Wilson. "Not
one between them. And Mrs. Taggerty came borrow-
ing something the very day after she moved in. *And*
hasn't returned it yet. Such an untidy woman, too.
Pleasant though. She had a dreadful dog with her that
simply *romped* all over my geraniums. And Mrs. Taggerty never said a word to stop him."

"Oh, dear!" said Mother again. "I'm afraid they
will be impossible as friends. I must warn the children
to have nothing to do with them."

"My dear, your three are so well brought up that I
am sure they wouldn't have anything to do with the
Taggertys anyhow," said Mrs. Wilson. "That little
Annette of yours now—a *sweet* child, with such lovely
manners. What a pretty little thing she is—and you
always dress her so beautifully, too."

Mother was pleased. "Yes, Annette is a dear pet.
Well, all of them are, really, though my husband does
complain sometimes that John isn't a real *boy*! He'd
like him to swarm up trees and tear his clothes, and
crawl through bushes and splash through puddles and
goodness knows what. Well, there's no need for children to do things like that, and I don't like it. I like

well-brought-up, well-behaved children, who like to be clean and tidy, and helpful to others."

"Well, yours certainly are all that," said Mrs. Wilson. "A pleasure to be with. Do let them come to tea with me one day next week. As for those Taggertys, don't you let your children mix with them. Yours might be good for the Taggertys, but the Taggertys wouldn't be good for *yours*."

When Mother got home she called the children to her. "I'm sorry to say that I haven't had a very good report about the Taggertys," she told them. "There's no need to repeat to you what I've heard, but all I want to say is this—the Taggerty children are not our sort, and I don't want you to play with them. You can be polite, and say 'hallo,' but no more than that."

The children were glad. *They* didn't want to know those rough children and their dog.

"I don't expect they go to church or to Sunday School, and I don't expect they even say their prayers," said Margery. "Do you think they clean their teeth, Mother?"

"Oh, I expect so," said Mother. "That's their business, not ours. Now, I'm going to go and see Granny. Who wants to go with me?"

Nothing more was said about the Taggertys that day. The three children spent the rest of the day with their granny, and she praised their behaviour to their mother.

"Really, they are a credit to you," she said. "You are lucky to have such good children. I don't believe they are ever naughty."

"No, they're not really naughty," said Mother. "Their father says sometimes he wishes they were. He thinks they're *too* good, you know. But that's only because he was a very naughty little boy when he was small, and he can't understand John's not wanting to be naughty and mischievous, too."

The children didn't go down to the bottom of the garden at all for some days. Annette wouldn't even go half-way down, she was so afraid of seeing Pat and having something rude called out to her. They couldn't help hearing the Taggerty children though, for they always seemed to be playing some exciting game.

"Red Indians, or robbers and policemen, I should think," said John. "I wish they were nice. I'd love to play those games with them. It's no fun playing them with Annette, because she screams at the least thing."

Then on Saturday something surprising happened. It was when the children were having their midday dinner. Daddy always came home for dinner on Saturdays, and the children liked that. He served out the stew, and then began to talk.

"Mother," he said, "I met a very famous writer yesterday. I meant to have told you. He was at school with me as a boy, and when he grew up he became famous as a writer of books. Very fine books they are, too."

"Really?" said Mother, busy taking the meat off the bones for Annette. "Where did you meet him?"

"Well, I went to a tea-shop I sometimes go to, to buy chocolates for you and the children," said Daddy, "and there, having tea, was old Dickie—and his family with him! My word, you'd have liked his children, Mother."

"What were they like?" asked Margery.

"Well, there was a boy, about John's age, I suppose," said Daddy. "A fine boy, merry and with plenty to say. A proper boy, too—won all the races at his last sports, can climb any tree, according to his father, and is as plucky as a boy can be. He broke his ankle last year, doing something mad, and never made a murmur about it."

"What were the others like?" asked Annette.

188

"There was a girl like you, Annette, an amusing little thing. She was quite squashed by the others, but she didn't seem to mind a bit. A little monkey, I should think. And there was another girl, too. I like her very much. So natural and friendly."

"They sound nice," said Margery.

"They were rather noisy and excited," said Daddy. "Their mother was there too—such a nice, friendly woman, enjoying the treat as much as the children were. Well, well, it *was* a surprise to meet old Dickie, I must say—and to find him with a family too. Of course, I told him all about you—and I do want you all to be friends."

"Oh yes!" said Annette. "I want a friend. I'd like that little girl to play with. But where do they live, Daddy?"

"Well, now I've got a surprise for you," said Daddy, beaming all round the table. "A real surprise. They've come to live here, in our village! They live next door but two to Mrs. Wilson, Mummy's friend. Isn't that strange? It *will* be nice to have old Dickie round in the evenings."

There was a silence. Everyone looked at Daddy. Mother asked the question they were all thinking. "Daddy—what is their name?"

"Taggerty," said Daddy. "Dickie Taggerty sat by me at school, and he was always first in composition, and vowed he'd be a writer one day. And so he is—at the top of the tree, too. I am proud to know him. Well, you'll call on Mrs. Taggerty, won't you, Mother, and ask the children round to tea?"

There was another silence. The children's hearts sank. Goodness! To think it was the *Taggertys* that Daddy had been talking about. That dreadful family.

"Oh dear," said Mother, at last. "Daddy, the Taggertys live in the house whose garden joins ours at the bottom. And, dear, they are *not* really very nice children. So rough and dirty and rude."

"Well—they seemed a little untidy, and they certainly had plenty to say, and could have done with a little better manners," said Daddy, "but they were thoroughly nice children, natural, jolly and friendly. I liked them. It would do ours good to know them. And it might do *them* good to know ours too. You'd like Mrs. Taggerty, I'm sure, dear. Most amusing, and so jolly."

Mother didn't look as if she would like Mrs. Taggerty at all. Whatever was she to do? She didn't want to make friends with the Taggertys at all—and now Mr. Taggerty had turned out to be Daddy's old friend at school! It really was too bad.

"Well, will you call on the Taggertys?" asked Daddy, sounding a little impatient. "I want to ask old Dickie round here, and we must ask his wife too. And the children would mix quite well together—exactly the right ages. There's a baby too, Mrs. Taggerty said."

"I don't think they *would* mix, Peter," said Mother. "Really, the Taggerty children are very rough and not well brought up at all. I don't want John and Margery to make friends with children like that."

"John's too girlish," said Daddy. "I want him to be more of a boy. That elder Taggerty boy will shake him up a bit. And the little girl will soon stand up to Annette and teach her not to cry so much."

John looked alarmed, and Annette looked ready to cry. Daddy looked at Margery.

"And I've no doubt Margery will get over her fear of this, that and the other," he said. "The Taggerty children have all kinds of pets—a dog, a cat, pet mice——"

Margery gave a scream. "Mice! I'll never never go near the Taggertys if they keep mice."

"I had twenty pet mice once," said Daddy. "and two of them lived in my trousers pocket for a week. It's a pity you children have no pets. You none of you seem to have my love for animals. I'd like a dog myself, but I suppose Margery and Annette would have a fit if it jumped up at them. Mother, it's time we did something about these children of ours. They're good and well-behaved, and truthful, and nice-mannered— but are they *proper* children? No, they're not! I tell you, they want a bit of shaking up."

"I don't agree with you, Peter," said Mother, in a smooth sort of voice. "But don't let's discuss it now, dear. I will call on Mrs. Taggerty, if you want me to, but please don't make us enter into any close friendship with them, if we do find they are not the kind of people we like."

"Well, we'll see," said Daddy, looking rather annoyed. "What's the pudding? Oh, cherry pie, good! I'll have a nice big helping, please, because I'm going for a long walk this afternoon. Anyone want to come with me?"

Nobody did. John knew he ought to say he would come, because Daddy liked boys who wanted to go for long walks and tramp through the woods and over the hills. But John didn't like walks. He wanted to stay at home and read.

"Well, I'm off," said Daddy, in a disappointed voice, when he had finished his pie. "Now, if only we had a dog I could take him for company. But we haven't. Good-bye."

CHAPTER FIVE

Over the Wall

THE children felt very gloomy after Daddy had gone. They went up into the nursery and talked about things.

"Isn't it bad luck?" said John. "To *have* to know those dreadful children. And how mean of Daddy to say I'm girlish. I'm not, am I?"

"Well—you don't climb trees or anything like most boys do," said Margery. "Of course—Mother doesn't like us to. So you can't very well help it."

"It will be awful having those children here to tea," said John. "You'll have to put away your best dolls, Margery. That girl called Maureen will probaby throw them about."

"And you'd better put away your new aeroplane," said Margery. "You never know what children like that will do with other people's toys. I bet they haven't a single unbroken toy!"

"I hope they won't bring that dog here," said Annette. "I shall hit him with a stick if they do."

"He'll bite you, then," said Margery. "He'll show his teeth—like this—and he'll growl—like this, grrrrr."

Annette screwed up her face to howl. "It's all right," said John, hurriedly. "Margery doesn't really mean it. I'll see the dog doesn't bite you. We'll send it away if it comes."

"I do hope Mother doesn't ask them to tea," said Margery. "Perhaps she won't. Good gracious, can you hear those children playing now? What a noise they are making!"

An angry voice came through the trees

It was rather an exciting noise. It sounded as if a big
drum was being beaten. Boom-boom-boom, diddy-
boom-boom-boom! Then there came what sounded
like a trumpet noise.

"They're having a band, or something," said John.
"Let's go down and see."

They went downstairs and out of the side door to
the bottom of the garden. Yes, there was certainly a
drum all right. Boom-boom-boom, diddy-boom-boom-
boom.

John couldn't resist putting his head over the wall.

He saw Maureen, dressed up in a flowing red cloak, with a crown on her head, parading through the bushes. Behind her came Pat, banging a drum, and Biddy, blowing on a small trumpet.

"Here comes Her Majesty!" shouted Pat, banging the drum. "Fall down before her!"

An angry voice came through the trees, and then someone appeared in a hurry. It was Bridget, the mother's help.

"Och, you naughty little ragamuffins, you, making all that din with the baby, bless his heart, just asleep after a bad tummyache. One more beat of that drum, Patrick, and I'll take the stick from you and lay it about you till you boom like a drum yourself!"

The beating of the drum stopped at once. "Oh, sorry, Bridget," said Pat. "I quite forgot about Michael. We'll play Red Indians instead."

"Indeed you won't, not till the baby's awake and happy," said Bridget. "War-whoops and what-nots, and dancing round like mad things, scaring the baby into fits. And your mother with a headache, too!"

She turned and went. John ducked his head down, for he didn't want to be seen. All was quiet for a few minutes, but then some other game started which had a lot of yelling in it.

"Aren't they awful?" said Margery. "Their baby is asleep and their mother has a headache—and still they can't be quiet. Most selfish children!"

"I'd like to have seen Bridget take the drum-stick and beat Pat like a drum," said John.

On the next Tuesday, Mother went to call on Mrs. Taggerty. The children waited eagerly for her to come back.

They met her at their front gate. "Mother! What happened? Were all the children there? How did they behave?"

"I *suppose* they were on their best behaviour," said Mother. "But I should be very sorry to think that any of you would behave as they do. Still, I suppose they can't help it. They've just been brought up like that. Mrs. Taggerty is rather easygoing. The baby is lovely."

"I'd like to see the baby," said Margery. "I do so like babies. Mother, did you ask the Taggertys to tea?"

"Yes," said Mother. "They are coming tomorrow. By themselves, without their mother. She says Bridget is out tomorrow, and she must stay with the baby. So the children will come alone, at half-past three. I do hope you will all get on together nicely."

Margery, John and Annette looked gloomy. "Mother, will you be with us all the time?" asked Annette. "I'm afraid of Pat."

"No, I can't be with you all the time," said Mother. "You must play in the garden by yourselves before tea, but I shall have tea with you, of course. And after tea I might have a game of snap or something with you."

That evening, when Annette had gone to bed, Margery and John heard someone whistling at the bottom of the garden. They went down cautiously to see who it was.

Pat's head stuck over the top of the wall. He beckoned to them. But when they came near he looked most astonished. "I say! So *you* are the children we caught here! I didn't know you lived over the wall. Did you know we were coming to tea with you tomorrow?"

"Yes," said John. "Don't go and say anything about us being in your garden. We'll get into a row if you do."

Pat made a scornful noise. "Tell tales about you! What do you think I am? I wouldn't dream of saying a word. Golly, fancy it being *you* we're coming to tea with. I say, your mother came to call on ours this afternoon, and she was so awfully polite and well-dressed and—er—er—well, stuck-up a bit, you know, that we got quite scared. So we thought we'd whistle you to-night, and see what you were like. We hoped you wouldn't be stuck-up too. We can't bear stuck-up people."

"Mother isn't stuck-up," said John stiffly.

"Well, we've heard people say she is," said Maureen, her head popping up beside Pat's. "I thought she was awfully pretty and I did like her dress. People say you children are rather awful too. Are you? Harry Lee told us you were prigs."

Margery wasn't sure what a prig was, but it sounded something horrid. She went red. John looked sulky.

"We're not prigs. People think *you're* pretty awful too. And so you are. We don't want you to come to tea a bit."

"And we don't want to come," said Maureen, her eyes shining angrily. "Horrible, having to dress up and wear gloves, and come in all polite and silly. And we shan't play any decent games, I bet, or climb a tree, or even have a game at 'he'. Just sit around and make polite conversation like your mother does."

"You're very rude," said John. "If it wasn't for our fathers knowing each other we wouldn't have to know you at all. We think you're an awful lot of children."

"We think the same about you," said Pat, his eyes shining angrily now too. "That's what we call you—those dreadful children."

"Oh—it's exactly what we call *you*," said John, surprised. "Well, don't come to tea if it's such a frightful bore."

"We shall jolly well have to," said Pat, gloomily. Then he brightened a little. "We might say we feel ill," he said, turning to Maureen. "Do you remember how we got out of going to see that great-aunt of ours once? We both said we had awful sore throats, and Mummy got alarmed and wouldn't let us stir out of the house."

196

John and Margery were really shocked. "But that was a frightful untruth," said Margery. "Do you really tell fibs like that? We never do."

"Our father says it's a cowardly thing to do, to tell untruths," said John. "He says people only tell them when they're too afraid to tell the truth. He says it's better to tell the truth and take what's coming to you than tell a fib to get out of it, because if you keep doing that you'll always be a coward, and wriggle out of things."

Pat and Maureen stared at him in silence. "We're not cowards," said Pat at last. "I can climb higher than any boy I know, and I can swim as fast as Daddy. Maureen's brave for a girl, too."

"All the same, you *are* cowards if you keep on telling fibs," said Margery. "You ask your father and see what he says. Now, if *we* didn't want to come to tea with you—which we don't, of course—*we* wouldn't be cowardly and go and tell Mother we'd got sore throats and worry her to death—we'd be brave and go and say we jolly well didn't want to, and why. See?"

"I bet you wouldn't!" said Pat, scornfully. "You'd just say, 'Yes, Mother dear,' and come. Pooh! I bet you're all three of you little cowardy-custards."

A bell rang. "That's our bell," said Margery, thankfully, for she didn't want to argue with Pat any more. "Well, I suppose we'll have to see you tomorrow."

"Wait a bit," said Maureen, urgently. "We wanted to ask you something. We know our father wants us to be friends with you because he likes yours so much—and we don't want to let him down if we can help it. So for goodness sake tell us what to wear, and does your mother like to shake hands with us, or is she the kissy sort?"

"She won't want to kiss *you*," said John. "Wear what you like. We don't care! But if you want our mother

197

to think anything of you, come with clean hands and faces, and don't shout at one another, or push one another like you do."

Maureen sighed. "It's going to be awful," she said. "All right, we'll do our best. Only for Daddy's sake though! I don't expect our mothers will like each other any more than *we* do—but Daddy's such an old dear we'd like him to think we're all friends together, so that he can have your father in whenever he likes."

"We must go," said John, as the bell rang again more urgently. "That's Mother ringing for us."

"I say! Wait! There's one more thing," called Maureen. "We can bring Dopey, can't we?"

Margery and John stopped in their run back to the house and turned shocked faces to Pat and Maureen. "What, bring that awful mongrel!" cried John. "Of course not! Mother would have a fit."

"But he *always* goes with us *everywhere*," said Maureen. "And he isn't an awful mongrel. He's the best dog in the world. He'll be heart-broken if he doesn't come with us. He'll bark the place down and keep Baby awake."

"Let him!" said John, hard-heartedly. "I tell you, Mother will send him home if he does come, and Annette will scream till she's blue in the face."

"Does she really go blue in the face?" asked Maureen, with interest. "I should like to——"

But, as the bedtime bell was rung impatiently for the third time, John and Margery fled at top speed down the trimly-kept path to their house. Pat and Maureen gazed after them.

"What frightful kids! Goody-goody and namby-pamby and priggy-wiggy. I wish we hadn't got to go to tea with them tomorrow. I liked their father awfully, didn't you, when we saw him at the tea-shop? I thought he must have really decent children."

"So did I. But you can never tell," said Maureen. "Anyway, we've got to go tomorrow, and do let's try to look tidy and clean, for Daddy's sake. I hope I've got a clean frock. I bet Biddy hasn't. She gets dirtier than any of us."

"Oh, well. Tomorrow won't last for ever," said Pat, as they went indoors. "But just fancy having to go out to tea with those dreadful children."

CHAPTER SIX

The Taggertys Come to Tea

Six children felt very gloomy the next day, and wished heartily that something would happen to stop the tea-party. But nothing did. The weather was fine. Everyone was quite well. And half-past three came nearer and nearer.

"Now are you clean and tidy, and ready for your visitors?" asked Mother, coming into the nursery. "Let me see your hands, John. And your nails? Annette, I must brush your hair again."

"But, Mother—the Taggertys won't care a bit if we're clean or dirty," said John, impatiently. "They'd *prefer* us dirty."

"I'm not thinking of what *they* like, but of what *I* like, and of what is right and proper," said Mother. "And don't talk in that tone of voice, John. There, Annette! You look very sweet with that big bow of blue. Now you'll be very nice with little Biddy, won't you? She may be shy at first."

Margery felt quite certain that Biddy wouldn't be at

all shy, but she didn't tell Annette so. She couldn't help wondering how the spoilt little Annette would get on with Biddy.

"There are the Taggertys now," said Mother, hearing the front-door bell ring. "Agnes will let them in and bring them up here. Then you can choose some toys to take out into the garden."

John wanted to say that he was sure the Taggertys would rather play catch or hide-and-seek—but he was certain Mother would forbid that, seeing that they were all dressed-up and clean. So he said nothing.

In came the Taggertys. They were clean, except that Biddy's knees looked as if she'd been crawling for half a mile on them in some muddy place. Their hair was brushed, and Biddy's ribbon for once in a way was done up. They had forgotten to see if their nails were clean, and not one of them had clean shoes.

Still, they had clean dresses on, and clean socks, and they advanced on Mother politely, holding out their hands.

"How do you do?" said Mother, smiling.

"Quite well, thank you," said all the Taggertys in chorus. They had evidently been practising this. John then advanced and held out his hand, too.

"Goodness! Do we have to do it to you?" said Maureen, surprised. "How silly!"

"Well, you needn't," said John, suddenly feeling that it was silly, too. But Annette wanted to. She loved showing off her manners in front of others. People so often praised her for them in public. So she went forward and held out her hand to Biddy.

But Biddy put her hands behind her and stared. "Hallo!" she said. "Are all these your toys?"

Then the Taggertys forgot any further politenesses and began to examine the nursery and all its toys with close attention.

"Look at this! Is it a musical box? Play it for us."

"What's this? It's a toy garage! Look at all the cars in it. Let's take them out."

"Oh, *Biddy*! See this dolls'-house! It's what we've always longed for. Margery, let's take all the furniture out!"

"I think it would be better if you all went to play in the garden this sunny afternoon," said Mother, seeing Margery's black looks at the thought of her dolls'-house being emptied.

"Well, we'll take the dolls'-house then—and the garage—and the musical box—oh, what lovely toys you've got!" cried Maureen. "And let's take this baby doll, too."

"No, you can't. She's mine," said Annette.

"Well, we're visitors. You have to let us play with your things," said Biddy. "I want to carry this doll."

"Shut up, Biddy," said Pat. "Don't talk like that."

Annette snatched the doll away from Biddy. "It's mine! I won't let you have it. Mother, she's not to have my baby doll, is she?"

"Let Biddy carry it down to the garden," said Mother. "She is your visitor, you know."

Annette burst into tears.

"Cry-baby!" said Biddy at once. "Isn't she, Pat? You told me she was, and she is! I don't want your silly doll, Annette. Cry-baby!"

"Now, don't quarrel," said Mother. "Oh dear, there's the telephone. Take the Taggertys down to the garden, John, and look after them till tea-time."

Mother went out of the room. Annette felt hurt and cross. Mother hadn't comforted her and fussed her as she usually did. She whimpered, feeling sorry for herself.

"Come on. Let's leave the cry-baby by herself," said

201

Maureen. "Help me to carry this dolls'-house down the stairs, Pat. Oh, I never saw such a beauty in my life."

"Haven't you got one?" asked Margery, feeling pleased at this admiration. "Oh, do be careful not to tilt it. All the furniture slides about if you do."

"We've got an old one belonging to our Granny," said Maureen. "But everything in it is broken now. It's not much fun to play with because none of the furniture stands up properly. The legs are broken, you see."

The dolls'-house and the toy garage with the cars were taken down into the garden. No sooner had they got there and settled down on the grass than there came a scampering of feet, and up the path from the bottom of the garden tore Dopey, his long, lanky body wriggling in delight to see the three children he loved. He rolled over on his back in a ridiculous way and threw all his legs in the air, working them about vigorously.

"Woof!" he said. "Woof!"

"Look—when he lies on his back and works his legs like that, we say he is riding a bicycle," Pat said, and gave the delighted Dopey a prod in the tummy. "Idiotic dog!"

Annette and Margery squealed in fright as the big dog came up and flung himself down beside them. They jumped up in horror. "Send him away!"

"Why?" said Pat. "He won't do any harm. He won't really. He's an awfully stupid dog—that's why we call him Dopey—but he's loving and harmless and he loves a game. Let him stay."

Dopey rolled over on his side and found his head near John's knee. He put out a great pink tongue and gave John a wet lick on his knee. And John liked it.

"I don't mind him staying," said John, and Margery and Annette stared at him in horror.

Dopey leapt up and ran to Margery

"He's to go," said Margery, beginning to tremble. "I'm afraid of dogs. You know I am."

"Cowardy-custard!" said Pat scornfully. "Hi, Dopey. Lick her then!"

Dopey leapt up, ran to Margery, and gave her a great fat lick on her bare arm. She squealed.

"Oh, how horrible! What a licky dog!"

"All dogs are licky," said Pat. "Lie down, Dopey, or you'll go home."

"Woof," Dopey said, and lay down most obediently. But he was up again in a trice and playfully ran at Annette's bare legs. She gave such an agonized scream that Mother came running down the garden at once.

"Annette, darling, what *is* the matter?"

Annette flung herself on her mother. "Mother, it's that dog! He rushed at me. He'll bite me."

Mother eyed Dopey, who laid himself flat on the ground and then squirmed towards her on his tummy, abasing himself most humbly. Mother gave him a very cold look.

"Is this your dog?" she said to Pat. "Well, you must take him home. I'd rather he didn't come into our garden."

"I want him here," said Biddy, in a piercing voice.

"Biddy! I'll take you home too if you butt in like that," roared Pat, making everyone jump. Biddy said no more. Pat got up. He was evidently still on his best behaviour.

"I'll take him round home," he said, and went off down the side-path to the front gate. He took Dopey home and pushed him into the washhouse. He shut the door on him and Dopey howled.

When Pat got back, the others were playing with the garage and the dolls'-house, and for a while all was peace. But suddenly there came the scampering of feet again, and up from the bottom of the garden gambolled

Dopey, looking very pleased with himself indeed. Somebody had opened the washhouse door, he had run to the wall, leapt right over it—and here he was, overcome with delight at his own cleverness. He lay on his back and did his bicycle act again.

"He's awfully good at that," said John, who was beginning to feel quite warmly towards this peculiar dog.

Dopey gave John a sudden slobbering lick. John patted his head. Margery watched in surprise. "Don't let him come near me," she said. "I don't like him. He's so floppy and clumsy."

"I'm going to tell Mother," Annette said, and got up. "Nasty horrid dog! I'm going to tell Mother."

"No, you're not," said Pat unexpectedly, and he took hold of her dress. "Sit down, tell-tale. Do you know what you want? You want a jolly good spanking— one that hurts. You yell just for nothing, and what you want is something to *make* you yell. If I were John I'd slap you every time you told tales or yelled. That's what we do to Biddy."

Annette was so shocked at this surprising speech that she couldn't even yell.

"Look at her," said Pat, to the others. "Mouth wide open again, ready to yell. Flies will get into it, cry-baby! Look out, there comes a bee! He's looking for a hole!"

Annette heard the bee and shut her mouth with a snap. Dopey flopped down on her feet, and she freed a foot and kicked him.

In a trice Pat was standing beside her, his face red with anger. "If I wasn't a visitor I'd give you such a spanking for that that you'd never forget it," he said. "What's John doing, that he doesn't make you behave? You're a spoilt little miss, that's what you are. Kicking a dog! When he wants to make friends with you, too. Coward!"

"Don't! Don't!" begged Annette, really frightened at being spoken to like this. "I won't do it again. John, tell him I didn't mean it."

But John too had been shocked at seeing Annette kick Dopey. "You *did* mean it," he said. "Sit down and behave yourself, Annette. We're all ashamed of you."

Annette looked as if she was going to yell, but, seeing five pairs of stern eyes on her, she suddenly sat down. She said nothing more. John and Margery looked at one another. It was the very first time Annette had ever been known to do something she didn't really want to do. Hurrah!

"Do you think I'd better take Dopey back home again?" asked Pat, in his ordinary voice. He seemed to have forgotten his sudden anger completely. "Blow you, Dopey. I'll be spending all the afternoon trotting you home!"

Everyone laughed except Annette, who still looked very solemn. Dopey gave a little whine and put his head on John's knee.

"He likes John," said Pat. "Look at him. He doesn't do that to everyone."

John felt terribly pleased. He patted Dopey's silky head again. Dopey licked him slavishly, and rolled his eyes in a most comical manner. He really was a peculiar dog, but John couldn't help liking him.

And when Mother came to see how they were all getting on, there was Dopey again, flopping his long length on the grass with the six children. And marvellous to relate, Mother didn't say a word. As for Dopey, he looked away and pretended he wasn't really there. He wasn't such a stupid dog as he looked!

CHAPTER SEVEN

Tea-Time and After

THINGS went very well until five minutes before tea. Then the Taggertys got tired of sitting about and proposed a game of hide-and-seek. In three minutes all of them were dirty and Biddy had lost her ribbon and torn her frock.

Pat had climbed a tree and got the seat of his shorts stained with black. Maureen had squeezed behind a big oil-can in the garage and had oil on her skirt and hands. John, excited by the game, had actually got dirty too and even Margery and Annette were not clean and tidy.

Dopey had gone quite mad over the game. He floundered about all over the place, and his big foot-marks were all across the rose-beds under the dining-room windows. Then he sat down on some snap-dragons to scratch himself, and broke them to bits.

"Look at him!" cried Annette. "What will Mother say? He's a bad dog."

"He doesn't mean to be," said Maureen. "He really has behaved awfully well, for him. Is that the tea-bell? I'm hungry."

Mother couldn't help exclaiming in horror when she saw them. "How *have* you got like that? Oh dear. John, take them to wash. I must mend your frock, Biddy. And what *have* you got all down that skirt, Maureen?"

"Have we really got to go and wash all over again?" said Pat, in dismay. "We've already washed once this afternoon, before we came here. Can't we have a picnic tea in the garden, Mrs. Carlton? I'll help to carry things out. It won't matter how dirty we are then."

"No," said Mother, rather stiffly. "Tea is laid in the nursery. Hurry and wash now."

Grumbling under his breath, Pat went to wash with the others. Dopey came bounding along too, but Mother shooed him out and shut the side-door on him. He sat outside and howled dismally. It was a dreadful sound. The Taggertys were upset.

"Dopey's feet are clean, John. Why can't he come in? Doesn't your mother like dogs? Your father does. He told us so."

Dopey had to sit outside all the time they had tea. He howled without stopping and Mother felt very cross. Dreadful dog!

The Taggertys were very hungry, for they had had an early lunch, as Bridget had wanted to go out to catch the half-past one bus. They looked at the plates of bread-and-butter and cakes.

The bread-and-butter was cut very thin. At home the Taggertys had thick slices. Goodness—six of these would only make one of the home-slices. Mrs. Carlton would think them very greedy if they ate all they wanted.

She did think them greedy. They really had no manners at all at table. They never passed each other anything. They didn't wait to be asked to take this or that, they just stretched out and took it. They didn't say please and they didn't say thank you. They were certainly not at their best at meals.

The buns were small. The slices of cake were only half the size of the ones they had at home. The Taggertys, afraid that they wouldn't have enough to eat, ate swiftly and silently. Outside Dopey howled and howled.

"How dreadful they are!" thought Mother. "Why

weren't they taught their manners? Such good-looking children too." Then she spoke aloud. "No, no, Biddy. Don't snatch the last cake off the plate like that. See if somebody else wants it first."

"I want it," said Annette, at once.

"You would!" said Pat. "Give it her, Biddy."

"No," said Biddy, and held on to it.

"GIVE IT HER!" roared Pat, making everyone jump. Biddy gave the cake to Annette. Pat looked round the table. "That's the way to treat them when they're spoilt," he said. "That's how you ought to treat Annette, John. Yell at her a bit. She'll soon grow a lot more sensible! What's the good of being an older brother or sister if you don't teach the young ones how to behave?"

"John has been taught to treat his little sister politely and kindly," said Mother, sharply. Pat stared at her.

"Well," he said, trying to find words that would not offend his hostess, "well—look what's happened! She's a screamer and a tell-tale."

Annette wept. "Don't be so unkind," Mother said, and put her arm round Annette. "Don't take any notice of him, dear. He doesn't know any better."

Pat looked uncomfortable. "I'm sorry," he said. "I shouldn't have said that. I didn't know how to say it without offending you, Mrs. Carlton. I'm very sorry."

"It's all right," said Mrs. Carlton. "Now stop crying, Annette. You don't want to make your pretty face ugly."

"Is she pretty?" said Biddy, looking hard at Annette. "I didn't think she was."

"Nor are you," said Pat at once. "Have we all finished? Can we go now, Mrs. Carlton?"

They all went off into the garden. "Really!" thought Mother, as she looked out of the window and saw Dopey, mad with joy, careering round them all again.

"Really! I never came across such children in my life. Never!"

She let them play for half an hour and then called them in. "Would you like a game of snap? I'll have one with you, if you like."

The Taggerty children would much rather have played out of doors. "Can Dopey come with us, then?" asked Maureen. "He'll only howl if he doesn't."

"Oh, very well," said Mother, feeling that she would allow anything rather than have that dismal howling again. "Or no—I know what we'll do. We'll take the cards out of doors and play on the grass. Then Dopey can be with you, and perhaps he'll be quiet and behave himself."

Soon they were all playing snap. But as usual, Mother let Annette have the cards when she really shouldn't have had them. "You don't mind, do you?" she said to Pat and Maureen. "She's so small, you see. She gets upset if she doesn't win a few times."

Nobody said anything to that. Pat looked sharply at Biddy, as if he wondered whether she, too, would expect to take cards when she hadn't really said "snap" first.

Soon Mother handed some cards to Biddy that really she herself had won. "You have these," she said.

"But I wasn't first in saying 'snap'," said Biddy. "*You* were!"

"Never mind. You've only two left. You can have these," said Mother.

"But isn't that cheating?" said Biddy. "Pat says it is. And anyway I'm not a baby like Annette. I shan't cry if I don't get the cards. I'd rather not have them, Mrs. Carlton. I like to play *our* way. Annette can play your way."

"I don't want to," said Annette, suddenly. "I'm not a baby either, I want to play Pat's way."

210

Mother was most astonished. After that, nobody had any cards given to them that they hadn't really snapped. Pat won the game. He was very sharp indeed, much sharper than John.

"Now what about a game of snakes and ladders," said Mother. "We've got two boards."

"I'm tired of sitting still," said Pat. "Can't we run about again? What about Red Indians? Dopey's awfully good at Red Indians, John. He can wriggle along on his tummy just like we can."

John was filled with admiration. "Tell him to, then."

They wormed their way along, and Dopey did exactly the same

"He won't, unless we're all doing it," said Pat. "Hey, Dopey! Red Indians. Shhh! Enemies ahead!"

He flopped down on his tummy, and so did Maureen and Biddy. They wormed their way along on the grass and Dopey did exactly the same. John shrieked with laughter, and even Margery smiled to see him.

"Your clothes!" said Mother, in despair. "No, John, don't you wriggle too. What will your mother say to your dress when you get home, Maureen?"

"Well, she did say it would be more sensible to put on old things to come and play," said Maureen. "But we knew you wanted us to be polite. Oh—here's Uncle Peter!"

Daddy came into the garden, beaming. He had come home early on purpose to see the Taggertys before they went home. They greeted him as if he was indeed a real uncle.

"You've come in time to see us! Look, Dopey knows you again!"

"Will you give me a piggy-back?"

"Uncle Peter, would you like to see me climb a tree?"

Dopey leapt up at Daddy and gave him a lick on the nose. Daddy patted him and tickled him behind the ears. Dopey went nearly mad with joy.

Soon Daddy was galloping round the garden with Biddy squealing on his back. Maureen ran after him, whipping him with a little twig. Pat shinned up a tree and yelled to him. "Here I am! Did you see me get up in a trice?"

Dopey galloped round madly, running over the beds and making Mother feel that he really was doing it on purpose. John, Margery and Annette watched all this half-jealously. They didn't like sharing their father with the Taggertys. And how those Taggertys liked him!

212

"It's time you went home, youngsters," said Daddy at last. "I'll pop you over the wall, and come over with you myself to have a few words with your father."

"Oh, not over the wall!" said Mother.

"Well, they're too dirty now to walk round home by the road," said Daddy, reasonably. "We won't be a minute."

The Taggertys and Daddy went off down the garden, talking nineteen to the dozen. Dopey followed them, barking.

"Well! Not a word of thanks! Not even a good-bye," said Mother. "What badly-brought-up children."

"I don't want them again," said Annette. "Pat was unkind to me. And I don't like Biddy. I don't want her for a friend."

"Clear up everything," said Mother. "Then you must come to bed, Annette. It's past your bedtime."

In twenty minutes' time, Daddy came back. And dear me, with him were the three Taggertys, still dirty and untidy, and all looking rather ashamed of themselves.

"Please, Mrs. Carlton," said Pat, "we forgot to thank you very much for having us and to say good-bye. So we've come back to apologize. Mummy did tell us to be sure and thank you. I can't think how we forgot. I suppose it was because we went off with Mr. Carlton like that."

"Thank you very much for having us," said Maureen.

"And for the nice tea," said Biddy.

"And please can John and Margery and Annette come to tea tomorrow," said Pat.

"Isn't that nice!" said Daddy, in a hearty sort of voice. "Of course they'll come, Pat. Now, off you go, Taggertys. Want a leg-up over the wall?"

"Good-bye," said Mother, faintly. The Taggertys were really too much for her.

213

"Good-bye!" yelled John—suddenly feeling pleased at the invitation to tea. "Tell Dopey I'll see him tomorrow. Good-bye!"

He went down the garden a little way after the departing guests. Pat slipped back to him. "I say," he said, "isn't your father a sport? He's wizard! I wish mine was as jolly as that—but he's the quiet sort. I do really like your father awfully."

John felt a glow of pride. He grinned at Pat. "He's not a bad sort," he said. "I'm glad you like him. Well, see you tomorrow. Tell Dopey to behave himself till I come."

CHAPTER EIGHT

Visiting the Taggertys

THE next morning Pat popped his head over the wall when he heard John playing with Margery.

"I say! My mother says will you put on your oldest clothes, please, when you come this afternoon, and we can really play some exciting games? Come early. Can't you come at three?"

John's eyes shone. Exciting games! Would that mean Red Indians—and crawling on his tummy, with Dopey crawling beside him? That would be fun.

"Yes, we'll put on old clothes," he said. "And we'll come at three. That's if Mother lets us."

"We're going to have a picnic tea under the weeping willow," said Pat. "Don't you think that's an exciting

214

sort of tree, John? It's like a big round green cave. We play that it's our home and we're quite safe there."

"That's what Margery and I said, when we came over into your garden before you moved in," said John.

Annette and Margery were not so keen as John on putting on old clothes. Annette loved dressing up and looking pretty. She enjoyed hearing people say how pretty and dainty she was. Margery felt a bit scared of the "exciting games". She was afraid that Dopey would get excited, too, and gallop about in his mad, clumsy fashion.

Mother didn't much like the "old clothes" idea either. "Oh, dear. I suppose that means you will play dirty rough games."

"And we're having a picnic tea under that big weeping willow," said John happily.

"How do you know there's a big weeping willow?" asked Annette, at once. "You've never been into the Taggertys' garden."

"Shut up," said John, in a voice exactly like Pat's. Mother stared at him in horror.

"*John!* How *can* you talk like that to Annette? Why, you sounded just like Pat, with his rough talk to poor little Biddy."

John went red. He really felt a little shocked at himself too. Still, Annette was so awful, the way she kept trying to find out things, and the way she told tales. He didn't say he was sorry, and Mother looked quite upset.

"That's what I was afraid of," she said. "I thought you would pick up all sorts of horrid ways from those Taggerty children. If only your father hadn't found out that Mr. Taggerty was his old school friend!"

"Dopey will be there to play games with us, too," said John, trying to change the subject. And, as if he had just heard his name, Dopey appeared, wagging his tail hard, looking at them sideways, as if not quite sure whether he was welcome or not. He had leapt over the wall, and come to see them.

"There!" said Mother, annoyed. "I knew that tiresome dog would keep coming here if once we allowed him in. Go away! Shoo, Dopey! Go home. HOME!"

Dopey rolled over on his back and did his bicycling act. He didn't seem to know what the word "home" meant at all.

"Oh, Mother! He's really very clever, the way he does that," said John. "Dopey, we're coming to tea this afternoon."

"Woof," said Dopey, rolling himself over on to his four legs, and springing upright. He butted John with his head. John was delighted. He patted Dopey, and tickled him behind the ears.

"John, take that dreadful dog back to the Taggertys," said Mother. "He ran all over the beds, look."

"Oh, *Mother*! Let him stay a few minutes," begged John. "Anyway, if I do take him back he'll only jump over the wall again."

"I believe you really do like that nasty dog," said Margery.

"I do like him and he isn't nasty," said John. "You and Annette are such babies. You never like *any* dog."

"Well, you never did till now," said Margery, crossly.

"Now don't quarrel," said Mother. "Oh dear. I do hope you won't grow like the Taggertys."

Dopey did not stay very long. He went back to his beloved Taggerty children in a few minutes. But at intervals during the day he leapt over the wall to visit John. John really felt very flattered. Annette would not go down to the bottom of the garden at all, because she was so afraid of being leapt on by Dopey, who sprang over the wall very suddenly indeed.

"Like a kangaroo," said John. "Honestly, he's a clever dog. He oughtn't to be called Dopey."

At half-past two they put on what Mother called "old clothes." Actually they were very nice ones, perfectly clean and tidy. John groaned.

"Couldn't I put on those shorts I've grown out of, and that faded jersey, Mother? And look at Annette! That may be her last year's dress, but it looks as good as new. She will never be able to play games."

"I don't want to," said Annette, primly.

"Oh, you're hopeless," said John, putting on Pat's voice again. Annette looked as if she was going to cry.

John was about to yell out "cry-baby" when he saw his mother's face. She looked annoyed and cross—not a bit like Mother, really. John felt sure she was about to say that he was getting just like those Taggertys, so he didn't yell out "cry-baby." He just gave Annette a scornful look and turned away.

They left at ten-to-three to walk round to the Taggertys' house. Mother wouldn't hear of climbing over the wall. She said that wasn't a proper way of going out to tea at all.

"Now remember your manners," she said. "Don't snatch and grab and gobble at tea-time just because the Taggertys do. And remember to thank Mrs. Taggerty for having you. I should be most ashamed if I had to send you back to say it, like the Taggertys last night. And come home at six, please."

They set off. There were no Taggertys to greet them at the front gate. So they walked primly up the path and knocked at the door. It was opened by a surprised Bridget.

"Well, now, to think you've come all the way round like this! The children are at the bottom of the garden, waiting for you to get over the wall."

She took them through the house. It was very untidy. Coats, books, papers, toys, lay about everywhere. Out into the garden they went, and down to the bottom. No Taggertys were to be seen.

"Funny!" said John, staring round. Then suddenly there was a terrifying chorus of screams and yells and whoops, and from under some bushes scrambled the three Taggertys, waving what looked like knives in the air. They fell upon the startled guests, and Annette gave a terrified scream as one of the knives came down on her chest.

"They're killing me! Save me, John!"

But the knives were only made of rubber that bent as soon as the blunt points touched anything. The Taggertys shrieked with laughter at their guests' frightened faces, and threw themselves on the ground to roll about in joy. Dopey rolled with them.

"You frightened me! You shouldn't do that!" cried Margery, her heart beating fast. Annette was crying, but not very loudly in case Pat should turn on her.

John was sorry for Annette. He put his arm round her. "Don't cry, silly," he said. "It was just their fun."

"We waited for you to come over the wall, and hid to jump out at you," said Pat, sitting up. "Why *didn't* you come over the wall? And I say! Why have you got on nice clothes? We told you not to."

"These are our old clothes," said John.

"Well, they look better than our newest ones," said Maureen. "I say, didn't we give you an awful fright?"

"Let's have a look at your knife," said John. He took one. It really did look exactly like a real one. "I wish I had one like this," he said. "It's marvellous!" He drove it into his knee, and the rubber point bent to one side at once. "Mother would have a fit if she saw this. She'd think it was real."

"My uncle sent us them," said Pat. "If you like I'll write and tell him I've lost mine, then he'll send me another, and I'll give it to you."

"But you couldn't write a fib like that!" cried Margery. "You're awful, Pat. You don't seem to think anything of lying and being deceitful."

"I'll tell Mother," said Annette, pursing up her mouth. At once Biddy flew at her and battered her with her small fists.

"You dare tell of my Pat! You're a tell-tale! I hate you! You dare tell of my Pat!"

Annette was taken aback and almost fell over. Then she lashed out with her fist too and caught Biddy an unexpected blow on her shoulder. Pat roared with laughter.

"Look at the two of them! Go it, youngsters. That's right, hit out, Biddy! Go it, Annette!"

John separated the two angry little girls. "Stop it," he said. "Annette, you're a guest. You can't behave like this."

"Well, she shouldn't either then!" panted Annette. "Oh, oh, make Dopey go away!"

Dopey had come up to join in the battle, and was now dancing round on his hind legs, looking alarmingly tall. "Get down, Dopey," said Pat. "Enough, you two kids."

Annette tried to slap Biddy again. She got a hard slap from Pat at once. "Didn't you hear what I said?" he roared. "I said 'enough'! And enough it is. You'll do what I tell you when you're here, see?"

Annette looked at him, shocked at being slapped like that. John expected her to howl, and to run home to her mother to complain. But she didn't. She went very red and turned away. She turned her back on them all and said nothing.

"Let her alone," said Maureen. "She's been so spoilt she doesn't really know how to behave. She hasn't been kept in order like Biddy has."

"What shall we play?" said Pat, in an amiable voice.

He seemed to forget his spurts of temper immediately. He grinned at John. "Like to play Red Indians and see old Dopey wriggling along?"

"Oh *yes*!" said John at once. "But I do wish we had really old clothes on. I don't know how we can wriggle in these without making them filthy."

"Well, your mother won't mind, surely, seeing that we did warn you we wanted to play exciting games," said Pat. "Now then—we'll divide into two parties. You can be Big Noise Chief John, and I'll be Big Feather Chief. Maureen, go and get all the Red Indian things you can find. Buck up."

Maureen sped off. "Oh, are we going to wear Red Indian things?" asked John, happily.

"You bet," said Pat. "And we've got a wigwam too, only we've lost it in the move. It'll turn up some time, and we can use that for our tent. Now, I'll have Annette for one of my tribe. Come here, Annette. She fights so well she'll be useful to me."

Annette was startled to hear this. She half turned round, looking in astonishment at Pat. He held out his hand to her. "Come on, kid. You can be on my side."

To John's immense surprise, Annette walked over to Pat, looking pleased. And indeed she felt *very* pleased. Pat seemed a very strong, rough, fierce kind of boy to Annette, and to be chosen by him like this, after he had given her that hard slap, was surprising but somehow very pleasing.

"Then I'll have Biddy," said John. "And Margery too. You have Maureen. What do we do? Go stalking one another? Who will have Dopey? Can we?"

"Nobody has Dopey," said Pat. "He'll just belong to whatever party he likes. He'll go mad in a minute, when we begin, and wriggle and leap about and do some war-whoops on his own. Here comes Maureen!"

Up came Maureen with her arms full of Red Indian

things. There were six feather head-dresses, two of them with trails of feathers that fell from the head to the ground. "Chiefs' feathers," said Pat, handing one to John. "And here's a little one for you, Annette."

Annette put it on. She loved dressing up. "Do I look nice in it?" she asked, pulling her curls out beneath the feathers.

"No, awful," said Pat at once. He always squashed any attempt at "showing off" as he called it. "A perfect fright. Better not wear it."

But Annette wanted to wear it. She scampered about, feeling thrilled. Dopey capered with her, but for once she didn't mind.

Everyone was soon dressed up. "It's a pity Dopey can't wear feathers, too," said Biddy, eyeing him. "He'd be a very good Red Indian dog."

"No, he wouldn't. He's too noisy," said Pat. "Now you go down to the cave-tree, John, with your tribe, and I'll go right to the wall. Then we have to stalk one another and pounce. Prisoners can be taken and tied up—and we'll scalp them!"

Off they all went. Margery was trembling. This game was too exciting, she thought. Oh dear, there was Dopey coming with them. What a very licky dog he was!

CHAPTER NINE

Margery Wants to Go Home

THE game was indeed exciting. There was a lot of stalking and wriggling over the grass and under bushes, and at the end of it not one single child had tidy or clean clothes. It didn't matter a scrap to the Taggertys, for they all had on the oldest things imaginable, which had been half-dirty anyhow.

But the clean Carlton children soon looked very bedraggled. Annette didn't like it, but she didn't dare to say a word because she was with Pat. As for Margery, she was quite horrified. Only John didn't mind. He was being a real Red Indian and thinking of nothing else at all.

There was a great deal of yelling and whooping, dancing round, struggling, brandishing of rubber knives, and rolling over and over, with Dopey in the middle of everything. He did some marvellous wriggling on his tummy, but as he was too excited he barked all the time, and wasn't really a good Indian at all.

In the end, John, Biddy and Margery were all captured. Margery and Biddy were condemned by Pat to be tied to trees. John had to lie on the ground and pretend to be dead. But this was very difficult because Dopey didn't seem to understand that he was meant to be dead, and kept pawing at him and giving him great slobbering licks all over his face.

Biddy was used to being tied up to trees. She bore it bravely. But Margery was frightened. Pat had smeared some dirt over his face, and looked most alarming. He yelled in her ear, and brandished his rubber knife over her when he had tied her up.

"You're my prisoner! I shall scalp you!"

"Grrrrr!" growled Dopey, entering into the spirit of the game, and leaping up at poor Margery. She screamed. "Don't! Don't! I don't like this game. I want to go home. Untie me, untie me!"

Pat thought she was acting. He became even fiercer. Margery screamed piercingly, and John sat up.

"Pat! Shut up! She's really frightened."

"Good!" said Pat. "She ought to be frightened. She's my prisoner."

Someone appeared through the trees. It was Mrs. Taggerty. She, too, had heard Margery's piercing screams, and had heard the real fright in them.

"Pat! The child is really frightened," she said. "Untie her. I told you not to play rough games with the little Carltons. They're not mad like you are."

"I want to go home!" wept Margery. "I hate this game. I hate Pat, I hate Dopey. I want to go home."

Mrs. Taggerty untied her. "Now, you come and see my baby," she said.

"I want to go home," wept Margery, trembling.

Mrs. Taggerty put her arm round her. "Now don't you mind that rough boy of mine," she said. "I'll tell his father to whip him tonight for scaring you so. You shall go home if you want to. But come and see our baby first."

The others watched her go off with Mrs. Taggerty. "She's a cry-baby," said Annette, pleased to see Margery crying when she herself wasn't.

"She's not," said John, loyally. "You'd have howled your head off too if you'd been tied up and had Pat yelling round you. It's just that she's not used to it."

"She's a coward," said Pat.

223

"I tell you she's not," said John. "She's only a girl. You've been treating her as if she was a rough boy. She's too gentle for this kind of game. I ought to have thought of it."

Pat stared at him scornfully. "Is *that* how you treat your sisters?" he said. "Making them namby-pamby little sissies? Pooh!"

John was angry. "Look here!" he said, "hasn't your father ever told you how to treat girls? They're not so strong and rough and brave as boys and we've got to remember that and look after them. See? And stick up for them. And not hit them."

"Well, I wish I'd given Margery a good slap when I had the chance," said Pat, gloomily. "Now I shall get a hiding from Dad tonight for treating her badly. How was I to know she was such a silly? Is she always like that?"

"She's scared of lots of things," said John. "Dogs and mice and bats and storms—really she is."

"Well, I hope she never comes here again," said Pat. "I don't expect she'll want to, anyhow. What shall we play at now?"

"Let's paddle in the goldfish pond," said Biddy. "It's so hot. It would be lovely to get our feet cool and wet."

"Ooooh!" said Annette, surprised. "Are you allowed to do that?"

"Of course!" Biddy said scornfully, and began to take off her shoes. Maureen and Pat did the same. John and Annette hardly knew what to do. Paddling in the pond! What *would* Mother say?

But it looked so tempting. John peeled off his socks and shoes, too, and so did Annette.

"Mind the goldfish don't nibble your toes, Annette," said Pat, paddling in the pond. Annette hesitated. She didn't want her toes nibbled.

"Go on! He's only teasing," said Maureen, giving

the little girl a friendly push. "Haven't you ever been teased before, silly? You'll have to get used to it if you play with us."

Soon the five of them were happily paddling in the cool water. Then they sat on the edge with their feet still in. "I wonder what's happened to Margery," said John. "I do hope she hasn't gone home. Mother won't like it."

"What a lot of things your mother doesn't like," said Pat, wriggling his toes in the water. "Shut up splashing, Dopey. Golly, look at the waves he's making. Your mother must be rather tiresome sometimes, John."

"Don't say things like that about my mother," said John, frowning. "You oughtn't to say things against your parents to anybody. It's a beastly thing to do."

"All right, all right," said Pat. "Look, there's Margery with Mummy. She hasn't gone home after all."

Margery had really meant to go home at once, without any delay at all. But Mrs. Taggerty took her to the pram where the baby lay, and showed him to her.

The baby, Michael, lay on his back in the pram with his brilliant blue eyes wide open. He had dark curls clustering all round his head. His lips were very red, and he was as brown as an acorn.

He looked up at Margery, puzzled. Hers was not a face he knew. Margery stared down at him solemnly, tears still wet on her cheeks.

The baby suddenly smiled at her, and chuckled. Then he reached out a small, plump hand, with wrinkles of fat round the wrist, and tried to touch her. She gave him one of her fingers to hold and at once his own baby fingers closed tightly round it. He gurgled.

"Oh!" said Margery in delight. "He's holding my finger as if he'd never let it go, Mrs. Taggerty. And look at him smiling at me! He's lovely—like a real live doll."

225

He reached out a small, plump hand

"He *is* a lovely baby, isn't he?" said Mrs. Taggerty. "They all were, the little rascals, every one of them. Ah, it's nice to see him lying so quiet and good in his pram there, but soon he'll be yelling and rushing round with the rest of them. He likes you, Margery. Hear him gurgling to you!"

"Coo," said the baby, "coo-coo. Gah!"

He suddenly tried to sit up, for he was a strong little thing. He still held Margery's finger.

"Do you think I could hold him for a minute?" asked Margery eagerly. "I've always wanted to hold a real live, warm baby, Mrs. Taggerty, but I never have."

"Of course you can," said Mrs. Taggerty. "It's nice to see you wanting to fuss him a bit. The others haven't much use for him yet, because he can't play, and he yells if they frighten him. They're a rough lot, the three of them! Now—hold out your arms—that's right! Here he is!"

The sweet-smelling, plump little baby was placed in Margery's outstretched arms. She sighed in delight. He felt so warm and cuddly—better than any doll she had ever had. "He's a darling," she said. "I love him. Can I sit down somewhere and hold him?"

"Well, would you like to sit down on a rug in the sunshine, and nurse him a bit?" asked Mrs. Taggerty, putting a rug down on the grass. "But don't you want to go home? You go if you want to, dear. I won't keep you here a minute if you don't want to stay."

"Well," said Margery, looking down at the smiling baby, "well—I think I'll stay a bit longer, if you'll let me hold Michael. I do love him."

She sat there in the sun, nursing the plump baby blissfully. She saw the others paddling, but she took no notice. She was much happier with this gurgling baby!

"I suppose I couldn't sometimes take him out in the pram for you, could I?" she said to Mrs. Taggerty, who sat beside her, knitting a blue coat for the baby.

"Well, that would be really sweet of you," said Mrs. Taggerty, gratefully. "You see, I'm always so busy, and so is Bridget, and none of the children will bother with Michael. They make such a noise in the garden, too, when he ought to be asleep. It would be lovely if you could sometimes wheel him down the road and back."

Margery felt very happy. She liked all little helpless things like babies and kittens, although she was so scared of even smaller things such as bats and mice. "I'll come every day of the holidays and take him out," she promised.

Bridget suddenly appeared with an enormous loaded tray. There were glasses on it, and a large jug of iced lemonade, with the lemon rings still floating in it. There were plates of thick bread-and-butter, and a great jar of golden honey. There were buns cut in half and smeared with jam and butter, and an enormous home-made cake.

"Tea!" yelled Pat. "Hurrah! I thought you'd forgotten us, Bridget! We're going to have it under the willow-tree."

John ran to help Bridget, though Pat made no move to go to her aid at all. Bridget beamed down at John. "Well, if it isn't nice to see some good manners in a boy! See, Mrs. Taggerty, madam, here's a boy who'll help my poor tired old arms. There's manners for you!"

Soon they were all sitting down in the cave-tree, its green light shining over everything. "Now for a good tuck-in!" said Pat. "My word, I'm jolly hungry."

CHAPTER TEN

After Tea

MRS. TAGGERTY took the baby from Margery. "Do you want to run home to tea now?" she asked. "I must take the baby in and change him. You run home if you like. And I'll see that rough Pat of mine gets a whipping to-night for scaring you so. He's no right to treat visitors like that and well he knows it."

"Please don't have him whipped," said Margery. "I don't want him to be. I feel better now and I don't want to go home. I'd like to go and have tea with the others. It did look such a nice tea."

"All right, I won't have him punished if you don't want him to be," said Mrs. Taggerty. "I'm glad you don't bear malice. Pat's got a good heart, really, but he's headstrong and he's got no manners at all. I'm hoping maybe you three will teach him some!"

Margery got up and walked over to the others. She went inside the cave-tree. "Hallo! Aren't you going home after all?" asked Maureen.

"No," said Margery. "And, Pat, you're not going to be whipped tonight. I asked your mother not to let you be. I don't know why I was so silly and scared."

Pat grinned his wide grin at Margery. "Thanks!" he said. "Sorry I scared you. Only my fun, really. Have a bit of bread-and-butter?"

All six children were very hungry, for the Taggertys had their tea late. They worked their way through the thick buttery slices of bread, and John discovered that he much preferred a good thick slice to the thin ones he had at home. You could really get your teeth into a thick slice.

The Taggertys had no manners at tea-time. Except for the one time that Pat offered Margery the bread-and-butter, nobody passed the Carltons anything. At first they sat patiently with empty plates, waiting to be asked. Then Annette got cross when she saw Biddy spreading honey on her fifth slice of bread-and-butter, without even asking her if she, too, would like some.

"You're awfully rude," she said to Biddy. "I've sat here ages with an empty plate. Why don't you offer me something? Don't you know you ought to look after your guests?"

"Can't you help yourself, silly?" said Biddy. "Grab, like we do, or you won't get anything."

Mrs. Taggerty's voice came across the garden. "Are you children all right? Pat, are you remembering to look after your guests? Pass them food when their plates are empty and see that they have plenty to eat."

"Yes, Mummy. We're looking after them well!" called back Pat at once.

"You are an awful fibber," said John, helping himself to a jammy bun. "Why can't you say you're not doing your best to look after us, but you will? Anyway, don't bother. I'll help myself. You gobble so fast that if we wait till we're asked we'll get no tea at all."

Everyone laughed. Maureen actually offered Margery a bun. The buns were lovely. So was the fruity homemade cake. Pat cut the slices, and they were enormous ones. Margery couldn't help comparing them to the thin little slices they had at home. These big, thick slices looked rude and greedy, but they really were lovely and big when you were hungry.

The lemonade was delicious too. The Carltons always had milk for tea at home, and it was a change to have this lovely sweet lemonade. They enjoyed themselves thoroughly. As for Dopey, he did very well indeed, accepting tit-bits from all the Taggertys in turn. Socks the black cat joined them too, and ate bits of bread-and-butter very daintily and primly.

"She's funny," said Pat. "Although she knows that if she doesn't eat quickly Dopey will gobble up her food, she never will hurry. She reminds me of Margery! You nibble, too, Margery."

"Does Socks scratch?" asked Margery, rather afraid of the big green-eyed cat, who suddenly stretched out her front paws and showed her claws.

"Rather!" said Pat. "Look out she doesn't give you a scratch all down your bare leg."

"He's only teasing," said Maureen, seeing Margery's look of alarm. "It's all right. Socks only scratches if you chase her or pull her tail. Would you like to see my pet mice? I've got three, Woffles, Wiffles and Wonky."

"Oh *no*!" cried Margery in horror.

"Let's put one down her neck," suggested Biddy. Margery squealed.

"Be quiet, Biddy," said John. "You can see she's afraid of such a thing."

After tea Pat suggested a spot of tree-climbing. "There's a fine chestnut at one side of the garden," he said. "Not far from the bottom. Let's go and climb it. Come on, girls. We'll pretend the tree is a pirate-ship— our ship—and that we're sailing to lands far away."

"What about all these tea-things?" asked John. "Oughtn't we to take them in?"

"Oh, let Bridget," said Pat, impatiently, and tore off down the garden. Bridget appeared at that moment, and John and Margery helped her to pick up the picnic things and load her tray with them. Annette had disappeared with the others.

"There now! Didn't I say those children had the best manners in the world," called Bridget to Mrs. Taggerty, who was rocking the baby gently in his pram. "Picked up all the tea-things for me, they have, and put them on my tray."

John and Margery went to join the others. Margery pulled at John's sleeve. "Don't climb trees! I know *I* can't. And Mother wouldn't like it."

"But we've got old clothes on," said John, suddenly feeling that he couldn't possibly say he wouldn't climb a tree, and face Pat's scorn. "You don't need to climb one. But *I* shall."

"You've never climbed one in your life." said Margery. "Never. You'll fall. You just see if you don't."

Pat was half-way up the tree when they got there. He called down to them, "Come on. It's fine up here. There's a bit of a wind and the tree sways just like a ship at sea."

Maureen was nearly up to him. Biddy was swarming up too, calling to Maureen to help her.

"Hey, John! Come on up quickly," shouted Pat. "We two will watch out for sails on the horizon. Buck up!"

John valiantly began to climb. He wasn't used to it,

and he was, besides, a little afraid of falling. He half-wished he hadn't begun, especially when his shirt caught on a twig and held fast there. He dragged himself away and the shirt tore. Bother!

"John's not very good at climbing!" cried Maureen, peering down. "Do come on, John. Where's Margery? I suppose Annette's too small to come."

"She's a baby," announced Biddy, from half-way up the tree. "*She* can't climb, can she, Pat? I'm a good climber. You always say so."

To Margery's immense astonishment Annette suddenly tried to swing herself up on the first branch. "I'm coming too!" she shouted. "I *can* climb. I'm a very good climber! It's Margery that can't climb."

Annette managed to get quite a long way up the tree. She felt very proud when Pat called down to her, "Jolly good, Annette. I didn't think you had it in you. Come up higher. John's here."

But Annette didn't want to go any higher. She was beginning to be afraid. She didn't say so, though. She sat just below Biddy, and peered out between the branches, holding on firmly with both hands.

It was exciting up the tree. John thought it was grand. He felt the tree sway in the wind. He looked down on his own garden, and it seemed very far below. He was excited and pleased. Why had he never climbed a tree before?

All the children forgot the time. Six o'clock had gone a long time before. Now it was a quarter to seven. Mr. Carlton was home. He and Mother walked down to the bottom of the garden to see if there was any sign of the children.

"I told them six o'clock," said Mother, vexed. "I wonder what they're doing. They made a frightful noise this afternoon. How that Taggerty baby ever manages to go to sleep I don't know."

They came to the bottom of the garden. They were tall enough to look over the wall, but there were no children to be seen.

Not far off, high above them, were the five children in the tree. Margery was at the foot alone. Pat suddenly saw Mr. and Mrs. Carlton and gave a loud and piercing yell.

"Hey! Uncle Peter! Mrs. Carlton! Here we are! Up in the tree! Annette is here too. HEY!"

What a shock for the Carlton children's mother! She stared in horror. "Come down at once!" she said. "Come down at once!"

The five children gazed down at her. "Hallo, Daddy!" cried John. "Look how high I am!"

Mr. Carlton laughed to see so many faces peering out at him from the tree. "Good for you, John," he said. "And is that really Annette I see up there too? Where's Margery?"

"She's afraid to come," said Annette, importantly. "But I wasn't. Margery wanted to go home before tea, Daddy."

"Shut up!" said Pat, John and Maureen all together. Annette shut up. Pat tried to reach her with his foot. "Tell-tale!" he said.

Mrs. Carlton was still looking up in horror. "John! You know I don't like you to climb trees—and I can't *believe* Annette is up there too! She might fall and break her leg. Peter, go over and get her down before she falls."

Mr. Taggerty came down the garden at that moment and the children hailed him eagerly.

"Daddy! We're up the chestnut tree! And look, there's Uncle Peter over the wall."

John saw his mother's displeased, anxious face and began to climb down. Mr. Taggerty lifted Annette

233

down. "There you are! My word, you're just as much of a monkey as Biddy, climbing trees like that!"

Mrs. Carlton gazed in dismay at her three children. They were so dirty, so untidy, their clothes were so torn —and surely they were wet, too? What *could* they have been doing, with those dreadful Taggerty children?

Daddy lifted them over the wall. Mother eyed them in silence. They looked down at their dirty, torn clothes, and felt very guilty.

"Well, Mother, we did ask you to let us have old clothes on," began John. "It's no good playing in the garden with the Taggertys unless we do."

"Come along to the house," said Mother, in a cold voice. "You're very late. I said six o'clock and it's nearly seven."

They followed her, feeling rather flat after their exciting afternoon. "Mother, I nursed the baby," said Margery. "He's so lovely and soft."

Mother said nothing. Then Mr. Carlton spoke to John. "I suppose you thanked Mrs. Taggerty for having you?" he asked. The three children stopped dead.

"Gracious, no! But it isn't our fault, Daddy. Mother made us come back so quickly we didn't have time."

"Well, go back and thank her at once," said Daddy. "I'm surprised Mother didn't say something about it."

The children went back to thank Mrs. Taggerty. Their mother turned to their father. "I was too upset to think of anything but John and Annette up that high tree," she said. "And oh, what little ragamuffins they look. Just like the Taggertys."

"Never mind. John looked a real boy for once in a way—and Annette forgot to be a spoilt baby," said Daddy. "I only wish Margery had been at the top of the tree too!"

CHAPTER ELEVEN

A Horrid Quarrel

THAT was the beginning of the friendship between the Taggerty children and the Carltons. Although John's mother was cross and disgusted at their appearance when they got back from tea that first time, she did allow them to put on really old clothes the next time. And the Taggertys too appeared in their oldest clothes when they came to play with the Carltons.

John soon began to revel in all the exciting games the Taggertys played, Red Indians, Burglars and Policeman, Pirates, Dragons, Witches and the rest of them. He became what Daddy called a "real boy", and actually asked to go with him one afternoon when Daddy was setting off for one of his long walks.

Annette, instead of hating Pat for his straight speaking, and the few slaps he gave her when she annoyed him, admired him immensely. She stopped telling tales. She stopped crying. She even stopped showing off, and that was very difficult for her. If only she could be with him she would stand anything, it seemed!

Margery was the only one who didn't like joining in their rough games. "Well, don't come with us then," John would say, impatiently. "Stay at home with your dolls!"

But there was one thing that drew Margery to the Taggertys more than any other, and that was the baby. She really loved him. All the Taggertys loved him, but only Margery would trouble to nurse him, and talk to him for hours, and play with him. He loved her.

235

The Taggertys never seemed to go to church or to Sunday School. They wore the same old clothes on Sunday as on any other day, and they made just as much noise.

"Why do you go to Sunday School this lovely sunny afternoon?" said Pat impatiently one Sunday, when he wanted John to come paddling in the pond with him. "It's so hot. A paddle would be lovely. And after tea we're going to play shops in the summer-house. We've got real money. We hoped you'd come."

"We always do go to Sunday School," said John. "And we like it. Why don't you come too? Doesn't your mother want you to go?"

"Yes. But she says it's too much bother to make us," said Maureen.

"Don't you say your prayers at night either?" asked Annette, who always prayed most fervently, and never forgot to ask God to bless even her smallest doll.

"Sometimes I do," said Maureen. "Mostly I forget. It doesn't matter."

"It *does* matter," said Margery, shocked. "Why, you behave like heathens, not like Christians. If you went to church, and listened to stories at Sunday School, you'd know lots of things you *don't* seem to know— like why it's wrong to tell as many fibs as you do, and why you should be kind to others, and why . . ."

"I don't want to know things like that," said Pat. "They're boring. You're goody-goody! Fancy wanting to go to Sunday School when you could go paddling in our pond. And I thought if Mummy wasn't about we might even bathe! Come on, do. You could pretend to start out for Sunday School, but really you could come round to us. You could always say you'd *been* to Sunday School, if your mother asked you."

All three Carltons were shocked at this. "You're hopeless," said John at last. "Sometimes I think you're really bad. You'll get an awful punishment some day, I should think. You can tell untruths all you like and be as deceitful as you want to be—but we *shan't*! We'd *like* to paddle, and we'd *love* to bathe—but not if we have to tell stories about it, and deceive Mother! That's not being goody-goody. It's just not being deceitful."

"You don't love your mother if you want to deceive her like that," said Margery to Pat.

"I do," said Pat, looking fierce. "She's the best mother in the world. And yours is awful!"

This was really the last straw. John went flaming red, and slapped Pat across the face. "I'll never speak to you again!" he said.

"Want a fight, do you?" said Pat, his face showing a red mark where John's hand had slapped him. "All right, come along. I'm ready!"

"Not on Sunday, John! Oh, John, don't fight now. It's time we went to Sunday School," said Margery, almost in tears. Annette watched in silence, half scared.

"All right," said John. He turned to Pat. "I'll fight you tomorrow. Not today. And if you ever dare to say again that my mother's awful, I'll give you an even harder blow."

"You're afraid to fight," said Pat scornfully. "Cowardy-custard! Afraid to fight! Wants to go to Sunday School instead. Pooh, baby! Go along, then. We won't fight today or tomorrow either, little funk. We Taggertys don't want to have ANY MORE TO DO WITH YOU AT ALL. Good-bye for ever."

Pat disappeared. The three Carltons heard footsteps running up the garden. They were all very distressed. "I shouldn't have hit him like that," said John. "But I can't bear him to talk of Mother in that horrid way. It's disloyal to listen."

"He's bad, but I do want to play with him again,"

237

whimpered Annette. Margery was white. She took Annette's hand.

"Come along. It's time we went," she said. "Oh, John—do you think Pat meant what he said? If we never go there again, I'll never see Michael."

"What's that matter?" said John. "You're silly over that baby. And I tell you this—and you too, Annette— we are *NOT* going to have any more to do with the Taggertys."

And off they went to Sunday School, where poor Margery prayed a very muddled and anxious prayer all about not wanting to play with the Taggertys any more, but please, please, God, could she still see the baby?

They heard the Taggertys screaming and yelling very loudly indeed that evening. "They can't be playing shops," said Margery. "Even *they* couldn't make such a noise over just shopping. They're playing some noisy game on purpose for us to hear."

"Shall we tell Mother what has happened?" asked Annette, who never could resist passing everything on to her mother, much to the annoyance of the others.

"Certainly not," said John at once. "That would be sneaking, Annette. Gracious, surely you wouldn't be a sneak, after all that everyone has done to stop you?"

"No, I wouldn't," said Annette. "Goodness, what a noise! I'm sure all the neighbours will complain."

They did, and in a short while there was silence at the Taggertys'. Margery said she thought she heard someone crying.

"Perhaps it was Pat, having a caning," said Annette.

"Pooh! You know he wouldn't cry out loud," said John. "Even if he cried at all! I've never seen him cry yet."

"*You* nearly cried yesterday," said Annette, "when you twisted your ankle jumping. I saw tears in your eyes, though you pretended to be laughing."

238

"Shut up," said John, fiercely, in a voice like Pat's. Annette shut up. Then the bell rang for her bed-time and she went off.

There was no sign from the Taggertys the next day. The Carltons played in their own garden, and they could hear the Taggertys play in theirs, though they were not nearly so noisy as usual. John, Margery and Annette were playing hide-and-seek after tea, and it was Margery's turn to look for the others. She stood by the wall, counting a hundred, when she heard a whisper.

She looked up. Maureen was peeping over the wall. "Margery! Our baby's hurt himself. He fell out of his pram."

Margery's heart stopped still. She forgot all about the dreadful quarrel. "Where is he?" she asked.

"In his cot," said Maureen. "He keeps crying. Mummy said she did wish you'd been in today, because he's always so good with you."

"I'm coming over," said Margery at once.

"But Pat says we're never to have anything to do with you again," said Maureen, looking woebegone.

"I don't care," said Margery. "I'm coming over to see Michael. Poor, poor little Michael. Oh, I do hope he'll soon be all right again. Did he hurt his head when he fell?"

She climbed over quickly. Annette, peering out of her hiding-place, was filled with astonishment to see her go over the wall. She called to John.

"Margery's gone to the Taggertys. I saw her!"

"Then she's a nasty, underhand, double-faced untrustable little beast," said John, trying to think of all the horrid words he knew. "I *said* we wouldn't have any more to do with them. Wait till she comes back!"

He wandered off up to the house by himself, very angry. He wouldn't speak to Margery for days, once he

239

had told her what he thought of her, the nasty little thing!

Annette was left alone at the bottom of the garden. She went to the garden-roller and stood on it, wondering if she could see Margery. But Margery wasn't there.

Biddy was there, on her way to the wall. She looked up and saw Annette. Annette was about to bob down with a scowl when Biddy hailed her in a loud whisper.

"Annette! Quick, Annette! I've got some news."

"What?" asked Annette, curiously.

"We've got four dear little kittens!" said Biddy, proudly. "One's all black, one's tabby, one's black-and-white, and one's *exactly* like Socks!"

"Do they belong to Socks?" asked Annette, thrilled.

"Yes. She borned them last night," said Biddy. "She's licked them till they're lovely. Come and see them."

"John said——"

"I know. So did Pat," said Biddy. "But you simply *must* see the kittens. Socks is so proud of them. She's in a basket in the kitchen. Do come. I know we're in the middle of a big quarrel but we didn't know Socks was having kittens, and you really must see them while they're so weeny."

Annette climbed over the wall. Soon she was in the kitchen with Biddy, and the two of them were looking with delight at the four tiny kittens beside Socks. Socks purred proudly and licked each one.

"Oh, how I would like that one that's just like Socks!" said Annette. "We've never never had a pet, not even a cat to kill the mice. I do wish I could have a kitten."

"I'll give you the one like Socks, if you like—if Mummy says so," said Biddy. "And I'm sure she will. You can have it for your own when it's old enough. It would be better than any doll."

"Oh, Biddy! Ask your mother," begged Annette. "And I'll ask mine. But mine will be the difficult one. Mother doesn't like 'animals."

"Well, ask your father then," said Biddy. "He simply adores animals, doesn't he? Even our pet mice. He'll coax your mother to let you have it. You ask him."

This seemed a very good idea indeed. Annette stroked Socks and began to plan all kinds of things for the kitten—a blue ribbon—a fine basket—a little ball!

John couldn't find Annette when he went down the garden again. He looked at the wall. Surely Annette hadn't gone over too? What were the two girls thinking of? He felt very angry indeed.

"I'll go over too!" he thought. "And I'll find Pat, and make him take back what he called me—a cowardy-custard indeed. If he doesn't—I'll fight him!"

CHAPTER TWELVE

Making It Up

HE climbed over the wall and went into the Taggertys' garden. No Annette, no Biddy, no Maureen, no Margery. Not even Dopey! How strange.

Suddenly he heard a dismal whining. It came from the washhouse. It was so very dismal that John couldn't bear it. Dopey was locked up. Why?

He crept cautiously to the washhouse door. He looked in at the window. Pat was sitting with his arm round Dopey's neck. To John's intense surprise Pat was crying. Yes, actually a tear rolled down his cheek. What was up?

He opened the washhouse door and went in. Pat glared up at him, and wiped away the one tear fiercely.

"Get out!" he said.

"What's up?" asked John.

"Dopey went mad this afternoon, when we were playing some jumping game, and he leapt on top of the pram and knocked it half over," said Pat. "Baby fell out and hurt himself. And Bridget got a whip and whipped Dopey till he cried. He's still crying. I can't bear it. Dopey didn't mean to knock the pram over."

Dopey whined dolefully. He didn't understand why he had been whipped. He nestled closer to Pat.

John forgot what he had come for. He was very upset about Dopey, too. "Didn't Bridget understand that he did it by *accident*?" he said indignantly, and sat down on the other side of the big dog. Dopey gave a ponderous sigh and licked John on the nose. "How mean of Bridget! How long is Dopey to be locked up?"

"Till he's given away," Pat said mournfully, and looked so miserable that John couldn't bear it.

"Given away! Do you mean to say Dopey's to go?" he asked in horror.

"Well, that's what they all say," said Pat. "I can't live without him. Nobody believes me when I say that, but it's true."

John felt quite certain it was true. He was sure he would feel the same if Dopey belonged to *him*. Dopey was so idiotic and lovable and eager and affectionate. John's heart sank when he thought that Dopey might be sent away and never come back again.

"Pat," he said, in a low voice, "we'll see that he isn't sent away. I could hide him in our shed, if only he wouldn't make a noise."

Pat looked hopeful for a moment. Then he shook his head. "But he *would* make a noise. You know he would. Thanks awfully all the same, John."

242

*John forgot what he had come for. He was
very upset about Dopey, too*

There was a silence. Dopey whined a little and the two boys patted him. "What did you come for?" asked Pat, after a while. "Did you want something?"

"Well," said John, looking uncomfortable, "I really came over to fight you, as a matter of fact. You made me so angry, you know."

"You made me angry, too," said Pat. "You'd better not slap me again like that."

"I'm sorry about that," said John, "especially now I know about Dopey."

"We'd better be friends again, hadn't we?" said Pat. "I take back all I said and apologize."

John felt better at once. "So do I," he said, and for once he bore no malice, but felt exactly the same towards Pat as he had done before the quarrel.

Margery was in the night nursery with the baby. Mrs. Taggerty was there, looking worried. But since Margery had come Michael was happier. He had stopped crying, and had taken hold of Margery's finger in the way she loved. Then he suddenly smiled at her.

"Look at that!" said Mrs. Taggerty, relieved. "He'd not smile like that unless he was feeling himself again, bless him. He's getting over the shock. Except for the bump on his head he'll soon be all right."

"I'd better go back home now," said Margery, getting up. "I didn't tell Mother I was coming, and she may be wanting me. I'm so glad Michael's better, Mrs. Taggerty. I'll come in tomorrow and nurse him, shall I?"

"Yes, you do," said Mrs. Taggerty. "He's always so good with you. Hallo, here's little Annette!"

Annette tiptoed in with Biddy. Margery looked at her in surprise. Why had she climbed over the wall? Had she disobeyed John too?

"Mrs. Taggerty," began Annette, eagerly, in a whisper, "could I have one of Socks's new kittens, please, when it's old enough—if Mother says I may? Please do let me. I'll take such care of it. I shall call it Whitefeet."

"Yes, of course you can," said Mrs. Taggerty, smiling. "You ask permission and you can certainly have little Whitefeet. What a pretty name!"

Annette's face glowed. She was just about to thank Mrs. Taggerty when somebody else tiptoed into the nursery. This time it was John. He looked most surprised to see Margery and Biddy there, and they both looked guilty.

"Mrs. Taggerty," began John, "Pat is so upset about Dopey being sent away. Couldn't you please keep him? He didn't mean to knock the pram over I'm sure he'll never do it again. Pat's so miserable."

Margery and Annette stared at John in surprise Why, surely John had a fierce quarrel with Pat, and was never, never going to have any more to do with him.

"*Will* you keep Dopey?" asked John, again. "Dopey would pine away if you didn't, Mrs. Taggerty. Do, do keep poor Dopey. Pat would die without him! You wouldn't like that."

"I would not," said Mrs. Taggerty, and a little tiny twinkle came in her eyes. "Well, we'll see. Maybe if Pat tries not to be so noisy when Baby is asleep, and keeps Dopey quiet too, I'll keep him."

"Oh, *thank* you, Mrs. Taggerty!" said John, fervently. "How's Michael?"

But without waiting for an answer he sped off to find Pat and tell him that Dopey might not be sent away after all. The others followed him. Soon they were all in the washhouse comforting Dopey, who enjoyed the attention very much indeed. Even Margery was glad

245

that he wasn't to be sent away, for she too knew he had upset the pram by accident.

"Well—the quarrel's ended," said Pat, looking round at everyone with his usual grin. "Funny! I was absolutely *determined* never to speak to any of you again—and here we are, the best of friends. You were very decent about it, John."

After that things went on much the same as usual. Dopey was not sent away. Michael soon recovered from the shock of falling out of his pram, and he really had not hurt himself very much. Annette's kitten grew rapidly, and she watched it squirming about in Socks's basket every day, and wondered when she dared ask her father if she could have it.

She had quite decided not to ask her mother. Mother would say "No!" at once. But Daddy liked animals. She wondered if Daddy would think she had gone behind Mother's back, if she asked him first and said nothing to Mother about it?

Fortunately her birthday was coming along soon, and people always asked her what she wanted most. Daddy would too. Then she could ask about the kitten.

Sure enough, one morning Daddy asked her the question she was waiting for. "Well, Annette? You'll be six soon. What do you want for your birthday?"

"There's something I want most terribly," said Annette. Daddy smiled.

"What is it? A new doll?"

"No. Something much, much nicer," said Annette. "And oh, Daddy, it won't cost you any money at all. But it's something I'll really *love* to have for my very own."

"Whatever is it?" asked Daddy, curiously. Mother smiled too, wondering what made Annette so serious.

"I want a kitten," said Annette, earnestly. "The one

I want belongs to Socks, and it's exactly like her. Biddy says I can have it, and Mrs. Taggerty says so too. Can I, Daddy?"

"I don't see why not," began Daddy, and the three children whooped in delight. Annette flung herself on her father. "Daddy! You darling! I'm going to call it Whitefeet and I'm saving up for a basket for it."

Mother didn't say anything. She didn't want a cat in the house, but how could she bear to disappoint her precious little Annette, when Daddy had already said he didn't see why she shouldn't have the kitten? Oh dear. Those Taggertys were at the bottom of everything.

Annette flew to tell Biddy. The two little girls told Socks, and she listened, purring. "I'll be very, very good to your kitten, Socks," said Annette. "You can trust me. I'll love it and look after it well. Just as well as you look after them all."

There were no more big quarrels after that. The two families were beginning to respect one another, and copy one another too. John was much more of a boy, to his father's delight. Margery was no longer scared of Dopey, and even consented to look at the pet mice. Annette was full of respect and admiration for Pat, who ordered her about and ticked her off just as he did Biddy.

Annette no longer told tales, and only cried when the others were not there. She didn't dare to show off any more in front of the Taggertys, and was a nicer little girl altogether.

And the Taggertys even copied the Carltons in a few ways! Their manners were better, they didn't think it was so clever to tell fibs, though they still told them. Pat was more mannerly and gentle to Biddy and Maureen, as John was to his own sisters. The two

247

fathers were pleased to see the effect each family had on the other.

"They're so different," said Mr. Taggerty. "Yours are so gentle, compared with mine, and I must say they are very well brought up, Peter, and have some very nice ideas. Mine are a set of ragamuffins, I know. Their mother hasn't had much time to see to them properly. She's been ill a lot, you know, and although she looks so well and strong she isn't really."

"Oh, they're a fine set of children," said Mr. Carlton warmly. "They've done mine a lot of good, as I thought they would. I got worried about John—a little mother's boy he seemed to me—but now that he climbs trees and goes for walks and rags about with the others, he's quite different."

The two fathers often smoked and talked together, renewing their old schoolboy friendship. The two mothers sometimes called on one another and talked too.

Mrs. Carlton grew to like the lively, cheerful, easy-going Mrs. Taggerty. She saw how much her children loved her and clung round her, though they were sometimes cheeky and disobedient.

And Mrs. Taggerty liked and admired the neat, well-dressed Mrs. Carlton, and sighed when she thought how beautifully she had brought up her three children, and how badly-behaved the Taggertys always seemed to be, compared with the Carltons.

"I suppose it's my fault," she said to Mrs. Carlton. "But I've really been ill so much, though I'm better now, and if children are left to themselves they just grow into little scamps. I don't believe mine know Sundays from weekdays!"

"Well, that's easily put right," said Mrs. Carlton. "I'd be very pleased to take them to church with us on

248

Sundays, and they could go to Sunday School in the afternoons with mine, too. They do so love all they do at Sunday School, you know."

"Oh, mine wouldn't go if I asked them!" said Mrs. Taggerty. "And there's their prayers, too, and all the other things they ought to know—they're little heathens, it seems to me."

Mrs. Carlton thought so too. What a pity! Well, her own three hadn't had much effect on the Taggertys in some ways. "You'll have more time to teach Michael, I expect," she said, as she rose to go. "Margery will help. She loves him, you know. Good-bye, Mrs. Taggerty, I *have* enjoyed coming to tea with you."

CHAPTER THIRTEEN

I Dare You!

THE cave-tree, the pond and the summer-house were all lovely places to play games in. The cave-tree could be a big wigwam, a cave inside a green mountain, a house and all kinds of things. The pond could be the sea, or a big lake. It was never just a pond. The summer-house could be a house to live in, a shop, a school, a castle, and half-a-hundred other things.

Compared with their own garden, the garden of the Taggertys seemed a perfect playground to the Carltons. Mother could never understand why.

"Our garden is so much *nicer*," she said. "The beds are full of flowers, the paths are trimly kept, the grass is properly cut. Why do you always want to go into the Taggertys' garden?"

"Oh—it's *much* more exciting!" said John. "But Mother, we're going to help Mr. Taggerty to tidy up the top part, near the house. He's asked us to. I do think Pat and the others might help him, but they won't."

It was a funny thing, but though Pat would tire himself out playing Red Indians, or chasing for hours up and down the garden, he was always too tired or too lazy to help to tidy up the garden, to carry things for Bridget, or even to fetch anything for his mother.

He didn't mind taking Dopey for long walks, but he didn't want to run down to post a few letters. He would climb every tree in the garden one after another, but he wouldn't wheel Michael down the road and back.

Still, that didn't matter, because Margery was always on hand for that. She never minded what she did for Michael. Mrs. Taggerty often said she wished she were her own little daughter, she was so useful.

"Don't you like Michael?" Margery asked Maureen. "You never do anything for him."

"Oh yes. I like him. I love him," answered Maureen. "But it's such a bore, always having to be quiet when he's asleep. And I hate having to wheel him out."

"You don't *really* love him, if you don't want to do things for him," said Margery. "You're rather selfish, I think, Maureen. Still, *I* don't mind, because it means I can do the things you don't want to do but which *I* love to do!"

Dopey came running up at this moment. He certainly

could be a very stupid dog, but stupid or not he seemed to realize that it was very important not to jump about anywhere near the pram now. He stopped short every time he came to it, and put his tail down. He was very interested in Socks's kittens, and bore several scratches on his nose which Socks had given him for his curiosity.

Annette was impatient because her kitten did not grow as quickly as she wanted it to. It took twelve days to get its eyes open. "Fancy, twelve days!" said Annette. "I thought it would be blind for ever! It's got dear little blue eyes just like all the Taggerty family have."

She was looking forward very much to having the kitten for her own. Mother had said that it was to be house-trained before they had it, and that if it was dirty she would not keep it. Annette was very anxious for it to behave itself well.

"I do hope it will have nice manners," she said to Margery. "But it can't learn very good ways from the Taggertys, really. I like them all, now, but I still think they are very dirty and untidy—and they do say such cheeky things to poor Bridget."

"Perhaps Socks will teach the kitten to wash itself and keep clean and nice," said Margery. "Socks always looks very tidy and clean, doesn't she? I wish we could buy a baby, too, Annette. A little tiny one, so that it would take a long time to grow. If Michael gets much heavier I shan't be able to lift him."

John could never do the daring things that Pat did, because, though he enjoyed climbing and jumping and wading in the river, he was always a little afraid of doing some of Pat's most reckless things.

"You're bigger than I am," he said to Pat one day. "And stronger. If I tried to do all the things you do,

I'd end up breaking my leg or something. So what's the sense?"

One afternoon Pat dared John to jump over a stream that ran in the meadow not far from their house. John looked at it. It was wide and deep just there, and ran strongly.

"You couldn't jump over it just here yourself," he said to Pat. "You do the dare yourself, before you challenge *me*, see?"

"I can easily do it!" said Pat. He went a little way back, measured the stream with his eye, ran forward swiftly and jumped. He sailed right over the stream and landed well over the other side.

"Jolly good!" cried John.

"I *could* do it, you see!" shouted Pat, triumphantly. "Oh, here comes Dopey. He can do it too. Well done, Dopey! You're braver than John. He doesn't dare."

"It isn't that," cried John. "I just know I *can't* do it! I shall only fall in the middle, and wet myself to the skin. Then I'll get into a good old row and not be allowed out with you again. It isn't that I don't *dare*. I'll jump the stream further down the field, if you like, where it isn't so wide."

But Pat was obstinate. "No. Jump it here. You say you won't because you're afraid. We always said you were namby-pamby, but I thought you'd grown out of it—and you haven't. Pooh!"

John flushed red. He looked at the stream. No, it was no good, he couldn't jump it. All right then, let Pat think what he liked. He turned to go home, sulking.

Pat laughed. "Old gloomy-face! You'll turn the milk sour and the butter rancid if you go home like that."

"Well, stop saying I don't dare to do this and that, then," said John furiously. "You can't tell the difference between being reckless and being sensible, that's

252

what's the matter with *you*. Why should I get myself soaked just to please *you*? It's nothing to do with my being brave. I could be brave enough if there was any need for it, you know that. I suppose you think you're brave enough for anything—you wouldn't be afraid of a single thing."

"No, I wouldn't," boasted Pat. "I dare to do anything!"

The boys went home. John was rather quiet. He was trying not to sulk, but it was difficult. Pat was lively and cheerful, in a teasing mood. The boys parted at the Taggertys' gate and John went home.

After tea he and Margery and Annette went down the garden to play. "Shall we go over the wall?" asked Annette. John shook his head.

"No. Let's play here for a change."

Over the wall an exciting game was going on. The Taggertys were doing something with a cricket-ball. There were shouts and laughter—and then a fearful crash! It came from the garden next to the Taggertys'.

"Whew! Their ball has gone into the Johnson's cucumber-frame," said John. They listened. There was a dead silence from the Taggertys' garden. Not a word, not a laugh.

"They've fled indoors, I should think," said John. "My word, I bet Miss Johnson will be angry. She's always complaining about the Taggertys."

Footsteps came down the Johnson's garden, and there was an angry exclamation. Miss Johnson leaned over the broken glass and picked up the cricket-ball which lay among her cucumbers.

She caught sight of the three Carlton children and called to them, "Is this your ball? Did you break my frame?"

"No, Miss Johnson," said John at once. "We didn't."

253

"Then who did?" cried Miss Johnson. "There doesn't seem to be anyone in the Taggertys' garden. Did you see the Taggertys throw the ball over into my garden?"

"No, Miss Johnson," answered John, truthfully. He

"Pat! Is this your ball?"

felt awkward. He couldn't tell tales of the Taggertys. He wished they would come out and own up.

Apparently Pat did come out. He walked whistling down the garden, his hands in his pockets. Miss Johnson hailed him.

"Pat! Is this your ball?"

Pat stopped, and looked surprised. "Oh no! That's not ours, Miss Johnson. Where did you find it?"

"In my cucumber-frame," said Miss Johnson, grimly. "Somebody threw it over the wall and broke the glass. Are you sure it wasn't you?"

"Oh yes, *quite* sure, Miss Johnson," said Pat, still looking very innocent. "I'm so sorry about it. Who could have thrown it?"

Miss Johnson snorted and went back into the house with the cricket-ball. Pat looked over the wall and grinned.

"Golly! We only just ran away in time," he said. John stared straight at him.

"I'm going to dare *you* to do something," he said, in a cold, scornful voice. "You laughed at me because I wouldn't jump the stream, but I knew I couldn't. Now I'm going to dare *you* to do something you *can* do—but you'll be afraid, and I shall laugh at *you*! We all shall."

"I'll take your dare," said Pat at once.

"Very well. Go and own up to Miss Johnson and tell her you broke the frame and told a lie," said John. "Go on. I dare you to!"

Pat looked taken aback. "That's a silly dare," he began, but John interrupted him.

"It isn't. I'm just showing you what a coward you are. You don't dare to own up when you've done wrong. That's much more cowardly than not daring to jump a stream that's too wide. *You're* not brave, Pat. You can climb a tree and jump a stream—but you can't own up to anything. Coward! I'm ashamed of having you for a friend."

John turned and went up the garden with Annette and Margery. Both girls thoroughly agreed with him.

They never could understand why Pat should be so cowardly and deceitful over things like this, when he always seemed so brave in other things.

Pat stood for a minute, thinking. At first he felt angry. Then he flushed. He saw that John was right. He *was* afraid of owning up. He always had been. And Maureen and Biddy were just the same.

John always owned up at once, no matter how he might be punished. He was brave and good that way. Pat suddenly felt ashamed of himself. He rushed indoors and found his money-box, and took out his birthday ten shillings. Then he ran round to Miss Johnson's front door and hammered on it. He must do this thing whilst he still felt so ashamed. If he waited he might change his mind.

Miss Johnson opened the door in surprise. "Miss Johnson—I bro .e your frame. I'm very sorry I said I didn't," said Pat, his words tumbling out in a hurry. "I've brought you the money to pay for new glass."

He thrust the money into the surprised Miss Johnson's hands and ran off again. He had owned up! It was horrid and difficult, but he had done it. He went home again and tore down to the bottom of the garden. He shouted loudly.

"John! Come here! I want you!"

John came, still looking cold and scornful. "I've taken your dare!" said Pat, grinning suddenly. "I've owned up and I've told Miss Johnson I told a lie to her. I've given her the money for the frame out of my money-box. Say you're not ashamed to have me for a friend, John. I won't make you ashamed that way again. You're quite right about it."

"Good old fellow!" said John, really touched, and he banged Pat on the back. "You're really brave. I always knew you were. Good old fellow! I almost feel I'll go and jump that stream now—and get right over it, too!"

CHAPTER FOURTEEN

Going to School

"ONLY two more days before we go back to school," said Pat, gloomily. He was swinging on a low bough of a tree in his garden, and John was sitting beside him.

"Well, I like school," said John. "You're coming to my school, aren't you, Pat? It'll be nice to go with you each morning. But you'll have to go clean and tidy, and I'd better warn you that our form-master goes up in smoke if we walk about with our hands in our pockets."

"It sounds as bad as the school I went to before," groaned Pat. "I hate school. Always having to do as you're told, and having to sit still, and swot at things you don't like and——"

"If you sit next to me I'll help you," said John. He guessed that Pat was lazy and difficult at school. It was likely that he would be cheeky too—and old Pots, the form-master, wouldn't stand that. Pat would find himself robbed of football, and having to stay in and write out "I must be polite" a hundred or more times.

"The only things I shall like about the new school

are Break and football," said Pat. "And I don't think it's *worth* going to school just for those two things. I wish I could run away to sea!"

This was one of Pat's stock wishes when he had to face things he didn't like. John laughed.

"If you went to sea you'd find things a lot harder than being at school, idiot, and you'd get plenty of shouts and roars and clips on the ear. Hallo, there's Maureen—and Margery with the baby as usual. She's mad on that baby."

"Well, *let* her be," said Pat, swinging himself so violently that John fell off the branch to the ground. "Hey, Margery! Can't you leave Michael alone even for a moment?"

"I shall have to in two days' time," said Margery, gloomily. "School opens then. Maureen and I are going to the same school, just as you and John are. There will just be Biddy and Annette left to play with each other, and poor Michael will be all alone."

"He'll have Dopey," said Pat, and the big dog came running up, hearing his name. "I wouldn't mind going to school a bit if Dopey could come too. He did keep coming to my last school, till the master complained, and then he had to be tied up all the morning. Shame!"

Dopey floundered round in his usual idiotic fashion. Margery pushed him away from Michael. She really didn't mind Dopey a bit now; she had got used to him and his silly, lovable ways, and except when he barked very suddenly she liked him. As for John, he agreed with Pat that Dopey was the nicest dog in the world.

Annette arrived over the wall, beaming. She no longer looked always as if she was about to go to a party. Mother had bought her some smocks, and she wore these for the garden, looking much more sensible in them than in her frilly little frocks.

"Hallo!" she said to everyone. "Mother's been writing out invitations to my birthday party. She's written one out for you, Pat, and Maureen and Biddy —and for lots of others too."

Pat and Maureen didn't look very thrilled. They didn't like the kind of parties they had to dress up for. "When is it?" asked Pat.

"Next Wednesday," said Annette. "And your mother says I can have Socks's kitten that day, because it will be old enough to leave its mother. That will be my very nicest birthday present."

Margery loved a party. "There'll be ice-creams, and crowds of cakes and jellies and blancmanges and a big birthday cake with six candles on," she said. "It will be a lovely party."

"I shall like that part of it," said Pat. "I suppose we shall go from school, John, shan't we? We won't have time to clean ourselves up much, or put on party things."

"Wednesday is a half-holiday," said John. "We'll have plenty of time to get ready."

"I wish Michael could come," said Margery.

"Goo," said Michael, staring up at the moving green leaves above his head.

"Well, he can't," said Pat. "You'll be mooning over him the whole time if he does, and won't join in any games at all. You spoil him. I'll have an awful time licking him into shape when he can walk and talk."

"You jolly well won't lick him into shape," said Margery fiercely, hugging Michael close.

"Well, I shall," said Pat. "I'd be a poor elder brother if I didn't. I shan't let him be a molly-coddle like John used to be."

"A Margery-coddle you mean," said John, with a

giggle at his own wit. "What shall we play? We'd better make the most of what time we've got left—school will soon begin."

Then they plunged into a terrifically noisy game of pirates, in which Annette joined with gusto, and Dopey enjoyed tremendously. He waited till first one child rolled on the ground and then another, then leapt on the heap, licking so ferociously that it was almost unbearable.

"We ought to keep a towel handy when Dopey joins in our games," said John, wiping his face with his handkerchief. "He really has got the wettest tongue in the world. Shut up, Dopey. If you lick me again I'll lock you up."

"Woof," said Dopey, which meant "fibber!" He knew that not one of the children would ever lock him up or tie him. It was only the grown-ups who did that.

School came two days later. Pat and John set off together. Pat looked unusually clean for him, and actually wore a new suit. His wavy hair was as smooth as he could get it. John stared at him.

"You don't look like yourself a bit. Did your mother make you look so neat?"

"Yes. She's taking a leaf out of *your* mother's book, and nags at us about clean hands and cleaning our teeth and keeping our clothes decent now," said Pat, in disgust. "She never did before."

Maureen set off with Margery, but to her disappointment she was put into a class below. And Pat, to his dismay, was also placed in a form below John. Now they wouldn't be together.

"Dad won't like hearing we're below you and Margery," he grumbled at Break. "He's so clever himself, he thinks we must be clever too. And now he'll think we aren't."

"Well, you can easily go up into my form, if you work hard enough," said John. "You're cleverer than I am in some things. Anyway, you'll be miles better at gym and games."

Pat was. He was soon one of the stars in the football team, sturdy, quick, fearless and a very fast runner. John was quite good, but too afraid of being hurt to be really first-class. He was not as reckless as Pat either, and his over-cautiousness made him miss many good chances of playing really well. Still, he was much better than he had been before, mostly because he was copying Pat and trying to be as plucky as he was.

Maureen grumbled about being below Margery. "I don't see why I am. I'm sure I could do the same work as you do. Why are you higher than me? You're the youngest in your form, but I shouldn't have thought you were as clever as all that."

"I'm not," said Margery honestly, "but Mother always helps me a lot at home, you know, and explains things to me I don't understand, and shows me how to do things. That's really why I've got on, I think."

"My mother never does that," said Maureen. "She just doesn't bother with us like yours does. Sometimes I think it's a jolly good thing not to be fussed over like you are—but other times I wish my mother would help us a bit more. I couldn't possibly go and ask her to help me with those awful homework sums for instance. And Daddy wouldn't bother either. Still, I'd hate to be fussed over always, as you are."

Margery said nothing. Neither she nor John would discuss their mother with the Taggertys. They loved her very much and were loyal to her, even though they sometimes wished she wouldn't fuss so. They liked Mrs. Taggerty too, and secretly thought that the three Taggerty children were very lazy and selfish and rude towards their mother.

"They don't do a thing for her," said John once to Margery. "Anyone would think they didn't love her."

"Sometimes I wonder if they do," said Margery. "How can you be so mean to somebody if you really do love them? Why, yesterday Maureen wouldn't even lay the table for her mother when Bridget was out. She just ran out into the garden. I was there and saw her. I think it's funny really the way Mrs. Taggerty treats those three. Sometimes she loses her temper and slaps them, sometimes she just says nothing."

"I don't think they love Mrs. Taggerty," said John. "Not really. Or their father either. I like them, they're fun, and it's nice to share Dopey and Socks with them, and play their exciting games—but they hardly ever think of anyone but themselves."

"They're not really Christians," said Margery. "I heard Mother tell Mrs. Wilson that. And Mrs. Wilson said they were little heathens, who didn't even say a prayer at night."

"Well, I can't possibly do anything about Pat," said John, "but I don't see why you can't try and help Maureen and Biddy, Margery. Be a sort of missionary. You don't want Michael to grow up into a heathen too, do you?"

No, Margery didn't. She had already planned to tell Michael all kinds of stories when he grew older. She would tell him the old Bible stories, too, that her mother had told her and John and Annette. And if Mrs. Taggerty didn't teach him his first little prayers, perhaps she, Margery, could.

She didn't tell anyone this. She knew that Pat would laugh and call her a goody-goody little prig, and Margery wasn't a prig. "All the same I mustn't fuss Michael too much," she thought. "Like Mother used to fuss us, always wanting us to be perfect. I must be careful."

Pat and Maureen soon settled down at their new school. Maureen liked it. She hadn't liked her other school, because she hadn't known how to behave, and had been a rough, ill-mannered little girl whom both teachers and children disliked. But now she knew better, and she enjoyed being liked.

Pat loved the gym and the football, but he groaned at the work. He scamped his homework and refused John's offer to help him. "No. If you come over and help me we'll be ages. *I* don't care if I'm bottom of the form or not so long as I'm in the football team."

"But your father will be wild when you get a bad report," said John. "He'll give you a hiding again."

"Well, perhaps if he'd taken the trouble to help me when I first began school, like yours did, I wouldn't be so bad at lessons." said Pat. "Now shut up preaching, John. Did you see me climb up to the very top of the gym rope today? I bet I looked like a monkey."

"You did!" said John, admiringly.

"And that's just what you are." said Maureen, unexpectedly. "You're a monkey!"

CHAPTER FIFTEEN

Annette Has a Birthday

ANNETTE'S party was a great success. Twenty children came, all bringing little presents. Annette was full of pride and delight. She had a new dress of blue silk with a lovely sash, and blue socks and shoes to match. She looked very pretty, and knew it.

"Don't I look nice?" she cried, dancing over to Maureen, who had just arrived with Pat and Biddy. "Do you like my new frock?"

"It's awful," said Pat at once, and Annette pouted.

"You don't really mean it!" she said.

"Well, *you're* awful, anyway, showing everyone how vain you are," said Pat. But Annette wouldn't listen. She would have burst into tears two months back, but now she had got used to being teased and was much more sensible. All the same she didn't show off any more, but welcomed her guests politely.

It was a lovely party. There were balloons and crackers and games. There was a glorious tea, but unfortunately Annette was so excited that she could hardly eat anything.

"She's always like that at parties," said Margery to Biddy, who was tucking in fast. "You don't need to gobble so, Biddy. There's plenty of time and plenty of food. You ought to have been a turkey, you're such a gobbler."

"Well, I'd rather be a gobbler than somebody like Annette who feels sick at parties," said Biddy. "What an awful waste!"

The birthday-cake candles were lighted. They were so pretty, two green, two red, one pink and one yellow. Annette cut her cake, with Mother guiding her hand, and soon everyone had a piece of the delicious cake on his or her plate. Pat and Biddy had two pieces each, of course. Maureen would have liked another, but just couldn't manage it.

"What bad manners those Taggerty children have!" said one of the children's mothers, who had come to help, to Mrs. Carlton. "Look how they grab and gobble."

"Yes. But they're *much* better than they used to be," said Mother. "Really they are. I do think my three have been a good example to them. If only they weren't such little heathens. I'd like them to go to Sunday School with mine, and I've offered to take them to church with us any Sunday morning—but no, Mrs. Taggerty just won't tell them to go, because they don't want to."

"What a pity!" said the other mother. "Such nice-looking children too—and I hear the baby is a beauty. But dear me, how Miss Johnson their next-door neighbour complains of them. Says they make more noise than any children in the place. I'm glad *I* don't live next to them."

Annette was a very good little hostess. She really did look after her guests well. Most of them were her own age, and she saw that each of them had a balloon and two crackers. She watched for anyone who was left out of anything, and went to make them join in. Mother was very pleased with her.

John was good too. He was always gentle with little

girls, for that had been his father's teaching. Maureen watched him picking up one who had fallen, and giving another his balloon when hers had burst. Then she turned to find Pat. He was teasing a small girl. He had taken her balloon away and was snatching it out of her reach every time she tried to get it.

She felt a sudden feeling of affection for good-hearted John and of annoyance with Pat. "Why must he always tease and be rough and annoying?" she thought. "Everyone must think he's so badly-behaved."

Of the three Taggerty children, Maureen was the one who most liked and admired the Carltons. Especially she liked John. He was always kind to her, even in the roughest of games, and never wilfully hurt her as Pat did. "He behaves like a gentleman," she thought suddenly. "And Pat doesn't. I wonder why. Perhaps it's something he learns at Sunday School or church. I can't think of anything else."

The party came to an end all too quickly. The Taggertys were, as might have been guessed, the very last to go, and they wouldn't have gone when they did if Mrs. Carlton hadn't firmly said they must. They remembered to thank her and Annette for the lovely party. Annette gave Biddy a hug.

"Thank you for Whitefeet!" she said warmly. "He's my nicest present of all. I've had three dolls and a doll's pram and books and games and toys—but I like my darling little kitten best of all. I do hope he won't miss Socks too much."

"Oh, Socks is tired of all her kittens now," said Biddy. "She smacks them hard when they jump at her tail. She'll be glad that one of them is gone. The others will soon go too. I don't expect Whitefeet will miss Socks at all."

But little Whitefeet did! He missed his big, warm,

comfortable mother and his playful brothers. He mewed pitifully and Annette could hardly bear it. She cuddled him in her arms after she had had her bath that night, and comforted him.

"Don't cry, Whitefeet. I love you. I'll take care of you just as well as Socks did. Don't cry! Mother, let me take him to bed with me, he's so unhappy."

Mother was shocked. Take a kitten to bed! What next? It was bad enough to have one in the house, without letting Annette take him into her nice clean little bed.

"Certainly not," she said.

"Not even on my birthday?" said Annette, pleadingly.

"Not even on your birthday," said Mother firmly, so there was no more to be said.

Annette went to bed and fell asleep thinking of Whitefeet. She remembered him especially in her prayers.

"Don't let him be unhappy tonight!" she begged God. "Look after him for me. It says in the Bible that You see when even a sparrow falls, and Whitefeet is bigger than a sparrow, so You can see him easily. Please make him happy."

Annette woke in the middle of the night. She remembered Whitefeet. Was he crying? Had God seen him and comforted him if he missed Socks?

Annette had to go and see. She slipped down the dark stairs and came to the kitchen, where Whitefeet had been put into a cosy basket. She opened the door and switched on the light.

Whitefeet was sitting up in his basket, wide awake. His eyes shone brightly. He gave a little welcoming mew and tumbled out of the basket. He was still so small that it was quite difficult for him to reach the

What did she see but a small, curled-up figure

ground. He ran to Annette, and she picked him up.
"Are you all right?" said the little girl. "Are you
happy? You don't miss Socks, do you?"

She sat down in Agnes's comfortable wicker chair,
with the kitten on her knee. Whitefeet patted a button
on her nightie, and then tried to nibble it. Then he

settled down in a little round ball, making a warm patch on Annette's knees, and went to sleep.

Annette loved feeling him there. "Margery may like to hold Michael and feel how soft and warm he is," she thought, "but *I* think a kitten is much nicer. I don't like to get up. If I do he'll wake and begin to mew. I'll just stay with him for a little while."

So she stayed—and, of course, she fell fast asleep too. And when Agnes came down, yawning, in the morning, what did she see but a small, curled-up figure in the arm-chair, with Whitefeet on her knee. Well, well, well!

She shook Annette gently. "Get back to bed, child," she said. "Your mother will miss you when she comes to wake you. Bless us all, fancy you nursing that kitten all night long!"

Annette stumbled up to bed, sleepy and stiff. Whitefeet, thoroughly awake, ran at all Agnes's brooms and pans as she used them, and was very happy indeed. Then he began to look for his brothers.

The kitten was a great success. All the children loved it and its funny, playful ways. It would hide under beds and jump out at people's passing legs. It would go to sleep on Daddy's feet, and it would sometimes go completely mad and tear round and round the room without stopping.

Daddy loved it, too. "I had a kitten as mad as Whitefeet when I was a boy," he said. "It was called Bimbo. And I had a puppy too, called Sandy, because his head was sandy-coloured. Dear old Sandy—he grew up into such a faithful, loving dog."

"Daddy, I want a puppy!" suddenly said John, feeling that he really *must* have one. It wouldn't be as nice as Dopey, of course—but it would be lovely to have something alive that was his very own to look after and love.

"Well," began Daddy, who had secretly wanted a dog for ages, "well, I don't see why . . ."

"Oh, Peter! It's bad enough to begin having cats!" said Mother. "Not dogs too, please. Margery will say she wants a parrot or something next."

"I shan't," said Margery. "If anybody is going to give me a pet, I'll have a baby, please. I do think the Taggertys are lucky to have a baby."

"Oh, those Taggertys!" groaned Mother. "Why must you want everything the same as they have?"

"*Can* I have a puppy for *my* birthday—or better still, for Christmas, because it's nearer?" asked John again, his eyes shining. "Mother, it won't be any bother, really it won't."

"It will chew up the rugs, make messes all over the place, bark and yelp and whine, upset things and be a real nuisance in the garden," said Mother.

"Well," said John, looking suddenly sad, "if it will upset you, Mother, I won't ask again. I can always share Dopey."

"Oh, Dopey might quite as well be our dog as the Taggertys'," said Mother, "the way he comes in at every hour of the day. He even came in yesterday when I was knitting all by myself here, and ran off with my ball of wool. He pulled my knitting right out of my hands."

The children roared. "Oh, I wish I'd seen him," said Annette. "Oh, Mother, John won't ask you again for a puppy, but *I* shall go on and on asking you for him, because I know how much he wants one. And it isn't fair for me to have a kitten if he can't have a puppy."

Mother looked round at the four earnest faces. Daddy was gazing at her, too, pulling solemnly at his pipe. Mother suddenly put down her knitting and began to laugh.

"*Don't* look at me like that!" she said. "You look like a lot of Dopeys, all gazing at me with big, doggy eyes. Don't! You shall have your puppy if you want him so much, John. I know Daddy will be thrilled to have a dog to go with him for walks, too."

There was an outburst of delighted squeals and shouts, and three children flung themselves on Mother with all their might. She was squeezed and hugged till she had no breath left.

"And now I'll have my turn," said Daddy, and gave her a hug too. "Thank you giving in to us, Mother. I promise you that if the dog is a nuisance we won't keep him."

"But I bet before long, Mother gets fond of him," said John in a low voice to Margery. "She's already fond of the kitten."

"So am I," said Margery. "I never wanted a dog before, but somehow Dopey has made me change my mind. I think if you really get to *know* a dog you can't help wanting one yourself. And I do know Dopey now, and though he's quite mad and awfully silly sometimes, I just can't help loving him."

"You're changing, Margery," said John, in surprise. "You used to be so scared of animals. Now you don't seem to mind nearly so much. I hope I get my puppy in time for Christmas, don't you? What a wonderful Christmas it would be!"

"Mother's changing, too," said Margery, answering the first part of John's speech. "Dear me—we've changed the Taggertys quite a lot—and perhaps they've changed us as well!"

CHAPTER SIXTEEN

All Sorts of Things Happen

A LOT of things happened the next week. John was top of his form, and Mother was delighted. Pat was bottom, and was forbidden to play in a football match he was much looking forward to, much to his anger.

Whitefeet wandered away and got lost for a whole day and Annette nearly went mad with despair. Maureen found her wandering round the Taggertys' garden, calling miserably, tears streaming down her cheeks.

"Where can Whitefeet be?" asked Maureen, putting her arm round Annette. "Don't cry so. He'll come back."

"Pat says he may be stolen," wept Annette. "Or he might have got run over. Or——"

"Oh, don't listen to what Pat says," said Maureen impatiently. "Whitefeet can't be far away."

"I simply don't know what to do," said Annette, tears pouring down her cheeks again. "I've done everything I can."

"Have you prayed about it?" asked Maureen suddenly. "God is sure to know where Whitefeet is, isn't He?"

"I never thought of that!" said Annette, and she stood under the weeping willow-tree and spoke directly to God who, she felt sure, was always ready to listen to her, no matter what she said. Maureen stood nearby, listening.

"Dear God, You know where my little kitten is, the one with the white feet like Socks," said Annette, wiping her tears away. "Please let me find him. Amen."

The little girls searched everywhere again and Biddy came to join in too. Then Dopey came prancing round. Suddenly he pricked up his ears, and leapt right over the wall into Annette's garden. He began to bark loudly.

"What's the matter with Dopey?" said Maureen. "He's awfully excited."

They climbed over the wall to see. Dopey was at the foot of a birch-tree, standing with his forefeet up the trunk of the tree. He barked loudly again.

And there came a tiny answering mew. Annette gave a shriek. "It's Whitefeet! He's up the tree and he can't get down. Oh, Dopey, you are *clever*. Whitefeet, I'm coming. Stay there till I come."

Up the tree went Annette, scratching her bare legs against the trunk, her hair catching in the twigs, and a branch tearing at her frock. But Annette didn't notice any of these things at all. Up she went till she came to where the terrified little kitten sat, clinging to a swaying branch.

"Whitefeet! How long have you been up here? Fancy climbing up when you can't climb down!" cried Annette, taking the kitten gently by the fur at the back of its neck. She placed it on her shoulder, where it at once dug in its claws. But Annette didn't mind. Whitefeet could scratch her to pieces for all she cared.

Down she went, and soon they were petting the kitten, and Dopey was trying to nose his way in too and share in the excitement, his long tail lashing against the girls' bare legs.

Annette rubbed her eyes. Her face was stained and smeary, her hair was full of twigs, her dress was dirty and torn. She might have been a Taggerty! But she was very happy because she had found her precious kitten, and had climbed a tree to rescue him. "I thought he was gone for ever," she said, cuddling him.

Maureen was very thoughtful after this little happening. "God heard Annette's prayer," she thought. "It was almost like a miracle. I think I'll go to Sunday School with Margery, and I think I'll say some prayers too."

So, much to Margery's surprise, and to Pat's real amazement, Maureen went off to Sunday School with Margery and John and Annette on the next Sunday. She liked it. She liked the teacher, who told them the story of the Boy with the Loaves and Fishes, and she wished she had been that boy, who had some little fish and bread to take to Jesus to feed all the hungry people.

"I'm going to say my prayers now, too," she told Margery. "Can I just say them in bed, or is it best to kneel down? Does it matter?"

"Well, it's best to kneel down properly," said Margery. "It seems more reverent somehow. And you can think what you're doing then, too. It's so easy to fall asleep in bed."

It was rather difficult for Maureen to say her prayers at night, because as soon as Pat discovered she was doing so he teased her. "Little Goody-goody! Look, Dopey, lick Maureen's soles! They're nice and bare, turned up all ready for you."

Then Dopey's tongue would lick Maureen's up-turned feet, and she would wriggle and squeal, because she was very ticklish there. "You're mean, Pat! God will be angry with you. Take Dopey away."

A little ashamed of himself, Pat did take Dopey away. Margery prayed very fervently, and Biddy was curious, to know what she was praying for. But Maureen wouldn't tell her. She wasn't going to be laughed at by Pat or Biddy.

274

During the next week Margery noticed that Maureen was very quiet. "Is anything wrong?" she said. "Don't you feel well? You don't think you're going to have the measles, do you?"

"No," said Maureen. "It's only that I keep on and on asking God for things and He never listens to me at all. It's not much use saying prayers, really."

"What did you ask Him for?" asked Margery.

"Well, you know that test-paper we had last week?" said Maureen. "One of the questions was 'Where is the river Amazon?' and I put down that it was in Italy, but it's in one of the Americas. So I prayed to God to make it be in Italy because that was the only question I got wrong."

Margery stared at Maureen in surprise. "But *Maureen*! What a thing to ask! Just imagine what would have happened if your prayer had been granted. Think of the river Amazon flowing through Italy all of a sudden. You're silly."

"You said the other day that nothing was impossible to God," said Maureen, half-sulkily. "Well, He could do that then, couldn't He?"

"He wouldn't want to," said Margery. "Be sensible, Maureen. Would a great loving Father like God do a stupid miracle asked for by a girl who had made a mistake in a test-paper! Your idea of God is all wrong. You'd better come to church with us and learn better."

"I shan't pray any more," said Maureen, crossly. "It's difficult enough, anyhow, with Pat teasing me, and Dopey waiting to lick the soles of my feet, and Biddy keeping on asking me what I'm praying, and you saying that God won't listen to me, and——"

"He will, He will," said Margery. "But you don't know what to pray for, nor how to pray either, I should think. You don't *understand*, Maureen. You see, our mother told us lots of things when we were little, and

275

she taught us our prayers, and everything—but nobody has taught you, have they? You're unlucky. But you can learn, if you want to. You come to church with us."

But Maureen wouldn't do that, though she went to Sunday School, and soon Biddy came too. Biddy loved it. Pat wouldn't hear of going.

"If I'm a heathen, then I'm a heathen and I like it," he said to Maureen. "You shut up. You're not going to make me into a goody-goody little pi-boy."

"John isn't like that," said Maureen.

"He used to be," said Pat, "till he got to know *us*. We've done him a lot of good. I heard his father tell Daddy that last week, so there!"

"Uncle Peter is nice," said Maureen. "I like him. I wish I could go off on a long walk with him too, on Saturday afternoons, like you and John and Dopey do."

"Well, you can't," said Pat. "Girls not wanted! Especially little pi-girls!"

"What's pi mean?" asked Biddy, who had been listening with great interest.

"Pious," said Pat. "You're both little pi-girls now. But don't you think you're going to make *me* pi too! Nothing in the world would make me that."

The term went on. Pat's work was still bad, and once more he was forbidden to play in an important match as a punishment for slack work.

"It's no good, Taggerty," said his master, tapping the blue-pencilled page before him. "I won't have work like this. This isn't homework. Why, even a kindergarten child could do better than this. I shall send in a report to your father soon, if you don't do better."

Pat scowled. He was ashamed of being bottom of the form, and out of the match, though he wouldn't try to do better. He vented his annoyance on Maureen, Biddy and Michael, and teased them continually. Michael

276

howled. Biddy was almost in tears. Maureen ran off to the Carltons.

"What *is* wrong with Patrick lately?" wondered Mrs. Taggerty. "So rude and selfish and noisy! What can be the matter with him?"

They soon knew for a letter came from the headmaster, telling Mr. Taggerty of Pat's bad work at school, and asking his father to take him away the next term, or to insist that Pat did better.

It was a great shock to both his parents. They had been proud of their good-looking Patrick, proud of his fearlessness and his prowess at games. Now, apparently, he was nobody to be proud of at all for in that same letter the headmaster had complained of Pat's untruthfulness and his deceitfulness too! "He will cheat if he can, and he will tell untruths to get himself out of trouble," said the letter. "He is not a desirable influence to have in the school."

Poor Mrs. Taggerty was so shocked and amazed that she sank down into a chair, looking white and troubled. "Our Pat!" she said. "It can't be!"

"It's partly our fault," said Mr. Taggerty. "We let them do too much as they liked. We've been so afraid of fussing them too much that we've gone too far the other way—we haven't guided Pat enough. and he's so young he's gone the wrong way without knowing it. This is terrible."

He spoke to Pat about it. The boy was sullen, and because he was ashamed he pretended to be defiant and not to care. Mr. Taggerty hardly knew what to do with him.

He thought of Maureen and compared her with Margery. Margery was sweet to Mrs. Taggerty. and always at hand to help with the baby. Even Bridget was always singing her praises and saying how helpful she was. But Maureen would never do a thing to help either

277

Bridget or her mother. And there was Biddy too—lovely, curly-haired Biddy, with her dimples and her smiles, a real little tomboy, but never wanting to do anything for anyone but herself. Really, those children seemed to love Dopey better than they loved anyone! Mr. Taggerty suddenly felt discouraged and disappointed.

"I'll have a talk with John's father," he thought. "Those Carlton children may be too much fussed-over, and too prim and proper sometimes, but they certainly are unselfish, kindly children. How do the Carltons do it? What is there in their home that there isn't in ours? There must be *something*."

"I'm going to bed, dear," said Mrs. Taggerty, to him, in a faint voice. "All this upset has made me feel ill. Bridget will manage Baby. Oh, dear—I keep on and on thinking of that dreadful letter, and Patrick's defiant face, and fearing that Maureen and Biddy will turn out the same. I must have been a bad mother."

"I'll come up and see to you," said Mr. Taggerty. "Don't worry too much. Tomorrow I'll go and see John's father, and show him this letter. I've no doubt we can do something between us to make things better."

He went upstairs with poor Mrs. Taggerty, who did indeed look ill. When she was in bed, he kissed her. "Now don't you worry," he said. "Things will be better tomorrow."

But they weren't any better. They grew worse.

CHAPTER SEVENTEEN

When Dinner was Late

PAT did not tell John anything about the letter. He went off to school earlier than usual, and John wondered why, because as a rule they always went together. When he saw Pat's sullen face he was surprised. It was not really like Pat to be sullen.

"What's up?" he asked. "Anything wrong?"

"Nothing," said Pat, attempting to grin. But it was a very poor sort of grin. There was plenty wrong. Not only that dreadful letter. He had been rude to his father that morning, and had been unkind to his mother at breakfast. She had come down looking pale and tired, and had asked him to call in at the grocer's on the way to school, with the grocery list, to save her going out that morning.

"I don't pass the grocer's," Pat had said, rudely.

"I know," said his mother. "But it's only a minute out of your way. I'm tired today, and I thought you could easily do that, Pat."

"Why don't you make Maureen go?" said Pat. "You're always asking me to do errands. Why shouldn't Maureen?"

"Well, I *do*," Maureen said. "I do lots more than you."

"You don't," said Pat. "You're lazy. Everyone knows that."

"I'm *not*!" said Maureen indignantly. "I think that's mean of you. *I'm* not bottom of the form like you, anyway! Dunce!"

Pat gave her a kick under the table, but caught his mother's ankle instead. She gave a cry.

"Sorry," said Pat, going red. "I meant it for Maureen."

Mrs. Taggerty was silent and upset. She had hardly slept at all. She looked at Pat sadly, but he would not meet her eyes.

"Well, Maureen, will *you* call at the grocer's for me?" she said, not wanting to argue with the defiant Pat.

"I promised Margery I would call for her this morning," began Maureen. "I'll go on my way back from school."

"That will be too late," said Mrs. Taggerty.

"Biddy can go, surely? She's quite old enough," said Maureen.

"I don't want to go," said Biddy. "I'm going to play shops in the summer-house."

"You said you would tidy up your bedroom for me today," said Mrs. Taggerty. "You've got your dolls' tea-set all over the floor."

"I want to play shops," said Biddy. "I don't want to tidy up the bedroom. Let Maureen do it."

It was a good thing that Mr. Taggerty was not at breakfast, but had gone off some time before to London, or he would certainly have had something to say about all this. Michael began to cry just then, and Mrs. Taggerty listened to see if Bridget was going to him. But Bridget was out in the garden hanging up some clothes she had washed, and did not hear him.

"You go, Maureen," said Mrs. Taggerty. "I expect he just dropped his rabbit out of his cot or something."

"I shall be late if I bother with Michael," Maureen said primly, and ran to get her satchel. Michael went on howling.

Pat went off to school, still sullen. He did not go near

the grocer's. *He* wasn't going to run errands for anyone if he didn't want to. Let Maureen go or that lazy little Biddy.

Maureen climbed over the wall to go and call for Margery. She didn't go near the grocer's either. Biddy never thought of it again. She ran out of the room and into the garden, down to the summer-house, to play shops with Dopey and with Annette when she came.

Her mother called her after a while, but Biddy pretended not to hear. This was a favourite trick of the Taggertys when they knew they would be asked to do some job. Presently she heard somebody's footsteps. Biddy ran to a thick bush, crawled under it and sat there perfectly still.

When her mother arrived there was no one to be seen but Dopey, who was sitting on the sunny step of the summer-house, snapping at a fly that was trying to settle on his nose.

"I suppose Biddy has gone over to play with Annette," thought Mrs. Taggerty. "Naughty little girl, when I wanted her to clear up her bedroom. Now I shall have to stoop down and pick up all those tea-things, just when my head feels like bursting."

She went away, and Biddy crept out of her hiding-place. Dopey greeted her with a lick. Dopey was very good when the children hid from grown-ups. He never gave them away, but simply sat still where he was, looking very innocent.

Mrs. Taggerty saw to Michael, and bathed him, and put him out into his pram after he had been fed. Then she did some of the housework, and at last went to put on her hat to go out to the grocer's.

"You look very pale, Mrs. Taggerty, ma'am," said Bridget. "Are you all right?"

"I don't feel too well," said Mrs. Taggerty. "It must be the heat. It's very hot today, isn't it? I'll leave

Michael behind in the garden, Bridget. He'll be all right there."

She set off with her basket. Biddy saw her go out of the front gate, for she was peeping from behind the side gate, hoping the ice-cream man would come by. He didn't come, and Biddy went down to the bottom of the garden again, where she was playing with Annette, Dopey and Whitefeet. The kitten went everywhere with Annette, and was growing into a bonny, playful little thing. He wasn't a bit afraid of Dopey, but smacked him on the nose whenever he sniffed at him, just as Socks did.

The little girls played happily with Dopey and White-feet at shops in the summer-house. They had an array of things to be bought and sold, and first one was the shop-keeper and then the other. Although Annette had been spoilt, and Biddy was a fierce little creature, they played quite well together. If Annette behaved in a spoilt manner, Biddy would fly at her, yelling something rude, so Annette never did behave in a silly way if she played alone with Biddy.

And if Biddy lost her temper and became unbearable, Annette would simply climb over the wall and go home, taking Whitefeet with her. So Biddy behaved herself too, because she didn't want to play alone.

A bell rang in the distance. "Our dinner-bell," said Annette, getting up. "I must go. Come on, Whitefeet."

"Oh, just finish what we're doing," said Biddy, impatiently. "You don't need to go at once."

"Good-bye," said Annette. "I'm going." And she went, carefully putting Whitefeet on the top of the wall whilst she herself climbed over, and then lifting the kitten down the other side.

John and Maureen arrived home just as Annette went into the house. "Where's Mother?" said John.

"Oh, there you are, Mother. I got one of my drawings up on the wall today!"

"And I got top marks for needlework," said Margery. Mother looked pleased.

"I got top marks for shopping," said Annette, with a giggle, "and Whitefeet got top marks for mewing."

"Idiot!" said John, laughing. "Hallo, Whitefeet! Been chasing your own tail this morning?"

Agnes brought in their dinner, and they sat down hungrily when they came back from washing their dirty hands. "I bet Pat's hungry for *his* dinner," said John to Margery. "He was kept in at Break for not having done his homework, and that means he wasn't allowed to eat the cake he brought."

Pat was indeed hungry. He ran home from school wondering what there was for dinner. He had already eaten the slice of cake that he was not allowed to eat at Break, but that didn't make him feel much less hungry. He joined Maureen, and they went the rest of the way home together. They burst in at the side gate, and ran indoors.

Mrs. Taggerty wasn't anywhere to be seen. The table was laid for dinner, but there was no sign of Bridget bringing it in, though there was a delicious smell from the kitchen.

Pat ran out to Bridget. "Why isn't dinner ready? I'm starving! Where's Mummy?"

"She's not back yet," said Bridget, from the stove. "She went out in a hurry to the grocer's, though why to goodness one of you children couldn't have gone for her on the way to school, I *don't* know!"

"Oh, bother!" said Pat, sniffing the smell that came from the pot on the stove. "Need we wait for Mummy? You can serve us, Bridget—or we can serve ourselves."

"You can well wait a minute or two for your mother," said Bridget, sharply. "And put that spoon

*"Oh, bother!" said Pat, sniffing the smell that
came from the pot on the stove*

down, Patrick. If you go taking bits out of that pot you'll burn the skin off your tongue—though maybe that would be a good thing, the saucy, rude boy that you are!"

"Oh, come on, Bridget, get the dinner in," begged Pat. "Maureen's starving, too. I don't see why we should wait for Mother. She's probably met some friend and is talking to her, the way she always does."

"It's mean of her to be late and keep us waiting," complained Biddy.

"And do you know why she was late going out, Biddy, then?" demanded Bridget, turning round on the little girl. "She went and tidied up that bedroom of yours, with all those messy little dolls' tea-things on the floor everywhere. It's a thing you should have done yourself. Ah, there's Michael crying. Go and see to him, Maureen."

"Let him cry," said Maureen. "I'm not Margery. I don't want to coo over him at every moment. He's a nuisance."

"Think shame on yourself to talk that way of your baby brother!" said Bridget sternly, stirring the pot vigorously. "You don't deserve the kind mother and father you have, nor a blessed darling baby like young Michael there—nor someone like me, either, always slaving for you and never getting a polite word, nor a civil thank you. You're a bad lot, and that's the truth."

The three Taggertys took no notice. They had heard all this many times before. Usually Bridget then went on to praise the three Carltons and their nice ways. But this time she didn't. She glanced at the clock.

"A quarter past one. Your mother's watch must have stopped, I'm thinking, and she's doing her shopping late, not knowing the time."

"But the shops shut at one," said Pat. "I expect she's

285

gone in to see a friend. You know how Mummy talks and talks and talks sometimes."

"I want my dinner!" wailed Biddy. "Bridget, can I have a piece of bread? I want my dinner!"

"Go to the front gate, Patrick, and have a look to see if your mother's coming," said Bridget, looking at the clock again. Pat shot off. He soon came back.

"The road's empty. There's no sign of Mummy or anyone else. What *can* she be doing?"

"You take in the bread, Maureen, and the jug of lemonade," said Bridget, making up her mind. "Go along now. Biddy, you get me the hot plates. Pat, take in the butter."

The children did as they were told. Bridget put the dinner on a dish and carried it in herself. The children sat down. Dopey laid himself down under the table, where he could receive unseen all the bits the children didn't like, and where he could lick as many bare knees as he wished.

Bridget served each of the children. Then she glanced at the dining-room clock. It struck half-past one as she looked at it. What *could* be keeping Mrs. Taggerty?

The children set to work hungrily to eat their dinners. Bridget put a little on her own plate, but somehow she couldn't eat it. She was worried. Dopey suddenly licked her ankle and made her jump.

Michael yelled again and she went to see to him. When she got back the children had finished and were drumming on the table with forks and spoons, impatiently.

"What's for pudding? Say it's suet pudding! With treacle!" said Pat.

"Well, it's not then. Your mother and I had no time to go making suet puddings this morning," said Bridget, gathering up the dirty plates. "It's stewed plums and milk pudding."

She brought the dishes in, and served the children again. She looked at the clock. A quarter to two!

"Mummy *is* late!" said Biddy. "Where *can* she be?"

"Maybe she's run away from the bad lot of children that you are," suggested Bridget. Biddy stared at her in alarm.

"No, she wouldn't run away from us! Anyway, she would never leave Michael. Bridget, where *is* she? I want her."

Bridget was silent. The children looked at her worried face, and fear suddenly made their hearts go cold.

"Something's happened," said Bridget. "I feel it in my bones. Yes, something's happened."

CHAPTER EIGHTEEN

A Terrible Shock

THE three children sat as if they were turned to stone. Dopey gave a little whine that startled them terribly, for they had all forgotten he was there.

"What do you mean—something's happened?" said Maureen at last, in a whisper.

"She was tired and pale," said Bridget, "and she didn't want to go walking out. She looked sad and it was a pity to see her looking like that, for it's not like her. I think I'll go along the road and see if I can meet her."

"Let *me* go!" cried Pat, jumping up. But before another word was said the sound of a shrill bell made them all jump.

"The telephone!" said Bridget. "Now we'll get some news—and pray God it's not what I feel in my bones."

She went to the telephone and took down the receiver. She put it to her ear. A voice spoke.

The children clustered round, listening. "No, sir, Mr. Taggerty is out," said Bridget. "He'll not be in till tea time. I'm Bridget, the mother's help. Is there any message I can take for the master? The mistress is out, too."

The children listened eagerly and watched Bridget's face. The voice said something else. Bridget gave little gasps of horror and sank down on the chair beside the telephone. Her hand began to tremble.

"Oh, the poor mistress! Oh, sir, is she bad? You'd best try and reach Mr. Taggerty, sir, he's at his brother's in London, Whitehall 66781. Yes, the children are here. I'll see to them. You get on to Mr. Taggerty, and he'll know what's best to be done."

She put down the receiver. There were tears running down her cheeks. Maureen clutched at her. "What's the matter with Mummy? What's happened to her?"

Bridget gulped once or twice. All three children were crying, even Pat. Bridget put her arm round Biddy.

"It mayn't be so bad as we think," she said. "Your mother was on her way to the grocer's, and was just crossing the road there, when she must have come over giddy. I told you she didn't look well. And she fell down in front of a car."

Biddy screamed. She shook Bridget's arm violently. "Is she hurt! Is she hurt! You've got to tell us."

"Yes, she's hurt," said Bridget, wiping her tears away. "She's at the hospital. But maybe she's not hurt very badly, so don't let's fret too much till we know."

"Will she be home tonight?" asked Maureen, who couldn't imagine home without her mother there.

"Oh no," said Bridget. "Of course not. Not for some time. Your poor father! This will be a terrible shock to him."

Pat was very white. He looked so queer that Bridget

drew him into the kitchen and sat him down by the fire in her chair. "Now don't take on so," she said. "There's clever doctors and nurses at that hospital, and she'll soon be home again, right as rain."

"You don't understand," said Pat in a whisper. "She asked *me* to go to the grocer's for her—and I wouldn't. It was all because of me she was knocked down."

Maureen and Biddy stared at him in horror. Then Maureen flung herself against Bridget. "I wouldn't go either," she cried wildly. "Bridget, I wouldn't go either."

"Ah, we never know what a moment's selfishness will bring," said Bridget, wiping her eyes again. "You've not been kind to your mother lately, and that's the truth."

Neither Maureen nor Pat would go to school that afternoon, and Bridget had not the heart to make them. She telephoned to Mrs. Carlton, who came round at once. Her calm kindness made everyone feel better.

"Now, we mustn't worry till we know there's something to worry about," she said. "It's quite certain that Mummy will be in hospital for a little while, at any rate, so we can plan all sorts of things to help her. She mustn't be allowed to worry one moment about anything, because if she does she will take longer to get better."

"I shall clean all Mummy's brushes and her mirror, in case she wants them at the hospital," said Maureen. "I feel as though I *must* do something for her."

Michael began crying again. Everyone had forgotten him in the upset. "Poor lamb! He'll be wanting his meal," said Bridget. "What I'm to do with him I don't know. He'll be crying for his mother all the time. Maureen's no good with him."

"I will be, I will be!" cried Maureen at once. "I'll be

as good as Margery is. I'll help with him, Bridget. I will really."

"Margery shall come and help with him, too, because he loves her," said Mrs. Carlton. "Agnes will come and help you in the afternoons, Bridget. She's a kind soul and will like to. And I'll slip along in the mornings. We'll manage, you'll see, till Mrs. Taggerty comes back."

Mrs. Carlton took all the children back to tea with her; Michael too. The Carltons were horrified to hear the bad news. They all liked kind, easy-going Mrs. Taggerty. Margery took Michael from her mother.

"Oh, Mother! He'll miss his own mother, so much. Mother, can't we have him here? I could look after him. I know exactly how to. I could even give him his bath, I'm sure."

"No, I'm going to look after him," said Maureen. "Mummy will like to know I'm doing that. He'll be happier at home with us, too."

Mr. Taggerty arrived at his house after tea, after having first gone to the hospital. He was glad to find that the children were not there for the moment. Bridget came to him, her face full of questions and anxiety.

"It's pretty bad, Bridget," said Mr. Taggerty. "The car hit her when she fell. The shock has been dreadful for her."

"Will she—will she be all right?" asked Bridget, her voice trembling.

"I hope so," said Mr. Taggerty. "I hope and pray so, Bridget. Where are the children? Do they know?"

"They're at the Carltons'. That kind Mrs. Carlton came and fetched them all," said Bridget, sniffing and blinking tears away. "They're terribly upset, of course. Poor Patrick, he went as white as a sheet. He's got some idea that he's to blame for the accident. His mother asked him to go to the grocer's for her and he wouldn't. So she had to go instead, and it was when she was crossing the road to the grocer's that the accident happened."

"Poor Pat. Yes, he will reproach himself terribly for more than one thing," said Mr. Taggerty, thinking of the letter from the headmaster that had upset his wife so much. "Can you manage, Bridget? My wife won't be back for some time I'm afraid. I could send Pat to my brother's if you could manage the others. We'll get someone to help you."

"Now, don't you worry your head about anything but Mrs. Taggerty," said kind, loyal Bridget, taking Mr. Taggerty's hand. "I can manage all right. I can manage fine, and I'll see to the children just as well as their mother did, though maybe I'll be a bit stricter than she is. As for Pat, send him off if you like. He might feel happier away from here."

But when Mr. Taggerty suggested to Pat that he should go away to stay for a while, Pat shook his head at once. "No, Daddy. Don't make me go. I want to stay here, near Mummy, so that I can see her when she's getting better. I can help Bridget with the others too. And Daddy, I'm—I'm most awfully sorry about that letter. I'll try and do better. Oh, if only Mummy comes back quickly I'll be top of the form, I'll do anything, anything! It's all my fault it happened. How could I be so mean to her? It was such a little thing she wanted me to do."

"Pat, so often the little things grow into great big things," said his father gravely. "Well, I shall not send you to Uncle Henry's, if you really will help with the others, and do what you can for Bridget too. I've been disappointed in you lately, terribly disappointed. Perhaps now you can show me a different side, and be a comfort to me in my unhappiness. I shall miss your mother much more than you will."

"Oh, Daddy!" said Pat, and flung his arm round his father's neck. "Daddy, I'll help you. Trust me again, and let me help. And if you see Mummy tonight, tell her I'm sorry about everything, and I'll show her I am when she comes back home."

The next day was a very miserable one for the Taggertys, and for the Carltons too, for they shared wholeheartedly in their friends' sorrow. The news was not good from the hospital, and Mr. Taggerty spent the whole day there. The children went to school as usual and everyone was especially kind to the two Taggertys. Pat worked grimly, meaning to make up now for every slack hour he had spent before.

That evening, when the children heard that their mother was not any better, they felt afraid. "We'd better pray very hard," said Maureen. "All of us, not only me. You must too, Pat. It's a pity you've always laughed at me so for praying. But it's the only thing left for us to do now."

Pat stared at Maureen. "I don't believe God would bother to listen to me," he said at last. "Why should He? I've been beastly. It doesn't seem fair that I should have laughed at the idea of praying, and now, just when we're in trouble, suddenly I think I'd better do it. If I were God I wouldn't listen to people who did that."

"Yes," said Maureen. "It does seem rather small and mean only to fly to praying when you want something very badly, like we do now. I shouldn't think our prayers would be worth much."

"Yours might," said Pat. "But Biddy's and mine wouldn't. Do you think—do you think we could go and ask the Carltons to do some praying, because after all they always do pray anyway, and their prayers would be heard more than ours. It might be some help if they prayed hard for Mummy."

"Yes, let's go," said Maureen. "Let's go now and ask them. I know they won't mind."

So the three of them climbed over the wall just before Annette's bedtime, with Dopey, and went to find the Carltons.

"Hallo!" said John. "We were just going to come and ask you if you'd like to have supper with me and Margery. Annette has hers in bed."

"We've come to ask you something too," said Maureen, seeing that Pat was tongue-tied. "John, will you pray for our mother, please? To make her better, you know. Pat and I don't think our prayers would be much good. I'm sure Pat's wouldn't because he's always laughed at the idea, and been afraid of being pi. But it's very, very important. We have to do every single thing we can for Mummy."

The three Carltons looked at the three serious Taggertys. "But we *are* praying for your mother!" said John. "How could you think we weren't? We all did last night, and this morning too. Even Annette prayed for a long time. That's the first thing we thought of."

"Oh," said Maureen. "Thank you, John. It's such a relief to know that."

"But you must pray too," said John. "And don't think your prayers won't be heard. They will. Mother says every single prayer is heard, the sinner's and the saint's."

The three Taggertys looked very much relieved. They couldn't help feeling much better now that they knew the Carltons were doing so much.

"I must get back to Michael," said Maureen. "It's his bed time. You come and help too, Biddy."

They went off. Pat stayed behind. Annette went in

to bed, and Margery decided to climb over the wall and help Maureen with the baby.

Pat was left with John. He looked so woebegone that John wanted to comfort him. "Cheer up," he said. "Maybe the news will be better tomorrow."

"John," said Pat, "I want to tell you something. It's very important. I've been thinking about it all day long. I simply *must* tell someone!"

CHAPTER NINETEEN

Pat Makes a Solemn Promise

"WHAT is it?" asked John, curious to know why Pat was suddenly so very earnest and solemn. Then it all came out—all about the letter from the head, and how upset his father and mother had been; how he hadn't said he was sorry or anything, how rude and unkind he had been to his mother the morning of the day she had had her accident, and how he had refused to go to the grocer's.

"So, you see, I can't help feeling it's all my fault," said Pat. "And John—if she doesn't get better, I shall never, never be happy again. Do you think that if I tell God I will turn over a new leaf, and work hard at school, and be good to Mummy always and always, and to the others too, He would let her get all right again?"

"I don't know," said John, slowly. "I don't see how anyone can make a bargain with God like that. It seems awful cheek, somehow. Like saying, 'You do this and

I'll do that. And if you won't, I won't.' There's something wrong about it somewhere.

Pat gazed at him in despair. "Well, there must be *something* I can do," he said. "And that's the best thing I can think of."

"Let's go and ask my father about it," said John, hearing his father in the hall. "Look, he's gone to sit in the study. Come on, let's ask him."

They went in. Mr. Carlton was filling his pipe. He was surprised to see the solemn faces of the two boys. "Come to ask me something?" he said. "Sit down then."

They sat down, Pat looking nervous and anxious. John poured out everything to his father, who listened gravely without saying a word.

"You see, Daddy, Pat can't think of anything better, but it does seem a bit as if he's trying to make a bargain with God," finished John. "And somehow that's a bit queer."

"You can't bargain with God," said Daddy. "And no one should try. What you *can* do, Pat, is to do all you say you will—turn over a new leaf, work hard and well, help your family all you can, and be kind and unselfish—whatever may happen to your mother. That isn't a bargain then, you see. It's saying you are really sorry, and that you are going to show it. It's a promise, not a bargain. You would keep that promise even if your mother didn't come back again."

"I see," said Pat, his face very serious. "Yes, I do see that. If I really am sorry, I should be willing to do that, no matter what happens. Well, I *will* do it. I'll promise. Shall I make my promise to you?"

"No. To God," said Mr. Carlton. "It's a very solemn thing to do, Pat. Think well about it, before you make it. And ask God for His help in keeping the promise, too. You will not be strong enough to keep it alone."

The boys went out of the room. Pat gave John's arm a sudden squeeze. "Isn't your father fine?" he said. "You know, he's an absolute sport—and yet you can go and talk to him about things like this too. Oh, John —I feel a bit happier now I can really *do* something. I shall make my promise tonight before I go to bed."

Pat kept his word. He made his solemn promise that night and got into bed afterwards feeling happier. He thought about his mother. How could he have been so mean to her? How could he have said he wasn't going to the grocer's? Such a small thing to do for anyone you loved! And there were other things too.

There was the time she had asked him to hold her wool for her, when she wanted to wind it into balls, and he had pretended he had forgotten, and had gone out without doing it. There was another time when she had asked him to bring the pram in from the rain, and he hadn't, and it had got soaked. She had asked him for so many little kindnesses, and so many times he hadn't done them.

"Not because I didn't love you, Mummy," he said to her in his heart. "Don't think that, will you? It was only because I didn't think enough. I was unkind and selfish. You were always doing things for me, and I hardly ever did anything for you. But you come back and see what I'll do!"

Maureen said long prayers that night. She, too, had felt very remorseful about her unkindness to her mother. She had taken advantage of Mrs. Taggerty's easy-going ways. She had told her untruths and deceived her. Now Maureen went red in the dark, as she remembered the mean little things she had done.

"Why didn't I take Michael out for her the other day? Why did I forget to leave the parcel she asked me to leave? Why didn't I make my bed when she was busy?"

Biddy heard her tossing about and muttering.

"What's the matter?" she asked. "Are you thinking about Mummy? So am I, too."

"I'm thinking how beastly I was," said Maureen. "And you were too, Biddy. We all were, except Daddy —and Michael, but he's too little to be kind or unkind. You didn't clear up those dolls' tea-things for Mummy, did you?"

"No," said Biddy, in a small voice. "I didn't. And when Mummy came down the garden, and called me, I hid under the bushes and didn't answer. And perhaps I could have gone out for her, instead of her going."

"We were all horrid," said Maureen. "It seems like a terrible punishment for us, doesn't it? Sometimes we've jeered at John and Margery and Annette because they never deceive their mother, or tell her fibs, or refuse to do the things she asks them to—but they're right, you know. If you love people, you've got to be decent to them. I wish I'd been decent."

"So do I," Biddy said, and began to cry. "I want Mummy. I want her to come up the stairs this very minute and tell us not to talk, and kiss us good-night. I don't like all the things that are happening. I feel sort of strange and queer."

"I do, too," said Maureen.

They said no more, and after a while Biddy fell asleep. But Maureen kept awake a long time, and Pat even longer. Bridget came in to look at them at ten o'clock, and Pat was still awake.

"You go to sleep now, boy," said Bridget, kindly. "We can only hope and pray for the best."

"Are you praying too, then?" asked Pat.

"Well, of course!" said Bridget. "Am I a heathen then, not saying my prayers? I'm a Christian woman, and you should know it, Patrick Taggerty. Now, you

297

go to sleep, and the morning will maybe bring good news."

The telephone rang next day at breakfast-time. Mr. Taggerty went to answer it, an anxious look on his face. He said, "Yes, yes," several times into the telephone, while the children listened breathlessly. Bridget appeared from the kitchen, her face anxious.

Mr. Taggerty put the receiver down. He turned to the children, and there was a faint smile on his face. "Just a bit better news," he said. "Mummy's had a fair night—and she has been asking about us. I'll go and see her this morning."

The children felt as if a load had rolled away from their hearts. If Mummy was actually asking about them, she couldn't be so very very ill. Surely very very ill people didn't ask about anybody at all?

"Daddy, will you buy Mummy some flowers for me?" asked Pat, taking down his money-box. "And some from Maureen and Biddy too—and a tiny bunch from Michael? And give her our very best love, and tell her we are all thinking of her and—and—loving her very much."

"I will," said Mr. Taggerty, and Pat saw the shine of tears in his father's eyes. "Poor Daddy," he thought. "This is awful for him. I'll never let him down again. It's not fair."

Dopey seemed to feel the better news too, and became more his old self. He had been very subdued and had gone about with his big tail down and his ears pressed back, which gave him a very odd look. He couldn't understand *where* Mrs. Taggerty was. He had looked for her everywhere.

"Better news, Dopey!" said Pat, and at the sound of the boy's more cheerful voice, Dopey rolled over on his back and did his bicycling act. Socks sat washing herself near by, watching Dopey scornfully. She thought him a very silly dog, though she didn't mind playing with him sometimes when she felt like it.

Mr. Taggerty came back from the hospital looking a little more cheerful. Bridget met him at the door.

"Well, the news is no worse," said Mr. Taggerty. "She's worried about us all, though, which is such a pity. You must go and see her tomorrow, Bridget, and tell her we're all getting on famously, and she must hurry up and get better."

"What about the children?" asked Bridget. "Can they see her too? Once they see her again they won't worry so much."

"Well—she's got a big bandage round her head," said Mr. Taggerty. "It would scare them to see that. We'd better wait till it's off and she's feeling a bit better."

The next day came and the next. Mrs. Taggerty mended a little, though no doctor would say she was definitely out of danger. The children were as good as gold. They did their very best to think of all kinds of ways to help Bridget and their father. Even Biddy tried.

Maureen amazed Bridget by the way she took charge of little Michael. It was true that Margery came to help, and even felt a little jealous when she saw how well Maureen was managing—but certainly Michael was well looked after, and hardly cried at all.

Pat surprised his masters at school by suddenly working harder than anybody. He was keeping his promise, and nothing was going to make him break it. And he wanted to do more still. What could he do?

"I'll clear away all the weeds from the part of the garden near the windows, where Mummy likes to sit," he thought. "I'll weed the path there, too. She'd like that. She's always said how nice it would look if only she could get down to the weeding. Well, I'll do it for her, for a surprise when she comes back. When she comes back! Doesn't that sound good?"

Biddy wanted to do something too. So she borrowed a pail of water from Bridget and a cloth and scrubbing brush and soap, and began to clean out the little summer-house with a great deal of splashing. "Mummy can sit here when she comes back," she told Bridget. "She always said she wouldn't because it was so dusty and dirty. I'll make it clean for her."

Mrs. Carlton helped a lot by having the children in to meals at times, to give Bridget a rest. Agnes went willingly to help in the afternoon sometimes. Everyone was very kind, even Miss Johnson next door, who had never had a good word to say of the Taggertys since they had moved in.

"People are good when trouble comes along," said Bridget. "You never know who your friends are till something happens."

She glanced at Pat, who was cleaning the pram for her. "And you never know what good there is in people till trouble brings it out!" she thought. "Look at that boy—I never knew anyone change so. But will it last? It all depends on himself."

The news grew better and better. At last the bandages were off and Mr. Taggerty said that he would take the three children to see their mother the very next day. They were overjoyed.

"It's ages since we saw her," said Pat. "Maureen, I hope to goodness you've got a clean dress."

"Well, I have," said Maureen. "And so has Biddy. And Bridget has washed your blue shirt and pressed your best shorts. We'll look as nice as the Carltons tomorrow!"

"I'll see that you do!" said Bridget. "Your mother will have told everyone her three children are coming, and she'll want to be proud of the lot of you. You'll go

300

with your hands clean, and your faces and knees clean, and your hairs brushed, and your nails clean too. Do you hear me, Patrick, my boy? Your nails clean, too!"

Pat laughed. "All right. I'll see they are. I'm just as anxious to make Mummy think we look nice, as you are, Bridget. It's the one time we shan't grumble about it!"

And, indeed, they did look nice when they set off with their father the next day. "I'm quite proud of my family," he said. "I've never seen you look like this before. I really feel that your name must be Carlton, not Taggerty!"

CHAPTER TWENTY

Going to See Mrs. Taggerty

It was a week since the accident had happened—a long, long week to the three Taggertys. They were all excited at the thought of seeing their mother again, but they somehow felt a little solemn too.

Mrs. Taggerty was in a little private room. The nurse opened the door and said, "Here are the children, Mrs. Taggerty—but mind, only five minutes—and don't get excited or I'll take them away!"

The children did not dare to do as they would have liked to do—rush in and fling themselves on their mother. They tip-toed in, wide-eyed and quiet. Mummy was lying in bed, very pale. The big bandage had gone, and only a small one was left. There was a bruise on her left cheek where she had fallen. The children couldn't bear to see it there. She smiled at them, with tears of joy in her eyes.

"Hallo, darlings! Aren't I silly to be like this! But I'll soon be better."

Biddy put her face down by her mother's on the pillow and pressed her soft cheek against hers. "Mummy, I love you! Mummy, are you hurt? When will you come back? I'm sorry I didn't clear up the dolls' tea-things for you."

Maureen could not say a word except for a choked-out, "Hallo, Mummy! Are you better?" She stroked her mother's soft, wavy hair with trembling fingers.

Poor Pat opened his mouth to speak but not one word would come out. He gazed at his mother as if he

"Mummy, when will you come back?"

could not look at her enough, and he knew in that one minute how much she loved him, and how much he loved her. "I didn't mean to be horrid to you," his eyes said to her. "I'm terribly sorry I didn't go the errand you wanted me to. It's all my fault. And oh, I kicked you too that morning, though I didn't mean to. Somehow I can't say a word to you, but you *must* understand, you've *got* to understand."

And his mother understood. She squeezed his rough little brown hand very hard and smiled through her tears, looking very happy. "It's all right, Patrick," she said. "I know what you're feeling and thinking, darling. We'll be happy together again when I come home. Now tell me about Michael. Is he missing me very much?"

"We all do," said Maureen. "Mummy, it's queer without you. You've always been there, and now you're not. I'm looking after Michael for you."

"Yes, Bridget told me," said Mummy. "I'm so glad. Love him for me, Maureen, won't you? And look after poor old Daddy and make a fuss of him. Let him know he's got a loving little family."

The five minutes went far too quickly. Biddy was really indignant when the nurse came to shoo them out. "Why, we haven't had *one* minute!" she said to the nurse. "And we haven't tired Mummy."

The nurse glanced at Mrs. Taggerty. She was looking happy but very pale. "You must all go now," she said briskly. "Say good-bye. You can come again next week."

"Good-bye, darlings," said Mummy. "You do all look so very nice and neat. I hope everyone in the hospital is looking out of the window when you go by!"

The Taggertys went, and Daddy slipped into the

room to stay for a while with his wife. She could hardly speak, she was so tired, but he saw she was happy.

"They're the nicest—children—in the world," she whispered, and took Daddy's hand in hers.

The Taggertys were so relieved at actually having seen their mother again, felt her warm hand and heard her soft, familiar voice, that their feelings got the better of them as soon as they left the hospital, and found Dopey waiting for them outside the gates, where Daddy had tied him up.

"Dopey! She's getting better!" Biddy yelled, and ran to untie him. "Hurrah!"

They tore home at top speed, Dopey leaping and bounding madly. They ran headlong into Mrs. Wilson and Miss Johnson as they turned the corner to go to their house. They almost knocked them over. The shopping-basket flew out of Miss Johnson's hand and Dopey pounced on it with joy. He took it by the handle very cleverly and pranced down the road. Biddy squealed with laughter.

"Oh, look at Dopey! He's gone shopping!"

Miss Johnson looked at the children in disgust. "To think they race along the road like this, shouting and laughing, when their poor mother's lying ill in hospital!" she said to Mrs. Wilson.

A week or two before Pat would have yelled as loudly as Biddy, and would have rushed off laughing to think of the collision they had had. But he didn't do that now.

He spoke to Maureen. "Go and get the basket from Dopey." Then he turned to the two disapproving ladies. "I'm so sorry we nearly knocked you over. You see— we've just been to see Mummy in hospital, and we felt so glad she was getting better that we just *galloped* along the road in joy!"

Maureen came up with the basket. She gave it to Miss Johnson. "I'm sorry we gave you a fright," she said. "Thank you for all your kindness about Mummy, Miss Johnson. Daddy said you sent her some lovely flowers."

Miss Johnson forgot her crossness and smiled. "I'm glad she's better. I am going to see her myself next week, I hope."

"Could you tell her we're getting on all right?" said Maureen. "So that she won't worry about us?"

"I'll tell her you're being extra-specially good!" said Miss Johnson. "I've seen you wheeling that baby of yours out every day, Maureen. Quite a little mother to him, aren't you?"

The children ran home to tell Bridget about the five precious minutes at the hospital. Bridget was making cakes, and she stirred the mixture and listened with great interest. "And did you tell her you were all as good as gold?" she asked, stirring vigorously. "A bad lot, you were, but you're good at heart, and that's worth something. Now stop putting your finger into the bowl, Biddy, do!"

"It tastes so nice," said Biddy, licking her finger. "Can I scrape the bowl when you've finished, Bridget? Mummy always lets me."

"Your mother was too soft with you," said Bridget. "There were times when I thought you hadn't one scrap of love for her between you. But maybe there's good in you after all. *Will* you stop poking your finger into my bowl, Biddy? I'll rap you with my wooden spoon if you do it again."

"Oh, Bridget, you always sound so sharp and cross but I do like you," said Biddy, leaning against her, and rubbing Bridget's floury arm with her cheek. "Daddy says he doesn't know what we'd all do without you."

"Well there now," said Bridget, stirring again vigorously, "what's come over you to say a nice word to poor old Bridget? It's just that you're wanting to scrape out my bowl!"

"It isn't, it isn't," said Biddy. "Is it, Pat? Is it, Maureen? We do like Bridget awfully much, don't we?"

"Of course," said Pat, gruffly. He knew better than the others what a brick Bridget had been lately. But then, Bridget always was a brick, no matter whether things went ill or well. He put a finger into the cake-mixture and got a sharp rap of the wooden spoon.

"Shame on you, being such a baby, licking your fingers like that!" cried Bridget, but her eyes twinkled. "Get away, the lot of you. Come back when I've finished."

And when they did come back, the cakes were in the oven, baking nicely, and the bowl was still on the table with quite an extraordinary lot of scrapings left in it. The children looked at it in surprise and began running their fingers round the bowl, licking them in delight.

"Bridget! I do believe you've left an extra lot on purpose!" called Maureen. "There's never been so much before. Why does cake-mixture taste so much nicer before it's cooked than after! Bridget, you *have* left us a nice lot."

"And it's on purpose, you think!" scoffed Bridget from the scullery. "Would I be as soft as that, now?"

The days went by. Mummy was still in the hospital, slowly getting better. But it seemed a very long time. Two weeks went by, and then another. They were now in the middle of November. Would Mummy never come home?

"*When* will she leave the hospital?" asked Maureen. "I want her back. Can't you get her back, Daddy?"

306

"She will be out of hospital at the end of November," said Daddy, "and then I am taking her away till she is quite all right again. So she won't be home yet."

Maureen's face fell. "But, Daddy! All that time! Oh, Daddy—she *will* be home for Christmas, won't she?"

"I sincerely hope so," said Daddy, smiling. "Oh yes, I think I can promise you that."

The children were very disappointed to learn that Mummy wouldn't be home for so long. Pat talked to John about it. "There's one thing," he said, "it gives me longer to work hard, John, and get a good report. If only it's really good! I could put it on the table on Christmas morning, and then Mummy would know I'd done my best."

"All our weeding will have been wasted," said John. "If she doesn't come home till Christmas she won't be able to go into the garden much, and she won't see how nice we've made the top part."

John had been helping Pat with the garden, and the two boys had cleared away weeds and cut back bushes, and trimmed the path edges well. Now they were busy each day sweeping away the fallen leaves.

"Never mind. She'll see it from the dining-room window," said Pat. "Is your father going for his usual walk this afternoon, John—or doesn't he go in dull, miserable weather like this?"

"Of course he's going," said John. "I'm going too. I used to hate walking, but now I like it, especially if you come too. And Dopey, of course."

Pat had a tremendous admiration for John's father. Neither of them had ever said any more about Pat's solemn promise, but Pat knew that Uncle Peter, as he called Mr. Carlton, was watching him week by week, and was glad that he was keeping his word.

All three Taggertys went to Sunday School with the Carltons now. Pat had joined them one Sunday afternoon without a word. The two girls went to church with John, Margery and Annette too, and their parents, and Pat came once or twice.

"I might come always," he said to John, "only somehow I can't bear to leave Dopey both morning *and* afternoon too. I do wish he could go to church as well. I'm sure it would do him good, even if it only taught him to be a bit quieter. I'm trying to make him quiet for when Mummy comes home."

Maureen was managing Michael beautifully, and he crowed to her, and held out his arms whenever she came back from school. She was pleased.

"He doesn't seem a nuisance any more," she said to the half-jealous Margery. "Isn't it queer?"

"Well, *I* thought it was queer when you said he *was* a nuisance!" said Margery. "Do let me hold him, Maureen. You hardly ever let me have a turn at him now."

"He likes me best now, that's why," said Maureen, a pleased look on her face.

"He doesn't," said Margery, fiercely. "Michael, don't you want to come to Margie?"

Michael turned to her and held out his fat arms. "There you are!" Margery said triumphantly and bent towards him. The baby put one arm round her neck and then one round Maureen's, and held them tightly with surprising strength, so that the heads of the two little girls almost met over him.

"He loves you both exactly the same!" said Biddy, who was looking on. "I love him too."

"Yes, but *you* love Dopey best," said Maureen. "No, I'm not calling you, Dopey, you idiot. Get *down*! Oh, look, Margery, Michael's trying to pat him. Isn't he the cleverest baby in the whole wide world!"

CHAPTER TWENTY-ONE

Christmas is Coming!

SCHOOL days went on and on. Time for work, time for
play, breakfast, dinner, tea and supper. Bedtime. The
weeks flew by happily, and John, Margery and Annette
enjoyed them, though Annette, of course, did not go to
school. Biddy came to play with her in her nursery, to
leave Bridget free in the mornings, with only Michael
to see to.

Biddy was a careless and destructive little girl, and
she and Annette had many a tussle because of the way
she treated Annette's dolls and other toys. But gradually she learnt to be careful with them and not to break
them. She even learnt to put them away!

She learnt to be tidier and cleaner too, for Mrs.
Carlton would not allow her to come and play in the
nursery, or to have meals with Annette, unless she was
at least clean and tidy.

"If you wear a hair-ribbon, then tie it up," she said
firmly. "Or don't wear one at all. And see that your
dress has all its buttons done up, and your shoe-buttons
too. No, that isn't being fussy, Biddy. It's part of good
manners."

All the Taggertys began to learn better ways because
they were now so much with the Carltons. Maureen
learnt to like their tidy, pretty house, and began to
compare her own untidy home with it—coats thrown
down on the floor, papers about, dead flowers in the
vases, everything higgledy-piggledy.

"It's just because we always throw our things about,

and nobody ever bothers to pick them up, till Bridget gets a fit of tidiness and rushes round tidying," she thought. "But as soon as she's done that, we all begin throwing things down again. Well, I'm going to copy Mrs. Carlton!"

She did, and tried to make Pat and Biddy do the same, and be tidy and neat. But they wouldn't, and Pat became very cross with Maureen.

"*You* can be as tidy as you like," he cried, "but don't try to make Biddy and me the same. And if you're so anxious to get things right, well, run round and pick *our* things up too. We shan't stop you!"

And lo and behold, Maureen even did that too, picking up Pat's things and Biddy's without a murmur, tidying Pat's room, putting his books away, and Biddy's toys. Soon the house was a pleasure to come into, and Mr. Taggerty noticed it.

"What a good little mother Maureen is," he said to Bridget. "I do hope they will go on behaving like this when their mother comes back. It would please her so much."

The time came for Mrs. Taggerty to leave the hospital. She was to go away with Daddy in the car. She had said good-bye to the children the day before, when they had gone as usual to see her.

"Do come back in time for Christmas, Mummy!" they had begged her. "We can't have Christmas without you."

Now Daddy wasn't at home either. There was only Bridget, getting a bit tired and sharp of tongue, but someone familiar, who could be depended on for help at any time. She would scold at the sight of a hole in a stocking, but would bind up a hurt knee kindly at the same time. She would be cross with Pat for losing his pen, but would go and try to find it for him before he left for school. They couldn't do without Bridget, that was certain.

All kinds of plans were on foot for Christmas. Bridget was making the puddings, and all the children, the Carltons included, had to stir and wish. The Taggertys, of course, wished fervently that their mother would be home for Christmas. John wished for a puppy, though he felt guiltily that he ought to wish that the Taggertys' mother would be home. Biddy and Maureen wished it for them, however, so he felt it would be all right.

Everyone was making cards and presents. The Taggertys, with Mrs. Carlton's help, were making a big streamer to hang over their front door, with "WELCOME HOME, MUMMY" on it in big red letters. Maureen and Biddy, who hated sewing, took their share in the work, and didn't grumble once. It was for Mummy!

"You never used to do a *thing* for your mother!" said Annette, sewing at a big letter L. "Not a thing. We used to think you were awful about that. Now you don't seem to mind anything, not even sewing. I remember one time when you told an awful story to your mother, and——"

"Shut up," said Maureen. "We don't want to be reminded of things like that. You wait till your mother has something awful happen to her, and see what you feel about things! It makes you different, somehow."

"All you Carltons are different too, anyway," put in Biddy unexpectedly. "Don't you remember what a dreadful tell-tale Annette was?"

"And a cry-baby, too," said Maureen. "Awful. And John was such a mother's boy—couldn't even climb a tree! And Margery used to scream if Dopey came too near—and she wanted to go home to her mother when she first came to tea."

Neither Annette nor Margery liked this kind of re-membering. Had they really been like that? Yes, they had. They looked uncomfortable, and Margery went very red.

Maureen saw her scarlet cheeks. "Don't let's remember horrid things," she said, giving Margery a little poke. "You could remember lots about us—how we told the most awful fibs—and how rough we were, and didn't even know our table-manners! Don't let's remember them. You showed us how beastly we were, anyway."

"And you showed us how silly *we* were," said Margery, generously. "I never thought we'd be friends."

"I've finished my letter L," said Annette. She gave an enormous sigh. "I must have a rest. Why are needles so small to hold? I'd like a much bigger one. Look at Whitefeet, Maureen. Do look. He's gone to sleep be-tween Dopey's front paws! Oh, I do wish he wouldn't grow so fast. I want him to be a kitten for always."

John hadn't said any more about a puppy. He was very much hoping for one at Christmas, but he didn't dare to ask about it in case it wasn't to be. But he couldn't help hoping.

The holidays came. Only four more days till Christ-mas now! The school reports came in. John's was excellent, and so was Margery's. Their parents read them out loud to them, as they always did.

"I wonder what Pat's report is like," said John. "I hope it's good. It ought to be because Pat has really tried hard for weeks."

Mr. Taggerty paid a flying visit to his home three days before Christmas, to make arrangements with Bridget about bringing back Mrs. Taggerty. She was still very much of an invalid, but otherwise a great deal better.

312

Pat's report had arrived, and so had Maureen's. Mr. Taggerty opened them.

Maureen had quite a good one, and the remark at the bottom pleased her very much.

"Has improved tremendously in manners and appearance lately," wrote her form-mistress. "Maureen is not nearly so untidy and careless now."

Pat's report was splendid. His father read it with great pleasure, and then beckoned Pat to him.

"You must read this with me, Patrick," he said. "Look at the list of marks you had in the first few weeks—and your position in form—bottom! And now look how the marks go up and up and up—and your position in form goes up too—till you are fourth from the top! And read what your form-master has to say of you."

Pat read the piece at the bottom, his heart beating fast, for his report meant a good deal to him that term.

"Patrick seemed quite impossible in every way, except at gym and football, at the beginning of the term," said the report, "and I considered him a very bad influence. Now, I am happy to say, he is quite a different boy, has worked extremely hard and well, is no longer undependable, but trustworthy and honourable, a credit to his class, and will, we hope, be a credit to the school as the terms go on. He deserves great praise for being able to change himself in this way, and I am proud of him."

Pat's face glowed. His father drew him to him. "I'm proud, too, Pat," he said. "Very proud. You have more than made up for the beginning of the term. How pleased your mother will be. We'll put this on her breakfast-tray for her on Christmas morning. It will be the best Christmas present she could have!"

Mrs. Taggerty was to come home the afternoon before Christmas Day. The children all made great preparations. Bridget cooked and baked hard. All the children's clothes were clean and mended. Baby Michael looked beautiful in a new white woollen suit, knitted by Mrs. Carlton.

The big white streamer, with its "WELCOME HOME, MUMMY" in big letters of red, was carefully put up over the front door. There was a special cake, with the same words on it in Bridget's best icing-writing. There were silver balls, preserved violets, and little yellow sweets all over the icing, too. It looked a lovely cake.

Daddy's car drew up at the door. Out stepped Mummy on Daddy's arm, her face radiant. How much better she looked now! The children ran down the path and flung themselves on her.

"Welcome back, Mummy! You've really come!"

"Careful, careful," said Daddy. "Down, Dopey. Bless the dog, he's gone mad. Down, sir, DOWN!"

Mummy was so glad to be home again that the tears rolled down her cheeks. She looked round as she walked inside. "How lovely it looks! How tidy and clean everything is! Why, Bridget, there you are! How can I thank you for all you've done! Where's my little Michael?"

It was a lovely home-coming. Everyone enjoyed it, even the three Carlton children, who had gone round by the road, and were watching from the pavement on the opposite side. They hadn't wanted to go any nearer for they knew that this was the Taggertys' joyful day, not theirs. But they just wanted a little share of it.

Michael squealed with delight when his mother picked him up. "Oh, he's grown! He's beautiful!" cried Mrs. Taggerty. "How well he's looking. You have taken great care of him for me, Bridget."

"Maureen's done her share. Mrs. Taggerty, ma'am," said Bridget, who could hardly let her mistress out of her sight. "Such good children they've been. You can be proud of them."

"Why, you always said what a bad lot they were!" said Mrs. Taggerty, smiling.

"Well, they are," said Bridget, twinkling at the three children clustered round their mother. "A real bad lot —but they're worth their weight in gold, all the same!"

Christmas Eve, with Mummy sitting in her usual chair again—the children could hardly believe it was true. And how nice to have her to come up and kiss them tonight!

Pat had told no one but John and John's father about the solemn promise he had made. But that night, with his arms round his mother, he told her. "It wasn't a bargain," he said, hugging her. "It wasn't something I said I'd do *if* you came back again, or *till* you came back again—it was a promise made for always, whatever happened. You'll see I kept my promise, Mummy, when you read my report tomorrow morning—and you'll see it when you get my report next term, and the term after, and always! And I'll never, never be unkind to you again."

"Oh yes you will—but I shan't mind, and you'll always be sorry and make it up to me again," said his mother. "I'm glad I can be proud of you, Pat. You're my eldest one, my first boy, and you have a very special place in my heart. I do so want to be proud of you— and I am!"

Christmas morning was lovely. There were all kinds of presents on the table, and these were saved up till Mummy came down after breakfast to help them to open them. The children had already had stockings, but they were only filled with small things. The real presents were on the Christmas table.

"Oh, what a lovely doll!" squealed Biddy. "Mummy, did you make the clothes?"

"Yes, I had such a long time in bed," said Mummy. "Oh, who gave me this beautiful mat? Maureen, you don't mean to say you *made* it—and embroidered all these daisies on it too. Well, I *am* pleased!"

"Dopey's given you something," said Biddy. "You haven't opened it yet."

Mummy opened the parcel and everyone yelled with laughter. It was a big bone! "Oh, Dopey!" said Mummy. "How can you possibly spare it? You must share it with me."

And Dopey was only too pleased, of course. He didn't understand that it was Christmas. He only knew that everyone was very happy and glad, so he was too. His big tail wagged without stopping.

Then Mummy opened Pat's report. Her eyes shone as she read it. "It's my nicest present," she said to Pat. "You couldn't have given me a better one. I like it more than the table-napkin ring you made me in your handwork class—and I do like that very much indeed."

"I wonder how the Carltons are getting on," said Pat. "Mummy, we've got a wonderful present for them. At least, he's for John really, but they'll all share him. We're fetching him this morning, in a short while. He's at the farm."

"It's a spaniel puppy," said Biddy, unable to keep the secret any longer. "We bought him between us for the Carltons, but Daddy paid the most money. He's lovely, lovely, lovely."

They went to fetch the puppy. He was glossy black, with drooping ears and melting brown eyes. In fact, as Maureen said, he was altogether beautiful.

"Not more beautiful than Dopey!" said Biddy jealously. Dopey was not beautiful, but all the Taggertys thought he was.

"We'll have to hurry," said Maureen, as they left the farm with the spaniel capering round them, and

Dopey making mad darts at him. "You know we said we'd go to Christmas Day church with the Carltons this morning. We've got to say a big thank-you there for getting Mummy back. Hurry up!"

They hurried. The spaniel hurried too, pleased to run with the children. Pat had tied a label round his neck, giggling as he did so. The spaniel thought it must be his name. But it wasn't.

They went round by road to the Carltons—and, hurrah, there were John, Margery and Annette just starting out to go round to *them*.

"We've got a present for you!" yelled Biddy. "Look! It's this puppy. It's for all of you, but especially for John."

And John, who had been surprised and disappointed at the non-appearance of a puppy after all for his Christmas present, gave a yell as loud as Biddy's. He dropped down on one knee beside the spaniel, who licked his nose with a little red tongue.

"Oh! So this is what Biddy and Maureen were so mysterious about! They kept on and on hinting to me and I was too stupid to understand. Isn't he marvellous? I'll call him Scamper, because look how he scampers. Biddy, Pat, Maureen, thank you, thank you, *thank* you!"

Then John looked at the label round the puppy's neck, tied to his scarlet collar. He read it and roared with laughter. "Look, Annette, look, Margery—see what the Taggertys have written—'Happy Christmas to THOSE DREADFUL CHILDREN'!"

"And look what *we've* written on *our* label to you!" squealed Annette, pushing a marvellous conjuring set into Pat's hands. "Do look!"

Pat looked, and laughed. "You've written just the same!" he cried. "'Happy Christmas to THOSE DREADFUL CHILDREN'!"

317

"That's what we used to call each other," said John. "However could we have? Come on, let's show Mother my puppy. Come, Scamper, come to your home."

In at the gate the spaniel scampered, his tail wagging and his ears flapping. Dopey dashed after him, almost knocking him over. All the children followed.

"Happy Christmas, Mrs. Carlton!" yelled Biddy. "Many happy returns of Christmas Day!"

And we will wish them a happy Christmas too, and leave them to their lovely Christmas day. Happy Christmas, dreadful children, happy Christmas to you all!